hard
TO QUIT

—mark mitten—

MILFORD
HOUSE

an imprint of Sunbury Press, Inc.
Mechanicsburg, PA USA

MILFORD
HOUSE

an imprint of Sunbury Press, Inc.
Mechanicsburg, PA USA

For information about special discounts for bulk purchases, please contact Sunbury Press Orders Dept. at (855) 338-8359 or orders@sunburypress.com.

To request one of our authors for speaking engagements or book signings, please contact Sunbury Press Publicity Dept. at publicity@sunburypress.com.

ISBN: 978-1-62006-748-2 (Trade paperback)
ISBN: 978-1-62006-749-9 (Mobipocket)

Library of Congress Control Number: 2017952955

FIRST MILFORD HOUSE PRESS EDITION: September 2017

Product of the United States of America
0 1 1 2 3 5 8 13 21 34 55

Set in Bookman Old Style
Designed by Crystal Devine
Cover by Mark Mitten
Edited by Olivia Swenson

Continue the Enlightenment!

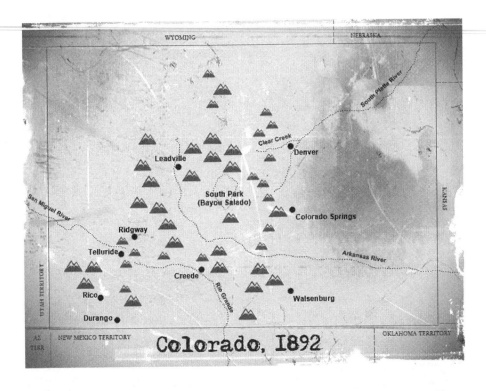

Colorado, 1892

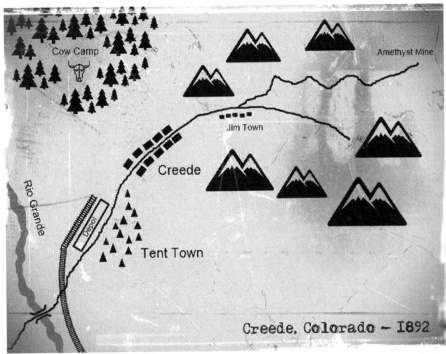

Creede, Colorado — 1892

— CHARACTER LIST —

(Complete character index in back)

 Cow Camp

LG and Davis are old friends
and bring in fifteen-year-old
Walker Blancett to help run cattle.

 Leadville

Horace "Haw" Tabor owns
the Matchless Mine.
Everyone calls him the Silver King.

Elizabeth "Baby Doe" is his young wife.

They have a toddler, a little girl
named Silver Dollar.

Big Ed runs the Stray Horse Brewery
but thinks he runs Leadville, too.

 The Smith Gang

Jefferson "Soapy" Smith
and his con men:

Banjo Parker
Joe Palmer
Old Man Tripp

 Young Horace

Horace Tabor, in his early years,
heads west with his first wife Augusta
and their son Maxcy.

Their homestead neighbor, Nathaniel,
leaves his sod house behind, too.

 The Sun Trail

Kahopi is looking for his father.
He meets three wandering Utes:

Greasewood
Bear Claw Lip
and a quiet kid, White Owl

Citizens of Creede

Bat Masterson runs the Denver Exchange, one of the biggest saloons in town.

Billy Woods is the barkeeper and a Saturday night prizefighter.

Bob Ford, the coward who killed Jesse James, often stops in for liquor and gossip.

— PART 1 —

— CHAPTER 1 —

SUMMER 1859
KANSAS TERRITORY

"I don't feel safe," Augusta scolded him. "I can't believe you left us alone."

Horace had just returned from town. He was tired, and in no mood for arguments.

"Gussie! You weren't alone. I asked Nathaniel to keep watch. You were safe the whole time."

"I never saw Nathaniel once."

"But he was *watching*. He can see our house from his own front door, clear as day."

Augusta's mouth fell open and she glared. She had dark brown hair. It was very curly and framed her face in tight. She also wore spectacles, which made her blue eyes seem severe. Especially when she was irked.

"Nathaniel lives two *miles* away, Horace. The only thing he would see is the smoke boiling up in the sky! We are homesteading in the middle of nowhere, in case you forgot. What if someone decided to burn us out?"

"Now, Gussie, no one is going to burn us out."

But that was a weak reply and he knew it. One of their neighbors *had* been burned out. In fact, they saw black smoke on the horizon the day it happened. It was the German family and their alfalfa field.

"What about Maxcy?" she whispered harshly, leaning in. "He's hardly a year old and where was his father when his home got burnt down?"

"Now, that's not . . . it ain't been burnt down. We're not in any . . ."

Horace wilted.

He did not like arguing with his wife. All he did was argue at the capitol building in Topeka ever since he got into politics. But for the moment, Horace was tired and simply wanted a friendly face. So he glanced past her shoulder, searching for one.

Maxcy was sitting beside the woodstove, nibbling on their broomstick. Teeth marks were all over it. Horace smiled and waved at the little boy.

Meanwhile, Augusta stomped over to the window and put her hands on her hips.

"On the bright side, I suppose if we got burnt out I wouldn't need to sweep up all this dirt."

Their home was a typical sod home—dim and dusty. They had one "window," which was just a hole in the wall with a rickety shutter. When the wind picked up, she always closed the shutter, but it didn't do much good.

"I have to sweep the whole floor, every single day. And *bugs*, Horace. They crawl right inside, like they live here. Ants and crickets and centipedes and spiders."

Horace wiggled his eyebrows at Maxcy, who grinned.

"Look at me when we're having a conversation, Horace!" Augusta snapped, and then snapped her fingers as well.

Maxcy tried snapping his own fingers, but they made no sound. This was because he wasn't doing it right. He just flicked his fingers—like he was flicking a bug. Maxcy liked to flick bugs. He stopped flicking his fingers and looked around for bugs. He spotted a spider web behind the woodstove and crawled over to investigate.

"I'm trying to make a life for us," Horace explained, and sighed. "I've tried farming, but I am no good at it. I've tried sod, but I'm no good at that, either."

"You can add windows to that list," Augusta suggested.

"People like me, Gussie. I do well in politics. They say I have gumption."

"I don't know about gumption, but you do have gall."

She kneeled next to Maxcy, who had found a spider and was plucking its legs off.

"You left me alone with our son!" she whispered, harsh again. "For what? To rub elbows with politicians?"

She took off her eyeglasses and rubbed the bridge of her nose.

"We're raising a family, Horace. Maybe we should move back to Maine."

Horace wasn't sure what to say that wouldn't make things worse.

He certainly wasn't going to tell her about the latest massacre. Everyone at the capitol building was buzzing about it. Some ruffians from Missouri, who were pro-slavery, simply walked across the border and took eleven men hostage—eleven men who were against slavery. They were marched into a ditch and shot.

A cold shiver ran through Horace's gut.

What if whoever burned out the alfalfa farm had meant to burn *him* out? He was a political figure, after all, and everyone knew he was a Free Stater. Maybe they were looking for the Tabor homestead and picked the wrong one?

Horace began to knead his temples.

"I have a headache, Gussie. Can we talk about this in the morning?"

"Let's move back to Maine, Horace. If you're worried about finding work, you know my father will give you a job again."

Horace wanted to pull his hair out when she said that. The man was intolerable.

CHAPTER 2

WINTER 1892
CREEDE

Squinting in the darkness, Davis tried to see if LG's eyes were open. But his hat brim was too low, and the light too dull. He resisted the urge to check his pocket watch. Davis didn't even want to know what time it was.

The two of them were huddled around a cast-iron stove with a big dent in it. The top of the firebox was so mashed in, the iron door did not close properly, and hot embers kept rolling out every time the fire popped or shifted. Just to keep the tent warm, someone had to stay up and feed sticks every half hour or so. Davis was mad about the whole situation. Every night they drew cards to see who stayed up with it. And every night, it seemed, LG drew a high ace. Why couldn't they just alternate?

"If I ain't getting no sleep, then you ain't getting no sleep."

He reached over and poked LG in the cheek but got no response.

LG's arms were folded, and his chin was resting on his chest. He appeared to be sound asleep, but Davis suspected he was just as awake as he was.

"Say, whatever happened to Emmanuel?" he asked in a loud voice. "That cook was one of the finest men that ever graced a chuck wagon. Top hand punching cattle, I'd add. He could fork any horse no matter how corrupt it was."

They had a long day ahead, and Davis was not looking forward to it. Building a cow camp in the middle of winter was a chore. Creede was a new boomtown. Silver had just been found, and people were flocking to the canyon creek to try their hand at mining. But LG and Davis had a different plan to get rich—beef. The only meat source in the backcountry was deer, maybe a bear, or fish from the half-frozen river. People would pay high dollar for steak.

The first step was to build a fence all around their new cow camp. They had chosen an open meadow in the middle of the forest. It would be perfect to hold beeves. All they needed to do was string wire from tree to tree to circle in the whole area.

Burning wood shifted inside the stove, and a lump of bright embers dropped onto the ground.

"What a foolish purchase," Davis pointed out unnecessarily. "Them boys at the Amethyst sure pulled one over on us, didn't they? They sure weren't straight about how it got bent in. *A big Kodiak thought it was a biscuit*—my eye! There ain't no Kodiak around here. I bet one of them drunks got soaked and whacked it with a sledgehammer."

He squinted at LG again, studying him in the dim light.

There was no way the man could be sleeping. This was pretend. He obviously wanted Davis to think he was impervious to hardship and could sleep through anything.

Without warning, the wind picked up.

Davis could hear the treetops sway and groan. The canvas roof rippled in the gusts. Behind them, the whole tent wall buckled and Davis twisted to see if he could get a look through the fluttering door-flap. He spotted a reddish glow outside and it made his heart sink. The sun was rising. It had been yet another long cold night without a wink of sleep.

"Remember that time Emmanuel couldn't find his triangle?" Davis said. "He pretended he was mad and accused the kid of stealing it. Poor kid denied it, of course. And then you said, 'We should have a law trial. To find the truth of the matter.'"

Davis took a quick sip of his coffee, but it was stone cold. He rocked forward and pitched it under the stove.

"So we pick a jury from the crew, and let the kid choose his own attorney. He picks Casey, who starts asking such dumb questions. 'Can anyone here even describe what a triangle looks like?' Then you point at Emmanuel and say, 'This here cook rings a triangle . . . three times a day!'"

Davis twirled his empty coffee cup by the handle.

"Then we tied him up and threw him in Beaver Creek. He was scared to death."

The wind howled and sent plumes of ice crystals pattering against the tent like a sandstorm. The sound sent fresh chills down Davis's back.

He reached over and poked LG in the cheek again.

CHAPTER 3

"Sun's up."

Davis's eyes snapped open.

"I almost didn't want to wake you," LG told him. "You looked as peaceful as the baby Jesus."

Sitting up, Davis cleared his throat.

"Now hold on," he said. "We can't go anywhere until the coffee's been drunk. I simply refuse to throw out good coffee."

He grabbed the coffee pot, but when he pulled off the lid he could see it was sludge—what little was in there had boiled down thick as molasses.

"Did you enjoy your beauty rest?" LG asked.

He pulled out a cigarette package from his pocket and fished one out. Then he struck a matchstick down the side of the stove and lit the tip.

"Are those Pinheads?" Davis leaned over to see the label better. "You were a Duke of Durham man for the longest time. 'Only Dukes,' you'd say. 'Only Dukes.' What made you change your tune?"

Pursing the cigarette between his lips, LG tightened up his neck scarf and grabbed his gloves. He stuffed the cigarettes back in his pocket without offering one.

"Oh, that's right," Davis recalled. "They plumb quit making 'em."

He yawned and rubbed his eyes, then he wiggled his cold toes inside his boots. He must have fallen asleep!

Outside, the wind was still screaming. He tried to think of a reason to keep from going outside.

"I can't *wait* to get that fence up," LG said out of the corner of his mouth.

Davis tried to balance the coffee pot on the dented stove, but as soon as he let go, it slid off and landed with a clang.

"I hate this piece of junk."

At that moment, hailstones began rattling the canvas roof. The whole tent began to quake. It was so loud, Davis put his fingers in his ears. Pieces of balled ice bounced in from under the tent walls. One rolled near their feet.

"Look at this thing," he shouted, picking it up. "Big as a cue ball!"

He tossed it back on the ground.

"Hope them horses find a tree to hide under."

The fabric popped and rattled. They both stared at the roof, worried it might rip apart any second. Finally, after what seemed like forever, it stopped. A few final hailstones plunked off the canvas as the storm wound down.

LG flicked his cigarette stub and put his hands on his knees like he was going to stand up.

"Look at us. A couple of sorry procrastinators."

But Davis didn't move. "If you want to go out and string wire in this mess, go right ahead."

Then he jumped up and went over to the doorway and pointed at the cords that tied the door-flap closed.

"And good luck trying. These dern knots are frozen solid. At four a.m., when the call came, I had to use the ash pail to piddle in."

LG shrugged. "We got cows coming in today on the train. We need to put up a crowding pen, at the very least."

"Aw, leave 'em at the stockyard," Davis said. "Who's gonna give a fig one way or the other?"

"No one might give a fig, but they'll happily charge us by the day to hold 'em."

They both stared at the mangled stove in silence.

The wind died down, but inexplicably, LG eased back down and took out the cigarettes again. He fished out another one—and this time offered one to Davis.

"Back in '84, I once spent a whole winter all alone in a line shack, up in Wyoming," LG said, striking a match. "Just me, pushing back beeves if they crossed the river. It was almost frozen over, but awful creaky in the centerline. That ice was thin enough to make a wooden Indian's hair rise."

Davis took the match and lit his cigarette, too.

He smiled slyly.

"Is that so?"

"You bet. Now, in the line shack, all I had for company was this lanky little mouser. I cut a hole in the wall and that cat could come in or out whenever it suited him. At first, he was wild as a deer. But I trained him to come running when I rang the supper bell."

"That's unbelievable."

LG took a quick puff.

"Well, one time some beeves got away in a storm, but I found 'em cooped up in a cutbank, hiding from the wind. I got 'em turned around, and pushed 'em back across that creaky old ice. But as I got close to the line shack, I heard something strange. I stopped and cocked my head, listening."

"What was it?" Davis asked.

"*Ring a ding. Ring a ding.* I could tell it was coming from inside that line shack. But no one was living there but me! Not one soul within a hundred miles. So, I eased out of the saddle and crept up. Slowly, I open up the door, and—*ring a ding!* There's that cat! Ringin' the supper bell!"

He hooted and slapped his knee, but Davis merely waved him off.

"I was smelling corral dust halfway through."

"True story."

"My ma gave me a dime to buy a liar with. But since I got you, I'll just hang on to it. It'll save me a trip to the store."

LG finished his laugh and wiped his eyes. Then, he picked out a wedge of knotted pine from the wood pile.

"Maybe one more."

He pushed the wood into the coals and puffed on his cigarette some more.

Suddenly, Davis snapped his fingers.

"I *knew* you were faking. Your eyes were closed when I brought up the chuck wagon triangle. And now, here you are, spinning some tale about a cat ringing a supper bell."

LG lit another cigarette. Davis held out his hand, but LG put the package back in his pocket.

Davis frowned.

"Well, you may wanna look beyond the pale and scope of this cold stank tent for your inspiration. That's all I'm saying."

LG tapped his forehead.

"It's all up here."

The coffee pot was still lying on the ground, where it fell. Davis picked it up and swished it around. There wasn't anything drinkable left. He stepped over to the ash pail in the corner of the tent and poured out the steaming sludge, right on top of his frozen four a.m. piddle.

— CHAPTER 4 —

GARO

"This would look sharp on you."

Til Blancett pointed at a stack of orange shirts.

His son, Walker, picked one up and examined it. It had big white buttons and felt starchy. It also had deep creases from sitting in a tight neat stack, along with the other shirts exactly like it. Puckering his forehead, the boy paused and considered the right words for a proper assessment.

"It's got some fine traits."

Til nodded in approval.

"And a good color to wear. It will remind you of your mother and her fondness for oranges."

Walker rubbed the fabric with his thumb.

"Now, Til, it ain't just plain old *orange*. The catalogue calls it Sundown," said Chubb, who ran the store. He turned to Walker. "Is Mrs. Blancett fond of sunsets? I bet every time she sees the sun go down she'll think of you in that nice shirt."

Walker held it up again and then glanced at Til.

"Poppa, why don't you own an orange shirt?"

"Well, I don't have a fondness for oranges," Til mused. "And sunsets are fine, but I prefer the sunrise."

"I do, too," Walker said and set the shirt down. "I prefer sunrises."

"Now, hold on a minute," Chubb said. He rooted through the same stack of orange shirts and pulled out one from the bottom.

"You're in luck. We've got one left in Sunrise."

Walker lit up and took it from Chubb.

"I do like this one."

Chubb went over to the store counter and began patting around and moving papers. He was always losing pencils. Customers would often discover them in unlikely places, frequently near the candy jars, so he rarely had to order new ones. But it was still a bother.

"Have you seen my dern pencil?"

"I saw one in the shirts, in the red pile," Til mentioned. "It was in the Grenadines. No, wait—maybe the Maraschinos. I find it hard to discern which is which."

Chubb gave Til a hard look on his way to the shirt table.

Though Walker managed to stand still, he was antsy inside. His stomach got butterflies each time he thought about the train ride. For the first time in his life, he was leaving home. He was going to work cattle in Creede. On his own. As a paid hand. Like a full-grown man.

"There ain't no pencil over here," Chubb muttered.

"And add in a pack of playing cards," Til called, and then winked at Walker—who was just as tall as he was. "Of course, your mother isn't to know."

Walker nodded solemnly.

Returning, Chubb reached beneath the counter and produced a brand new set of cards.

Walker felt the butterflies again. He couldn't believe his father was buying him playing cards. His mother would certainly not approve, not one bit.

Til pointed at the deck.

"I'm willing to wager LG still has the same ol' greasy six-ace pack he's had since he rode for the JA's."

"I remember LG," Chubb said. "Where did he end up? Is he still in South Park?"

Taking out his money, Til shook his head.

"Naw, he's up in Creede running beeves."

Chubb looked like he had been bit by a wasp.

"He's in *Creede* and he ain't panning for *silver*?" Chubb exclaimed. "You've gotta be pulling my Johnson!"

Til shook his head again.

"Nope."

"He's a damn fool, then. They say there are lumps of ore in that creek the size of an old whore's milkies."

Til put his hand on Walker's head and mussed up his blonde hair.

"Watch your language, Chubb."

But Chubb was too shocked to care.

"If I was LG, I'd give up cowboying directly," he continued. "That ain't no way to earn a living. Not when silver ore is lying among the river rocks, and all you have to do is lean over and pick it up with your bare hands. Invest in some waders, I'd say. Get on in there! What are you by now, Walker? Twelve?"

Walker frowned and combed his fingers through his hair, trying to fix it.

"Fifteen."

"Want to buy some waders?"

"No, he doesn't want to buy no waders," Til objected.

Walker frowned.

Everyone in Garo treated him like he was still a kid. He felt like he was stuck in time. He had been ten years old the day they moved into the area, and he would be a kid forever—as long as he stayed in Garo. Worse, his own mother was the schoolhouse teacher. It was hard to do anything without getting scolded, switched, or cuffed. So the purchase of playing cards—the devil's cards—and Chubb's crass talk was a refreshing change.

"I'm *fifteen* years old," he repeated. "And maybe I will come back for the waders when I've earned a proper wage."

Chubb slapped the counter.

"There you go. Big enough to head off to a mining camp all by his dern self. Big enough to work cows all by his dern self. He don't need to be coddled no more, Til. Time to cut the apron strings."

He leaned across the counter and locked eyes with Walker.

"Now mining camps are rough. So, here's some free advice—*He who sups with the devil ought to use a long spoon.*"

Chubb held the gaze, waiting for a response, but Walker wasn't sure what he meant.

Til started to muss his son's hair again but checked himself.

"Now he's trying to sell you a spoon. Let's get out of here while we got what we came for."

He held up some cash.

"How much for the shirt and cards?"

But Chubb pointed at the candy jars.

"How about some sweets? I got those red cherry candies you like. I know they're your favorite, and the train ride to Creede is a long one."

Seeing the red cherry candy, Walker almost said yes. They were indeed his favorite, and they would make for a nice treat on the train. But candy was for children.

"No, sir, I do not care for any."

Chubb was shocked.

"Peppermint puffs, then?"

"I do not care for that either," he replied.

But in his heart, he did.

CHAPTER 5

LEADVILLE

It was when the hail started clicking off the carriage top that Elizabeth "Baby Doe" Tabor knew her husband's talk about a leisure day trip was tommyrot. She turned and swatted him in the chest rather briskly.

"What are you really up to, Horace?" she demanded. "We can't see the countryside in the middle of a hailstorm."

Horace dug deep and worked up a mighty frown.

"Baby Doe!"

All over Leadville and beyond, Horace Tabor was known generally and affectionately as the Silver King. Ever since they got married, Baby Doe had grown accustomed to certain ways, and anything that even smacked of lower class banality frustrated her. Plus, she had grown adept at sniffing out his sneaky ways.

"It's a coach ride, for goodness' sake," Horace stammered. "Can't you merely appreciate the good life? Must you always shuck my good intentions?"

But her eyes were cast, and he knew his little game of subterfuge was over.

"Like corn," he explained.

She had caught his attention when she was only twenty-six. They were both married back then, but not to one another. Her first marriage was to the plain and uninspiring Harvey Doe. The only thing she kept from that relationship was her nickname. But only when she was in the mood to be called by her nickname—and she was not in the mood.

"We only go on coach rides *in* the country to *see* the country, which we cannot *see* in a hailstorm. The writing is on the wall, Horace," she said contemptuously, and proceeded to scratch at his eyes.

Batting at her with both hands, Horace scooted as far away as he could on the tiny bench. She was right, however. Whenever he took her on a country outing, it was always when it was sunny and warm. This was never the case in February in Leadville. And it was February in Leadville—a regrettable oversight to an otherwise ironclad duplicity.

"What are you planning?" she demanded. "Tell me!"

Horace stared at her, his mouth working to form a variety of shapes, as he wondered exactly what to divulge.

At times, the Silver King had business to conduct that might not be considered "above board" in polite company. And Baby Doe might not think so, either.

He often felt conflicted whenever he had to deal with unsavory folks, those of a murky disposition. Like Big Ed Burns, who he was secretly going to see—the true reason for their carriage ride. Horace had devised a crafty plan. He would dash inside the Stray Horse Brewery, telling Baby Doe he was picking up bottled refreshments for their country outing. Once inside, however, he would meet covertly with Big Ed, who had a secret message to pass on.

"You are *twenty* years older than me," she said, watching his wheels turn. "You should be far more clever by this point in your life."

At that moment the coach riddled through the icy ruts and skidded to a stop, and their driver called out above the hail.

"Stray Horse!"

Wiping the fog off the window with a silk hanky, Baby Doe peered out and instantly knew her suspicions were correct.

"We risked our lives in the hail for *this*? I'm not going in that dingy little plank-sided beer house."

"I just wanted some refreshments to make the ride more enjoyable."

"They sell *swill*, Horace."

He shrugged his shoulders helplessly, turned up his collar, and hunched out into the icy blur. It was true, the beer at the Stray Horse was barely palatable, but at least his crafty plan had worked.

CHAPTER 6

Once he got inside, Horace shook the ice pellets off his coat.

The Stray Horse Brewery was on the outskirts of town, in Stray Horse Gulch. The bartender was a man named Dirty Johns, who always wore dirty johns—covered by equally befouled dungarees.

"Your bottles are in the back," Dirty Johns said and winked.

The room was barely bigger than a barn aisle, and Horace had to cross it to get where he was going. However, there was a sour-smelling puddle in the middle of the floor, blocking his path.

"Did you see this?" Horace asked.

Dirty Johns leaned over the bar and looked.

"Don't mess your fancy shoes."

Grimacing, Horace inched carefully around the puddle. It was no easy task, given the sheer volume of retch he had to navigate. Once across, Horace sighed, relieved, and then marched into the backroom.

Dirty Johns watched him go.

"I wish I had a pair of fancy shoes."

The backroom was where the big copper brewing vats were housed. Like the saloon area, it too was cramped quarters. But at least it didn't stink. The scent of boiled grains was in the air, like someone was baking bread. It reminded Horace of the old days, when his first wife Augusta baked bread. She used to make a cinnamon bread that was both sweet and delightful . . . two traits she lacked.

"Howdy, Haw."

Big Ed was sitting on a crate, cradling a beer bottle.

"What is it, Ed?"

It annoyed Horace that Big Ed called him Haw. Only his good friends called him Haw.

"What is it that's so blessed secretive I had to come all the way out here in a hailstorm?"

But Big Ed guffawed.

"Look at you. Such a big man in this town. Can barely spare a minute for your ol' friends."

Horace had never liked Big Ed. In the past, the man had been one of Soapy Smith's lackeys. Soapy was the most well-known con artist in the state. He used to have Leadville under his thumb but

had since moved on to dominate Denver. In Soapy's absence, Big
Ed tended to think *he* ran Leadville.

"Just tell me the damn message."

Big Ed took a sip of beer and got serious.

"Teller is comin' through."

"Teller?" Horace repeated. "You mean Henry M. Teller, our state
senator? Coming here?"

"That's the gist."

After staring at Big Ed for a moment, trying to gauge the reli-
ability of the news, Horace began to pace. Well, that certainly *was*
news—if Big Ed wasn't pulling his leg. Without fail, Big Ed always
tried to manipulate him or play coy games whenever he thought he
had some kind of leverage. But Horace was tired of the shenani-
gans. And of Big Ed in general. Without Soapy Smith to tie onto, the
man wasn't as intimidating as he used to be.

Yet today, despite his faults, Big Ed had actually contributed
something useful.

"Did he say why he wants to meet?"

Big Ed's face creased into an off-putting smile.

"Oh, Haw. Should I let it be a surprise? Surprises are more fun."

Horace frowned. These were the kind of games he was tiring of.
The man was trying to play mob boss. It wasn't working, though.
Clearly, Teller's men had not told Big Ed Burns why he wanted to
meet.

"You got nothing, do you?" Horace asked, feeling his oats.
"That's because you're just the errand boy, Ed. Errand boys don't
know piss or pooter."

Big Ed stopped smiling. He stood up and inched close.

"Don't push what you can't pull, Tabor."

Horace did not feel the gut flutters he used to feel in moments
like this. Perhaps time had hardened his resolve. Or perhaps he
was just seeing clearer than he had in years.

"Set it up, Ed. Just set it up. Maybe you'll get a little something
for your orchestration. A bauble of some kind. Something shiny."

PART 2

CHAPTER 7

SUMMER 1859
KANSAS TERRITORY

When Horace saw the front page of the *Kansas Tribune*, he could barely sit still.

"This is it, Gussie!"

Spreading butter on a slice of bread, Augusta ignored him.

"Listen to this," he said, and tapped the newspaper. "They found gold in the Rocky Mountains. It's everywhere. In every creek and canyon. All we need is to take a pan and dip it in the water!"

Augusta rolled her eyes.

"Every time there's a gold rush, they always say that. Don't be gullible, Horace."

He tapped the newspaper again.

"This is our ticket out of here."

He grabbed the bread out of her hand and wagged it in front of her eyes.

"I'll give this back once we get to Denver."

Jumping up, he raced out the door.

Augusta simply sliced off another piece of bread and spread butter on it. She licked the knife clean and pulled the newspaper across the table.

Deciding to investigate the spider situation, Maxcy crawled across the dirty floor. The woodstove was very hot, and he knew better than to touch the metal. On the other hand, he saw a new web back there. It was just out of reach.

As soon as he pressed his cheek against the woodstove, Maxcy knew he had made a big mistake. He squalled.

Instantly, Augusta ran over and scooped him up.

"Maxcy!" she cried. "When are you going to learn not to do that?"

But he howled and wept, so she held him until he settled down.

Every morning, no matter how hard she cleaned the day before, their house was *covered* with fresh spider webs. Holding her son in her arms, Augusta walked back over to the kitchen table. She stared at the headline.

"If I was rich, I would hire a maid to sweep this dang floor and all these dang cobwebs."

Maxcy blubbered and wiped his eyes with his little knuckles.

She set him on the floor and gave him the piece of bread.

Then Augusta went and stood in the doorway. It was a bright, cool morning. The grass sparkled with fresh dew. The sun was inching up above the wide, empty prairie. And her husband, Horace, was halfway to their neighbor Nathaniel's house.

"So gullible."

Then, quite suddenly, fear racked her gut.

Dashing across the corral, she climbed the manure mound. The top of the mound was the best place to scan the entire horizon for smoke. It was her morning ritual, but with all the gold rush talk and the stove incident, it slipped her mind! She looked north, south, east, and west. But the sky was clear. No one was being burned out today.

She looked again at Nathaniel's home, two miles away.

"Don't you tell him about that gold!" she shouted.

Horace was almost there and too far away to hear her voice.

Sighing, Augusta started walking back toward the house, but then stopped and stared at it. It didn't look like a house. Not at all. It looked like the manure pile. A giant pile of manure filled with bugs. And a poorly hung window.

CHAPTER 8

WINTER 1892
LEADVILLE

When Baby Doe Tabor strode into the great room, it just so happened Horace was already hiding behind the drapery folds. It was an unexpected convenience, because now he was hidden from the wrath of *two* Tabor women.

His original intention was to evade his daughter Silver Dollar's rage. A tangy little toddler, her temperament was already disturbingly similar to her mother's.

"Horace! Show yourself!" Baby Doe demanded loudly.

Horace did no such thing.

After checking beneath the dining table, Baby Doe peeked behind the settee and the arm chairs. But she did not find her elusive husband hiding in any of his usual places.

From the staircase in the foyer, she heard a dull but distinct *whump whump*. She knew immediately it was Silver Dollar sliding on her rump one step at a time. Baby Doe waited, and it was but a moment before the girl dropped into view. Her face was tomato red, but it softened to a lesser, strawberry coloring the moment she saw her mother.

"Necklace!" Silver Dollar shouted.

"Silver. Come," Baby Doe said and waved her over.

"Necklace!"

Baby Doe knew that her daughter was enamored by pretty things. She had taken a particular interest in jewelry, and an even more particular liking to Baby Doe's more expensive pieces—especially the Isabella Necklace. It was made of pearls. It used to belong to Queen Isabella, and Horace had bought it the very morning of their marriage for ninety thousand dollars. It had been a smashing addition to her wedding ensemble.

Given their current state of marital tumult, Baby Doe had decided to let the child have at it like a toy. After all, that was how Horace was treating her—like a toy. A toy he liked to show off to his illustrious comrades in consumerism, and then toss aside when the liquor and cigars came out.

When, at a recent Sunday brunch, Horace saw Silver Dollar sitting in her dinner table highchair with the Isabella Necklace in one hand and a fistful of buttery peas in the other, he was appalled.

"She can't play with *that*."

He reached for the necklace.

"She can if she wants to!" Baby Doe countered and slapped Horace's hand fiercely.

It instantly became a bitter point of contention.

Thus, when Horace went upstairs to get his emerald-studded stick pin and found Silver Dollar whipping the Isabella Necklace against the baseboards, he knew the moment was his. Shimmying the object from the girl's grip, he turned and hustled down the staircase as fast as he could. Dodging through the foyer into the great room, he made a beeline for the draperies—which all had led to the present predicament.

"Necklace!" Silver Dollar cried out, wobbling on her feet.

Baby Doe turned slowly around the great room, her eyes narrowing.

Then, in one swift motion, she swept up her furious little daughter and plunked her on the settee. In a second swift motion, she took up the wrought-iron poker from the fireplace and skewered the nearest drapery fold. Fortunately for Horace, it was not the drapery fold he was hiding behind. But the violent thrust was cause enough to unseat him from his camouflage.

"Cease your stabbing, woman!" he cried and dashed across the room.

"I *knew* you had it!" she roared, pointing the poker.

"Necklace!" Silver Dollar hollered and jumped off the settee. Unfortunately, her launch was not governed by foresight, and she clocked her forehead on the coffee table. Instantly, she began to wail.

"Now look what you've done," Baby Doe snarled at her husband, and was, for a moment, conflicted as to which direction to rush.

Horace, seeing her hesitate, bolted for the door like a jack rabbit.

"*It cost ninety grand!*" he yelled over his shoulder as he wrestled the knob. He had to yell to be heard above Silver Dollar's pulsating screams.

Scooping up the nearest vase, Baby Doe hurled it in his direction. It arced through the air and collided heavily with his buttocks, and then fell to the floor with a thud. However, it was not enough to slow his escape. Horace slammed the door behind him and ran down the street.

CHAPTER 9

Horace spent the afternoon barricaded in his office at the Tabor Grand Hotel. It appeared he had successfully absconded with the Isabella Necklace. But, just to be safe, he remained at his desk until dark.

There was a second reason Horace was waiting for nightfall. He needed to sneak down to the train depot without being seen. Henry M. Teller, state senator of Colorado, was at that very moment waiting in a caboose with the curtains drawn.

So, once the sky turned black, Horace went down to the hotel stables and took a carriage ride to the depot, even though it was just a couple blocks away.

Horace hadn't seen the senator for years. In fact, some years back, Teller had actually stepped down from his station to become Secretary of the Interior. When he did, Horace seized the moment. He pulled every string he could and won a thirty-day appointment, albeit nominal, as the new Colorado state senator.

But those were a glorious thirty days.

Ah, Horace thought, *the days of public scandal.*

Those same thirty days were not only lively, but morally ambiguous, as he changed over from his first wife to his second.

He tried to be discreet, at first, with his interest in the former Mrs. Doe. After separating from Augusta, Horace moved into a Leadville hotel. But then, Baby Doe *coincidentally* moved into the same hotel a few days later.

Augusta certainly did not take the news very well.

Red-faced about being cast off for a younger thing, she simply refused to sign off on a divorce. So Horace went around her. He pulled some more strings. He got the divorce down in Durango. The snag was, it wasn't legal. And therefore, neither was getting wed to Baby Doe. Which was why they held a private ceremony—in Saint Louis.

Then Augusta found out about their forbidden nuptials, legally and otherwise, and made a big stink about it. Enraged, she left town and moved to Denver, vowing never to return. Not too long after that, she got the idea, probably from one of her equally dour high-society lady friends, to invite a newspaper reporter over for a "chat." Being a millionaire made Horace a prime target for the media. The gossipy Augusta rants made for a juicy read, and soon everyone in Colorado was talking about the Silver King's checkered goings-on and goings-behind.

Finally, they negotiated a real divorce.

It was costly, of course. Not only did Augusta get hundreds of thousands of dollars, but she got to keep their second home in Denver. It was a $40,000 mansion!

But when tempers cooled, Horace and Baby Doe got married again, this time legitimately, and this time in DC—just a few days before his senatorial stint expired. It was a big bash. Even the president came.

Now, all of that was long since over.

And here he was, sneaking off to meet Henry M. Teller himself, the state senator *encore une fois*, in a train caboose.

"Are you aware that the price of silver has been falling?" Teller asked as soon as Horace snuck in the door.

The senator was sitting on his bunk in his shirtsleeves and suspenders, holding a notebook.

"Here are the numbers," he continued, adjusting his bifocals. "119, 104, 99, and now 87 cents an ounce. Do you realize what that means?"

Horace considered himself an optimist and refused to be cowed by mathematics.

"Do *you* realize I have been in Leadville for thirty-odd years? I was here from the beginning, when it was just a muddy creek and a handful of prospectors. I've seen a gold rush, and I've seen a silver boom. So whatever the trouble is now, I assure you things will turn around."

Teller set the notebook down and took off his eyeglasses.

"We're headed for a silver crash, Tabor!"

Walking over to a small table across from the bunk, Horace took off his hat and sat down.

"What about all that legislation you got passed?" he asked with a heavy sigh. "I thought it was set in stone."

Horace was conflicted. On one hand, Senator Teller was his strongest ally in the realm of politics. On the other hand, he was a bit dramatic.

"I know for fact the US treasury is obligated to buy four *million* ounces of silver every single month," Horace continued. "The mines of Leadville are churning it out night and day, so what's the worry?"

But Teller looked irritated. He itched his cheek, which was covered in a thin sheen of gray whiskers.

"I've been in this train for a week straight. Did you know that, Horace? I haven't bathed once, and these chin hairs are itchy as hell."

As soon as he heard that, Horace broke into a magnanimous smile.

"Well, come on up to my hotel, Henry. I'll put you in the Millionaire Suite. Silk sheets from the Orient, and we'll smoke cigars in the parlor until dawn. How does rib-eye strike you?"

Teller slammed the notebook shut, and then threw it against the wall.

"You're not thinking clear! Don't you understand the danger you're in? The politicians out east know Leadville is flush with silver *and they don't like it*. All this easy money. They're jealous, sneaky, legislative bastards. Can't you see what's going on? They're devaluing the silver!"

Horace shifted in his seat and sat up a little straighter.

"Damn Democrats," he grumbled.

"There's only one way we can stop them. The presidential election is this November. They have to be defeated at the ballot box. We need all the votes we can get . . . every miner in Leadville *must* be on the same page."

Horace nodded, trying to follow along. Politics often made his mind feel garbled.

"Okay. So how do we do that?"

"Create a fraternity—call it the Leadville Silver Club. Tell everyone that whoever signs on gets a bonus of some kind. You figure it out."

"Not a problem." Horace said, and snapped his fingers. "I can get that going."

The senator was fuming mad and obviously unimpressed with Horace's nonchalance.

"Good. Because if silver crashes, then so does every silver miner in this town, state, and country, including *you*—along with every farmer paying his bills with a silver dollar!"

Pulling back the curtain, Horace peeked outside.

The street lamps were on, casting a soft yellow glow in the darkness. The last train of the evening had already left, so no one was standing around waiting. The depot was quiet. A light dusting of fresh snow covered everything—the platform, the rails, and even his carriage. Horace could see his driver, up on the driver's bench, shivering in the chilly night air.

CHAPTER 10

DENVER

John Arkins stepped out the front door of the *Rocky Mountain News,* where he reigned as chief editor, and yawned.

It had been a long day and he was ready to go home.

Then he noticed Banjo Parker outside, waiting, and forgot where he was going.

Sporting long limbs and blobby hindquarters, Banjo Parker was hard to miss. He looked like a banjo. And, like the folksy fiddle, his neck was even a little stringy.

The sight of Banjo was disturbing, not because of his odd conformation, but because of his reputation as a Smith Gang heavy. Then Soapy Smith himself seemed to materialize from nowhere, with a cane, and batted John Arkins upside the head.

"Got you, sucker!" Soapy shouted. "Right in the ivories!"

Soapy swung again, this time at the kidney area.

"Damn chatterbox."

As a crowd gathered around them, Banjo put a hand on Soapy's shoulder.

"People are gawking. We should have done this in the alley."

Before he passed out, John Arkins smiled. He smiled because he had finally gotten to Soapy Smith, baited him out in the open— for all the world to see.

All summer long Arkins had been writing articles, trying to expose the man for what he really was. Most people thought Soapy Smith was an average con artist. A lot of hoodlums ran shell games on the street corners of Denver, and indeed, that was how he started out. But John Arkins figured out that Soapy wasn't interested in simply taking people's money. He wanted to take over the whole city.

It began with simple bribes to get out of jail. He paid off policemen, judges, and lawyers. Whenever Soapy got arrested, he somehow turned up on the street again the very next day.

Then, as time went on, Soapy set his sights higher.

When he had enough money, he opened up a gambling hall, the Tivoli Club—but rumor had it the tables were rigged. When the gaming commission looked into it, Soapy paid them off, too.

And when anti-gambling legislation was introduced, he "donated" to certain campaigns and the politicians made it all go away.

Well, John Arkins realized what was going on. He sent out reporters to dig around, and as the truth came to light, he published it. Denver was being poisoned, but the editor of the *Rocky Mountain News* was fighting back.

With headlines.

He tried everything, but nothing seemed to work. Insinuations, exposés, even outright insults. But in the end, all it took was a little family research. Anna Smith, it turned out, was living in a nice, sensible cottage right there in Denver, raising three wonderful children. In order to maintain the veneer of a normal life and a warm welcome in the community, she told everyone her husband sold textiles.

So John Arkins wrote about it and irked Soapy into showing his hand.

And by caning the editor of the very newspaper that was investigating him, Soapy had just fallen on his own sword.

CHAPTER 11

CREEDE

When Davis was about two sentences in, LG found he could restrain himself no more.

"You don't have to read your love letters out loud."

Davis gave him a look.

"A girl didn't write this. Lee did."

"She has a lovely name. Put that away."

Gritting his teeth, Davis quietly folded it up and put it back in the envelope. Then he took off his hat, dropped it inside the crown, and mashed the whole thing back on his head.

"I was just getting to the good part."

LG snorted.

"If there ain't cash money in there, there ain't no good part."

"Hell, you worked with the man and you *know* who I'm talking about. He wrote to warn us about heel flies. It's an epidemic in Texas."

"Well, there ain't no flies up here," LG said and snickered. "There's six feet of snow."

"We are headed to the train depot at this very moment to receive a shipment of cattle—from Texas. I'd say that is cause for concern."

"They ain't *from* Texas. Their feet won't barely touch the ground. They'll come off an ocean ship and get right on a train."

Davis knew LG was just ribbing him, but it was still a frustration. Lee, whom they both knew, had gone to the effort to write a letter and mail it all the way from Texas. Heel flies were causing a great deal of trouble for the cattle at the big XIT ranch. Davis himself used to punch cattle down there, once upon a time. However, he left after getting knifed in the back by a fellow named Billy Ney. It occurred during an argument over whether or not Davis had caused a stampede by striking a match in the darkness and spooking the herd. In fact, Davis had not struck a match—but Billy Ney was in a foul mood and produced a knife anyway.

LG and Davis were riding to town. It was late in the morning, but the sun was bright.

They took their horses down a narrow forest trail and then out into the river valley. The river itself was mostly frozen, except in spots where they could hear the water pouring by. In the distance, they could easily see the big cliff rising above the trees, just a couple miles away, where Creede was.

Hailstones were everywhere. They filled in the muddy wheel ruts and speckled the snowpack. With every awkward step the horses took, there was a brittle crunching sound.

"Our dang broncs are gonna get footsore," LG noted.

But Davis was not through with the argument.

"You know, flies can ride on trains just as easy as beeves," he pointed out.

LG looked him up and down.

"It's winter time, in case you're blind. Plus, the railmen dip every single one before they load 'em on the train."

At that, Davis laughed victoriously.

"Dipping a cow is for disease. That don't keep flies off their heels."

CHAPTER 12

Tent Town was a group of tents all around the train depot. Creede proper, made of actual wood-framed buildings, was up the road directly beneath the cliff.

"I think every single one of these is a saloon," Davis said, indicating the tents.

He began reading off the business names, which were painted right on the canvas.

"The Gold Nugget, Bonanza, Old Prospector, Lode Hill. I don't think half these were here last time we came through."

One unsteady fellow was urinating on the Bonanza, leaving streaks up and down the canvas wall.

"Write your name!" LG called out.

Davis looked thoughtful.

"When I was a kid, I used to work a buffalo camp out past Dodge. An old frontiersman used to come around with a wagon full of booze. He called it his rolling saloon. It was full of jugs and jars and bottles and they all had chili peppers floating inside. One even had a rattlesnake head."

LG spotted another drunk miner, pale as a ghost, yacking in the muck.

"What did you have for supper?" he called. "Looks like hard boiled eggs!"

When they reached the train depot, they both parked their horses. Davis hiked right up the steps and nearly slipped. The whole platform was slick with the melting hail.

"Why are you going in there?" LG asked him. "The train ain't even here yet."

"I want to see if we got any more mail."

"You and your love letters."

Heading inside the station office, Davis was accosted with a blast of heat and promptly forgot about the mail.

"It is paradise in here."

He went straight over to the big iron potbelly stove in the corner. It was burning so hot the wall boards around it were charred black and sap was sizzling.

As soon as LG came through the door, Davis called to get his attention.

"Look at this. A stove that actually puts out heat."

He knelt down and examined it closely.

"And look at this. The door shuts proper."

LG unbuttoned his coat.

"You bet," he replied. "And it cost top dollar, too."

The station agent was sitting at the desk, quietly reading the newspaper. LG leaned over and flicked it.

"What's the *Creede Candle* got for us today?"

Irritated, the station agent yanked the paper away.

"The Denver Exchange is advertising butter from the Red Cliff dairy."

"No wonder you look so morose. Is that what qualifies as news around here? Butter?"

The man squinted spitefully.

"No, but that is what I was reading when you interrupted me."

As if summoned, the door opened and Billy Woods stuck his head in. Billy tended bar at the Denver Exchange.

"Did you hear about the Swedish sheepherder? He got killed dead last night by the hail. Him and his thousand sheep. All dead from hail."

LG turned and pointed at the station agent.

"Now *that* is news. Put that paper in the privy so it can serve a higher calling."

Davis pressed his wet gloves against the big hot stove.

"A man just went to meet the Lord," he said as they sizzled. "So sad."

But Billy Woods did not look sad.

"The Denver Exchange got all the dead sheep. We're serving mutton all day long!"

"The man ain't even buried yet."

Billy shrugged.

"Not true. We buried him in a snowbank out back. Come on by if you're hungry."

With that, he disappeared out the door. As soon as he was gone, LG began buttoning his coat back up.

"Hot damn. We better get over there quick—before all them buttery lamb chops are gone."

Davis looked at the wall clock.

"When is the train supposed to get here?"

There was a chalkboard with the schedule written on it, and the station agent tapped it with his finger.

"Noon, it says."

"But it's well past noon already."

"Probably got slowed down on account of the hail. Or maybe there are trees down on the tracks. How should I know?"

"It's your job to know."

But the station agent ignored them and went back to his newspaper.

CHAPTER 13

ROCKY MOUNTAINS

"What are you reading there, boy?" Soapy Smith asked.

Walker held up his novel to show him the title.

"*The New York Detective Library—Frank James: The Avenger and His Surrender*," Soapy read off. "Well, that sounds like a good one."

The boy nodded.

"I am enjoying it immensely."

"I don't know how you can read on this bumpy ol' train. I'd be seasick if I tried."

Closing his book, Walker turned and looked out the window. They were in a snowy mountain canyon in the middle of nowhere. Big, craggy peaks stuck up in the sky, and he had no idea where he was.

Walker did feel sick to his stomach. But it wasn't the train.

One time, when he was still a child, Walker had gotten to ride on a train. Back then, it had been a fun adventure. But this time, it wasn't fun at all. He was so worried about leaving home that he hadn't slept the night before. He couldn't get his mind to stop working, either, or the butterflies to stop messing up his gut. At least reading a book took his mind off the whole ordeal.

"I think Frank James is working in a theater up in Saint Louis," mentioned Joe Palmer, one of Soapy's men. He was seated across the aisle, next to Banjo Parker. "Selling tickets. Or an usher, I think. Somehow he ain't in jail, I know that much."

Immediately, Walker started to feel better. He loved talking about the James gang. Even with complete strangers.

"The last time he killed a man was in Northfield, Minnesota, back in '76. The year before I was born," Walker explained. "The cashier was a Mr. Joseph Lee Heywood. He told Frank the safe had a time lock and could not be opened—it really did have a time lock, but it wasn't engaged. The safe was open the whole time but Frank didn't know it. He *did* know that Mr. Heywood was being difficult. So he put a gun to the cashier's head and pulled the trigger."

Soapy thought about it.

"So he shot the man in the head for being difficult."

He winked at Banjo, who was sitting nearby.

"Maybe I should go back to Denver and pay another visit to John Arkins."

Joe was confused.

"If the safe was unlocked the whole time, why didn't Frank just go over there and try the handle?" he wondered.

"Well, the cashier tricked him," Walker replied. "Plus, the people in town realized the bank was being robbed, so they started shooting. He had to get out of there fast."

Joe frowned.

"So they didn't even get the money? That's a terrible story."

"They made off with twenty-six dollars in nickels."

"Twenty-six bucks!" Soapy said, chuckling. "What a waste of time. I'm glad I ain't a bank robber."

Joe and Banjo grinned at each other.

"So, where are you from?" Soapy asked the boy.

"South Park. A little town called Garo. My family runs Hay Ranch. Have you heard of it? We gather hay and ship it all over the place. We even ship it out of state, and my poppa says next year we're gonna ship it to England."

Soapy shrugged.

"Never heard of it."

Suddenly, Joe leapt out of his seat, crossed the aisle, and crawled across Soapy's lap to get at the window.

"What are you doing?" Soapy yelled.

To avoid getting pinned, Walker slid down and squirmed into the aisle.

"Get off me," Soapy growled at Joe. "You're standing on my foot."

"There's a deer right outside the window. Banjo, give me my gun, quick."

Sure enough, just outside, there was a doe. It was right beside the tracks, nibbling on a twig. Banjo handed him his rifle.

"This one's mine!" Joe called.

He slid the barrel into the cold air and drew a bead on the animal.

Walker put his fingers in his ears.

The gun went off and the smell of burnt powder filled the car. The deer seemed to leap, but then fell flat in the snow, in the underbrush.

"Hey Garo," Joe said. "Go tell them to stop this train."

"Me?"

"Hurry up before we get too far."

Walker ran up the aisle and went outside. The passenger car was hitched behind the coal car, and he had to stand on his toes to see over the black heap. A man was shoveling large lumps of coal into the firebox.

"Hello the engine!" Walker shouted.

"What is it?"

"A fellow just shot a deer."

The man gave him a thumbs up. Turning around, Walker went back inside. The steam whistle blew and the train came to a stop.

"Where the hell is Old Man Tripp?" Joe asked, looking around. "I need a hand with that carcass."

"I put him in the luggage car to guard our gear," Soapy said.

"He's probably dead drunk, anyway, and I need someone who ain't dead drunk."

Banjo frowned.

"Don't ask me."

So Joe went over and patted Walker on the shoulder.

"It's you and me, Garo. Come on."

They climbed off the train and slid into the snow. Walker went in up to his waist. It was deep. He grabbed onto some willow branches for balance.

"It's over there," Soapy hollered, pointing from the window.

The two of them began wading through the snow towards the dead deer.

"That was a good shot," Walker remarked, breathing hard.

Joe grinned at him.

"Frank James couldn't have done it better."

— CHAPTER 14 —

TERRITORY OF ARIZONA

It was in a dream that the Spider Woman spoke to Kahopi and told him she had turned his father back into clay.

Kahopi was at first shocked by her smug explanation. The Spider Woman was old and her face and arms were wrinkly, crosshatched like an old sunken apple. Her eyes gave him the cold shivers, but her power was strong and he could not look away.

Kahopi knew then that sleeping out on the mesa was foolish, like people always said.

There was an old shrine on the south end of the mesa. Right next to the shrine, there was a hole in the ground, a *sipapu,* where the Spider Woman was said to live. It was the entrance to the underworld. No one ever dared to crawl inside, but many people left her offerings. There were always plates lying at the entrance.

While the sun god, Tawa, was the one who ruled the sky, it was the Spider Woman who ruled the underworld. In the beginning, Tawa and the Spider Woman had made the earth. The Spider Woman sculpted animals from clay, but they did not have life in them until Tawa spread a white blanket over them and they began to wiggle. The Spider Woman then took clay and sculpted men and women, too. But just the same, the men and women had no life in them. So, she scooped them up and clutched them tightly. Both Tawa and the Spider Woman sang a song. As they sang, the men and women began to wiggle.

"Where is he now?" Kahopi asked. "That I might bury him properly?"

"Way up there in the mountains. Where the Whites dig like ants."

"Where is that?"

The Spider Woman smiled a crafty smile.

"The Whites dig to find the Third World. But they will not find it."

Kahopi shook his head in disgust. Everyone knew the Third World had been destroyed by a flood! But Kahopi also knew why the Spider Woman was being so difficult with him. One time, his father had defecated in the *sipapu.* His father was drunk when he dumped there, but of course the Spider Woman would be offended whether he was drunk or not.

When the sun rose in the east sky and cast its warmth, the dream ended and Kahopi sat up, shaking. His ears were ringing, and he trembled. To see the Spider Woman was dangerous. Perhaps she wanted to trick him, and lead him into the underworld in his dream. But Tawa had intervened at the last moment, waking him, and he had escaped.

Quickly, he stood and hurried down the trail toward the rising sun.

Whereas the Spider Woman was deceptive, Tawa was trustworthy. And Kahopi knew Tawa would lead him to where his father was. Kahopi wanted to bury him properly so he could hasten to the Skeleton House.

CHAPTER 15

SOUTHWEST COLORADO

The further east Kahopi traveled, the more lonely he became. And so, when he came across three Utes sitting around a campfire in a ring of juniper trees, he immediately sat down.

"What are you discussing?" Kahopi asked.

"We are discussing the best way to deal with White thieves," Bear Claw Lip told him.

His lower lip was missing and Kahopi found it difficult not to stare.

Greasewood, an older man with gray streaks in his hair, shrugged.

"There are some Whites up in the canyon right now," he explained. "They found the sacred cliff houses, where the Ancient Ones used to dwell."

The third Ute was just a boy in his teens, listening quietly. His name was White Owl. He had a long branch that he used to stoke the campfire.

"They are scratching around, looking for treasures," Bear Claw Lip said. He looked indignant and fidgety. "We need to get up there right away."

But the older man merely yawned and rubbed his eyes.

"What can we do, anyway?" he asked.

"We have to do something. They even brought shovels."

As soon as he said that, Kahopi felt his ears tingle.

"Are they digging like ants?"

"Digging like ants," Bear Claw Lip said. "And stealing like raccoons."

He pointed at Greasewood.

"And only *he* knows where the secret entrance is."

"But I am old and tired," Greasewood explained. "I want to go home and take a nap."

Bear Claw Lip gaped at him.

"What? You just woke up a few minutes ago."

"Are they looking for the Third World?" Kahopi inquired.

But the Utes were too busy arguing.

Since he had never met them before, Kahopi decided to keep his mission private—but he wanted to learn more. He suspected that this was the place where the Spider Woman had left his father. She said Kahopi would find his father's body where the Whites were digging like ants, searching for the Third World. And what better place to search for the Third World than in a sacred place where the Ancient Ones used to dwell?

"Let's tie them to the rocks and unwind their entrails. Tack them straight out to the four winds," Bear Claw Lip said, splaying his fingers. "Like spokes on a wagon wheel."

Greasewood elbowed Kahopi and winked.

"Last year, some cowboys let their cows graze on our land. Everyone discussed it, and we decided to butcher the cows. But Bear Claw Lip wanted to butcher the cowboys instead!"

"We should have," grumbled the disfigured Ute.

Suddenly, he jumped to his feet and took out a knife.

"Help me find a good stone to sharpen my blade."

But no one did.

When he was out of earshot, Greasewood elbowed Kahopi again.

"Bear Claw Lip is an angry man. Ever since he lost his lower lip."

"How did he lose it?"

"A black bear swiped it off when he was a boy," he explained, and pointed at the young Ute sitting next to him. "He was about White Owl's age when it happened. And even though it's had plenty of time to heal up, it still looks eerie. Like someone scalped his chin! None of the girls were very interested in him after he lost his lip."

Kahopi nodded.

"Such a thing would make any man bitter."

Then Greasewood leaned over and patted White Owl's knee, who was still listening quietly.

"Stay away from bears."

The boy nodded thoughtfully but said nothing.

Trotting back, carrying a stone, Bear Claw Lip sat back down and began to sharpen his blade.

"Let's cut off their hands as punishment for stealing."

But Greasewood shook his head.

"If we do that, the White government will send in another big White general to deal with us. Like when they made us leave our hunting grounds. They might even destroy the sacred ruins entirely."

He patted White Owl's knee again.

"Even though you are only fifteen years old, you are a better listener than your elders."

He shot a dark look at Bear Claw Lip, but he was too busy sharpening his knife.

A peel of thunder shook the canyon.

Kahopi studied the sky. The clouds were rolling in. They looked thick and gray, like an upturned skillet full of puffy biscuits.

"It's going to rain," he mentioned.

"I doubt it. It's too chilly. Maybe sleet or snow," Bear Claw Lip replied skeptically.

But Kahopi stood up and spoke firmly.

"We need to get out of this canyon."

Greasewood got up and brushed the sand off his legs.

"Okay. Let's go home."

But Bear Claw Lip was shocked at the suggestion.

"What! But what about the thieves? We need to go up there right now and teach them a lesson. Their innards ought to be removed. And perhaps their eyes as well. Certainly their hands, at the very least. No one can argue against their hands."

Kahopi went over and stood next to him.

"I will go with you."

Putting his hands on his hips, Bear Claw Lip glowered at Greasewood.

"You have to at least show me the secret entrance," he demanded. Then he turned to Kahopi. "The old man knows a secret way in, from the top of the canyon. Otherwise, the only way is to climb up from the ground. There are stairs cut in the rock face, but the Whites will see us coming and we will be easy targets. They'll throw rocks on our heads. Or shoot us dead."

Greasewood turned to White Owl.

"What do you say we should do? Go home, or chase off the thieves?"

The boy thought for a moment.

"The Ancient Ones will be angry if we don't do something."

"Alright, then. You win," Greasewood replied with a heavy sigh. "Even though I am old and need a nap, I will climb all the way up that steep old canyon and show you the way."

Reluctantly, he started up the slope. He avoided the snowbanks and angled up where it was dry. The higher they got, the steeper it got. It soon became so steep they had to use their hands, and hold onto tree branches and rocks for balance.

Suddenly, the wind began to gust. It whipped at their hair and clothes and was so cold it took their breath away.

Kahopi looked up at the sky nervously.

The Six-Point-Cloud-People were not pleased. Back in the desert where he came from, rain was normally welcome, for it made the crops grow and filled the cisterns. But these were ugly storm clouds. And Kahopi suspected the Cloud-People, who were departed ancestors, were angry at Kahopi's father, just like the Spider Woman and everyone else back in his village. The Cloud-People clearly didn't want his father, who defecated in the *sipapu*, to arrive at the Skeleton House. But Kahopi was determined to find his father and bury him properly.

Before long, the four of them made it onto the canyon rim. Here, the wind was even stronger, with little to block its path. Big chilly drops of ice cold rain splattered the ground and their shoulders.

"Down here," Greasewood said, and he crawled into a dark cleft in the rocks.

Without hesitation, the other two Utes slid down after him.

Alone on the cliff top, Kahopi knelt in the gravel and listened. He could hear the soft scuffle as the others climbed down. He looked up at the sky for the sun, but the sky was black now. Tawa was nowhere to be seen. Kahopi was alone in a strange land.

He felt the hair rise on his neck. This cleft in the rocks reminded him of the Spider Woman's shrine on the mesa, where she lived in a hole much like this one.

"Are you coming?" White Owl called, his voice hollow and distant.

Kahopi began to wonder if these men were Two-Hearts, witches, luring him into the underworld where he would be trapped. But Kahopi always carried a pouch of cornmeal. To be safe, he sprinkled several pinches of cornmeal at the entrance. That way, if it was a trick and he was murdered, his spirit could find its way back out.

— PART 3 —

— CHAPTER 16 —

AUTUMN 1859
KANSAS TERRITORY

"Let's stop for the evening," Augusta suggested. "The oxen need a break."

Horace turned and gave her a look.

"The boys don't need a break. They can go on forever."

Grabbing the reins out of his hand, Augusta pulled the wagon to a stop and jumped down into the prairie grass. She walked around in a circle, rubbing her lower back.

"I wasn't thinking very clearly when I agreed to this," she said, wincing. "And what little good sense I got is getting rattled right out of my head."

Horace climbed down and went over for a hug, but she pushed him away.

"Don't touch me. Two weeks without a bath, and you smell like a bowl of onions."

He took off his hat and blotted his whole head with a handkerchief. Day after day in the sun had turned his face and neck a ruddy red. But somehow Augusta's skin, despite the exact same conditions, was still chalk white.

Horace reached into the wagon and pulled out Maxcy, who was just waking up. When he opened his eyes and saw who it was, the little boy reached out and grabbed Horace's mustache.

"And you need a shave," Augusta added, watching. "It looks like a caterpillar died on your face."

"I will not. Maxcy likes it."

He knelt down and put the boy in the tall green grass. Seeing moths, Maxcy tried to pounce, but they all fluttered away.

Their neighbor, Nathaniel, drove up in a small buckboard with a white pony in the traces. Moving like a decrepit old man, he crawled out of the wagon and immediately lay down.

"Six hundred *miles*," he groaned.

Horace got out the boiling pot.

"You just need a little coffee in you."

"I hate coffee," Augusta mentioned. "You know that!"

"I was addressing my good friend Nathaniel."

"It is a stimulant and isn't healthy. What about Maxcy? Don't you want to live long enough to see your son grow up? Some of my friends back in Maine have become vegetarians. You're lucky I am not against meat. But I do believe in avoiding coffee and ardent spirits, and eating good, healthy breads. Slow digestion is good digestion. The body is a temple, Horace."

Ignoring her, Horace got out the spade and began digging a fire pit. He whistled as he worked.

CHAPTER 17

WINTER 1892
LEADVILLE

"Why does this seat smell like piss?" John Campion asked, sniffing the leather. Like Horace Tabor, John Campion was one of the richest and most successful mine owners in Leadville.

The new leather chairs in the parlor at the Tabor Grand Hotel had arrived just that morning. Horace spotted them in an advertisement in a catalogue and knew he had to have them. Horace liked exotic things, and these were handmade in New York City with imported leather—all the way from India! Horace discovered, far too late of course, that leather workers in India soak their cowhides in horse piddle.

"Maybe your steed got you? Those beasts drain out like a waterfall."

Horace lit up a cigar to help his guest forget he was seated in body fluid. He drew hard to get the smoke swirling.

"Rumor has it, one of your mines struck good ore," Horace said, puffing like a chimney. "Which one is it?"

The Tabor Grand Hotel was designed with luxury in mind. On the first floor was the private parlor room, one of Horace's favorite places. It provided a clear view of the Downtown District through its oversized windows. Horace's eyes always lit up when he looked outside. Unlike every big city out East, everyone walking the streets of Leadville carried a pickaxe or a spade, or led a string of burros. No matter what the season, the place was buzzing like a beehive. Buckboards and stagecoaches had to crawl and weave just to get up the street. Black smoke churned into the sky. Tailings and timber alternated with houses and cabins like hopscotch—after all, half the lots in Leadville were active dig sites. Everyone shared one common goal. And Horace, the Silver King, got to watch it unfold every day over cigars and bourbon.

"Maybe I did."

"Tell me, then."

Carefully, Campion's eyes surveilled the parlor. There were several other businessmen sipping and smoking, plus the bartender and waitress. Horace always found Campion's crustiness partly amusing and partly annoying. But this was the Tabor Grand Hotel—not a seedy saloon in the red-light district.

Cupping his hand over his goat-bearded mouth, Campion whispered at Horace.

"Are we being spied upon?"

"Well," Horace said, wiggling his eyebrows. "One never knows."

Sinking back in his leather seat, Campion crossed his arms and pursed his lips.

Other conversations drifted in the air.

Deciding to feign camaraderie, Horace looked both ways, then cupped his hand around his own mouth.

"Which one is producing?"

But Campion kept on brooding.

Finally, Horace sighed.

"Just tell me, dammit. I'll buy you a whiskey."

Campion perked up.

"Fourth Street," he revealed, resorting again to a throaty whisper. "The Lucy B. Hussey property."

Horace leaned closer.

"Go on."

"I sunk ten shafts, but only one hit good ore. And not just a pocket, but a *vein*. Had to dig down seven hundred feet to get beneath the glacial wash, but it's there. And I guarantee you, that vein runs right underneath this whole blessed town."

Horace flagged over the waitress.

"What's your name, dear?"

"Mollie."

"Hello, Mollie. Would you be so kind and bring this man three fingers of Old Nectar?"

"Sure!"

The waitress went straight to the bar and got a glass decanter of amber whiskey. Returning, she poured a glass for Campion and set it on an end table.

"This man hit the pay dirt," Horace confided. "Look out that window. You see that mine right there, on Fourth—you can see it from here. Pay dirt!"

"Congratulations, sir," Mollie said with a nice smile.

Pursing his lips again, Campion ignored her. But Horace did not.

There must have been something shiny outside, because sunlight flickered through the window and lit her face for one delightful moment. She had rich green-blue eyes, just like turquoise.

"Why, you've got the prettiest eyes I have ever seen. Look at her eyes, John."

But Campion did not look. He continued to brood in silence.

Winking, Horace carefully placed a small stack of silver dollars on her tray.

"That, Mollie my dear, is for helping us celebrate."

"Wow!" she exclaimed.

Balancing the tray so the coin stack did not collapse, Mollie smiled again, and then headed back to the bar.

Horace watched her go. He felt pleased at his own magnanimity. Miners only made three dollars a day. He just gave this waitress five. And all she did was serve one polite drink. Also, she was very pretty.

"Now John. Here's what I'm thinking," Horace said, giving up on the absurd whisper. "Leadville needs a silver club. Since you just struck pay dirt at the Lucy B., why don't we get one of your boys to head it up? A man who can lead effectively. Who do you got running that operation?"

"Why would I wanna do that?"

"Why? Because we need enthusiasm to carry the day! Verve! What's more exciting than a big silver strike right here in the middle of town? We'll throw a big bash Friday night and announce both things at once—The Lucy B.'s success and the silver club. We can even give out lapel pins and think up a secret handshake."

Horace worked his cigar again to get the smoke churning.

"The Leadville Silver Club," he continued. "The word will spread like wildfire and we'll get the votes of this whole town locked up tight come November. We can't let them damn Democrats win."

"But what about you?" Campion asked. "Let's use *your* mine manager instead. The Matchless is the biggest silver producer in Leadville. That makes more sense to me."

Horace cringed.

"People need to be properly enthused. My mine manager, Major Bohn, while an efficient leader, is dull as ditchwater."

"I don't know. My fellow's got enough on his plate already."

"We all must saddle some of the burden, John."

In actuality, Major Bohn had a sanguine personality, but he was a busy man. The last thing Horace wanted was to bog him down with the silver club. The Matchless Mine was churning out thousands of dollars a day, and it required the Major's full attention. Why jeopardize the man's productivity?

Shifting uncomfortably, John Campion picked up his whiskey glass and drained it in one gulp. Then he got to his feet and examined his trousers, looking to see if they were damp. He felt like he had been sitting in whiz the whole conversation. He wanted to argue more with Horace, but he could no longer stand the smell, and Horace's cigar didn't help.

"Fine. We can use my guy."

CHAPTER 18

"Hey, dummy."

Big Ed looked up—and was shocked. He saw his older brother, John Burns of all people, standing in the front door of the Stray Horse Brewery.

Ed frowned.

"That ain't my name."

"Sure it is, dummy."

John took off his hat and looked around at the bar and the tiny room, unimpressed.

"This reminds me of that ratty little tavern down by the docks. I'm surprised it ain't boiling over with Micks on the make."

"This ain't Chicago," Big Ed stated. "There's more chinks than paddies."

John walked up to the bar and pushed aside some empty bottles. Besides the two of them, the room was empty—except for Dirty Johns, who was mopping the floor.

"Get me some whiskey."

"This is a brewery," Big Ed told him, walking around the bar. "But you're in luck."

Hidden under an old tarp, between two pallets of beer bottles, was a whiskey barrel.

"You always were a sucker for cheap rye," John said. He reached into his pocket and took out a glass flask. "Better than nothing."

As his brother filled it up, John turned to watch Dirty Johns mopping. The floorboards had many stains and discolorations. The mopping clearly wasn't doing much.

"What died in here?"

"You're a long way from home," said Big Ed, ignoring the comment. "You get run out?"

He handed the flask back to his older brother.

"Nope."

They went over and sat down at a table and stared at each other. They hadn't seen each other for a number of years. Big Ed didn't know what to say, so he said nothing.

"You should come back home," John said finally. "It's time."

Letting his eyes fall, Big Ed shrugged.

"Why now?" he asked. "I thought the alderman wanted me gone for good."

John grinned at him.

"Well, dummy, he hears you run Leadville."

Big Ed looked up, eyes glinting.

John raised an eyebrow. "Do you?"

Gritting his teeth, Big Ed said, "Of course I do. I've got this whole city buttoned up. Why?"

Turning around, John glared at Dirty Johns.

"Does that filthy mopstick need to be here while we talk like this?"

Pointing at the backroom, Big Ed snapped his fingers and Dirty Johns took his mop and disappeared.

"See that?" he said. "That's all I have to do to get things done."

"Good, that's what I was hoping."

John leaned forward and, even though they were alone, spoke in a low voice.

"It's an election year. We need to fix things so they go right. Your big senator paid a sneaky visit up here. Did you know that?"

"I did."

"You know why?"

"You tell me."

John chuckled and looked around to make sure Dirty Johns hadn't returned.

"Teller wants to create a silver club right here—so he can tell the whole city how to vote for president of the United States. Leadville lives and breathes silver . . . but in Chicago, it's gold that makes the world go round. So all you gotta do to make the alderman happy is make sure that silver club don't happen."

He leaned back in his chair, confidently.

"To make it easy on you, I met someone who can help," John added, standing up and pulling out his flask. "There's a toboggan slide up past the train station. Meet me there tomorrow at noon."

CHAPTER 19

CREEDE

After leaving their horses in the livery corral, LG and Davis walked up the road to the Denver Exchange. Inside the saloon, there were four game tables in the middle of the room, and they were all full—poker, faro, casino, and pool. They spotted Billy Woods standing behind the bar and went right over.

"The train ain't here yet," LG told him. "Cook us up some sheep."

"Tell it to the cook, I'm bartending today," Billy said. "Why are you waiting for the train?"

"Got a shipment of beeves, plus a new cowhand to help."

Billy looked intrigued.

"Does that cowhand need a mule? I'm selling mine."

LG leaned against the bar.

"How much are you selling it for?"

"Ten bucks. And I'll throw in the tack."

LG burst out laughing.

"Is it ready for the glue factory?"

Looking both sly and indignant, Billy took a rag and wiped down the bar top.

"It's just a little spirited, is all."

"Well, we are going to need a saddle mount for Til's kid." Davis pulled out a ten-dollar bill. "Sold."

There was a young prospector with long sideburns playing pool. He was lining up a shot, but it was obvious he was flat out drunk.

"There he goes again," Billy said, shaking his head.

The man took the shot but missed entirely. The cue stick rolled out his hands, then he collapsed on the tabletop. Billy sighed, and then went over to roll the young man onto the floor so someone else could play.

Bat Masterson popped out of the kitchen and came over to check on them.

"You want venison or rainbow trout? And we got that famous dairy butter."

"We want those lamb chops," LG replied. "What are *you* doing in the kitchen?"

"The cook woke up ill, so me and Billy flipped a coin."

He was wearing a nice lavender-colored corduroy suit and tie covered by a greasy white apron.

LG looked him over and smiled.

"Don't say anything," Bat grumbled, and went back into the kitchen.

They leaned against the bar and watched Billy prop the young drunk into a chair. When he returned to the bar, Billy wiped his hands on a wet rag.

"Who is that, anyway?" LG asked.

"I don't know his real name, he's always too drunk to tell me. We call him the Corner Pocket Drunk. Every day he passes out on the pool table like that. I don't roll him off quick, he leaks all over the velvet. Then me and Bat flip a coin to see who cleans it up."

At that moment, Bat came back out of the kitchen with two steaming plates of food. He set them on the bar and glanced over at the pool table nervously.

"Did he leak on it?"

"No, we got lucky this time."

Picking up a fork and knife, LG cut into a lamb chop.

"This is tasty."

Davis took a bite, too, but frowned.

"Hard to enjoy it knowing that poor sheepherder got beaned to death. What a way to go."

As they ate, Bat went back for a platter of hot buttery rolls.

"I can't believe you boys are going to run cattle up here," he said when he returned. "If they don't outright freeze to death, they're going to shiver the meat right off their bones. It'll make for some awful thin steaks."

LG picked up a buttery roll and bit into it.

"You ever heard of Scottish Highlanders? They're big, shaggy things."

"No, but I have heard of Scotch."

LG finished the roll and licked his fingers clean.

"They ain't regular beeves. They were made for the cold."

Bat thought about it.

"The closest thing to steak I've even seen in months is a cold piece of jerky."

LG held up the bone shank he just cleaned.

"You should try the sheep."

CHAPTER 20

When the steam whistle blew, Walker felt butterflies swirl around in his stomach again.

Joe Palmer got to his feet, even though the train was still pulling into the station.

"End of the line, Garo."

However, Walker decided to stay on board, in the same seat. He figured if he just remained in place and didn't move, the train would turn around and take him back home. His poppa would be there waiting, sitting in the saddle, with a cloth bundle in his hands. Unfolding it, Walker would find his favorite meal—a cheese sandwich, which his mother made. While he ate the sandwich, he would rub Bit Ear's neck. Bit Ear was his father's saddle horse, a sleek-looking bay. He always liked it when Walker rubbed his neck. But never his nose. Bit Ear hated that. The horse was smart, too. If Walker happened to have a cherry candy in his pocket, Bit Ear always knew, intuitively. He would bump his nose against Walker's jacket, and it was always the correct pocket.

"End of the line," Joe repeated. "I've got a deer to collect. What about you?"

"Just my bag."

The boy reached under the seat, pulled out the bag and held it in his lap.

Soapy looked him over.

"Don't forget your Frank James book."

The train jostled and finally rolled to a stop. Walker glanced out the window nervously. They had finally arrived in Creede. Deep in the Rocky Mountains, far from civilization. And far from home.

"Here," Joe said, and he presented Walker with a shiny quarter.

"What's this for?"

"For helping me drag that deer through the snow."

Soapy got up from his seat, and as he headed for the exit, he gave Joe a hard shove. Falling into Banjo's lap, Joe looked up, confused.

"What did I do?"

"Ever since you touched that carcass, I've been getting ripe whiffs."

Cautiously, Joe stood back up and sniffed his hands.

"I don't smell nothing."

"Well, I smell it. And it disgusts me."

Not knowing what else to do, Joe stuck his hands in his pockets.

"Now, head out to the luggage car and see if Old Man Tripp is sober," Soapy muttered darkly. "And you need to either burn those clothes or get them laundered proper."

As Soapy stalked off, Banjo stifled a laugh and Joe checked his hands for stink again.

Meanwhile, Walker was studying the quarter Joe gave him. It was his first real wage for doing a real job! He had never gotten paid to do anything before. Back home, Walker helped out a lot. He fed the horses, and shoveled out the corral, and swept out the bunkhouse, and oiled the leather tack. But all those things were just chores.

He squeezed the quarter tight in his palm.

"See you out there, kid," Joe mumbled, grabbed his rifle, and left.

Banjo got off the train, too, along with everyone else—except Walker.

Through the glass, he had a good view of Creede.

Just beyond the depot platform, he saw a sea of dirty tents. *This must be what Colonel Custer felt like at the Bighorn River,* he thought. *Indian teepees everywhere.*

But he knew, of course, that they were not Indian teepees. The main giveaway was that there were no Indians. Just a whole bunch of men with mustaches and beards, and many of them looked like they had been drinking. One tent had a woman out front, crouched over an open fire, roasting peppers and onions in a frying pan.

Then the big cliff caught his eye.

It was a massive granite wall. Up and up to the clouds. It dwarfed everything. It went up so high, Walker couldn't even see the top from inside the train. He wondered what was up there. The top of the world? Maybe a renegade band of Apaches hiding out, making arrowheads?

Someone tapped on the glass, which startled him.

"Yep, I knew it—Til's boy," LG said, his voice muffled by the glass. "Looks just like Til."

Davis was standing next to him, and he waved pleasantly.

When Walker recognized Davis, he felt very relieved and waved back. He remembered Davis. Every now and then, the man had visited the Blancett house in Garo and occasionally helped cut hay during the summers. It was good to see a familiar face. The butterflies in his stomach began to settle down. He collected his book and bag and headed up the aisle.

CHAPTER 21

Davis called to LG.

"Don't fall down!"

"The hell I will!"

LG was clinging to the side of the stock car to avoid getting trampled. The cattle had come racing out like it was the Kentucky Derby, and he barely got out of the way in time.

The herd charged down the timber-framed chute and barreled into the stockyard. Without slowing down, they plowed down a cross-fence like it was made of papier-mâché.

"They're wild!" Davis shouted. "And stout as buffalo."

LG shimmied along the boards until he was clear and jumped down.

Wood posts snapped like firecrackers, and another cross-fence went down. The cattle bellowed, kicking up clods of mud and snow as they ran by. The outer fence shook and rattled.

Davis cringed.

"If they bust out, we'll be chasing them down the Rio Grande, all the way to Mexico," he said.

Even LG looked nervous.

But the herd veered and circled around and at last began to settle down. Coming a little closer, the two of them peered through the fence slats. The Highlanders didn't look like regular beef cows. They had long hairy coats and thick, sharp horns. The hair even drooped down and covered their eyes.

"How can they see?" Davis wondered. "If that was me, I'd get a haircut."

Suddenly, he got worried.

"What happened to the kid?" he asked.

"Up here," Walker called. "I thought it would be safer than on the ground."

The boy was watching the chaos from up on the depot platform. He was not alone. A small crowd of curious people had gone up to get a good view. Even the station agent had come out, still clutching his newspaper.

"I hope you plan on repairing those fences," he complained.

Now that it was safe, Walker jumped down and cautiously approached the stockyard. The sound of the cattle blowing and snorting made him feel queasy, even though the danger had passed. They were big, bizarre-looking creatures, and he wasn't quite sure what to think.

"Where in the world did they come from?"

"Scotland," Davis said.

World geography had never been one of Walker's strengths, but he didn't want to appear both frightened and foolish on his first day on the job. So he said nothing.

"Let's let them cool off for a while," LG suggested, and then grinned at him. "Want to meet your new saddle mount?"

They went up to the town livery to retrieve their horses, and the big brown mule they had bought from Billy Woods for ten dollars. When Walker saw it, he hesitated.

"Is she friendly?"

"Jump on up there," LG said. "Fork that saddle."

He gave the boy a boost so he could get his foot in the stirrup. The moment Walker put his weight in the seat, the mule pinned its ears. Instantly, the boy dropped the reins and seized the saddle horn.

"Relax," Davis told him.

Grabbing the bridle, LG studied the mule's eyes, as if searching its soul.

"I seen this before, many times," he said confidently. "It's these quiet ones what are sly. Just waiting for you to ease up, and then *whomp!* Send you where the woodbine twineth."

Turning pale, Walker wiped his palms on his pants leg and gripped the horn even tighter.

"What do you think?" Davis asked, but Walker said nothing.

LG took off his hat and held it aloft.

"They say a cowboy has nothing on his mind but his hat."

Ignoring him, Davis patted the mule.

"If Billy Woods can ride her, you won't have any trouble. Billy rides like a rag doll."

CHAPTER 22

Zang's Hotel was two stories high. It only had three rooms for rent, and they were all on the second floor.

"Lady Luck!" Zang said. "One left."

Soapy took off his black hat and ran his hand through his dark hair.

"Seems everywhere I go, Lady Luck has got there first and got things ready."

The Chinaman grinned in a friendly manner and turned to Joe and Banjo.

"Tent out back," he told them. "Half price."

Soapy tapped his toe against his traveling trunk, which was sitting on the tiny rug in the tiny lobby. It was bright bumblebee yellow. Soapy had bought it back in Denver once he realized that public sentiment had turned against him after beating John Arkins unconscious in broad daylight.

When he first came to Denver, which was many years ago, Soapy was just a kid. He didn't have any luggage at all back then. Just the clothes he wore. His black hat and black coat. He wore it so much people began to notice him for his dark look. *There's that charming young man who sells soap on the corner—the one in the nice black suit*, he would hear.

When Soapy could finally afford to purchase a new set of clothes, he stuck with the same look. It was like a uniform by then.

So when it came time to finally leave Denver, and leave behind all he had struggled for and accomplished, bled for and achieved, Soapy chose a bright-colored trunk. He refused to be depressed, and that bright yellow color would always serve as a reminder of how colorful life should be. Despite the disappointments.

"Take that up to the room."

Lifting the trunk, Joe and Banjo took it up the steep wooden staircase.

"You boys be careful. And set it near the window so I can sit on it," Soapy called up the stairwell, and then grinned at Zang, who was still grinning himself. "I like to pull my boots on with a good view of the camp."

Zang nodded.

"Ten dollar is one week."

"Here's five hundred," Soapy replied and counted out the cash. "That should carry me for a while. Make sure I am not disturbed overnight, nor surprised at any hour. And have a fresh cup of coffee sent to my room every morning at sunrise."

Gathering the bills, Zang turned and snapped his fingers at a young Chinese girl peering from the kitchen.

"You—coffee!"

The girl disappeared.

"In the morning is fine," Soapy said. He was ready to head upstairs and rest.

But Zang merely bowed.

"Coffee."

"Alright, then."

She returned and obediently set a cup on the counter. Soapy took a sip, just to be polite. Rapping his knuckles on the counter, he put his hat back on and then climbed the stairs.

The stairwell had no windows and was very dim. At the top of the stairs, there was a musty hallway and three narrow doors. Banjo and Joe had already found the right room, and were hissing and muttering at each other, trying to get the trunk inside without scraping it against the jambs. Once they got it in, they set it on the pine plank floorboards right beneath the window. Banjo pushed open the drapes to let sunlight in, even though there wasn't much left.

"Where are the rest of us gonna sleep, Soapy?" Joe wondered, looking around.

The room was not very big. There was a narrow bed with a new copper frame, a plush chair in one corner, and a free-standing mirror with flowers etched on the glass.

"Zang said there's extra rooms out back," Soapy told them.

Joe frowned.

"I believe he said there was a *tent* out back."

Soapy frowned.

"Are you telling me you don't want to sleep in the tent? I suppose you require comfort and solitude?"

"That train was pretty bumpy, and I could use some decent sleep. Plus, it is the middle of winter. I prefer a warm featherbed over a cold tent."

Soapy raise his eyebrows slowly.

"A warm featherbed? Joe requires a warm featherbed, Banjo, did you hear?"

He put his hands on Joe's shoulders and looked him in the eye.

"Why don't you take the room, Joe, and that nice warm bed. You deserve it. Why don't I go sleep in the cold tent. I have too many good things, too many of life's comforts, as it is."

Joe's mind reeled. He must have said something wrong. Soapy had been in a good mood on the long train ride from Denver, but now it seemed the good mood was gone.

"Well hold on a minute," Soapy said, sniffing his cheek. "You still smell like that dead deer."

He glanced at Banjo.

"Banjo, do you think Zang wants someone sleeping in his warm featherbed that smells like dead deer?"

"No, he wouldn't like dead deer stink in his featherbed, I suppose."

Suddenly releasing his grip, Soapy took a step back and sniffed his fingers.

"Why, this is my good Sunday coat, Joe. If you got dead deer on my good Sunday coat . . ."

His eyes grew hard.

"Banjo, did you bring my cane?"

Moving quickly, Banjo grabbed Joe by the arm and dragged him into the hallway.

"You take that nice warm featherbed, Soapy. You deserve it most. I can't wait to sleep in that ol' tent, myself. And Joe, too."

They closed the door and rushed down the stairwell. At the bottom, seated in the lobby, they found Old Man Tripp nipping on a bottle of booze.

"What happened?" he asked, noticing their hasty descent.

"Soapy needs to rest up," Banjo explained. "His mood took a turn. Plus, Joe stomped on his boot on the train ride in."

"Where were *you* this whole time, dern it?" Joe asked, still flustered.

Tripp held up the bottle.

"Purchasing bourbon."

"You were supposed to be watching our gear."

Joe looked out the window, but it had gotten dark and in the gloom he couldn't see much through the glass.

"You better hope no one jacked our gear or you're a dead man."

The street lamps, gas-lit, were flickering yellow. And there, in the dusk and shadows, piled on the walkway where they left it, was all their stuff—canvas bags, a folding table, and a black trunk full of soap cakes.

"You're lucky it's all still here."

The deer that Joe shot from the train was lying there, too, in the snow. Its black, glassy eyes were empty and void. Just seeing it made Joe feel guilty. He turned and glanced up at the second floor. There was a light in Soapy's window.

"Maybe I best go apologize."

"You best go get cleaned up instead," Banjo said. "Take a hot bath, and get those clothes wrung out. And next time you see a deer, don't stomp on Soapy's boot."

"Where's my room?" Tripp asked with a mouthful of bourbon.

Banjo shrugged.

"Around back, I guess."

Sure enough, there was a big canvas tent set up around back. As they were walking by, a door opened in the rear of the hotel. The Chinese girl appeared and dumped out a pail of entrails onto a trash heap. The heap was right by the tent, and a colon string oozed under the canvas wall like a snake.

Without raising her eyes, she quietly vanished inside and the door clicked shut.

"I know deer gut when I see it," Tripp pointed out. "I bet they're serving mincemeat tonight."

Banjo turned to Joe.

"Well, Soapy won't like that. You ought to take your supper elsewhere."

"Maybe I will."

Grabbing the dead doe by the legs, Joe dragged it over to the kitchen door and dumped it on the trash heap. Tripp was stunned.

"You don't want that?"

"What I want is a nice warm featherbed. But instead, I gotta sleep in this cold damn tent."

"Well, so do we."

Behind the hotel, there was a steep snowy hillside. A big gust of wind whipped down the slope and peppered them with sharp ice crystals. They all hunched and clutched at their hats until it died down.

"Criminy!" Tripp shouted. "That stings."

Fighting to be first, they all rushed inside the dark tent. Inside, they found several old military cots with thin blankets. The wind blew again, which caused the canvas sides to flap—and snow crystals blew right in underneath the walls.

"Not only ain't there featherbeds," Joe complained. "But Zang don't know how to stake out a dern tent properly."

— CHAPTER 23 —

Joe was shivering so bad he couldn't sleep.

The wind kept gusting beneath the loose tent walls. The sound of skittering ice crystals made him cringe. Even with his gloves and scarf on, huddled under a blanket, Joe simply could not get warm. Plus, the intestines the Chinese girl had dumped out had wormed beneath his cot and froze to the ground.

Giving up, Joe took the thin gray blanket and wrapped it around his shoulders. Why not go for a walk and get a warm cup of cocoa somewhere? Maybe that would help him feel better.

Outside, the street was empty. The street lamps were lit, all the way up the road, but no one was out. It was bitterly cold. In fact, it was so cold Joe almost changed his mind. But then he noticed the window of the Denver Exchange. A warm, yellow light radiated out and fell softly on the snowdrift out front, and he heard boisterous voices and a variety of saloon sounds in the lull between gusts. It sounded so inviting that he trotted right over.

Pausing to look through the glass, Joe realized why the street was empty. Everyone was in the Denver Exchange! The game tables were crowded and people were lined up at the bar. He spotted Billy Woods pouring beer, and Bat Masterson was scolding an angry drunk.

When Joe tugged open the heavy wooden door, he was met with a warm blast of air, the smell of roasting mutton, and a chorus of protests.

"*Shut that door!*"

Quick as he could, Joe pulled it tight and headed straight for the bar.

"I said, gimme another beer, damn you," the drunk said to Bat.

"Why don't you take a break, Bob."

"Why don't I take another *beer.*"

With a stern look, Bat took away Bob's empty beer mug and set it out of reach.

"Go play some poker for a while."

Bat turned to Joe and started to ask what he wanted, but Bob leaned forward and swatted him across the cheek.

"Oh my Gawd!" Billy Woods shouted. "Bob Ford slapped Bat Masterson!"

The room fell silent.

Even the men at the game tables who didn't see it happen turned in shock.

Bob's face, red with alcohol, twisted from anger into confusion. He studied the palm of his hand, like he didn't recognize it.

"Did you . . . what?" he asked his hand.

The gas lights hissed, and for a long moment, that was the only sound in the room.

All eyes were on Bat Masterson.

Joe felt sure this mouthy drunk was about to die. Every time Bat's name came up, someone would invariably remark that Bat Masterson killed twenty-six men before his twenty-seventh birthday. Whether it was true or not was beside the point.

Joe looked down at Bat's hands, which were resting on the smooth polished bar top. He was supposed to be a quick shot with either his right or his left hand, and always deadly. Joe wondered which hand would move first.

But instead of shooting the drunk, or throttling him, Bat merely chuckled.

"Go home, Bob," he said.

Billy Woods was shocked.

Joe was shocked.

Everyone in the Denver Exchange was shocked.

"But if you do want some trouble, I'll be right here," Bat added grimly.

Bob Ford began to slink away, looking lost. But instead of going home, or even across the room, he threw his arm around Joe's shoulder.

"A beer for my partner, then," Bob shouted. "Charge it to my account."

Calmly, Bat poured a beer for Joe and set it in front of him.

"Alright, Bob, it's on your bill. But all *you* can have is coffee."

As the room relaxed, Bat moved down to the other end of the bar. The Corner Pocket Drunk wandered over, carrying the cue stick. His words came out slurred.

"Any more mittens?"

"No more mutton," Bat replied, gently correcting him.

"Did that sheep man ever recover?"

Pulling out a cloth, Bat wiped down the surface of the bar.

"People don't recover from death."

When he said that, the Corner Pocket Drunk began to sob.

"Don't you remember?" Bat asked. "We buried him in the snow drift, in the alley out back. You yourself helped with the shoveling."

The young man, using the cue stick as a crutch, hobbled back to the pool table. As he left, Bob leaned into Joe's ear to whisper.

"See that spineless exchange? Masterson ain't so tough."

Since Bat wasn't looking, Bob tried to grab Joe's beer but Billy Woods rushed over and grabbed his wrist and twisted.

"Ow, damn you!"

"You can have coffee," Billy reminded him. "But that's all."

"Fine. Get me coffee then, you bastard. Go!"

Rubbing his wrist, Bob took a step back. He stared at the beer like he was going to grab it again, but then gave Joe a dismissive wave.

"If you want it, you might as well drink it. I don't care."

Shaking his head in disbelief, Joe took a cautious sip.

"I can't believe you slapped Bat Masterson."

But Bob shrugged, like he didn't have a care in the world.

"Aw, it ain't nothing. I'd do it again in a heartbeat."

Billy Woods began to get a ceramic cup from the stack, but as soon as he heard Bob's remark, he turned around and gave him a hard look.

"Hurry up, *Billy*," Bob shouted, slapping the bar. "I like my coffee *hot*."

His watery eyes came in and out of focus, and then gravitated back to Joe.

"Hey. You're dressed in a blanket."

"That is true," Joe said.

"Like a dusky red heathen."

Joe pulled it tighter around his shoulders.

"I can't get any sleep in Zang's horrible tent. It ain't staked down right, and the wind zips right through there like there ain't no walls at all."

Still looking mean, Billy set a ceramic cup in front of Bob and glared at him as he poured. It filled up and overflowed, and Bob pulled his hand away just in time to avoid getting his fingers scalded.

"I hope your boxing skills are better than your pouring skills," Bob said, being snide. He glanced at Joe. "Every Saturday night, ol' Billy Woods puts on the gloves. What a sorry little weakling."

Billy grit his teeth but said nothing.

"Can I get some, too?" Joe asked, pitifully. "I am chilled to the bone."

Leaning down to sip from the rim, Bob took a slurp of coffee.

"I had a saloon myself, you know. Down in Walsenburg. Sold it to come up here." Then he aimed another sour look at Billy. "Though at the moment, I am pained to remember why."

Abandoning the coffee, Bob spun around and leaned back against the bar.

"You know why Bat didn't throw down?" Then he waved his arm at the room, irritably. "It's because *I boss this whole damn camp!*"

The Corner Pocket Drunk lined up a shot at the pool table. He slid the cue stick but missed the ball entirely.

"Hey!" Bob shouted at him. "What's your stupid name?"

But instead of replying, the Corner Pocket Drunk crawled onto the pool table and fell asleep.

Joe studied this fellow named Bob Ford. His face looked rather cherubic—like an angry little angel baby. But he had wide blood-shot eyes that rolled back and forth like a spooky horse. And, like a spooky horse, every time someone walked by Bob tensed up until they passed.

"Bat knows better," Bob muttered. "He knows what I am capable of."

Suddenly, Joe realized something.

"Are you the same Bob Ford who killed Jesse James?"

"The one and the same." Pleased, he clapped Joe on the back. "Just for that, I'll buy you another beer. Where's that fool Billy Woods?"

Spinning around to face the bar again, the smile fell from his face when he realized he was staring at Bat Masterson.

"Damn, you startled me," Bob said. "You're like a phantom."

"Are you still here?" Bat asked, bristling. "I thought I told you to go home."

Walking away, Bob grabbed Joe by the sleeve.

"Come on, partner. This ain't the only place in this godforsaken camp that sells booze."

CHAPTER 24

SOUTHWEST COLORADO

It was when rainwater began cascading down the tunnel that Kahopi realized he had been tricked.

"I should never have come down here," he muttered, terrified.

As the cold water rushed over his feet, he heard Bear Claw Lip cry out in the darkness.

"Why did you bring us here, old man? We will be drowned!"

"No we won't," Greasewood replied in a calm voice. "Trust me."

"Not only are you old, but you're stupid!"

The water was extremely cold and poured faster and faster.

"We're going to drown!" Bear Claw Lip shouted again.

After it had been discovered what his father had done in the village, Kahopi had been deeply embarrassed. In fact, even though it was his father's shameful behavior, others began to mock Kahopi as well. His uncles and aunts and neighbors began to question whether his mother had even given birth to him. Perhaps his father had dumped him as well, they suggested.

It was when these relentless taunts became too much to bear that Kahopi began to spend more time alone on the mesa. He even began sleeping among the boulders and cholla, taking a blanket with him.

"Are you not afraid of what could happen?" his mother asked him once. "You could be snatched by a Two-Heart. Or you might even see Masau'u, the Fiery Spirit!"

Kahopi was indeed afraid. But his desire to avoid their taunts was greater than his fear of witches, or even the bloody-headed god of death.

However, late one night, Kahopi saw a blazing flame float across the mesa. After bobbing along for a time, it disappeared over the rim. It was Masau'u, the Fiery Spirit!

Everyone knew Masau'u patrolled the mesa at night.

The cold shivers ran down his spine, yet he did not run home. Masau'u sometimes carried his own bloody head in one hand and a torch in the other. While it was true that to meet the Fire Spirit was a sign of death, it was also true he guarded the village at night.

Having an ear for the old stories, as a boy, Kahopi used to listen closely to his grandfather and always paid rapt attention during ceremonies in the kiva and the dances in the plaza. Therefore, Kahopi knew he was safe. Although he had *seen* the blaze of the Fire Spirit from afar, he had not been close enough to unwittingly *meet* him.

Night after night, sleeping out on the mesa, Kahopi learned how to move quickly across the rocks in the darkness without stumbling. And so, even though the rushing waters made the footing slick, Kahopi had great confidence. He raced down the tunnel. He ran by White Owl, and pushed past Bear Claw Lip, who clutched at him. Greasewood was startled when he passed, but did not clutch at him like Bear Claw Lip had done.

He sped down the narrow passageway, deeper into the earth, slapping blindly at the sandstone walls.

Suddenly, the darkness softened.

Kahopi emerged from the tunnel and found himself standing in ankle-deep water in a square, brick room. But he was not alone. A small group of Two-Hearts were there, waiting. It was a trap after all! Was this the underworld?

Greasewood, Bear Claw Lip, and White Owl popped out of the tunnel.

Kahopi felt betrayed. Trapped. There was nowhere to go.

However, Bear Claw Lip produced his knife. He slashed at the nearest Two-Heart, and the man's fingers sprinkled into the churning water.

"Thieves," Bear Claw Lip cried out.

He sliced at another man who was cradling a clay pot like a newborn baby. Blood squirted, and the pot fell from his grip.

The White thieves began to cry out in terror. They bolted for a low doorway in one of the brick walls. They hunched down to get through—but it was only half a man's height, and only big enough for one at a time.

One wiggled through, but Bear Claw Lip, in a fury, poked and jabbed until the rest lay still.

"Maybe you should kill us, too," White Owl suggested. "I'd rather get stabbed than drown."

The cold water continued to swirl around their ankles, but strangely, it never got any deeper. Looking around in the gloomy light, Kahopi saw why. There was a small hole in the middle of the floor. The water poured down like a drain.

"No, we won't drown," Greasewood told them. "There is a kiva below. For collecting drinking water. The Ancient Ones designed it this way on purpose."

Bear Claw Lip glared at him. "You could have told us all this beforehand." Then, he knelt down and crawled through the doorway.

Following him outside, Kahopi took a look around. The Ancient Ones had chosen this place well. It was situated on the deep ledge of an open cave in the middle of the cliff face. The rock curved overhead like a roof and provided shelter from the elements. The falling rain seemed to hang like a blanket, enshrouding the cliff dwellings in secrecy. It was also high above the canyon floor—which was now roaring with muddy water. It was good they had left the canyon when they did.

While Bear Claw Lip darted in and out of the brick buildings, the other two Utes came and stood by Kahopi.

"Do they have no shame?" White Owl wondered. "Don't they know this place is sacred?"

"They are searching for the Third World," Kahopi explained, staring down at the muddy waters. "But they will not find it. It was destroyed in a flood."

Greasewood was surprised.

"How do you know?"

"The Spider Woman told me in a dream."

Dragging the thief who had escaped by the hair, Bear Claw Lip called out to them. "I cornered him like a field mouse. Now, help me remove his ears."

But Greasewood shook his head.

"No, he will need them. The Whites are looking for the Third World. Someone must tell them it was destroyed in a flood. Then they will leave this place alone."

Bear Claw Lip pulled the man to the edge.

"There's no one left to tell."

He flung the White Man into the air. He wheeled his arms as if to fly—but he merely plunked like a stone into the churning brown waters below.

On one of the adobe walls, Kahopi suddenly noticed a crow. It was perched just above them, watching quietly, safe from the rain.

It could simply be a crow, Kahopi knew. Or it could be the Evil Power, which sometimes appeared as a crow.

Regardless, Kahopi was there for a reason. To find his father!

He began searching. He checked the rooms and the kivas, one by one. But as he made his way from one end of the cliff village to the other, his hopes slowly dwindled. While the others settled down and built a warm fire in a dry place, Kahopi kept looking.

The Whites may have been digging like ants, but his father was not there.

— PART 4 —

CHAPTER 25

AUTUMN 1859
ROCKY MOUNTAINS

When Horace opened his eyes, the first thing he noticed was the roof of his tent. It was sagging so low he couldn't sit up. He had to scooch around on his elbows to check his pocket watch. It was eight a.m. The air was so chilly he was tempted to stay under the warm quilts.

Instead, he poked his head outside to see what was going on.

There was snow everywhere!

The day before had been a normal, crisp fall day. The aspens were gold, the granite glittered in the sunlight, and the canyon echoed with the squawking of magpies and crows. Now, literally overnight, it was winter.

He crawled all the way out and stared at the landscape, shocked at how much snow had fallen. It was more than ankle deep. His tent had a thick load on top, which was causing it to sag.

"That could have smothered you in your sleep."

Spooked, Horace whipped around.

There was a grizzled old man sitting on a stone, watching him.

"Who are you?" Horace asked.

"Everyone just calls me the Old-timer. And I been doing this a long, long time."

The old man pointed at the mountainside.

"You see them slopes up there?" he asked. "Snow will slide. Gonna break loose and bury you flatter than a flapjack. You better head on back to Denver like everyone else with a brain."

Then, he got up and came closer.

"Say, you got any bacon? I'll trade you for this cheese," he said and opened a tin.

Looking closely, Horace gagged.

"That's not cheese. That's butter. Or it used to be."

The Old-timer shrugged.

"Well, it can pass as both."

But Horace was appalled.

"I don't think it can."

Putting the tin back in his pack, the man started hiking downstream. He turned around and pointed at the mountainside again.

"Flatter than a flapjack!"

Then he wandered off.

After he was gone, Horace broke down the tent, loaded up his backpack, and hustled down the creek as fast as he could. But the Old-timer was gone.

CHAPTER 26

WINTER 1892
LEADVILLE

Horace had wisely hidden a brandy bottle in the bookshelf in the quiet sun room earlier that afternoon, once he learned about Baby Doe's tea party and the "illness" that prevented the nursemaid from watching Silver Dollar—leaving the responsibility in Horace's hands.

"You just watch her, Horace," Baby Doe insisted.

It took him off guard.

"There's no time to find someone else," she went on, noting the glazed look in his eyes.

Smiling slyly, she wove her arm around his waist.

"You'll be fine, my sweet husband," she said. "You and Silver Dollar will have a chance to hash out that ugly necklace fiasco."

Hoping to assuage his sprite little daughter, Horace dropped by the store and got some candy. It was rare that Baby Doe called him her sweet husband, and that was what gave him the idea. In fact, it was so rare he could recall the last time with clarity—ironically, it was when he bought her the Isabella Necklace.

Horace chose rock candy. It caught his eye. Rock candy came in several colors and it looked just like minerals. Crystallized clumps of sugar on tiny sticks. It was genius. The more he thought about it, the more Horace wished he had been the one to invent the idea. Leadville was a city that was synonymous with ore. Mines were everywhere. *If you pick up a rock and throw it, you'll hit one,* he liked to say.

It wasn't long, though, before he regretted bringing the candy.

"Dadda. What does a marmot sound like?"

In addition to her airy wail, little Silver Dollar could achieve a spectrum of other alarming sounds. She was constantly developing new ones in her repertoire, and the newest was a piercing marmot pip. She took off around the desk pipping as loudly as she possibly could.

Kneeling like a penitent priest, Horace held out his arms as she raced by.

"Silver!" he implored. "Silver, please. Come to Dadda! Shush!"

But instead, after several twists and turns, she vanished into the closet.

A wave of uncertainty washed over Horace when, after a few moments, he realized his daughter had gone silent. At first, he was relieved and wiggled his fingers in his ears. Then, worried at the abrupt cessation of marmot pips, he cautiously tiptoed over to the closet and peeked in. Silver Dollar, a young tot with curly hair, was slumped in the shoes. Even more cautiously, Horace closed the door.

It was at that point he sought out the liquor.

Collapsing on the cushions in the window seat, Horace sighed. He suspected Baby Doe had deliberately saddled him with Silver Dollar. The nursemaid never got ill—not that he could recall. This was obviously punishment for liberating the necklace.

Horace felt a little shade of guilt, given that Silver Dollar had a silver-dollar-sized lump on her forehead from the other day.

Feminine voices began to carry through the wallboards as Baby Doe's party began.

He easily recognized Maggie Brown's nasally vocals.

"I've been trying to get my husband to carve out enough room in his schedule so we can plan just *one* visit to London. Even a short one will make me happy. But you know how he is."

"My dear," Baby Doe replied. "They are all like that."

"He always says, 'Sea travel does not agree with me.' Yet I struggle to remember even a single time when we were on board a ship."

Horace could hear them carrying on candidly, and he wondered if they realized how thin the walls were. Baby Doe certainly did.

"Horace used to travel," she said, casting her voice at the wallboards, and huffed. "He's turned into a pathetic sop."

If he hadn't been shanghaied into playing nursemaid, Horace would be playing a hand of poker with the other tea party husbands. They were undoubtedly laughing at his misfortune at that very moment.

"What kind of tea is this?" Maggie Brown wondered. "It is an absolute delight."

"Is this Earl Grey's Mixture?" Janey Campion asked, but sounded quite assured that it was. "I've got John adapted to drinking Earl Grey's Mixture, and he absolutely adores it."

Baby Doe scoffed at the comment.

"Horace, of course, *refuses* to drink tea. He is thoroughly untrainable. I'm just lucky he knows how to use the privy."

There was no denying that Horace was a social fellow. He enjoyed a good chatty scenario. Yet there were times when all he yearned for was a quiet moment. Between the Matchless Mine, his hotel and other businesses, not to mention his political machinations, quiet was hard to find. With the child asleep in the closet, his wife entertaining, and the sun about to dip below the ridgeline, Horace realized this was as close to a quiet moment as he was likely to get.

He wished he had stashed a cigar in the bookcase as well as the bottle.

"Is this Earl Grey's Mixture?" Horace muttered in a dainty, yet almost inaudible tone, and took a nip of brandy.

CHAPTER 27

Big Ed was watching kids ride toboggans down Capitol Hill, right down the frozen city street. In the cold air, their laughter and chatter sounded very crisp and distinct. He saw two brothers. One was older, and he was helping the smaller one tie his bootlace. It had come undone and he was worried his little brother would lose his boot on the toboggan ride.

"Hey, dummy."

It was Big Ed's brother John, walking up the street. He had a girl on his arm. She was bundled up in a thick brown furry coat, matching knit cap, and a milky white scarf.

"You look like a wooly mammoth," Big Ed told her, trying to be charming.

"This is Mollie," John said. "She works at Tabor's place. She hears things you might find useful."

"You work for Haw?" Big Ed asked. "Where, at his opera house?"

Mollie smiled a pretty smile.

"Oh, honey! Who cares about Haw's boring ol' theater?" She laughed. "Have you been to Ben Loeb's? He's got the Human Corkscrew, the Spanish Dagger Dancer, and the Miranda Sisters who do their Iron Jaw Trapeze Show. They hang on with their *teeth*."

"You're gonna lose your job, girl, talking like that," Big Ed warned. "That is, if Haw hears you. The man gets prickly when you talk up the competition."

Mollie let go of John, leaned close and pecked Ed on the cheek.

"Oh, honey, I'm taking the next train out."

She giggled and held up a small paper sack.

Immediately, John scowled and looked around to see if anyone was watching.

"Now, put that away."

Instead, Mollie smiled even brighter and opened it up to show Big Ed it was full of cash.

"Your big brother is *flush*."

"Tell him what you heard at the hotel," John said.

Mollie giggled, and then gave in.

"Okay . . . Haw has buddied up with Johnny Campion, and they're gonna start up a silver club. They're tight with that senator, too, what's-his-name. That way, they can tell *everyone* how to vote."

John nudged her.

"He knows that already. What else?"

She pointed up the street.

"You know the Lucy B.? Johnny says he dug deep and struck it *big*. And they're gonna get the fella who manages it to run the silver club. Pay him to head it up. They're gonna have a big bash Friday, so if you want to make a move, you better move quick."

Turning, Big Ed cast a cold look at the mine. John Campion had been digging there since last summer, sinking all kinds of shafts—although up till now nothing serious had come out of it.

The sound of kids hooting cut through the air.

Big Ed turned to see the two boys hurtling down the cross-street in the toboggan.

He glanced at John, who was making eyes at Mollie, and wondered what it would have been like to have a big brother who didn't call him dummy.

Mollie heard the kids hollering, too, and pointed as they passed.

"Look at them go!" she shouted, and waved. "What fun!"

John hardly glanced.

"Just some damn kids."

Mollie gave him a pouty frown.

"If you never rode a sled, you wouldn't understand."

Big Ed felt a lump in his throat. He turned his eyes away from the kids, back to the Lucy B. mine.

"What time is it?" Mollie cried out, looking frightened.

Digging out a watch, John tried prying it open, but he was wearing gloves and didn't want to take them off. He handed it to Big Ed.

"Open that up, dummy."

"Be nice to him," Mollie scolded and whapped him on the shoulder.

Big Ed took off his own warm gloves and, using his fingernail, popped it open.

"Top of the hour. Four o'clock."

She lit up and clapped.

"I gotta go, honey!" she said, and gave Big Ed another peck on the cheek.

"What about me?" John asked, shocked.

Mollie giggled again and shrugged.

"You're too devilish."

John grabbed at her, but she jumped aside and ran off with her paper sack full of money. The street was slick with ice and snow, and she slid every few steps but somehow managed to keep from falling down.

"I gotta go!" she called and blew John a kiss.

They watched Mollie slip and slide down Fourth Street.

"That's the prettiest wooly mammoth I ever saw," Ed noted.

Frowning, John gestured at the Lucy B. property.

"The river only runs one way," he said, and his eyes were hard. "You get my meaning?"

Big Ed nodded and cleared his throat.

"I'll take care of it."

"You do your part, and then come on back home. Where you belong."

Behind them, in the distance, the simple sounds of the carefree toboggan ride receded in the distance. Then they heard the steam whistle at the Midland Depot.

CHAPTER 28

CREEDE

While LG went inside the Hardware & Stoves store, Walker sat with the wagon. It was his job to make sure no one stole it. LG warned him it was a boom camp. There was no real law there. No sheriff or police force. No rules. Some ruffian might try and steal the wagon, so it was up to him to be the lookout.

Walker was just glad he was in the wagon and not riding Billy Woods's cranky mule. Somehow, he had made the ride from town to their camp without incident. But every morning since, when he saddled the animal, it tried to buck him off. So when LG asked him to help with a supply run back to Creede, he eagerly volunteered. It was nice to sit on the wood bench, and not worry about getting pitched on the ground.

Glancing down, Walker stared at the handgun. It was LG's big, heavy Colt Army revolver—the old cap-and-ball style. The leather belt holster was too big for his waist, so he kept the gun in his lap. It looked really old and he was certain it was going to misfire if he jostled it. What if it hit one of the horses on the wagon team? Or a passerby? The mere thought was too awful to contemplate. So he remained very still, like a statue.

"Who you betting on?"

Curious, Walker turned his chin, ever so slowly, to see who was talking.

Two miners were examining a sign in the store window, which advertised an upcoming prizefight at the Denver Exchange.

"Why, Billy Woods, of course," one said.

The other shrugged.

"Is he any good?"

"He's undefeated. He fights every Saturday night and Bat Masterson himself plays the referee."

The sky overhead was gray and there was a chill in the air.

Straight ahead, rising up behind the buildings, was the big cliff. The clouds were so low, the highest portion vanished in the mist.

What was up there?

Walker let his eyes wander upwards, hoping the clouds might break for a moment, and if they did, he might see something. Maybe handholds carved in the rock like a ladder. Or a secret rope dangling down. What if Butch Cassidy had a hideout up there? Maybe that was where he stashed the money he robbed from the Telluride bank.

Walker also hoped the clouds would stay dry. If it started spitting sleet, he was supposed to cover the bed with the tarp. LG warned him not to let the flour or provisions get wet. If they did, they would be ruined.

It was nerve-racking.

Guarding the wagon was a dire responsibility. There were strangers everywhere. Almost every one of them carried six-guns or shotguns or rifles or pickaxes or shovels or jagged knives.

"Get this wagon outta here, you son of a bitch."

Walker felt his gut twist.

A man had come up on him, and he hadn't noticed.

"Look at me when I'm talkin', you little bastard."

Turning to look, Walker was stunned. It was Bob Ford! The man who killed Jesse James! He would recognize that face anywhere. Walker felt his gut twist even tighter.

"Move this thing!" Bob yelled. "I swear to God, I'll whip you right now."

His eyes were hard as stone.

Walker looked desperately at the Hardware & Stoves store, but all he saw was his own reflection in the big window, next to the prizefight sign.

"That does it."

Bob began taking off his overcoat.

Walker didn't know what to do. Of all the people to be angry at him, it had to be Bob Ford. And here he was with LG's Colt Army revolver in his lap. If Bob Ford realized he had a gun, Walker knew he would be dead for sure.

"What is going on here?" Soapy Smith said, coming up.

Bob pointed a finger at Walker.

"This street is chock full of folks goin' about their business, and this kid is parked right slap damn in the middle of it all. Cloggin' up the street!"

Adjusting his black hat, Soapy didn't even glance at Walker. His eyes were locked on Bob Ford.

"And what's that to you?" Soapy asked icily.

Flustered, Bob turned to face him.

"Who the hell are you?"

"A friend."

"Well, *friend*. You better pass on before I give you a whaling like you wouldn't believe."

Then Banjo Parker snuck up and threw Bob to the ground. Kneeling on his chest, Banjo seized his throat—and Bob began to thrash and gasp like a caught fish.

Soapy leaned down.

"I didn't say I was *your* friend." He spat on the ground next to Bob's head. "Now, who the hell are you?"

But Bob could not speak with Banjo's hand squeezing his windpipe.

"That's the man who killed Jesse James," Walker said weakly, finding his voice. When he realized he had spoken out loud, the butterflies roared around in his stomach. He thought he was going to be sick for sure, but somehow he kept it all down.

"The coward, you mean," Soapy said and smirked at Bob Ford. "The *coward* who killed Jesse James."

At that moment, Old Man Tripp and Joe Palmer walked up carrying a large trunk full of soap. Noticing Bob Ford on the ground getting choked, Joe dropped his end and rushed over.

"That's just Bob," he said and tapped Banjo. "Let him up, he's harmless."

Glancing at Soapy for approval, Banjo let him go.

Bob scrambled to his feet, disheveled from being pinned in the mud. Coughing, he wasted no time and scampered off.

Soapy looked at him quizzically, mildly amused.

"How do you know Bob Ford?"

Joe shrugged.

"He bought me a couple beers the other night. He's a likable cuss. A little ornery at first, till you get to know him better."

Soapy chuckled.

"Didn't seem very likable to me. What about you, Banjo? Did you find him likable?"

"Nope," Banjo replied.

"Would you get back over here?" Tripp said, who was still holding his end of the trunk. Then he looked to Soapy for approval. "You saw it! He dropped his end, but I held onto mine."

"Just pick it up. And let's find a good place to set up the show," Soapy told them, and then tipped his hat at Walker. "Have a pleasant evening, Garo."

CHAPTER 29

"Buy this soap," Soapy declared. "And wash away your sins."

He held up a small cake of lye soap.

Several gritty miners were walking by and stopped, trying to see what he was holding. One of them, a short man with a dark mustache, came closer.

"What is that?" he asked. "Some kind of preacher soap? Looks like regular toilet soap to me."

Soapy laughed musically.

"To some standing here today, it might seem so. But perhaps you've heard it said . . . cleanliness is next to godliness. Well let me tell you, a pocket full of cash is even better."

Soapy was standing behind a folding table. On his right, there was a box filled with soap cakes. To his left, a stack of sky blue wrapping paper.

"Why would I wanna buy preacher soap?"

"What's your name, sir?" Soapy inquired.

"I ain't telling you my name."

Soapy was unfazed.

"By your apparel, I imagine you spend your days laboring over a sluice box?"

The man looked offended.

"Hell, no. I work a drift shaft up at the Amethyst."

Reaching into his coat, Soapy pulled out a twenty-dollar bill and held it up.

"This is twenty bucks. Now watch close."

Folding the cash around the soap cake, Soapy took a piece of blue paper and wrapped it around both the cash and the soap, making a pretty little package, and tied it snug with twine. He did the same with two fifties and a hundred-dollar bill. Finally, he bundled up a small pile of soap without cash and mixed them all together.

"My friends—tomorrow you can slog up that canyon, wade that cold creek, and freeze your fingers off rooting through a damned rocker box. But today, make some easy money."

"I just told you I don't work that cold crick," the miner snapped, but he leaned over the table curiously.

"Pay me five dollars, and I'll let you pick one package from this pile. Some of this is just plain soap. But who knows, you might just pick the right one."

Across the street, Joe was smoking a cigarette. Banjo was right next door, pretending to window shop. And, right on cue, Old Man Tripp strolled past the table whistling.

Soapy spotted him and hollered. "Sir! How about you? Take a chance, make some easy money."

Old Man Tripp stopped whistling and came right over.

"What's going on?"

"This fellow is trying to sell us nickel soap for five bucks," the miner explained.

Soapy pointed at the soap.

"Some of these have cash inside. Only five bucks per try."

Tripp's jaw fell open.

"Well, shoot, I'll take that chance," he said, and handed Soapy a five-dollar bill.

Soapy was pleased with his performance. Tripp had been useful back in Denver, too, but here the man really shined. Just seeing the old fellow itch his beard in contemplation, or hook his thumb behind his oversized suspenders, was pure magic.

Old Man Tripp chose a certain bar of soap, turned so everyone could see, and tore it open.

"Hundred bucks!" he hooted, jumping up and down, waving the bill.

Joe dropped his cigarette and came straight over.

"I'm next."

Banjo turned from his window shopping and ran over too. "No, I'm next!"

Seeing Banjo and Joe and the hundred-dollar bill in Tripp's hand, the men from the Amethyst Mine quickly pulled out their own cash and bought cakes of nickel soap for five bucks each. And that's all they walked away with.

CHAPTER 30

LG parked the wagon and hopped down. It was well after dark by the time they arrived, and he could barely make out their cow camp. He pulled back the tarp and held the lantern high so he could find what he was looking for.

"You want the candy?" he asked.

But Walker didn't move. He remained on the driving bench, shivering, with his chin buried deep in his scarf. He wasn't sure what LG was talking about. Did he buy candy? Walker couldn't remember. Everything had been a blur after the terrifying incident with Bob Ford and Soapy Smith.

"Did you get a new stove?" Davis called from inside the tent. "Because I surely hate this one."

LG angled the light and held up a paper package with a yellow label.

"In every bag of Arbuckles, they put in a peppermint."

He opened it up and fished out a thick red and white peppermint stick from among the coffee beans, and handed it to Walker.

"Should I wait till later?"

"I ain't your momma."

Then LG went over and yanked open the tent.

"Davey, you'll be pleased to know we got bacon, butter, syrup, and eggs."

Huddled in a blanket, Davis came out and examined the wagon bed in the lamplight.

"But no stove? Well, I ain't staying up feeding sticks till dawn no more, no matter how many aces you pull from that filthy old deck of cards."

Going back to the wagon, LG began unloading the supplies.

"I checked, but a new one is too costly. Maybe I'll see if the boys up at the Amethyst have a better one for sale."

Davis hung his head.

"This is the most miserable cow camp I have ever lived in."

Biting off a piece of cold peppermint, Walker realized he hadn't had sweets since he left home. He couldn't even remember how long ago that was. It was hard to think about anything, at the moment, besides Bob Ford's mean face.

Walker looked up at the sky. It was opaque. There wasn't any starlight, or moon, and the night was as black as he had ever seen it. He was glad LG had been driving the wagon, because he had no idea where they were until they pulled up to the tent. It was also bitterly cold. Even though he was wearing an overcoat and thick chaps, the chill cut to the bone.

"You okay?" Davis asked, noticing he was unusually quiet.

The boy shrugged.

"I nearly got killed. It's all I can think about."

Davis was concerned.

"How did you nearly get killed?"

But Walker got quiet again.

"Ol' Bob Ford started an argument when I was in the stove store," LG explained. "Got all swelled up at the kid because we parked the wagon in the street."

Davis climbed up on the driving bench and sat next to Walker.

"Don't you worry about Bob Ford," he assured him. "That fellow is all hat and no cattle."

Then he glared at LG.

"What we *do* have to worry about is freezing to death."

LG chuckled and flicked his wrist in contempt.

"This ain't nothing."

Then he climbed up on the driving bench, too, and boxed Walker in.

"Now, you're too green to know the cussidness of trail life. Months of lonesome country. Nose to the polestar. Perturbed by the elements. A body rides in from night guard, teeth a'chatter or all rain-sopped till you're half near froze."

Then he handed Walker the Arbuckles package.

"But this right here makes it all better. Go get the skillet. And parch the beans before you run 'em through the mill. I won't drink no belly wash."

CHAPTER 31

"Place your bets," Jeff Argyle announced, who was running a faro game in the Denver Exchange.

The table always had the same thirteen cards laid out on the green velvet. Starting with the ace and working up in order all the way to the king. It was a simple game, really. Each round, he would draw two cards—a losing card and the winning card. Usually, when Argyle announced a new game, players would place chips all over the thirteen cards. But ever since Soapy Smith walked in and started playing, everyone avoided the faro table. Except Frank Oliver, an ornery gambler and a habitual drunk.

"I sure could use another whiskey sour," Soapy mentioned to Bat, who was milling around the game tables.

Then he set a hundred-dollar stack of chips on top of the king card.

Frank Oliver guffawed.

"How much have you blown through tonight, Smith?"

"It's all in good fun, Frank."

"Always betting on the king, aren't you?" he sneered. "There are thirteen cards to bet on, plus the high card, and you always just bet the same stinkin' card over and over. No wonder you lose so much. Ol' Bat Masterson must light up when you come in to play, 'cause he knows he's gonna win every penny you got."

Bat walked back over and dropped off the requested glass of liquor.

Soapy took a quick sip.

"And there you go again," Frank Oliver said, sneering some more. "Sipping your booze. Sip, sip, sip!"

He looked disgusted.

"Like a *woman*. A true man will gulp it down like dynamite."

"That's where you're wrong, Frank," Soapy replied. "Only hasty people gulp. And if you gulp it down, you can't enjoy it properly."

"That's the most addle-headed thing I ever heard."

"Betting is closed," Argyle announced, though no one else was betting.

He turned over the cards, and the winning card was a king.

"There it is!" Soapy said and clapped his hands. "Did you see that, Frank? I do win sometimes. And on the king, you'll notice. That's because I am a king."

He raised the whiskey sour in a silent toast to himself.

"I'm gettin' in on this," Frank said.

He patted his vest pockets, but only turned up a couple bent cigarettes and a pocket watch.

"Run out of dinero, Franky?" said Bob, walking up.

Soapy turned to see who spoke, and when he recognized it was Bob Ford, he cackled.

"Oh hell, look who it is. Didn't recognize your voice apart from the rasp of strangulation."

"Run along, Frank, shoo," Bob said.

Frank Oliver got up, since he had no gambling money.

"You got a match?" he asked, trying to straighten out a cigarette. But Bob ignored him and took his seat.

"I'd offer to buy you a drink, but I suspect it's hard for you to swallow," Soapy mentioned to Bob in an offhand way.

Meanwhile, Jeff Argyle shuffled the deck. Then he reset the abacus so he could keep track of the cards as they were dealt.

"New game. Place your bets."

Quick as a cat, Bob reached over and placed a thousand-dollar stack of chips right on top of the king.

Soapy's face turned dark.

"Move it. That's the card I bet on every single game."

"Ah, don't look so down in the mouth," Bob said, and grew quite serious. "Looks like *I* get to be the king."

Jeff Argyle felt a chill.

He glanced over at Bat, but Bat had moved on and was observing the poker table. Turning around, Argyle cast a hopeful look at the bar but could not catch Billy Woods's eye, either. He was facing the whiskey barrels, filling up a shot glass. The room was full of gamblers, chatter, and cigar smoke. The entire time he had worked at the Denver Exchange, which was every night since it opened, Argyle never once heard a gun go off inside its walls. All the gamblers carried guns and knives regularly, but no one had gotten killed. Yet.

"Tell you what," Soapy said, standing up. "You can pretend you're king tonight, Bob."

He scooped up his remaining chips and his liquor.

Bob arched an eyebrow at Jeff Argyle.

"He's as dumb as he is ugly. Now, turn that card."

"Bets are now closed," Argyle announced, though again, no one else was playing or even thinking about it.

Then he flipped over the losing card. It was a king.

"Dealer wins," he said.

Bob Ford glowered at the dealer, and then up at Soapy, who was hiding a smile behind his whiskey glass.

"You better be playing fair!" Bob shouted at Jeff Argyle. "You in cahoots with him?"

Sensing trouble, Bat Masterson strolled over to see what was happening.

"Simmer down, Bob. He's a straight, square dealer. He ain't in cahoots with nobody."

"I just lost a thousand dollars!"

"Next time, don't bet so much," Bat suggested.

CHAPTER 32

SOUTHWEST COLORADO

Stretching out on the cold ground, Greasewood tried to get comfortable.

"Where can we go *now*?" he moaned. "We can't go back to the reservation. When word gets out what we did back at the cliff houses, we will be arrested. The government will search for us, that's for certain."

Bear Claw Lip took a drink from a bottle.

"Who cares? Where did White Owl go?"

They were camped on a ridge among juniper and oak. Before they left, Bear Claw Lip had raided the Whites' equipment at the cliff houses and found several bottles of liquor. He finished off one and opened another.

"To look for something to eat," Greasewood said miserably. "Maybe he will stumble on a cabin—and we can sleep indoors tonight."

"Why do you even *want* to go back to that stupid reservation?" Bear Claw Lip asked, sneering. However, his lip was so mangled, no one could tell.

Greasewood rolled onto his back and shook his fist at the sky.

"I want a bed to sleep in."

Sitting by the fire, Kahopi snacked on piñon nuts. "Why did you leave in the first place?"

Stalking around the fire, Bear Claw Lip looked menacing.

"Those greedy Whites!"

Greasewood propped himself up on an elbow.

"There was a rumor there might be gold on the reservation," he said. "So the White government sent agents to poke around."

Flopping back in the dirt, he let out a heavy sigh.

"And the railroad sent in surveyors, too. I better get used to this cold hard ground."

Bear Claw Lip took a deep swig, but whiskey drizzled through his bottom teeth and down his chin.

"They're going to move us again," he shouted. "They herd us around like cattle!"

Then he pointed at the piñon nuts.

"Can I have a few?"

Kahopi shrugged. He handed Bear Claw Lip a handful of nuts, who in turn handed him the whiskey bottle.

"Here, brother, drink some of this."

Even though Kahopi was not Ute, none of the other three treated him like an outsider. They treated him like a brother. It had been a long time since Kahopi had felt accepted like a brother. His own brother always treated him poorly. So did his uncles and aunts and sister's husband. Everyone always jabbed at him with jokes.

Returning to the fire, White Owl set down a pile of mushrooms.

"I found these," he said.

Greasewood looked up, hopefully.

"Did you stumble on a cabin?"

"No."

"Give me some," Bear Claw Lip demanded. He sniffed a mushroom and then ate it. And then a few more.

Greasewood moaned again.

"Where can we go now?"

White Owl shrugged, but Bear Claw Lip clapped his hands.

"North! To the mountains. To the old hunting grounds."

But Greasewood was not so sure.

"The old hunting grounds must surely be overrun with Whites by now."

"Then we will make them leave. Just like we did at the cliff houses."

Sitting up on his elbow again, Greasewood appeared very concerned.

"No. This is not right. Let's return to the reservation and accept our punishment. There is no future for us if we run. At least we will have beds to sleep in."

"You must be getting senile," Bear Claw Lip said. "There is no future for us if we return."

Then he picked up a few more mushrooms and ate them. As he gobbled them down, he observed the moon rising. It was coming up in the east, like usual, but it was twice its normal size and the color of bone. A look of understanding passed over his face.

"I know what we must do."

He spat in his hands and rubbed them together and held them out toward the moon.

"We are in the End Times. We must dance the Ghost Dance," he told them in a faraway voice. "It was not long ago that all the People danced. The Paiute and Apache, Hopi and Navaho . . . even the Cheyenne and Lakota. Ancient enemies united as one. It was said Kicking Bear did this, and Sitting Bull—everyone who believed. We danced the Ghost Dance all night long. Every six weeks we did this. Do you remember? Do you recall why we did this?"

He inhaled a deep breath of spirit power, and cried out, "*Give us back our arrows!*"

Then he began singing a magic song.

Feeling his spirit moved, Greasewood sat straight up.

Kahopi was shocked at the change in the old man's countenance. His eyes, once dull, now flickered with fire.

"*Give us back our arrows!*" Greasewood echoed.

Reaching down, Bear Claw Lip gripped his forearm and pulled the him to his feet. Together they danced around the fire and chanted. Joining them, White Owl danced too.

Father, I come.
Brother, I come.
Mother, I come.

Then Bear Claw Lip reached out for the bottle and Kahopi handed it to him. He drank, and then raised his hands to the moon again.

"When the springtime comes and the grass is high, the earth will shake. New soil will fall like rain and bury all the Whites. New grass will appear, new trees and fresh running water. And the buffalo will return and once again cover the plains. And all who dance the Ghost Dance will be taken up into the sky and remain there while this is accomplished. Then they shall float back down, and our ancestors shall descend, and we shall reside in peace, and hunt there forever."

Bear Claw Lip trained his gaze on Kahopi.

"We dance to hasten the End. Join us, brother."

— PART 5 —

CHAPTER 33

AUTUMN 1859
DENVER

Augusta pulled a small handgun out of her purse and held it out.

"Where did you get this?" Horace gasped. "How much did it cost?"

It was a Philadelphia Deringer with smooth, glossy walnut grips.

"Take it, Horace."

He weighed it in his palm and stared at it.

"In case you run into trouble."

They were sitting next to each other on a bed in a Denver hotel room.

"You better hold onto it, Gussie," he said, kindly. "There are two thousand men right here and not a single female anywhere. Well, except the whores."

He smiled his most winning smile.

"Such salty language," she commented. "Keep it. I have two. They were a wedding gift from my father."

Stunned, Horace couldn't believe what she said.

"He gave you *guns* on our wedding night? That man has always despised me!"

Then he crossed his arms and huffed indignantly.

"We have been married two whole years. And you had two pistols in your handbag this whole time?"

She pinched his mustache.

"Don't feel blue. I don't tell you everything."

Horace did feel blue. But mainly because he had been duped by the Old-timer.

"I'm sorry to hear he tricked you. And I'm sorry to hear all the men in the tavern laughed at you," Augusta said with another mustache pinch. "But Horace, you *are* gullible."

Clenching his jaw, Horace tried to hold in all his feelings.

"It was humiliating."

Augusta patted his knee.

"I know it was, Horace."

"Snow slides are a legitimate danger," he went on, feeling wretched.

"I know they are, Horace."

Hiding his eyes in a handkerchief, he fought to sound normal, despite the lump in his throat.

"That old cuss took my claim. He waited till I left—and even set up a sluice box!"

Finally, getting irked, Augusta rolled her eyes and pointed at the tiny pistol.

"Are you going back up that canyon or not?"

Horace swallowed hard and hefted the Deringer again.

"No."

Then he gave it back to her.

"I hate your father."

She took the gun, put it back in her handbag, and patted him on the knee again.

"I know you do, Horace."

CHAPTER 34

WINTER 1892
LEADVILLE

"Where's that pretty waitress?" Horace asked the bartender.

He looked around the parlor of the Tabor Grand Hotel, but did not see her.

"Which one?"

"The one with the turquoise eyes," Horace told him. "Mollie."

The bartender shook his head.

"Quit and gone."

Horace sighed. He was hoping to see her again. He had even filled his vest pockets with silver dollars.

"Well, shoot."

He looked around the parlor. He spotted John Campion at the same time the man saw him, and Campion walked straight over with another man at his heel.

"Haw, meet my mine manager at the Lucy B.," Campion said. "This is Wheezy Jones."

"How do you do?" Horace asked.

Wheezy Jones dabbed his nose with a handkerchief.

"I'm doing well, thank you," he said, and dabbed his nose a second time.

Noticing his penchant for nose dabbing, Horace decided not to shake hands. He did not care for other men's drippings.

Then, concerned, he leaned over to whisper in Campion's ear.

"Is he fit enough to run the silver club?"

"He is."

Horace was disappointed. He was expecting a fellow who exhibited verve. Charisma. The only thing this man seemed to exhibit was mucus.

"Why don't we all have a seat?" Horace suggested and pointed at the parlor chairs, the ones made of leather imported from India, glistening near the windows.

But Campion frowned, eyeing the seats with disgust.

"I prefer to stand."

Just then, another man entered the parlor, and Horace waved him over.

"Here comes the Major. Let's get these two acquainted."

The Major came and, nodding curtly, planted himself next to Horace.

"Mr. Jones, this is Major Bohn. He is the manager at the Matchless Mine—my biggest silver producer."

"It's a pleasure," Wheezy Jones said.

A bead of snot bubbled from one of his nostrils.

"I suppose," the Major replied skeptically.

The two mine managers could not appear more different. Wheezy Jones had poor posture and eyes like a doe, whereas the Major had eyes like a hawk. Jones carried a handkerchief. The Major carried a steel sword.

Horace leaned over and pinched Campion's sleeve.

"Perhaps we should go with my man after all," he whispered.

Bristling at the suggestion, Campion pulled away from Horace's grip.

"No. I already told Janey so we can't change it now."

"What does she care?" Horace asked.

Looking pained, Campion cupped his hand over Horace's ear. "He's her brother."

Horace sighed.

"Fine," he said and rolled his eyes. "Friday night, when the day shift ends, get all the boys at the Lucy B. to gather in the yard. We'll bring all the Matchless boys over at the same time, and make a big hoopla out of it."

Campion nodded, looking tense.

"This better work," he said. "You provide the libations, and I'll organize some fireworks and entertainment."

"It *will* work," Horace assured him. "I happen to know Teller is setting up silver clubs all over the state. He's going to every camp and boomtown he can find. Have some faith, John!"

Then Horace looked Wheezy Jones up and down.

"We need some incentive," he said. "Let's offer a wage hike for everyone who joins the silver club. If we say four dollars a day, I guarantee every single miner in this whole city will show up."

But Campion frowned.

"I don't like it. The price of silver is way too low, and it's still falling."

Horace *pshawed*.

"You need to stop drinking so much Earl Grey tea," he chided. "Don't get bogged down in political horse pucky. The price will shoot up like a rocket on the Fourth of July—as soon as we elect the right president."

Then he clapped Campion on the back.

"You get all your boys over to the Lucy B. on Friday night and just see what happens."

CHAPTER 35

When Horace heard the knock on the door, he assumed it was his carriage driver. So when he opened the door, he was amazed to see his son Maxcy instead.

"Maxcy?" Horace said. "What are you doing here!"

"Hello, Pop."

Throwing his arms around his father, Maxcy gave Horace a big hug.

"I wasn't expecting you. Did your mother wire? If she did, it never made it and I'm gonna sue that damn telegraph office."

Maxcy looked uncomfortable.

Fearing the worst, Horace looked around to see if Augusta was lurking nearby. Not seeing her in the icy street in front of his house, Horace studied the snowdrifts, in case she was crouching behind one of those.

"It's just me," Maxcy assured his father. "I told her I was taking a business trip to Colorado Springs."

Horace took him gently by the shoulders.

"I did not know a tall tale was in your constitution."

"I didn't want to hurt her feelings, but I just needed to get away."

"Son, you are well into your third decade . . . you should have gotten away a long time ago."

At that moment, Baby Doe appeared behind Horace, holding Silver Dollar in her arms. She looked through the doorway curiously.

"Who's in their third decade?" she said. "Me or him?"

Ignoring her, Horace reached over and twirled his finger in one of Silver Dollar's curly locks.

"This has got to be Maxcy," Baby Doe said. "Horace, he looks just like you. Only *much* younger. In fact, he may very well be my senior."

Maxcy smiled politely.

"How do you do, ma'am?"

She frowned.

"Ma'am makes me sound like the old crow. You *better* call me Baby Doe."

"You better, Maxcy," Horace told him. "She throws things."

Then, reminded again of Augusta's existence, Horace cast another fearful look up and down the street.

"Where is the old crow? Are you sure she's not here?" he asked, and then pointed at a carriage coming up the street. "Oh, dear Lord, is that her!"

"No, Horace," Baby Doe said. "That's *our* carriage. You sent for it, remember?"

They watched as it skittered up the slippery hill.

Horace shrugged but was clearly relieved.

"Mother is still in Denver. Don't worry, Pop."

"Sitting in my forty-thousand-dollar mansion," grumbled Horace. "It is a crime she won that in the divorce. Is she taking good care of the colonnades in the foyer? I got those shipped in from Greece! They're solid marble. She *knows* they chip easily."

"The colonnades are intact," Maxcy said.

"That woman is living in a forty-thousand-dollar mansion?" Baby Doe griped and gave Horace a cold stare. "Then why am I living in this hovel?"

The carriage parked in front of the Tabor home, and the horses snorted in the brisk air.

Horace turned to his son.

"Alright, well, come with me. We'll go for a ride and we can talk some more."

"Where are you off to?" Baby Doe asked, suspiciously.

Horace winked at Maxcy.

"I'm taking a business trip to Colorado Springs."

She shifted Silver Dollar from one hip to the other. The little girl was sound asleep and almost too big to hold anymore.

"You better not go to that filthy little beer barn!"

But with Maxcy standing on their front porch, and Silver Dollar sleeping in her arms, Horace knew she wasn't going to throw a tantrum—or a vase.

"Bye, bye," Horace told her. He gave Baby Doe a kiss on the cheek and Silver Dollar a kiss on the head. "Let's go, Maxcy!"

He trotted ahead through the crusty snow and opened the carriage door so his son could climb in first. Then he cast a quick glance back at the house. His wife was still standing on the porch, watching his every move. To be coy, Horace pulled up onto the side of the carriage so he could whisper the destination.

"Take us to the Stray Horse Brewery."

Then he slid down, waved, and got inside.

"Stray Horse!" the driver called out, whipped the reins, and the carriage was off again.

"*I knew it!*" Baby Doe roared.

Jarred awake, Silver Dollar began to wail.

Horace ducked away from the carriage window nervously, and so did Maxcy.

"Is she as mean as Mother?"

Horace chuckled, but it sounded a little hollow.

"No one is mean as Mother."

Then Maxcy sank back in his seat, turning melancholy.

"I apologize if I showed up at a bad time."

"It's never a bad time for you. I miss spending time with my favorite boy."

"I'm your only boy."

Horace gave him a wry smile.

"You're not a boy anymore, anyhow. Long since grown up. Yet somehow, unimaginably, still living with his mother."

After a few minutes, Maxcy sat up so he could see the scenery. The sun was bright and there were hardly any clouds in the blue sky. Covered in white snow, the mountains were almost too bright to look at. The carriage turned a corner and went down another street. Maxcy looked at all the different houses and cabins, studying each mine they passed with curiosity.

"This town sure has exploded since I was here last. It was barely a row of saloons back then."

"It's been a number of years, hasn't it?"

They sat in silence, enjoying the sound of the horse hooves clopping along, and the creak of the carriage.

"Are we really going to a beer barn?" Maxcy wondered.

Horace nodded.

"More or less."

"Mother dislikes beer."

Horace smiled at him.

"Do you?"

Horace's ex-wife Augusta was not easy to get along with. Horace certainly did not get along with her. And apparently, even the long-suffering and sweet-spirited Maxcy needed a break now and again.

The carriage made a few more turns, and at one point they had to cling to the walls when the wheels lost purchase and skidded around a corner. After a while it slowed and stopped.

"Stray Horse!" shouted the driver and thumped the roof.

They got out and went inside the brewery.

Dirty Johns was sweeping up peanut shells with a broom. He glanced up dully and, when he saw who it was, moseyed off into the backroom.

"This is it," Horace announced.

Maxcy looked around.

"It does feel like a barn."

"And the beer does taste like cow trickle."

A soft smile spread across Maxcy's face.

"Well, I better try it and see for myself."

No one else was standing at the bar, so they went up and leaned on it and waited for Dirty Johns to reappear. He did reappear, but he brought Big Ed Burns along with him.

"Well damn, Dirty Johns," Big Ed said. "You ain't *that* drunk after all. There really are two Haw Tabors."

He smiled his creasy-eyed smile.

"He even has the same big brushy soup strainer for a mustache. I swear I can't tell the difference."

Horace ignored him.

"How about a couple beers, Ed? For me and my son."

"Sure, sure, Haw. Wait, I wasn't looking," Big Ed said, pointing from one to the other. "Which one of you said that?"

Then he burst out laughing and slapped his thigh.

Maxcy, getting nervous, looked to his father. But Horace seemed completely at ease.

"I'm about to give you some big business."

"Yeah, what's that?"

"I am here to order every single bottle of beer you got."

Waiting for a punchline, Big Ed tried to gauge if he was serious.

"That's a lot of beer, Haw. You got a big party coming up? I don't recall being invited, myself. Dirty Johns . . . were you invited to Haw's big party?"

"Nope," Dirty Johns mumbled, still holding his broom.

Horace leaned forward and his face got hard.

"What *I* recall is ordering a damn beer for my son."

Big Ed's calculated smile faded. He bristled at the Silver King for a moment, and then pointed at his dungaree-clad employee.

"You going deaf, Dirty Johns? Get the man and his son a beer."

Then he leaned across the bar, looking sly.

"I swear, I'm gonna have to take him out back and wring his neck like an old crippled chicken one of these days."

Maxcy sat very still, hands folded neatly, and stared at all the cigar burns in the bar top.

Big Ed studied him for a moment, and then Haw, and back again. They both had the exact same receding hairline, weak chin, and mustache. But the son oozed fear like a jellyfish. It reminded Big Ed that Haw himself used to be spineless. He used to stare down at his lap whenever Big Ed came in the room, and he used to gobble magnesium tablets like they were made of sugar. Ed missed those days.

"Do you want my business or not?" Horace asked him.

Big Ed held his hands up in the air.

"I surrender! You got me!"

Then he laughed again, a little too loudly.

Horace sighed under his breath. This entire experience was not unexpected. Once again, Big Ed Burns was trying to pretend he was bigger than his britches. But Horace needed to order as much beer as he could find for the silver club event. It was only a few days away. Horace did not feel like scrambling to find what he needed in such a short amount of time from the good breweries in Denver. He knew Big Ed had it. So, for the moment anyway, he could put up with his circus act. However, Horace fully expected that one day, soon probably, he would need to evict Big Ed from Leadville. The man's usefulness had dwindled down to a last-minute beer sale.

Dirty Johns brought out two dusty bottles and set them on the bar.

CHAPTER 36

CREEDE

"Who?" Soapy asked.

"Persimmons," Banjo told him.

"Who's that?"

Banjo blinked, looking confused.

"Called himself Persimmons. Said he was your best friend."

Soapy mulled it over.

"I bet it's a Pinkerton."

The low morning sunlight was just starting to cut through the canyon trees, making them squint at each other on the boardwalk outside Zang's Hotel. Soapy was so tired all he wanted was his warm featherbed. His eyes were red and sore, which made him squint even harder.

"Did you play faro all night?" Banjo whispered.

Patting his coat pocket, Soapy felt the lump of his pistol exactly where it should be.

"Don't tell me you put him in my room."

"Course not!" Banjo assured him. "I imagine he's in there eating. It is breakfast time. I suggested he take on a bite while he waits."

Soapy tried to get a look through the plate glass window, but the sun was just right and he only saw his own muddy reflection.

"Did you eat already? What is Zang serving?"

"Calf's head jelly and vinegar pie."

Soapy was shocked.

"I don't know what they eat in China, but that ain't breakfast food."

Banjo shrugged.

"That's what he served me."

After rubbing his red eyes, Soapy blinked a few times and cleared his throat.

"Dammit. Let's go put a hole in that Pinkerton's head."

He pulled open the door and went inside. The dining table was completely empty, except for one man with a fork in his hand, probing a plate of calf's head jelly.

Soapy's eyebrows shot up in surprise.

"Is that Joe Simmons?"

Then he turned on Banjo, cuffing him like a schoolboy.

"Clean the *wax* out of your *ears*."

Banjo's face fell.

"How do, Jefferson," Simmons called out, using Soapy's given name. He wiped his sleeve across his mouth, and stuck his hand out for a handshake.

"Well, I'll be!"

Soapy swept off his black hat and swatted it against his thigh.

"Thought you were a Pinkerton."

Simmons shuddered.

"I am vile, but not *that* vile."

"Banjo, get over here. Meet Joe Simmons. We used to punch cattle together, back in the early days, in Texas."

But Simmons chose not to meet Banjo, and in fact ignored him entirely. He kept grinning and pumping Soapy's hand.

"It's been a long ol' time, Jefferson."

Feeling like the odd man out, and scolded to make things worse, Banjo hung his head and found himself staring at Simmons's plate. Zang didn't serve regular breakfast food, but always the evening's leftovers. Every morning, it was something inappropriate for the hour. Never eggs. And Banjo liked eggs.

He finally looked up from the calf's head jelly and examined this man, Joe Simmons. He didn't look as well dressed as Soapy. In fact, he looked like a disheveled drunk. He even had dried puke on his lapel. Then Banjo studied his boss again, dressed in his usual press-creased black suit. Neither one looked like they knew the first thing about punching cattle. Not like the cowboys down at the stockyards.

"Jeff and Joe," Simmons said in sentimental awe. "Old pals together again."

"We already have a Joe," Banjo mentioned. "Joe Palmer."

"Now how in the hell did you suss me out?" Soapy asked, ignoring him. "Did Bascomb tell you?"

"I read *silver boom* in the papers, and I say, well where else would the man be?"

Noticing Zang moving around in the kitchen, Soapy flagged him down.

"Zang! Why are you serving my best friend this garbage? Go back in that kitchen and fry us up some damn eggs. Eggs! Go!"

Without a word, Zang disappeared in the kitchen again and they heard him yell at the Chinese girl. Then Soapy Smith and

Joe Simmons sat down at the table. Banjo pulled out a chair and started to sit, too, but Soapy held up his palm.

"You already ate."

"I did, but I would prefer a fried egg."

"How about you run around to that tent, and go wake up the boys instead. Get them in here."

Slowly, pathetically, Banjo pushed the chair back into place and left.

Watching him leave, Soapy suddenly felt bad.

"What's wrong?" Simmons asked.

"Maybe I should apologize to Banjo. He seemed a bit crestfallen."

"You mean that string bean fella?"

Soapy shrugged.

"I was harsh. I thought he let in a Pinkerton."

"Apologize? What for? A bark instead of a handshake? A wink's as good as a nod to a blind mule."

Simmons took a moment to dig out a cigarette.

"Like all good lackeys," he said with a grin, "he lacks."

"Aw, he ain't too bad."

"The string bean shall recover," Simmons said and handed Soapy a cigarette. "So, I went through Denver and stopped at the Tivoli Club. Your brother tells me you beat the hell out of some big time newspaper editor and had to skip town."

He struck a match and lit Soapy's cigarette first, and then his own.

Soapy sucked in the warm gray smoke and blew it out through his nose like a bull. He smirked.

"Yeah, that's true enough."

Simmons looked amused.

"Hey, some folks are good listeners, and others need some sense beaten into them."

Zang brought out two plates heaped with fresh fried eggs.

Soapy gave him a disappointed look.

"Where's the coffee?"

"Coffee!" said Zang. He rushed into the kitchen, and they heard him yell at the poor girl again.

Simmons took a bite and began to reminisce.

"Remember that little saloon we ran, back in Texas?"

Soapy squinted at the ceiling, thinking back.

"The Chisolm Trail."

Simmons thumped his fist against Soapy's shoulder.

"That was it! We ran that place till we got ran out ourselves."

"Those were fine times."

Soapy took another puff on the cigarette, thinking back.

"Remember that dance girl from New Orleans? You were sparking on her. What was her name?"

"Hell, I don't know. I recall I took her to the fair to watch the fireworks. I bought that girl lemonade and ice cream, and she slapped me across the face. But I can't remember why."

"Well, you were always a little grabby when you got lit up with bad whiskey."

Simmons took another bite of the eggs.

"That could be it."

Bringing out two cups, Zang poured them each some hot fresh coffee.

"He does do coffee right," Soapy said and patted Zang on the arm.

Zang grinned and left just as quickly as he came.

Simmons watched him go. When they were alone again, he leaned close.

"It doesn't sound like you're heading back to Denver anytime soon, does it?"

"Nope," Soapy replied. "I like it here. And I'm just getting started."

"So then, you got a place opened up yet?"

Soapy glanced at him sideways.

"A saloon? Not yet."

"Well, let's get one open, then."

"Did you notice the sign I had, hanging above the door?" Soapy asked him. "At the Tivoli?"

"Yes I did. Was it something in Mexican?"

Soapy held his hands up like he was announcing a carnival attraction.

"*Caveat Emptor*—Let the Buyer Beware."

Simmons nodded in awe.

"You were always quick with words."

"I am."

"Well, think up a name right now. For our new saloon. I'm going to count to ten."

Before he got to three, Soapy snapped his fingers.

"The Orleans Club. Amusements and Top Hat Likker."

The door opened and cold air swirled in, along with Banjo, Joe Palmer, and Old Man Tripp. Soapy waved them over.

"Boys, this is my oldest and dearest friend, Joe Simmons. He's come all the way up here to help me open up a new saloon."

All three of them gazed at the eggs with longing eyes.

"How come you got eggs?" Old Man Tripp asked. "All Zang had for us was vinegar pie. I hate vinegar pie."

Soapy pointed at Old Man Tripp.

"There's no time to waste. Go buy that open lot down by the bank, and then meet me at the Hardware & Stoves. We'll order some lumber."

Then he pointed at Joe and Banjo.

"You two saddle up. Go find those cowboys that brought in all those shaggy beeves on the train. We'll need a steady supply of beef for the restaurant." He glared at Joe Palmer. "We won't be serving no rancid deer meat."

CHAPTER 37

"Do you hear that noise?" Joe Palmer asked.

Banjo cocked his head.

"Sounds like a goose to me."

"It's a ratty old cow," Joe continued. "I know that sound a mile off."

"All I can hear is my stomach rumbling."

They were following the narrow stock trail that led through the forest to LG and Davis's cow camp. Their horses carefully picked their way along the path.

Joe wrinkled his nose.

"This whole trail is nothing but turd."

"Better than dead deer. Did you ever get those clothes wrung out?"

Joe twisted around in the saddle so he could glare at Banjo.

"Would you shut up about that dern deer! I've heard as much of that fiddle-faddle as I'm gonna take."

"You're cranky this morning."

Banjo was right. Joe was cranky. He hadn't gotten any decent sleep. In fact, he hadn't gotten any decent sleep since they came to Creede in the first place. He had never slept anywhere that was as drafty as Zang's Hotel. It did not help that there were intestines oozing beneath his cot. Joe missed having a nice warm room, like he used to have at the Tivoli Club back in Denver. He wondered if he would ever have a normal bed to sleep in again.

The morning air in the forest was extra cold. Joe pulled at his wool scarf to snug it up around his throat. The scarf was special. His mother had knit it for his tenth birthday. That was back when he was young and his chore was to milk the family cows at sunrise and sundown. The winter, when the sun was late to rise, was the worst time of the year to milk. The only light he had on days like that was an oil lamp and the stars. He would tremble the moment he left the warm house, and his freezing fingers made the cows jump when he gripped their udders. Every time the wind gusted, it blew right down his neck and swirled around in his shirt, no matter how tight he clutched the collar. So when his mother made him a thick wool scarf for his birthday, it was a welcome gift. The wind never again blew down his shirt. Also, instead of clutching at his collar, he could warm his hands in his pockets—which in turn made the cows less jumpy. Still, sitting on an old tin pail in a drafty shed, grabbing the teats of a dairy cow that didn't want its teats grabbed, was something Joe did not reflect upon with any fondness.

Finally, the stock trail fed into an open, snowy glen. They came upon LG and Davis stretching barbed wire between two ponderosa pines.

"Hello there," Joe called.

"A ki-yote stole our bacon," LG remarked. "Do you fellows got any?"

Joe shook his head sadly.

"Afraid not."

"And we ain't got no eggs, either," Banjo added.

Davis sat down on a heavy spool of wire, looking confused. He was holding a hammer but couldn't seem to let go. He shook his hand a few times, but the hammer stuck in place.

"Why can't you find trees that don't secrete so much sap?"

Joe looked around the glen curiously. He spotted the Highlander herd at the far end of the glen.

"You the fellows who brung in them shaggy beeves?"

"Yep."

"I'd like to contract beef from you. We're gonna build a saloon. It'll be a restaurant too—and the boss wants beef."

As the others talked, Banjo studied the curious cattle. He had never seen a shaggy cow before, not even at the circus, or any of the wild west shows for that matter.

"Which outfit do you fellas rep for?" Davis asked.

"We work for Soapy Smith. Gonna open the Orleans Club. We want to make sure our kitchen gets what it needs."

At the mention of a kitchen, Banjo's stomach gurgled, and LG heard it.

"Why don't you two come on over to the ranch house. We'll get the kid to cook up some flapjacks and a gallon of coffee. Now, where did that kid go?"

Walker was on the far side of the meadow, near the herd, riding Billy Woods's big brown mule. LG put his fingertips in his teeth and whistled sharply. He waved his hat, and Walker waved his back— which spooked the mule. It bolted.

"It's not much of a ranch house. Don't let him fool you," Davis explained. "As you can plainly see from here, it's just a shabby old tent. Which is why the ki-yote got off with our bacon."

"Did you let Zang stake it out?" Joe asked. "That dumb Oriental don't know how to stake out a tent proper. I've got entrails oozing under my cot."

"Do you have any eggs?" Banjo inquired hopefully.

But LG shook his head.

"Nope."

Leaving the wire and hammer with Davis's glove stuck to it, they headed off across the glen. Joe and Banjo followed along, still on horseback.

"At least you're running beef cows," Joe told them, clutching his scarf tighter. "You don't want anything to do with milk cows, trust me."

Davis looked wistful.

"I don't even remember the last time I had fresh milk."

But Joe was adamant.

"I'd rather pay thirty cents for a can of condensed milk then place my hand on a filthy cow teat for free."

The cattle began to bellow and they turned to see why. Walker's mule was galloping as fast as it could, racing around the meadow, kicking up snow. Clearly terrified, the boy had dropped the reins and was gripping the saddle horn with both hands. Pounding back and forth, the mule made several sharp turns, scattered the cattle, and then angled straight for the men like it was going to run them all down.

"Watch out, boys!" LG shouted and ran for the trees.

Racing by, the mule circled back around the glen and kept running. Finally, after blasting through the cattle one last time, it eased into a snorty trot.

Walker looked ill. He slid off, shaking, and took the reins. Then he started dragging the animal along as he walked back to camp.

"Is that the Salty Jackass?" Joe wondered, watching in disbelief.

"It's Billy Woods's mule," Davis said. "That thing is wild."

Joe nodded in sympathy.

"That's the one. Billy named it the Salty Jackass. I hope you didn't pay more than a dime for it."

Davis frowned.

"Nope," he lied.

When Walker returned, LG pointed at the cook fire.

"When you catch your breath, make us some flapjacks."

The boy tied the mule to an aspen tree and went inside the tent to find the skillet. But once he got inside, and no one could see him, Walker collapsed on his bedroll. What a bad day. Not only did a coyote steal the bacon and his mule go cavorting, but he had forgotten to bring in the flour sack after supper the night before. When he woke up, he discovered it had gotten wet and turned to paste.

Walker felt butterflies race around in his stomach. How was he going to make flapjacks with no flour? Not sure what he was going to do, Walker rooted around the cook supplies in desperation. Then, he discovered the cornmeal. Why not make flapjacks out of cornmeal? Perhaps no one would notice the difference.

Pouring some into a bowl, Walker took a spoon and headed outside to the water barrel. But LG was standing right there, taking a drink, and saw what he was carrying.

"I said flapjacks, not corn fritters."

Walker blanched. LG was no fool. He must have seen the ruined flour. He must have known all along. The boy braced for a reaming, but instead, LG pointed at his mouth.

"I think you got some on your lip."

Walker blinked.

"What?"

"You got some cornmeal on your lip."

Walker rubbed his mouth with the back of his hand.

"Did I get it?"

"No, it's still there."

Walker blushed and clenched his jaw.

"Are you referencing my mustache?"

Turning to Davis with a lopsided grin, LG shrugged.

"Is that what that is?"

"Leave the kid alone," Davis told him. "Corn flapjacks will be just fine."

But Walker was upset about the joke and the comment.

"I ain't a *kid*. I'm fifteen years old."

CHAPTER 38

"It's day all day in the daytime, and there is no night in Creede."
Simmons folded the newspaper in half and dropped it in the frozen mud.

"Who writes this ballyhoo?"

Soapy leaned over and spat on the paper.

"The *Creede Candle* sure as hell ain't Shakespeare."

After the whole John Arkins incident, Soapy found that he no longer liked newspapers. Whenever he saw one, he cringed, half expecting to see a bad headline. Even in a small silver camp like Creede, with the smallest newspaper he had ever seen, he worried about bad press.

The knock of hammers was like gunfire from where they sat on a pile of fresh lumber. There was equipment and supplies in the middle of the street, but no one complained. Half the people who walked by asked what they were building.

"Good thing this lot was still open," Simmons said, looking up and down the street. "Ain't too many good spots left."

They were sitting on their winter coats to avoid splinters. Simmons held a canteen, and he took a long sip of cold water.

"At least it ain't snowing today," Soapy said, shielding his eyes. "Perfect weather for construction. We'll get this thing up in no time."

Slowly, he eased off the planks and landed directly on the newspaper. He gave it an extra twist into the mud.

"Let's head over to Bat's for lunch."

The Denver Exchange was just a short walk down the street.

"He's gonna be mad when he finds out we're opening a saloon a stone's throw away," Simmons said. "We'll be cutting into his profits."

"Oh, I don't know. I feel like Bat should be giving us a cut of his profits anyhow."

Simmons grinned.

"Maybe we call it fire insurance."

Nodding thoughtfully, Soapy held the door open for him.

They went inside and saw Bat Masterson standing by the poker table. He glanced up.

"Don't you ever sleep?" he asked Soapy. "You just spent the whole night losing at my faro table and now you're back for more."

Soapy laughed.

"Bat, you are too much. Say, I want you to meet Mr. Joe Simmons, who may be my oldest and truest friend. You won't meet a finer fellow."

Bat indicated the faro table.

"Jeff Argyle had to catch a wink of sleep. But Billy's sitting on the inside, if you want to play another game."

"Naw, we're just here for a bite to eat."

"Well, come on in, then."

Bat led them over to a table by the wall. Sitting down, Simmons frowned and thumbed his lapel. It was crusty—a mustard spot of dried puke dimpled the fabric. The train ride in was just a drunken haze in his memory. Both Soapy and Bat were wearing nice suit coats.

"Now Bat," Soapy began. "Don't be off put, but Simmons and I are right this very moment overseeing the construction of our own establishment. And we will be offering similar services."

Bat's expression remained unchanged.

"Now, don't hit me!" Soapy joked and ducked his head a little.

But Bat Masterson didn't throw a punch or even raise an eyebrow.

"We're back to venison and trout on the menu," he said. "All out of mutton, I am sad to say."

Soapy smiled warmly and pinched the man's sleeve as if admiring the corduroy texture.

"Always dapper, my friend. Always dapper."

Simmons sat up straight, feeling self-conscious, and used his fingers like a comb. While he was grooming himself, Soapy leaned forward and tried again.

"In case you're worried, we won't infringe on your clientele. This camp is growing like a damn weed. The mines run twenty-four seven, there ain't enough booze to keep up, and the train keeps shittin' out folks like it runs on prunes."

He held up his hand as if to stop Bat from protesting, even though Bat did not protest.

"Now, now, hear me out. I'd say the camp is going to *benefit* from two such places. The more venues available, the gentler our town will be. Virtue is its own punishment—that's in the Good Book. Tell you what, in these past few weeks since this camp was born, it's been pretty peaceful. And I do believe it's because any poor soul who might be susceptible to pent-up urges is able to find a suitable outlet. A little steam-letting, if you will."

Bat sighed and shifted.

"I don't like this silence," he said finally. "It augurs ill."

He gestured at the game tables.

"In every other boom camp I've been to, violent scenes unfold like clockwork. And I don't think gaming or whoring has a pacifying effect. Sooner or later, we're gonna see a big display of carnage. A little blood-letting, if *you* will."

Soapy applauded and laughed.

"Ha! Well said! Yes, that may very well be true. It may not be our services at all."

He winked at Simmons.

"It could be one other thing, however, keeping this place in check. It could be as simple as *Bat Masterson is in town.* They sense your presence like field mice sense a barn cat."

Breaking into a small grin, Bat softly shook his head.

"Venison or rainbow trout?"

"Surprise us," Soapy said and slapped the table.

As Bat went into the kitchen, they watched him go.

"Look at him," Soapy said. "There's a nut that won't crack easy."

Simmons nodded, but his attention was back on his crusty lapel. He picked at it with his thumbnail.

"The man is polished."

CHAPTER 39

"Soapy Smith is doing *what?*" Bob Ford hollered.

"Opening up a gambling hall."

Bob turned on Joe Palmer and shoved him hard and Joe almost lost his balance. He did lose his beer bottle.

"I heard you the first time. It don't bear repeating!"

"My beer!"

They had just emerged from one of the saloon tents in Tent Town. The sun was barely above the ridge. They had spent the whole night drinking. First, they started the evening drinking at Bat's place, until Bat kicked them out. Then they went down to the depot, where all the tents were. They stood on the platform and tried to count how many little one-jug saloons they could see. Since it was too dark for an accurate count, they decided the best way to know how many there were was to go to each one. It became a game. They alternated between a shot of spirits and a bottle of beer, and tried to see how many saloons they could drink at before the sun came up.

As he leaned down to pick up the bottle, Bob swatted Joe's hat off his head.

"Dern you, Bob."

Sometimes, Joe wondered why he spent any time with the man at all. He was prone to fits and outbursts and no one else in town seemed to like him. On top of that, Soapy hated Bob too, and didn't like it when Joe went drinking with him.

But Soapy always seemed to be mad at Joe these days, for no good reason.

Joe got his beer and reached for his hat, which had fallen into a puddle. Picking it up, Joe sniffed the brim.

"Dern it. My hat fell in piss."

Holding his hat out like a dead possum, he looked around for a barrel or water trough that wasn't frozen solid. There wasn't one anywhere he could see, but he did remember he saw a bucket outside the horseshoer's tent. Joe looked around, but all the tents looked the same. His memory was foggy, too. One of them belonged to the horseshoer, but which one?

Without explaining himself, Joe stalked off, his boots crunching in the snow.

Watching him go, Bob Ford whipped about and pumped a fist into the air.

"I swear!" he yelled.

Bob paced a few times until his breathing slowed. This was getting ridiculous. Every time he turned around, Soapy Smith was doing something that mussed his feathers.

"Thinks he can open a damn booze hall. Elect himself mayor next."

The years had begun to weigh on Bob's shoulders. They left him with a bitterness regarding how unfair life was. He should be a bona fide hero. People ought to shower him with admiration when he stepped into a room. He killed Jesse James! No one else did that. No one realized how much it took to do that. To get close enough, trusted enough, to be brazen enough, to plug such a dangerous killer. To seize the moment when it came. But people turn, don't they? They jump on the wagon. And the wagon wasn't carrying Bob Ford into the annals of history. It was dragging him. And that's how he felt.

"Tired of bein' dragged!"

He glared about but he only saw a few sleepy looking drunks. One was taking a leak on the side of the Mexican Lady's tent. The Mexican Lady came out with a handful of tomatillos and pelted the drunk away.

"By Jove, I can tap my *own* fire water."

Maybe he would do just that—open his own saloon. After all, he had done it before. Down in Walsenburg, he ran a little dance hall. He could do that here, too, just as easily. Besides, all he was doing in Creede was drink booze anyhow. He didn't own a mine. He didn't work a job.

Nearly a decade had passed since he shot Jesse James in the back of the skull. Ten years of disappointment and resentment in the public eye. Ten years of derision and chastisement. Well, Bob had had enough. Creede was supposed to be his escape. His redemption. But he needed to be somebody important—someone people respected and wouldn't ridicule.

It wasn't too late.

He could run this town, still.

As he weaved in and out of the tents, he almost got run over by a horse-drawn cart carrying a large black potbelly stove.

"Don't you run me down!" Bob shouted, dodging out of its path. "Where you going with that thing anyways?"

The man braked and stopped.

"All the way up the canyon, past Jim Town. Got to make a delivery and get back before dark," he replied, indicating the stove. "The boys at the Amethyst broke another one."

"Well, watch where you're going next time. People cross this dern street and don't need to get run over by some dumb bastard."

"I apologize."

He popped the reins and got the horses going again.

Bob had never been up the road very far. He knew Jim Town was another tiny camp a little further up the canyon. Beyond that, there were some mines that were hard to reach—burrowed up on the mountain slopes.

"Hold up!" Bob shouted.

The driver halted the heavy wagon a second time and glared at him in clear frustration.

Climbing up next to the potbelly stove, Bob waved him on.

"I may be too drunk to walk and I don't want to pass out in a snowbank and freeze to death. Wake me when we get to the Cliff Hotel. That's where I live."

The man popped the reins again, and got the horses moving. The cart rocked over the bumps and ruts and Bob found himself getting very sleepy. He laid down next to the stove, and patted it.

"Good boy."

He wasn't sure what he was going to do, really. Maybe he *would* open a saloon. Or maybe he would try and get *himself* elected mayor before anyone else thought of it. Or maybe he would shoot Soapy Smith in the back of the skull, just like Jesse James.

CHAPTER 40

ROCKY MOUNTAINS

The moment the mail carrier spotted four grim Indians in the aspen grove, his face lost all its color. That was the moment Bear Claw Lip had been waiting for.

He let out the worst war cry he knew, *ahu-ahu*, mimicking the Navaho, and succeeded in startling the horse the man was riding. The mail carrier went tumbling from the saddle and the horse bolted. It headed straight across the valley, whinnying as it ran.

Post-holing through the wet snowpack, the four Indians rushed forward and immediately surrounded the man—who didn't even try to get up. He lay flat on his back and remained very still. They circled around and stared at him.

White Owl picked up the satchel the man was clutching and shook it out. Envelopes fell out onto the snow and the wind took several of the light ones and swept them into the trees.

"Help," the man whispered. He was clearly frightened.

"What is he saying?" Bear Claw Lip asked.

Kahopi bent over him, listening, but the man became silent.

"He probably lost his wind in the fall," Greasewood said. "Let him catch his breath."

Instead, Bear Claw Lip began leaping up and down on the man's kneecaps. There was a loud popping sound. Like a chicken bone, the man's legs snapped at the joint and he howled.

"There!" Bear Claw Lip said. "He caught his breath."

Pulling his knife out, Bear Claw Lip waved it in the air as if deciding where to begin.

Kahopi stepped back. Getting blood on his clothes would bring bad luck into his life.

Meanwhile White Owl was opening letters.

"Look!"

He held up several dollar bills from one of the envelopes, showing Greasewood, who lost interest in the mail carrier and immediately began tearing open letters, too.

Kahopi stood in silence, observing his companions and reflecting on their behavior. Bear Claw Lip was a man who enjoyed violence, so it was no surprise he was abusing the mail carrier. But White Owl, usually very reserved, was acting frantic over the money. That seemed bizarre. And Greasewood, too, was acting frantic. He normally moved slow and only when he had to; he was mostly interested in just taking a nap. What did this mean?

Rubbing his hands together for warmth, Kahopi looked up and down the valley. There was so much snow! It was hard to believe. There were dark, pine-covered slopes and mountains and hills all around them. And everywhere he turned, he saw snow that went up over his knees—and much deeper in many places. The further north they traveled, the more snow they found. He had never seen so much of it in his life. Back home, there was sometimes a light dusting of snow on the mesa in the winter months, but never this much.

Kahopi spotted the mail carrier's horse all the way on the other side of the valley, pawing at the snowpack to get at the brown mountain grasses hidden below. He marveled. Even the horse knew how to forage and survive in this cold place.

Then, Kahopi noticed a large hawk sitting in the branches of an aspen almost directly overhead. It was silent, with its dark eyes and fluffy white chest feathers, observing them from above.

Without a doubt, Kahopi knew it was the Hawk Deity—given its sudden appearance right above them in such a cold, empty grove. One moment it was not there. The next moment, it was.

Then, from the corner of his eye, Kahopi spotted a big black crow. It was sitting in a different tree than the hawk—but close by, *in the same grove*. This was very strange. There had not been any birds in the branches earlier, while they were hiding out waiting for the mail carrier to pass by. Now, quite suddenly, there were two!

Kahopi reeled with dizziness.

It dawned on him that he had seen this crow before. It was at the ancient cliff dwellings, perched on the adobe walls while he searched the kivas and rooms for his father.

Two powers existed in the world from long ago—one good and one evil. The Evil Power often lived in the form of a crow.

As a child in the village where he grew up, Kahopi heard stories about the Evil Power. It was known to live on the mesa. Sometimes, as a crow, it would sit quietly on the mesa's rim, watching the people plant corn. Once the corn began to grow, the crow would fly down and eat the green leaves as they sprouted from the earth.

Sometimes, the crow could be seen flying around the village and over the plaza. Just as he watched the corn being planted and knew which fields had been planted first, the crow would watch the people closely to see how weak or strong their hearts were. The crow had the power to stir up trouble. He could send evil thoughts into people's hearts and even sickness into their bodies. It was common knowledge that anyone with a weak heart could be turned evil by the crow.

Glancing at the three Utes, Kahopi considered all of this.

Of the three men, Bear Claw Lip was the most evil. Perhaps the Evil Power was following them, projecting evil into Bear Claw Lip, causing him to be violent—and sending greed into the others. This made good sense to Kahopi, given that the crow had been present at the sacred cliff houses, where the Ancient Ones used to dwell. Also, it was well known that Utes, like the Hopi, were known to be peaceful. Of course, it was also true that being forced onto a reservation by the White government had stirred up much grief among the people, and frustration.

At the same time, it provided protection from the vicious Apache. It was a two-sided coin that many struggled to accept.

Another thought struck Kahopi. Dizziness had washed over him when he spotted the crow. That was another thing to consider. Back in his village, when he was growing up, his mother would remind him constantly that everyone had a Guardian Spirit. A spirit guide was unseen, but it would watch and always try to lead a person on the right path—the Sun Trail.

"Did you feel bad just before you ate them?" his mother asked one time after Kahopi got in trouble for eating peaches that were meant for the evening meal. "Have I told you . . . the Good and Evil Powers wrestle all the time over each one of us. Just before you do something, if you feel dizzy, stop and think! It could be your Guardian Spirit trying to keep you from falling off the Sun Trail."

Still busy tearing open envelopes, White Owl and Greasewood had not noticed the hawk or the crow. Neither had Bear Claw Lip, who was busy slicing off pieces of the mail carrier.

Perhaps the Good Power and the Evil Power were wrestling over them at that very moment. This was an important realization, but one he probably would not be able to communicate to the others— not if they were being influenced by the crow.

The thought crossed Kahopi's mind that maybe he should strike out on his own and continue the search for his father by himself. The crow might just follow the three Utes and leave him alone. In fact, these three did not even know the reason for his journey. He had kept it a secret. Perhaps Kahopi had simply gotten caught up in the Ghost Dance, their warm welcome and friendliness?

Perhaps their path was the path of the crow. In which case, he would do well to part ways. Unless—the crow was following *him?*

There was much to consider!

Fixing his eyes upon the hawk, Kahopi decided to stay with these men for a while longer. At least until he understood the crow's plans a little better. And he could take comfort knowing that the Hawk Deity was watching over him. He would certainly swoop in and carry Kahopi away if the danger became too great.

— PART 6 —

CHAPTER 41

WINTER 1860
DENVER

The tavern was lit by a row of fiery oil lamps on the wall. Everything looked red in the light, which helped conceal Horace's blushing cheeks after he walked in the door and everyone burst into laughter.

"Look, it's Snow-Slide Tabor!" hooted a man named George Stevens.

Slinking across the room, Horace sat at a table by himself.

Another man, named Kelley, came over and joined him.

"It's no disgrace to be dead broke," he said, and then gave Stevens a rough glare. "Or have some cad try and steal your claim!"

Horace felt defeated and glum. He was indeed broke and his claim had, in fact, been stolen.

Kelley leaned across the table.

"That weasel George Stevens," he muttered. "I know how you feel, Tabor. Because that man right there wants to steal my claim."

"He does?"

Kelley nodded grimly.

"Just before the snow began to fly, I found good colors in the backcountry. I marked the spot so I could find it in the spring, and hustled down here. But it turns out he was watching me the whole time. And now, that weasel has sordid plans to get there before I do."

He shook his fist at George Stevens.

"Claim jumper!"

"You leave it, you lose it," Stevens replied, looking around for support. "That is the rule, right boys?"

Horace leaned forward.

"What can you do about it?"

"Get there first. That's all I can do."

He pointed at the window. Outside, the sky was gloomy and gray, and big blots of white snow dropped past the glass.

"But I ain't waiting for the spring thaw," Kelley confided. "Want to come with me?"

Horace raised his eyebrows.

"You mean, share your gold claim?"

"I will share it with you. I just won't share it with weasels."

The barkeeper brought over a mug full of hot coffee. Horace took a sip, thinking it over.

"When do you want to leave?" he asked, as quietly as he could.

Kelley got up and huddled near Horace's ear.

"Tomorrow."

Horace was shocked. He looked out the window again. The snowflakes were still falling, and falling thick.

"I know," Kelley said, following his gaze. "It's too deep for a wagon, and all the grass is covered up so what are my horses going to eat? Well, they ain't, so I'm going in on foot. But, by God, I'm gonna get there first!"

He glared over at George Stevens, and shook his fist at him again.

"Weasel!"

Putting his head in his hands, Horace felt torn. This was exactly what he needed—but what about his wife and small son? There was no way they could hike through miles and miles of waist-deep snow. Plus, Augusta had just gotten ill.

That same feeling, the one in his gut when he first read the *Kansas Tribune* article, coursed through his body. This was it. This was how they were going to make it! But, he couldn't leave his family behind in a tiny hotel room in Denver.

What was he going to do?

It was a pickle.

CHAPTER 42

SPRING 1892
LEADVILLE

As Maxcy entered the Tabor home, the first thing he noticed was that everywhere he looked, he saw the color pink. The settee and the arm chairs had pink shawls draped over them. Decorative pink paper banners had been strung back and forth overhead. The runner on the dining table was also pink—and when he got closer to the table, Maxcy was stunned to find a pink teapot, pink ceramic cups, and pink serving platters. Even the sugar cookies were pink with pink icing.

It was all quite emasculating.

"Can you guess what color the tea is?" Baby Doe asked in a theatrical voice.

Her wardrobe consisted of a pink dress, pink gloves, and a pink wide-brimmed hat. Two other women arrived, almost immediately after Maxcy did, and they, too, wore the same color.

"This is all so lovely!" said Maggie Brown and gripped Janey Campion's forearm. "Isn't this lovely?"

Thankful he wasn't the only male invited to Baby Doe Tabor's tea party, Maxcy spotted another one, and strolled right over.

"Hello, there," Maxcy said, but decided not to initiate a handshake after noticing a dewy handkerchief clutched in the man's hand. "Maxcy Tabor. I am Baby Doe's brother-in-law."

"Wheezy Jones," said Wheezy Jones, dabbing his nose. "Manager of the Lucy B. Mine."

"It's quite colorful in here."

Jones, who wore a pink rose in his lapel, and a pink necktie, looked around the room and shrugged.

"Last week, my sister threw a Green Tea at her place. Every single decoration was green."

Maxcy felt a twinge of panic and wondered if he was supposed to have worn a pink accoutrement as well.

"I feel inadequately dressed. I did not realize there was a color scheme."

Baby Doe appeared and hugged him.

"You're so *adorable*, Maxcy! Horace wouldn't be caught *dead* at a tea party. And here you are, having a sartorial crisis. Bravo!"

Smelling liquor, Maxcy realized she was sauced.

He doffed his hat.

"I hope you like tea, because that's what we're serving." she said. "Horace *hates* tea."

"Oh, not to worry. I have developed a taste for it," he replied. "Mother hates coffee and only serves tea at the boarding house."

At that, Baby Doe swooped in like a pixie.

"What boarding house?"

He gulped and looked stricken.

"I shouldn't say."

Her eyes narrowed.

"But you should say."

"Perhaps I've misspoke."

"You better tell me!" Baby Doe insisted.

Perspiring, Maxcy looked at Wheezy Jones for assistance. But the mine manager was busy managing his lapel flower.

"Is this in the wrong buttonhole?" he mumbled.

Maxcy opened his mouth, and then closed it again. He had revealed something he hadn't meant to reveal. In the divorce, his mother had wrangled a sizable financial settlement. She also fought Horace, a fight which at times got quite ugly, so she could keep the expensive Denver estate—if for no other reason than spite. Since Horace was living in Leadville, the judge determined that Augusta would get the keys. Predictably, Horace was not happy about the decision. The property was pristine and richly decorated with handpicked objects and paraphernalia from around the world. It also had corridors lined with empty rooms, which Augusta had no need for—so she rented them out.

She did it for two reasons. Not only would the knowledge be an irritation to Horace— imagining unkempt transients defecating in the siphonic closet—but she could also generate a good chunk of income in the process. Augusta had no intention of ever begging for a handout from her ex-husband, as other divorcees whom she knew did. She also had no intention of ever speaking to Horace again. Since his mother had ceased communicating with his father, Maxcy never volunteered the information—in an attempt to distill the hostilities. So the secret of the mansion-turned-boarding house had been, up until this point, well kept.

Sensing his reluctance, Baby Doe jabbed her finger in his sternum.

"Don't tell my father, please," Maxcy whispered, a little pale. "But . . . Mother has turned the Denver estate into a boarding house."

"What! Augusta is renting out Horace's forty-thousand-dollar mansion? To homeless drifters?" she asked in a loud, delighted voice. "Horace will pitch a *fit*."

Cackling, Baby Doe reached out and pulled Janey Campion into the conversation.

"Janey, get over here and meet Horace's son."

Encountering Maxcy up close, her eyes grew wide.

"Has anyone ever told you that you are a mirror image of your father?" Janey asked. Then she snatched the pink rose out of Wheezy Jones' lapel. "Just don't tell me I look anything like my tramp of a brother."

"Sorry," Jones moped. "I didn't know which buttonhole to use."

But Janey ignored him and tucked the flower into Maxcy's lapel instead.

"There," she said, satisfied. "Now, you are ready for tea."

Wheeling over to the dining table, stationed near a grandfather clock, Baby Doe grabbed the edge for balance. Then she squinted to read the time.

"It is four o'clock!" she announced and made a shaky dash into the kitchen.

Wheezy Jones looked forlornly at his sister, Janey.

"What am I supposed to do now? My lapel has no flower."

She frowned at him.

"Wipe your nose."

Returning from the kitchen with a large platter, Baby Doe angled sideways across the room, and, since the dining table was not in her orbit, set it on the coffee table instead. She stuck her tongue out at Janey, who was watching in dreaded suspense.

"Don't worry. I didn't *drop* it."

Seating himself in one of the arm chairs with a pink shawl draped on it, Maxcy examined the platter. It was filled with little cucumber sandwiches made with pink-colored bread.

CHAPTER 43

Watching a gaggle of scowling, frumpy-skirted women lug baskets of dirty clothes into the laundry, not normally something worth watching, turned out to be a useful distraction.

"Buy a comb!" Big Ed called, heckling a frazzled-looking mother.

"I *have* a comb!"

"Try using it!"

Big Ed had a flask filled with whiskey in the crook of his arm and sat outside the Western Union nipping at it. The rye burned going down. Big Ed smirked as he thought about it. He had been drinking cheap rye for years and years, and it still burned going down.

The laundry was run by two young black women, sisters, named Merna and Eve. There was a sign on the building with their names on it, along with simple paintings of the sun and fresh green grass. As Big Ed watched, they came outside to help unload linens from the uncombed mother's wagon.

"You two girls must be giving it away," Big Ed declaimed in a loud voice. "Because every alley cat in Leadville is bringing you every stitch of clothing they own. I'm surprised this whole town ain't naked as a robin."

The sisters disappeared inside but came right back out, each carrying a broom.

"Gonna have us a talk!" Merna warned.

But Big Ed was not concerned. He did not care what they had to say. What he did care about was what Soapy Smith had to say.

While there were telephones all over Leadville, there were none in Creede. It was too new and too remote. The only way to communicate quickly was the old fashioned way—telegraph.

Big Ed needed advice. He wanted to disrupt Horace's silver club. So, Big Ed went down to the Western Union and composed a canny message: *Haw shindig Friday; what should I wear?*

There was some animosity between Soapy Smith and Haw Tabor, and Big Ed knew all about it. For a few years, Soapy's reach had extended all the way into Leadville. He ran the street cons and the criminal rackets from afar, and Big Ed was his eyes and ears—and his right hand. And back then, Horace Tabor had been easy to steer.

Those were good times.

It all went south, unfortunately.

One day, Soapy visited Leadville to dispose of a problem. As fortune had it, he happened to dispose of it in a deep dank shaft in the bottom of the Matchless Mine. The problem he disposed of, was of course, a rival.

Horace was sick to death about it.

And then, after Soapy left, Horace got angry. Once Soapy returned to Denver, the Silver King started running all the con men out of Leadville. Before Big Ed realized it, he was the last man standing. One day, he woke up and discovered that all he had left was a gang of one—Dirty Johns. The walls of the Stray Horse Brewery became his headquarters, home, and sanctuary, and unfortunately, the outer boundaries of his influence.

It was a bitter pill to swallow.

Given all that, Big Ed knew Soapy Smith would have good advice. And he desperately needed good advice, too, because he had a serious problem. Horace was advertising his silver club party in the newspaper: "Friday Night At The Lucy B! A Raucous Event Of Great Import, And Free Booze."

The genie was out of the bottle.

Not only was every miner in Leadville talking about it, but, to add insult to injury, Horace had asked *him* to provide the beer.

But all these thoughts were whisked out of his head by a broom.

"Whatcha doing here?" Merna demanded. "Scat!"

"We don't need you here," Eve added. "Making all them ladies feel creepy!"

Big Ed held up the bottle of rye.

"The genie is out of the bottle."

Eve and Merna looked scandalized.

"Don't you *dare* flash yo meat!"

Merna whacked him on the head with the broom. "Scat!"

Eve swung her broom, too, and knocked the liquor out of his hand.

"You talkin' creepy!"

Big Ed watched the flask skitter into an icy puddle. But he had no chance to retrieve it, since he was being broomed. Scrambling to his feet, Big Ed lumbered off—but he did not lumber far. Ducking behind the Western Union shack, he hid behind a telegraph pole.

However, the sisters were not fooled that easily.

They followed his footprints in the snow and spotted him instantly. Before they could catch him, Big Ed circled around once more. But this time, he went inside the telegraph office, slammed the door and leaned heavily on the latch.

"We know you in there. Don't you come out!"

"You stay put!"

Big Ed heard the sound of straw bristles raking the door.

"Okay, I will," he promised. "I won't come out."

The whisking continued for a few moments, and then it got silent.

"I imagine they are gone," said the telegrapher, who was sitting at his desk.

"Hear anything yet?"

He looked hopefully at the telegraph machine, with its lever and knobs and wires.

"Not yet."

Then, as if being summoned, the telegraph began beeping its electronic signals. The telegrapher leapt for his pen and stuck his ear near the receiver.

"Is it Soapy?"

But the telegrapher squeezed his eyes shut, so he could focus on the Morse code.

Since he was being ignored, Big Ed began looking around for his bottle of rye. But then he remembered it was outside in a puddle.

The beeping finally stopped, and the telegrapher parsed the letters into a sentence.

"What God hath wrought, a forked tongue might undo."

He took off his spectacles and looked at Big Ed.

"You get that?"

"How much do I owe you?"

"Twenty-four cents."

Counting out the coins, Big Ed added an extra dime into the mix.

"Well, thank you very much," said the telegrapher. "I can't wait for the party Friday. Free booze!"

Tucking the message in his coat pocket, Big Ed ran outside and bolted down the street.

CHAPTER 44

CREEDE

It was only after LG told him to tack up that Walker realized his bridle reins had been chewed up sometime in the night.

The early morning air was brisk, and his breath floated like fog. At first, he thought he was just too sleepy to think straight, and maybe he misplaced the reins the night before. But then he discovered them lying in the snow—chewed to pieces.

Being a cowhand, Walker discovered, was hard work. When he wasn't scattering feed or hay, or checking the fence line for broken wire, he was boiling coffee or chopping firewood. And it seemed like something was always going wrong. The axe head fell off, the flour got wet, the coffee tasted burnt . . . and now his reins were ruined! LG was sure to have something to say.

He looked around the meadow. The sun was barely up, but light enough to see the shaggy steers, still bedded down in the snow. While it was certainly possible, even likely, that one of the Highlanders had found the reins while he was sleeping and gnawed on them, Walker suspected the Salty Jackass was the culprit.

"Why ain't you saddled yet?" LG asked, coming out of the tent with a pail of oats.

He had his horse, Specter, already tacked up.

While LG waited for an explanation, Specter nickered to let everyone know he was ready to eat his grain.

Walker stood there shivering in the brisk morning air, trying to figure out what to say.

"I'm gonna give my saddle girth one last jerk, and then I'm ready to leave."

Reluctantly, Walker held out his chewed up bridle reins.

LG stepped closer to see what the boy had in his hand, and Specter followed right along behind him, to keep the pail of oats in sight.

The rest of the remuda heard the gritty shake of the grain pail and came right over. Davis's saddle horse, Big Sunday, was the first to get there, but the wheel team was close behind. Curiously, the Salty Jackass was not among them.

"I think it was that dang mule," Walker said, dispirited.

LG nodded.

"It don't take much detective work, does it?"

He dumped the pail out. Specter immediately began eating, and pinned his ears when Big Sunday got too close. The wheel team knew better than to even try.

Walker felt frustrated. The Salty Jackass was always causing him headaches. Several times a day, it tried to throw him. But it was always sly about it, waiting for the best opportunities. After being chunked enough times, Walker finally learned to keep his seat, even when the mule pitched at the worst possible moment. The most embarrassing thing was when it happened in front of LG and Davis, who immediately started clapping and making loud wagers as to how many jumps it would take until the boy came off.

"Can I drive the wagon instead?" Walker begged.

"Sure."

Relieved, Walker ducked into the tent to find the traces.

In the dim light, LG spotted the Salty Jackass. The cantankerous mule was at the far edge of the meadow. Now that the wire was up, it couldn't hide in the forest anymore—which was one of its favorite tricks.

Reemerging with the tack, Walker caught the wheel team and led them to the wagon.

Waking up, Davis pried open the bottom of the tent and poked his face out.

"Where are you off to?"

"You can't even be bothered to get out of your hot roll?" LG asked him.

"Nope. Where are you off to?"

"I'm going to buy an open lot in town. It's time to expand our operation. We got beeves, we got a fence, and we got a cowhand. Now we need to build a meat market. Pretty soon, we'll be selling beef to every restaurant, saloon, and kitchen in town. Go look for the hammer and whipsaw."

But Davis dropped the canvas and went back to sleep.

CHAPTER 45

The coin toss fell in Joe Palmer's favor, and he won the pool table for a bed. But while the fuzzy velvet surface certainly looked like green grass, it was nowhere near as comfortable to sleep on. It seemed like every hour on the hour, Joe woke up with a sore hip and flipped over. Then he would wake up again when both hips were sore and try sleeping on his back. To top it off, the fire in the corner stove must have gone out. The Orleans Club was freezing.

"Got a dern crick," Joe complained but got no response.

It was starting to get light outside—finally. The plate-glass picture window, frosted over completely, was starting to look blue instead of black.

Joe had been staring at a big brown bear skin tacked to the wall. It looked so warm, he wanted to pull it down. But he was too nervous Soapy would get mad and accuse him of smelling like a dead bear.

Banjo was sound asleep on the floorboards by the stove. Joe wasn't sure how he was able to sleep so well. Not only was the blanket too short for Banjo's lanky form, and his feet stuck out past the knees, but Joe knew the wood floor was ice cold. At one point during the night, Joe was so sore he decided to try sleeping on the floor himself. But as soon as his feet touched the frigid floorboards, he changed his mind.

Old Man Tripp had taken his blanket behind the bar, even though there were other game tables in the room. There was faro, which was too oval to sleep on, and there was three-card Monte, which was too small. But, he had chosen his bed ground well, Joe realized when he heard a whiskey cork pop open around one a.m.

Sleeping on the rock hard pool table in the half-built Orleans Club was turning out to be just as bad as Zang's drafty tent.

Rolling onto his stomach, Joe stared at the corner stove. Maybe there were still some hot coals inside. Maybe all it needed was some fresh wood, and it would be roaring hot again in mere minutes.

"Banjo . . . can you stoke up the fire?"

"Shut your yap," Tripp yelled and threw a glass bottle up and over the bar.

It bounced off Joe's stomach.

"You hit me, you skunk!"

Joe was irritated. He was sore and cold and tired, and now Old Man Tripp had flung a bottle at him. But he was also irritated with Soapy Smith. At that very moment, Soapy was sound asleep in his nice warm featherbed in his nice warm room at Zang's Hotel. And to make matters worse, he insisted the entire gang move into the Orleans Club to cut costs on hotel rentals—except his new buddy Simmons. One of the other nice warm rooms at Zang's magically opened up, and Soapy gave it to him, expensive as it was. Those upstairs rooms had soft fluffy pillows, too. There were no pillows on the pool table. In fact, Joe had to roll up his coat for something to rest his head on. But it kept unraveling, which was a constant frustration. He suspected Soapy was still mad at him for stomping his boot on the train ride in.

"Banjo . . . wake up."

Tripp growled again from the shadows.

Joe braced for another bottle attack but nothing happened.

Giving up on Banjo, he slid off onto the cold floor. He was in his socks and had no idea where his boots were but did not waste time looking. He rushed across the room, grabbed a piece of wood and tore open the iron door. He pushed it inside, but there were not any hot coals after all. There was only white ash and cold black cinder chunks.

"How in the world can you sleep?" he asked, prodding Banjo with his toe.

Since the lanky man refused to awaken, and every footstep sent a fresh chill through his body, Joe focused on starting a fire. He looked around and spotted the match box.

The frame construction of the Orleans Club was complete and it was almost ready to open for business. There wasn't much left to do. Soapy's brother, Bascomb, was set to deliver the wood planks for the dance floor, the dance girls themselves, more game tables, and of course extra booze. One final delivery, then the doors would open. Joe could hardly wait! Soon, they could stop wasting time on small-time cons—like selling soap. Even though it was easy money, running a saloon was even easier money. Once cash began rolling into the coffers, the first thing Joe planned to purchase was his own room at Zang's.

Someone walked past the frosted window and dropped something at the door.

Wary, Joe looked around for his pistol. It was nestled in a side pocket on the pool table. He cocked the gun and hustled back over to the front window. Scratching a peep-hole on the frosty glass, he spotted the paperboy. He was placing newspapers at every front door along the avenue.

Cracking the door open, Joe snatched up the paper, which was only two pages, front and back. Wadding it into a ball, he stuffed it directly inside the corner stove and struck a match.

CHAPTER 46

"What a goof!" Mollie giggled and poked Bascomb in the side.

But Bascomb did not open his eyes.

A long string of saliva oozed from his lower lip, down his chin, and all the way to the floor. His forehead was pressed against the glass, and the last thing he said before passing out was "chuck-a-luck paddle wheel"—and that had been over an hour earlier.

Whereas Mollie thought it funny, Ella Diamond found it disgusting.

"Wake him up already," she said.

Ella was seated in the row directly in front of them, so she scooted around and faced backwards, so she could watch. Even though the drooling was gross, it did make the train ride less boring.

"What has he been eating, clover?" Ella asked, making a face. "It's so slimy."

When she was growing up, she had a horse that ate clover in the summertime, and for some reason that particular plant always stimulated immense amounts of drool.

Mollie giggled.

"I don't think he ate anything at all since we left. But he did drink that entire bottle of rye all by himself."

Craning her neck so she could look out the window, Ella thought she could see trickles of gray campfire smoke in the distance.

"I think we're almost there. We better wake him up or his brother's gonna be mad."

Mollie poked him again.

"He's out cold."

A silly thought struck her, and Ella's reservations melted away. She got up and moved around into Mollie's row and, nearly sitting in Mollie's lap, whispered in her ear, "Let's put on rouge and kiss his cheeks."

Mollie burst out laughing.

When the train finally rolled to a stop at the train depot in Creede, Bascomb Smith, Soapy Smith's younger brother and bequeathed proprietor of the Tivoli Club in Denver, had two red lip smacks on each side of his face.

When Soapy saw him, he pinched his brother's jowl.

"Did you have to pay extra for this?"

But his brother didn't wake up, or even hear the question. He was suspended between the two girls. His knees buckled with each step, and it was clear he had no idea where he was or who any of them were.

Whistling, Simmons winked at the girls.

"Who do we have to pay to get the same treatment?"

"Surely you don't mean us?" Ella told him, and curtsied.

Both of the girls were dressed in their traveling clothes. Mollie wore a drab burlap colored skirt and a silky blouse, and Ella Diamond wore a black dress and hat.

Simmons made a show of straightening his collar.

"Well, these can't be the dance hall girls. Soapy, you must have made a mistake and ordered a church choir."

Soapy merely grinned at the banter and took Mollie's free arm as they all walked together. Simmons linked up with Ella Diamond.

"We look like a row of toy soldiers," Mollie laughed. "Straight out of the Nutcracker!"

Out of nowhere a small Chinese boy with a pit bull on a short rope ran right between Bascomb's buckling knees. His eyes snapped open.

"Watch out!" he mumbled. "There's a puppy in Shangri La."

Then he passed out again.

Mollie and Ella cracked up.

"It appears my brother is sauced. Now, I know he can't say, but maybe you know," Soapy said to Mollie. "Is everything I told Bascomb to bring on that train?"

She rolled her eyes to one side, thinking.

"Well, I remember seeing a couple gambling tables get loaded up. And a whole bunch of crates, which I'm sure had booze. The only thing I really kept an eye on was the boards for the dance floor. I watched as they put every single one on there, and I counted to make sure."

At that, Ella leaned over to catch her eye.

"You lost count after a hundred!"

Mollie frowned in a pouty way.

"No, I didn't."

"Yes, you did!"

While the two girls argued, Soapy glanced over his shoulder at the freight car. He spotted Joe Palmer and Banjo talking with one of the railmen. They would tell him the final count later, as well as the final tally for the liquor, beer, and wine. From the sound of it, he felt pretty good that everything had arrived on the train. And if it had all made it, and wasn't busted or lost, then the puzzle was complete. The Orleans Club was ready.

"Let's put the word out, and open the doors Friday night."

He glanced at his inebriated little brother.

Bascomb had only come along to oversee the delivery in person and was supposed to head right back down to Denver when the train turned around. Even if he didn't sober up in time, it didn't really matter.

"You know," Soapy said. "I don't know why we're even carrying him this far. We should stick him right back on the train and let him sleep it off."

"Aw, let's not," Mollie pleaded. "I wanna see his eyes when he wakes up and sees his reflection."

"And someone needs to wipe his slimy chin every five minutes," Ella added.

Soapy shrugged.

"Fine by me."

"I kind of wanna see that, too," Simmons said, pinching Ella Diamond in the rear.

She smiled, but only a weak smile. The crusty puke stain on his collar caught her eye. She wondered why every man she met was either drinking, drunk, puking, or puked on.

CHAPTER 47

"The Creede Silver Club?" Soapy asked.

"That's right."

Senator Henry M. Teller found himself holding his breath to see how the man would react to the idea. Teller didn't know Soapy Smith personally, though he had heard and even read a number of stories over the past few years. It was hard to know what was true.

A single oil lamp was ensconced on the wall, flickering yellow light. They were in Zang's Hotel, in a backroom behind the bar and the shades were drawn.

"And that's why you've secreted yourself here? Why our dialogue is conveyed in hushed tones?"

Soapy leaned forward and looked Teller straight in the eye.

"At the witching hour?"

The senator cleared his throat.

It was something in Soapy's eyes that made the hairs on his neck twitch. Was Soapy Smith the good-natured sleight of hand salesman who had bumbled and glad-handed his way to the top of the bunko heap? Or, like Arkin's articles in the *Rocky Mountain News*, was he a controlling, iron-fisted mob boss? Something about his manner gave Teller a sudden chill. And Teller was not easily chilled.

Without breaking his gaze, Soapy reached inside his jacket and pulled out a shiny revolver.

Teller cleared his throat again.

"It would be an organization," he said in an uncharacteristic blurt. "Pretty much all the big mine owners in camp—the ones you trust, the ones with clout. To really talk up the cause. *Our* cause, yours and mine—the silver cause. So when it comes November, the votes go our way."

Soapy reached out and pressed the gun barrel against Teller's chest.

"Who sent you?"

Taken aback, Teller raised his hands. He glanced around, but the others simply stared at him. In that moment, Teller realized these men weren't the other mining luminaries of Creede. This was the Soapy Smith gang.

"I sent me."

As his mind reeled, Teller began to wonder if he might have gotten a little ahead of himself. He always viewed himself as a master puppeteer. Politics were all about power. He found pulling strings to be rather satisfying—up until the present moment. And in light of the sudden down-spiral of events, he chided himself for arriving in this rowdy mountain camp without a retinue of armed gunmen.

Soapy gave Teller's chest a sharp jab with the gun barrel.

"*You* sent you?"

"I am the state senator of Colorado."

Soapy squinted.

"Was it Bob? Ever since I got here that little prick has been after me."

Leaning against the wall, Joe Palmer shook his head. In spite of everything, he liked Bob Ford.

"I hope it wasn't," he lamented.

"I bet it was!" Soapy snarled, and he spat at the senator. "You son of a bitch, I'm gonna shoot you through the guts."

Teller was not used to the feeling of creeping fear. Or spittle.

"I'm not here to cause you grief, Mr. Smith. The Democrats are doing that all by themselves. I am here to avert it."

The oil lamp made a soft sizzling sound.

The small room was dark and silent except that sizzling, which made Teller feel like his chances were also sizzling.

"There is a bigger fight going on," he said, very carefully and very seriously. "I am not here to take away your silver, or the silver of Creede. I want you to have it all. Every last ounce. But there is a great disturbance happening in Washington. A great disturbance that will affect you and me and everyone in this camp, in this state, and it may very well redefine the West. We must prepare for a battle."

"Politics?" Soapy asked with a sort of half smile.

Teller nodded.

"That's right."

Soapy leaned back on the stool and let the revolver sag onto his thigh.

"What do you think boys?"

Simmons, Joe Palmer, Banjo, and Old Man Tripp looked around at each other in silence.

"Damnation—I am pulling *teeth* in the Senate," Teller went on, desperate to keep the conversation moving. "I am doing all I can in Washington. And I will mention to you now, the National

Republican Convention is congregating forthwith, and I shall push
with all my might for bimetallism and the free and unlimited coin-
age of silver. Gold is our enemy, gentlemen. Our *enemy*. And it is
looming large and threatens to destroy everything you've accomplished here."

Scratching his white beard, Old Man Tripp looked confused.

"What's he saying, Soapy?"

"Why, I think he's saying he's on our side, boys."

Teller sighed and relaxed a little.

"Correct, sir. That is it."

Leaning back, Soapy studied him. Finally, he put the revolver
back inside his jacket.

Teller hoped the slight tremble in his fingers was going unnoticed.

But Simmons was unconvinced.

"I don't know, Jefferson. Look around. What I see when I poke
my head out that door is a long ol' row of ore cars stretching down
them rails—right through this whole damn town."

Soapy looked from Simmons to Teller, waiting for a response.

"Things are far more dire than they seem, I can assure you," the
senator insisted.

But Simmons seemed unswayed by his logic.

"And you need us to whip up a silver club?"

"A hundred silver clubs!" Teller said, but addressed Soapy. "All
over the state. In every town and camp you can think of. But Creede
will be one of our strongest voices. People will listen to you. You are
Soapy Smith. You do run this place."

"I am," said Soapy. "And I do."

Teller tried to keep calm. He was surprised at how dangerous
organizing a silver club had turned out to be.

"Even Leadville has one," he added.

When he said that, Soapy's face clouded over again.

"Leadville has one?"

Teller felt a chill again.

"Yes. They do."

"Who's running it?"

"Horace Tabor."

Soapy's eyes narrowed.

"He put you up in his fancy hotel?"

Teller raised an eyebrow.

"Yes. The Tabor Grand."

"The Silver King and his quaky conscience," Soapy cooed in a sing-song voice. *"My tummy feels oogy, where's my magnesium tablets?"*

It was clear to Teller that he had just said something wrong. His eyes involuntarily flicked down at Soapy's jacket pocket, where the gun was tucked away.

Suddenly, fingers wrapped around his throat from behind in a tight grip. It was Banjo. Teller was shocked at what a firm grip the man had, given his gangly conformation.

Soapy leaned in close while Banjo throttled him.

"Did Horace send you to spy on me?"

Teller blinked and his face got red and he croaked for air but there was no air getting through. Fighting the urge to flap around, Teller remained composed—even though his windpipe was not working. It was not easy to sit motionless while he was being choked out, but somehow he did.

Soapy's eyes were flat.

He merely sat on his stool like a statue.

Then suddenly his face became very ugly. His arm snaked out and he slapped Teller hard across the cheek.

"Did Horace send you? Did you come here to die? Because you will die here tonight in this very room!"

Looking livid, Soapy leapt to his feet and shouted in Teller's face, "Every man for himself and may the devil take us all!"

Banjo braced for a struggle. But except for making toad sounds, Senator Henry M. Teller remained stock still.

Banjo looked up.

"He ain't wrastlin' me, Soap."

Red and puffy faced, Teller folded his hands neatly in his lap. There was no longer any air in his lungs. His vision began to blur.

Finally, Soapy relaxed and even patted Teller's knee.

"Banjo, you may release our guest."

The pressure came off his neck and Teller could breathe again. He gagged and coughed and massaged his throat.

Smiling easy, Soapy spread his arms as if to embrace the world.

"The Silver Club of Creede," he announced in a warm, generous tone. "That is absolutely splendid. Let's do that."

CHAPTER 48

ROCKY MOUNTAINS

"Elk, deer, mountain sheep, turkey," Greasewood reminisced. "The river was our traditional hunting grounds. Until the Spanish came. Then trappers. Then miners. And at last, the government made us leave for good."

Kahopi listened as Greasewood talked. It helped pass the time.

"This smell is making me sick," Bear Claw Lip said, referring to the heavy acrid scent of creosote.

They were walking along railroad tracks in the afternoon sun. They found it was much easier to make progress following the rails instead of remaining in the trees. While travelling through the forest provided secrecy, the snow was also very deep.

"How long will it take us to get there from here?" Bear Claw Lip demanded.

Greasewood shook his head.

"I don't know for certain. All I know is we must first pass the Lizard Head. After that, we will arrive at the river."

The mood of the entire group was low. Kahopi knew why. They all did. The rail line they were following was a help, but it was also a continual reminder that the White Man had already intruded here. They all knew where train tracks led. To busy little towns crawling with White activity. It was easy to follow, but it also meant that their hopes for reclaiming the old hunting grounds were farfetched.

The longer they walked, the more somber they all became. Even Bear Claw Lip wasn't talking much, and he was normally very chatty.

All around them were mountains. The further they went, the taller they looked. Up ahead, they could see jagged peaks reaching even higher than the ones they were passing.

Kneeling, White Owl scooped up a handful of snow and put it in his mouth.

Kahopi also knelt and ate some snow. It tasted good.

"The Whites don't take into account the seasons," Greasewood grumbled. The more he thought about the old hunting grounds, the more unfair life seemed. "Our people would spend the summers up there, all along the river. The game was always plentiful. But when the snows came, the game would head down to the lowlands—to the desert with its red rock canyons. Not the Whites. They do not care for the rhythm of the seasons. Instead, they keep working. Digging at the cold frozen earth like ants."

Hearing this, Kahopi perked up. That reminded him of the Spider Woman's words. She turned his father into clay, and said Kahopi would find him *where the Whites dig like ants*. Kahopi looked up at the sun and thanked Tawa for reminding him of his purpose.

"It does not matter," Bear Claw Lip grumbled. "I hope they *have* taken the hunting grounds for themselves. So we can clear them out, once and for all."

Greasewood shook his head.

"Yes, we know that would be fine with you. You like to maim— this is not news," he said. "Where do you think these train tracks are leading? We know what we will find."

But Bear Claw Lip was frustrated at the old man's talk and weak attitude.

"The times are upon us, you fool. This is why we danced the Ghost Dance. We must be ready. It is wintertime now. But in the springtime, everything will happen that is supposed to happen."

At that moment, they all heard a chugging and hissing sound. Turning, looking back down the tracks, a plume of steam and smoke could be seen in the distance.

"Here comes another one," Greasewood said in disbelief.

In the course of the day, since they had been following the tracks, at least ten trains had come up and down the rails.

Quickly, the four of them ran down the slope into the trees, wading through the snow. They found a large blue spruce and crawled under its thick branches, which sagged very low to the ground.

"This is a nice spot," Greasewood said. "It's like a cozy little cave. Fairly dry. Good place to rest. We could even build a small fire under here."

But Bear Claw Lip did not like the suggestion.

"Don't start talking about naps again."

The train inched by their hiding place, chugging slowly up the grade. It was very loud. Peeking through the branches, Kahopi watched it go by. It was a freight train. Some of the trains that passed had people inside, while others had freight. He could easily see the engineers inside the cab. Their window was wide open. There were two of them in there. One was older with white hair and spectacles. The other one was young with brown hair and a cap. Both wore white shirts and black vests. The young one held a coal shovel.

There was an engine, a coal car, three box cars, a flat bed with timber, and a bright red caboose. It must have been carrying a lot of weight because it was going very slow.

Kahopi glanced at Bear Claw Lip. The Ute had a wild look in his eyes.

"I'm not spending the night in here," Bear Claw Lip muttered. "And I'm not going to spend the next week walking along those stinky railroad ties."

After waiting for the train to pass by, he wiggled out from under the spruce.

Greasewood looked alarmed.

"What are you doing?"

They watched as Bear Claw Lip dashed over to the tracks and chased the slow train. He easily reached the caboose and climbed aboard.

Without any discussion, White Owl slipped out from the spruce and ran after him, and Kahopi followed, too. Not wanting to be left alone, Greasewood scrambled to catch up.

Pulling open the door, Bear Claw Lip entered the caboose. He found himself standing in an aisle way. There was a man in the cupola, in the look-out chair. Grabbing his ankles, the Ute yanked the man down. He landed hard in the aisle and cried out.

Greasewood, White Owl and Kahopi clustered in the doorway, watching.

Bear Claw Lip leaned down and gnashed his teeth.

"Please! I'm just the flagman!"

Grabbing him by the shirt, Bear Claw Lip hoisted him up.

"Step aside, I'm going to chuck him onto the tracks."

But Greasewood held up his hand.

"Wait—let's hang onto him."

"Why?"

"He may be willing to tell us things," Greasewood suggested, and then turned to Kahopi. "Do you speak the White language? Where does this train go?"

"How many Whites are up ahead?" Kahopi asked the flagman.

Focused on Bear Claw Lip's mangled lip, the flagman was too afraid to speak. So the angry Ute gave him a good shake.

"How many?" Kahopi asked again.

"I don't know exactly. Next stop is Rico. Got to be thousands. Maybe five thousand?"

"Big town up ahead," Kahopi told them.

Greasewood took a deep breath and released it slowly. That was bad news.

"Don't do anything to me," the flagman begged. "I've got to watch that timber. If it shifts, we could derail!"

Bear Claw Lip slapped him sharply. Then he glanced at Kahopi. "What did he say?"

"He's worried about the train."

Stunned, Bear Claw Lip could not believe what he was hearing. Pressing the man against the floor, he drew his knife and gave him several quick jabs to the chest. The flagman sputtered blood and wiggled, but the Ute was very strong and would not let him go.

"Not too much," Greasewood warned. "He may have more useful things to say."

Bear Claw Lip gave him another jab for good measure.

Examining the interior of the caboose, Greasewood spotted a bunk at the far end with a soft mattress. He also spotted a piping hot wood stove with a coffee pot hissing steam.

"Move aside," he said and fixed himself a cup of coffee.

— PART 7 —

CHAPTER 49

FEBRUARY 1860
DENVER

Augusta rolled onto her side and vomited cheese soup onto the hardwood floor.

"Horace," she said, looking bleak. "No more talk. I want to lie here in silence."

They were in the hotel room in Denver, listening to the cold winter winds pummeling the thin walls.

"Can I have that napkin?" Augusta asked weakly. "I need to blot my mouth."

He looked at her in horror.

"No! Kelley drew the map on it."

Draping her forearm across her face, Augusta groaned.

"Who?"

Leaning over the bottom of the bed, Horace spread the napkin map out on the blankets.

"Kelley," he told her. "He is down in the tavern right now, and he showed me how to find his gold diggings. He drew a map on this napkin. Sit up, Gussie. Look at this."

But she only groaned again.

"We're running out of time!" Horace said with a feeling of dread. "Kelley is leaving first thing in the morning. He's walking in on foot and going to cut straight across the mountains to get there. But not us. I have a plan so we don't have to walk. We'll head south a little way, and then circle around. We may have to cut down a few trees to make a road for the wagon, but there is a way up this mountain pass."

He kept tapping the napkin as he spoke, causing the bed to shake.

"Quit it, Horace!" Augusta pleaded. "I am feeling green enough as it is."

He glanced at Maxcy, who was by the door playing with a box of matches. He struck a match and smiled as it flared up.

"Gussie, this is our one chance," Horace whispered. "But we have to leave tomorrow if we want to stake a claim. That other fellow, that weasel George Stevens, is watching everything we do. So we can't wait. Or there won't be any gold left to claim!"

Augusta said nothing.

Horace watched her for a few minutes. Surely she could travel in a wagon. He could arrange a nice bed for her inside, among their belongings. It might even be more comfortable than the hotel room.

"There is another town a couple day's ride to the south. You can do that, can't you? We'll find a hotel and you can rest there. Me and Nathaniel can get to work cutting trees. I even bought a whipsaw."

He paused and stared at her.

"That's the kind with handles on both ends."

Pulling the blankets over her head, Augusta rolled over to face the wall.

With a sigh, Horace folded up his napkin map and put it in his pocket.

"Okay, then. We don't have to leave tomorrow. Let's give it a day, and see how you're feeling."

It would only be a matter of time before George Stevens figured out what was going on. When he did, the race would be on. Horace didn't want to be last, whatever happened. But he was sensitive enough to know his wife was in no condition to travel. He could tell because her eyes were soft like a puppy's instead of hard like stone—her normal look.

The smell of partially digested cheese soup filled the room. Horace started to feel a little green, himself.

"Should I stay?"

"Get out, Horace."

CHAPTER 50

SPRING 1892
LEADVILLE

Since John Campion was too cheap, Horace decided to foot the bill for electric lighting himself. He wanted to lure the entire city to the silver club announcement, and the best way to do that was to create a bright, festive atmosphere that no one could ignore. What better way to make people feel bright about the future than bright lights? That and free booze.

So Horace paid a company to rush up from Denver and install several rows of tall, ornate lamp posts with big carbon arc light bulbs.

They weren't cheap, but they had panache. Decorative curves and floral patterns were fashioned in the metalwork, and the bulbs were the brightest ones available. They were far brighter than the standard gas-fed street lamps in town. To look at, they made the Lucy B. property seem more like Paris than Leadville.

Next, Horace looked into booking some music. Sousa's New Marine Band was on tour, performing a series of Civil War Yankee tribute ensembles along the east coast—too far away to arrive in time, even if he paid them enough to try. Instead, Horace wired the bandleader at the Broadway Theater in Denver and found that the theater orchestra was available.

The Broadway Theater was only two years old and still in the honeymoon phase of good artistic expression. Unfortunately, it was located right down the street from Augusta's $40,000 mansion. Even though his ex-wife's unseen presence cast a pall, Horace still rented a private box at the theater for the season—so he already knew how good the orchestra was. He took Baby Doe there for a show whenever they visited the city. However, he took pains to make sure the driver avoided Augusta's residence. The carriage did drive by there once, the first time they went, but it put Baby Doe in such a foul mood that she clawed at his tuxedo. From that point on, they took a side street. One of the more memorable concerts was called Pills to Purge Melancholy. The orchestra played absolutely bawdy songs, with titles like "A Tory, a Whig, and a Moderate Man," "Monsieur Looks Pale," and, "Ah, Phyllis, Why Are You Less Tender?" Since they were upbeat, catchy tunes, Horace requested the same material.

"This is gonna be a frolic to beat the Dutch," he chirped.

It was Friday night and Horace was standing next to John Campion at the Lucy B. mine, waiting for it to get dark. The sky soared overhead like a vast orange dome.

"Get dark already!" Horace shouted at the heavens.

Then he nudged Campion.

"Wait till these new street lamps are going. The Lucy B. is going to shine brighter than a dozen full moons. No one in town will be able to stay away, I guarantee that."

"I hope so," Campion muttered. "Is this even necessary?"

Horace looked shocked.

"Of course it is."

Then he gave him a conspiratorial wink.

"What kind of fireworks did you arrange?"

Looking uncomfortable, Campion crossed his arms.

"There were none to be had, given the time frame."

Horace was astonished.

"What? You should have told me. I know every vendor in Denver. I could have gotten an entire New Year's Eve rocket display trailed up here in twenty-four hours, easy. Dammit, John!"

Shrugging it off, Campion pointed at a group of men in baggy clown suits, over by the shaft house.

"We'll have a parade, instead."

Horace followed his finger and felt his heart sink. The clown suits were obviously hasty constructions, and all of the "clowns" were miners on Campion's payroll. None of them looked pleased to be suited up.

"Is that *Wheezy Jones*?"

"He's the lead clown," Campion explained. "Janey says he can juggle oranges like a professional. Been doing it since he was twelve years old."

Without saying goodbye, Horace stalked off toward the beer wagon. He grabbed a bottle and drank it down. Sometimes, he felt like the only one in the city with any vision.

Glancing at the clowns again, Horace winced. Wheezy Jones, the mine manager of the Lucy B., was supposed to introduce him on stage later that evening. The man Horace was looking at did not inspire confidence. Of course, the nasally fellow could not inspire confidence even if he was photographed with Abraham Lincoln, should he rise from the grave.

However, Horace's mood spruced up as soon as he heard the orchestra begin to tune their instruments.

At that very moment, the lamp posts flickered and buzzed, and came to life.

Horace clapped his hands.

"Come over here, John!"

But his voice was lost in a cacophony of trumpet toots and violin plucks, and Campion did not hear him.

Feeling his heart soar, Horace checked his pocket watch. It would not be long now. Soon, the Major would lead over the crew from the Matchless Mine, and every man crawling in the bowels of the Lucy B. would surface to ribald, dancy jigs.

In anticipation of a sizeable crowd, all the snow had been shoveled back. A big bonfire had been lit. Flags and bunting were hanging from the ore bins and the head frame. Food vendors were sizzling meat and popping corn.

The bell rang to announce the shift change.

It was time.

The bandleader signaled to Horace, and he signaled back. Immediately, they launched into their first number.

Since he had hung posters all over the city and advertised in the paper, Horace was not surprised when townsfolk began to flood in. There were miners, of course, but also families with small children, and business owners who locked up early.

He noticed a lot of familiar faces.

The crews from all the mines were pouring in—the Matchless, Chrysolite, Little Chief, Ibex, and more. The Western Union telegrapher made a beeline for the beer wagon. Laundresses Merna and Eve led a troop of small children straight for the Fairy Floss candy machine. The owner of the wallpaper shop, the schoolmaster, and the fire marshal surrounded the popcorn vendor. Horace even spotted his business rival Ben Loeb and his red-light girls congregating around the bonfire.

Privately, Horace congratulated himself. He had put this whole thing together in a matter of days. It was already sizing up to be the most memorable social event that Leadville had ever seen. Except there were no fireworks. And the "clowns." Campion was such a miser. Horace got angry as he thought about it. He had gone to great lengths to make the silver club announcement a success. He invested in advertisements, food, and beer. He even spent a small fortune on those fancy lamp posts—and the Lucy B. wasn't even his property. It was Campion's!

Horace's frustrations, however, were quickly doused as the orchestra launched into that punchy polka, "Blowzabella, My Bouncing Doxy."

CHAPTER 51

Milling about Horace's "Raucous Event Of Great Import," Big Ed spotted Sylvander Sawney, president of the Knights of Labor, chewing on a sausage roll.

Big Ed leaned in for a whisper.

"You know what I heard?" he asked.

Sylvander continued to chew but appeared to be listening.

"Haw Tabor ain't gonna offer no one a pay *hike*. Tonight, he's going to announce a pay *cut*."

Sylvander stopped chewing.

"It ain't going from three bucks an hour to *four*," Big Ed continued. "It's going from three to *two fifty*. God's honest truth!"

The president of the Knights of Labor, the miners' union in Leadville, swallowed his bite. He studied Big Ed for a moment, and then turned to scan the crowd. He spotted Horace on the stage, seated near the podium, tapping his toe to the music. Baby Doe and Maxcy were seated next to him, clapping along. Meanwhile, in his own world, Wheezy Jones was walking around the stage juggling oranges.

"Think about it," Big Ed hissed. "The price of silver ain't going up. It's going down. Everyone knows that. All this free food, free booze . . . what do you think that is? A reward for all your hard work?"

"Where did you hear those numbers?" Sylvander asked, suspicious.

Big Ed straightened up, looking offended.

"I got a girl working at the Tabor Hotel, in the parlor. She heard it straight from John Campion and Haw Tabor himself. They were trying to be sneaky about it, but my girl heard every damn word."

Sylvander dropped his half-eaten sausage roll onto the icy ground and licked his thumb clean of sauerkraut.

"The Silver King's got some mighty blurry ethics, I'd say," Big Ed mentioned sadly. "If you don't believe me, go ask his carriage driver. The fellow was privy to the whole conversation, too. In fact, that's him right over there."

Big Ed pointed at the Fairy Floss machine. Standing there, eating a tuft of candy, was Dirty Johns. But Dirty Johns was unrecognizable. His hair was watered down, and he was wearing an immaculate suit coat with a white hanky in the pocket. He also had a top hat, fresh black trousers, and a pair of hundred dollar boots.

"Damn, I wish I had some fancy boots like that," Big Ed said to Sylvander. "That fellow must make a pretty sizable salary, wouldn't you say?"

Then, just as quietly as he came, Big Ed melted into the crowd. But he did not melt completely away. He slipped behind one of the new fancy lamp posts, where he could still see what the president of the Knights of Labor would do next.

Big Ed waved at Dirty Johns, whom he had deputized for the deception.

Dirty Johns, doing his best to seem mannered and aloof, pinched off another wisp of sugary soft candy.

Unfortunately, Sylvander Sawney began walking in the wrong direction.

Big Ed swore under his breath. He looked at Dirty Johns again and shrugged. However, as he watched, Sylvander muttered in a man's ear, and another man's ear, and then a third, and together they all marched back over to Dirty Johns and began to question him.

It was obvious, even from a distance, that the line of questions was severe.

Worried the man might not be able to maintain his pseudonym and false pretense under duress, Big Ed started swearing again. He held his breath and watched.

But Dirty Johns, God bless him, kept a cool head.

When Sylvander and his crew stalked off, he gave Big Ed an "okay" sign. Relieved, and also excited, Big Ed came back with a "shove off" sign. Looking crestfallen, Dirty Johns, in his top hat, immaculate coat, and hundred dollar boots, took his Fairy Floss and headed down the street.

Scanning the crowd, Big Ed tried to see where the Knights of Labor went.

The orchestra was playing a jaunty waltz. It was a song that everyone seemed to know, and people began to sing along.

After the ball is over,
After the break of morn,
After the dancers' leaving,
After the stars are gone;
Many a heart is aching,

If you could read them all,
Many the hopes that have vanished,
After the ball.

As people clapped and whistled, Wheezy Jones carefully set his oranges on the stage and went to the podium.

"Speech!" someone shouted. "Speech!"

Jones gripped the podium, awkwardly.

"Uh, hello," he mumbled.

"Speak up!"

His audience pressed closer to the stage to hear him better.

"Good evening," Jones went on, barely.

"Louder! Louder!"

He held his hand up to shade his face, since the new electric lights were so intense. Then he cleared his throat to conceal the fact that his mind had gone blank. The Matchless miners, sensing weakness in their competitor, began booing.

"Perhaps you've heard the rumors," he began.

"What rumors?" the telegrapher shouted, free booze in hand. He also had a pretzel, and he lobbed it.

Jones ducked behind the podium, and the Matchless miners began booing again.

Muttering about the shame of incompetence, Baby Doe got up from her seat and exited the stage, abandoning the ever-faithful Maxcy.

The telegrapher, for some reason, started making beeping noises, as if mimicking a telegraph machine. The free booze must have played some part.

Putting his face in his hands, Horace felt embarrassed. He had envisioned an eloquent, even patronizing introduction, followed by warm applause as he sashayed across the stage.

The irritating buzz of the arc lamps did not help. Beneath their all-revealing glare, there was no possible way Horace could slink off unnoticed. So, he tried the opposite approach. He picked up an orange and hurled it at Wheezy Jones, bouncing it off his head. This got a good laugh from the crowd and they cheered Horace, whom they all recognized.

Jogging to the podium, Horace flushed the mine manager out from his hiding place like a quail. The man promptly hopped off the stage and vanished. Horace waited for the clapping to subside before speaking.

"Citizens, Romans, and countrymen!" he shouted. "The reason you are here, as you may have guessed already, is that I am inaugurating the Leadville Silver Club. How does a pay hike sound? All you shaft workers have been getting three bucks a day for the past decade. That ain't right. I'll tell you what. Every single man among you who works a shaft in the city of Leadville, each one who signs on to the Leadville Silver Club tonight, will get *four* bucks a day!"

There was a smattering of applause, but not as much as he was expecting. Horace's grin faltered, and he looked around again.

"How does *four dollars per day* sound?"

"It sounds like a politician's lie!"

Pushing his way forward, Sylvander Sawney, president of the Knights of Labor, climbed right up on stage.

"Syl?" Horace asked, confused. "Are you playing a joke on me?"

He offered his hand, but Sylvander did not shake it.

"We are being duped here tonight, people. Let me tell you something. No one approached me about a price hike. No one!"

The crowd booed.

"I must admit, Horace, this is quite a soirée!" Sylvander went on, obviously angry. "You've gone to a lot of trouble to fool a lot of people. But we all know the price of silver is crashing. There ain't no money for a raise. Who are you fooling? And more important, why?"

The Knights of Labor started chanting, "Strike! Strike! Strike!"

CHAPTER 52

CREEDE

"Did you hear about that mail carrier?" Joe Palmer asked. "He got speared and scalped by injuns."

Soapy had not heard, but he was not particularly interested, either.

"No, that's not what happened. They cut off his skin and hung it like wet laundry on an aspen tree," said Old Man Tripp, who scratched his white beard.

But Banjo disagreed with both of them.

"I heard they barbequed him black as the ace of spades."

Pacing back and forth, Soapy hooked his thumb behind his necktie and wiggled to loosen it up.

"Dead is dead," he said curtly. "Now forget about that. I want everyone paying close attention. Simmons pours drinks, Tripp deals faro, Palmer's on pool, and Banjo is on poker. Watch for trouble. Stay sharp, know your place, and don't nobody fool with me today!"

At the front of the building, people were tapping on the window and pressing their faces against the glass.

"Friday night, boys!" Soapy said. "Like bees to the honey, they've been lined up since noon and now they're chomping at the bit. They want to gamble, to drink, and to eat the only steak Creede has to offer—and we better have it all ready to go because today is the day and this is the hour."

He went behind the bar and pushed Old Man Tripp out of the way.

"Why are you back here? I said you're dealing faro."

Then he glared at Simmons, who was polishing a row of shot glasses.

"I don't see the girls. Where are the girls?"

Simmons looked around.

"Right back there," he said. "Painted up and purty as dolls."

Sure enough, Mollie and Ella Diamond were leaning on the piano wearing brightly colored dresses. Then Joe came out of the kitchen carrying a blue ceramic plate and set it on the bar.

"Taste this, boss."

There was a thick steak nestled among steaming potatoes, green beans, and stewed tomatoes. Soapy cut off a piece of meat and chewed it thoughtfully.

"Good Lord," he said, relaxing. "I don't even recall the last time I ate an actual steak."

Joe smiled and spread his hands.

"What did I tell you?"

Soapy poured himself a shot of rye and raised the glass in a toast.

"Alright boys. Let's shove the booze across the boards!"

He gulped it down, marched over to the front door and flung it open.

"Welcome to the Orleans Club," he shouted.

Elbowing and arguing to get through the doorway, the room quickly filled to capacity. Joe went over to the pool table and racked up a game. One miner ran right up and grabbed a cue stick.

"Well, it is about time. I'm tired of playing pool at the Denver Exchange. That table always reeks. Look at this plush new velvet."

He leaned down and sniffed the tabletop.

"It don't smell like whizz, let me tell you."

"It's a dime per game."

The man handed Joe a dime.

"By way of introduction, my name is JJ Dore. A lone prospector, but a man of great fortune."

Bending over the table, he lined up his shot, and then hit the cue ball hard. The pool balls scattered, but none went in any of the pockets.

"Alright, I'll bite," Joe said, feeling obligated to keep him happy, as a paying customer. "What kind of great fortune?"

Leaning on the stick, JJ Dore looked around to make sure no one was listening in on their conversation.

"Let me tell you something. A fellow prospector, feeling hope-less at his claim, sold it to me for a dime—just like the one I gave you. I started digging, and not two feet down, struck a find like you wouldn't believe."

Joe rubbed his eyes, getting irritated. Apparently, the Smith Gang was not the sole purveyor of false dreams roaming the streets of Creede.

"Is that so?"

"And I'll sell it to you, right now, sight unseen, for only a hun-dred bucks! Can you believe that?"

"No, so shut up and shoot."

Joe was trying to keep an eye on Soapy. He was worried about him. It was rare to see Soapy Smith unnerved or rattled even in the slightest, no matter the situation. In fact, Joe struggled to remember a time when he had seen him get riled up like this. Nerves were a familiar thing, and on many occasions Joe himself felt uneasy. But Soapy was always the confident one. No matter what happened. How many times had scams gone wrong back in Denver? Through police raids and turf wars, no matter how tough the situation, Joe always leaned on Soapy's strong constitution to carry the day.

Now that the club was busy, now that Soapy was mingling and chatting, it was clear he was becoming more at ease. His smile seemed more natural. His eyes had softened. The piano music, the girls dancing and singing, the click of the pool table and the shouts at the bar all seemed to help. Now that the Orleans Club was open, Soapy was in his true element. Joe knew everything would get back to normal. He sighed, relieved. Plus, now that there was steak to eat, there would be nothing to remind Soapy about Joe's dead deer stink. They could be friends again.

At that thought, Joe began to relax himself—until he saw Bob Ford walk through the door and head straight for the bar.

"Whiskey and a beer," Bob demanded.

Simmons set a shot glass and a beer bottle down, took his money, and turned to help the next man in line.

Glaring around the room with a suspicious eye, Bob took it all in.

Joe abandoned the lone prospector of great fortune, JJ Dore, and hustled right over.

"Hi Bob."

"Look at this piss hole."

"You really shouldn't be in here."

Draining the shot glass in one quick gulp, Bob put his arm around Joe's shoulder.

"You're probably right, partner. I shouldn't darken the door of some third-rate cupboard like this. Why, this place is downright shoddy."

Licking his lips, Joe felt his nerves getting jumpy. He glanced around the room and saw Soapy standing by Mollie while Ella Diamond sang and played the piano. A gambler Joe recognized as

Frank Oliver was telling a joke to Soapy, and Soapy was already grinning before he got to the punchline.

"Why don't we head over to Bat's place instead," Joe suggested urgently.

"I ain't goin' to Bat's place," Bob replied in a smug voice and ordered another whiskey. "What's wrong with you anyhow, that you put your chips in with Soapy Smith? The fellow's a simpleton who runs a soap scam on the boardwalk, for Pete's sake. *A soap scam.* Gawd, that is ridiculous."

He drained the second shot and sniffed the empty glass, crinkling his nose.

"Whiskey shouldn't taste this weak. Gotta be a secret house recipe."

Busy bartending, Simmons heard the comment and came back down to investigate, but Joe waved him away.

"I imagine, since I have such finely attuned senses, I could guess the amalgamation," Bob continued. "One part liquor, two parts horse squirt."

"Now Bob, that's not nice."

"You got me all wrong—I'm a nice fellow with nice things to say," Bob countered. "Like this fine compliment: Your boss is a very good at what he does. Very good at fleecing the common man. Just look at all the poor fools in this piddly room. Cheating them outta what little they got."

Turning to the nearest man standing at the bar, Bob leaned close as if he was going to whisper, but shouted in the man's ear instead.

"You been fleeced, you damn sucker!"

"Why, hello Bob," Soapy said, walking up.

"He's just got some liquor in him," Joe said, hoping to intervene.

"Is that right, Bob? You got some liquor in you?" Soapy asked and patted him on the cheek.

Bob's face turned beet red and he slapped away Soapy's hand.

"Keep off! You can't fleece me like you fleece all these suckers."

The other drinkers standing at the bar got annoyed, took their bottles and shot glasses and stalked off, casting dark looks over their shoulders.

Banjo came up and leaned his lanky elbow on the oak top.

"Did you bring my cane, Banjo?" Soapy asked him.

"It's in the back."

Bob Ford took a quick sip from his beer bottle and smirked.

"You think you run this town? You are slick, I'll give you that."

In a quick movement, Bob Ford raised the bottle and swung it at Soapy's head, but Banjo grabbed his arm even quicker. Bob yelled and tried to pull free.

"Ow, you dullard! Unhand me."

A splash of beer foam sloshed out of the bottle and spattered Soapy's jacket. Looking down, he examined the mess in dismay.

"Why, Bob. This is my good Sunday coat."

Without another word, Soapy marched directly into the back-room. Following along, Banjo dragged Bob Ford by the arm. Seeing Bob getting hauled off, the drunkards and gamblers of the Orleans Club raised a cheer.

"I killed Jesse James!" Bob shouted, glaring around with wild eyes. "I can take any one of you!"

CHAPTER 53

Bob Ford lay very still on his bed in the Cliff Hotel.

His entire body was black and raw.

After getting dragged into the backroom at the Orleans Club, Soapy Smith informed Bob that he was a nobody. Then, so there wouldn't be any confusion, Soapy coronated himself the king of Creede—and proceeded to cane Bob quite severely.

When Soapy tired of whacking him with the cane, Banjo choked him until he passed out.

Waking up on the railroad tracks, Bob crawled back to his hotel, which was located beneath the big cliff. No one helped him on his crawl, although a number of miners passed him by and noted, "Look, it's Bob Ford." It was only when his inert body blocked the stairs at the hotel that someone finally lifted him up and carried him to his room.

It was humiliating.

At least the fog of inebriation had acted as an opiate, dulling the pain.

Yet, as he thought about what had happened, a wave of anger washed over him. It roused him, and gave him the strength to sit up in bed. But once he sat up, he found himself looking at his own reflection in the dressing mirror.

Even though he was dismayed at all the bruising, what gave him pause was his forehead vein. It always bubbled up to the surface when he was mad. His own brother Charley, before he killed himself, had pointed it out one day. *You have a vein there,* Charley mentioned. *Where?* Bob asked. *Running right there, up 'n down. It's quite unseemly.*

That happened one night after the curtain fell on their roving theatre production. It was billed as "The Outlaws of Missouri," and they took it from town to town. At first it had been quite the hoot. Bob got cocky as a rooster when they counted up each night's ticket sales—and as his name began to spread into the public consciousness.

But after that night, things started going bad.

Hecklers began dogging the shows. They interrupted the performance with anonymous shouts from the darkened theaters. This was, of course, because he shot Jesse James. When his back was turned. While the man was unarmed. Having laid aside his guns on the sofa to straighten a picture frame. In his own house.

So it was an unpleasant thing for Bob, to realize folks did not consider him a hero after all. His own show seemed to highlight that self-same fact to all who watched—that he'd shot the famous Jesse James, who was unarmed, in the back of the head, in his own home.

Well, Charley shot himself, too, a couple years after all that.

But he was a goner anyhow since he had consumption and blew his earnings on morphine and strong drink. Add to that, his wits were constantly on edge for fear of Frank James's threats of revenge. The James boys had always lived for revenge. The odds were good that Frank might appear unannounced from the audience with a gun in his hand, and each performance left their nerves wrecked. So that was the end of the show tours. And the end of Charley.

The infamy Bob garnered along the theatrical path had become so pesky that he decided to head west and disappear from the public eye.

But even in the mountains, in the mining camps and saloons, people figured out who he was. There was no disappearing. So he decided that disappearing was for the birds. He wanted *everyone* to know who he was. He strutted around Creede, drinking and gambling, and if anyone said anything bad about him, he would curse and squabble, and even fight if necessary. But Bob wasn't an expert at fisticuffs. So he relied heavily upon intimidation. And it seemed to work, until Soapy Smith showed up.

Bob raised his hand and massaged his forehead. It hurt just to raise his arm, but he had to do it because the vein gave him the willies.

There was a knock on the door.

"What?" Bob grumbled.

The door squeaked open, and Joe Palmer poked his head inside.

"Don't shoot," he said. "It's just me."

"Come on in, then."

Bob didn't even know where his gun was, or his knife. He had been armed when he went into the Orleans Club. But his weapons were gone now.

"How you feel?" Joe asked.

Bob tried to sit up straight but gasped in pain.

"I've been pounded to a beefsteak. I expect you can imagine how I might feel."

Joe came closer and studied Bob's bruises.

"You took some terrible licks."

In several spots, the skin was broken and his clothes were sticky. Bob felt sore all over his face, neck, shoulders, and sides. His left eye had some blood in it, too. The white part was red.

"Why in the *world* would you walk inside Soapy Smith's saloon and insult the man to his face?" Joe asked. "You tried to bash him in the head with a bottle! Have you lost your mind? Hell, you even slapped Bat Masterson in his own place, just the other day. You're lucky to be above ground!"

"No thanks to you," Bob retorted, spitefully.

"Wrong. I tried to steer you out the minute you walked in the door, if you can remember."

"Help me up," Bob said, and beckoned him for assistance.

Joe sat down on the bed so Bob could hook his arm around his neck.

"Alright," Joe said. "Up we go."

Groaning, Bob managed to stand as Joe rose to his feet.

"You sure you feel up to this?"

Gasping at the pain, Bob nodded stiffly.

"I need fresh air."

Even though each step was agony, somehow Bob had the fortitude to make it all the way out the door and down the hotel stairs, through the lobby and into the morning sun.

Joe led him over to a bench and they sat down.

Feeling his head whirl, Bob blinked and gasped. Everything was pretty blurry and his ears rang.

"I'll be right back," Joe told him and went back inside the Cliff Hotel.

Each time he breathed in, Bob's chest hurt like hell. Flexing his hands, he knew he had a couple broken knuckles, and a pinky finger was bent a little funny. At least his legs seemed to be fairly unmolested. He had gotten struck on the thighs and shins a few times, but not as bad as his chest and head.

Somewhere off to his left, Bob could hear some voices. They sounded excited, like they were watching a dogfight. Bob tried to turn his head, but his neck hurt and his bad eye was extra blurry.

"Here," Joe said, handing him a tin cup. "Hot coffee. Don't spill."

Lifting it slowly, Bob took a painful sip. His lips were both split and puffy, and it stung. But it smelled good, tasted good, and warmed him up.

"Many thanks," Bob said, softly but sincerely.

Joe did not reply. Hearing Bob thank him was a little awkward. He wasn't used to hearing anything but curses and condescension come out of Bob's mouth.

"What's going on over there?" Bob asked.

Joe leaned forward to see.

"Looks like a shell game."

Bob tensed up.

"Soapy Smith?"

"No. I don't know who that is."

Joe frowned.

"Soapy won't like a stranger running a shell game in town."

Exhaling slowly, Bob was glad it wasn't Soapy. Or any of the Smith gang.

"Let's go watch," he suggested.

Leaning on Joe again, Bob got to his feet.

"Let me try walking on my own."

When they got closer, Bob found he could see clearer. It was some blond-haired teen running the shell game. His hands were quick, and he moved the shells around on the table so fast it made Bob's head spin.

"That one!" someone said, and tapped on one of the three shells.

"This one right here?" the teen asked.

"I know that's the one. You ain't that quick."

Lifting the shell, the teen revealed there was nothing beneath it. The man booed, but his friends laughed. As they walked off, Joe and Bob moved up to the table.

"Who are you?" Joe asked.

"The New Orleans Kid," he announced proudly. "Direct from the muggy climes of Louisiana. Try your luck."

He showed them a pinto bean and set it on the table. Placing one of the walnut shells over the bean, he slid the shells around and around.

"Keep your eye on the bean, and if you guess right, I'll give you a silver dollar. If you guess wrong, you give me one."

His hands were a blur, and Bob felt his head spin again.

"You are fast. I'll give you that."

"I ain't paying you nothin'," Joe informed the youngster. "Let's go, Bob."

But Bob was smiling.

"The New Orleans Kid?" he said thoughtfully.

The teen grinned back at him.

"That's right."

Bob looked at Joe and winked, but then cringed. He had winked his bad eye, and it hurt.

"You shouldn't be here," Joe warned the Kid.

"No, you should not," Bob said, smiling again, and dug out a silver dollar. "You're set up next to a damn hotel. People sleep in hotels—they don't play shell games."

The Kid shrugged.

"Is there a better place?"

"You should be where people are drinking and gambling and whoring, not outside a sleepy hotel. What better place for the New Orleans Kid than right out front of the Orleans Club?"

Joe was shocked. He looked at Bob in amazement.

"There's an Orleans Club?" the Kid asked.

"That's right. It's perfect. They got a big sign, and you can put your table right beneath it and people will line up for a mile."

"They won't mind?" the Kid asked.

"Hell no, they won't mind," Bob said and paused to spit out a string of blood. "They're real nice folk."

CHAPTER 54

When Old Man Tripp burst into the backroom and told Soapy there was a shell game operating on the boardwalk right outside the Orleans Club, Soapy laughed at him.

"You have to get up pretty early to fool me."

But Tripp was dead serious.

"I ain't joshing."

Soapy's smile faded. Slowly, but still wary about a practical joke, Soapy got up and put on his hat. Clearing his throat, he exited the backroom and strolled across the Orleans Club curiously. But Banjo brushed past him, wove around the poker and faro tables, and beat him to the plate-glass window.

"What do you see?" Soapy called.

Pressing his face against the glass, Banjo jerked back like he saw a ghost.

"It's some blond boy. People are giving him silver dollars."

Turning red, Soapy glared around the room.

"Who authorized that boy to run a shell game?"

Everyone stopped what they were doing and glanced around at each other.

"Did someone say it was okay to set up a shell game—on my front door?"

Simmons, who was tending the bar, shook his head.

"Wasn't me."

All the gamblers and miners avoided eye contact whenever Soapy looked their way.

"Where in the hell is Joe Palmer?" Soapy asked. "He better not be boozing with Bob Ford!"

Mollie pointed at the alley door.

"He's in the shitter. I saw him take a newspaper and head outside a few minutes ago."

"Do I have to do everything myself?"

His face getting even redder, Soapy marched past the game tables, thrust open the door, and began shouting at the New Orleans Kid. In the crisp winter air, his breath came puffing out in great white clouds.

"I want this outfit moved! And damn quick!"

There were several carefree prospectors looming over the Kid's table, trying to guess the correct shell. As soon as they realized what was happening, they ran away.

The New Orleans Kid watched them go and frowned.

"What do you think you're doing?"

"No one runs any game in this town without my say so."

The Kid did not move or even seem scared. In fact, he merely brushed his blond hair back with his fingers and gave Soapy a rather cocky glare.

"Ain't no rules in this camp. Don't see no signs, neither. Now, unless a bona fide city marshal comes and informs me I have broken a bona fide city law, and shows me that law in a dang law book, I ain't gonna relocate. And I certainly don't need your say so."

Banjo came out and heard what he was saying and was shocked at the Kid's bold words.

His first thought was to go get Soapy's cane. Soapy would surely want to beat some sense into this young fool.

But Banjo noticed the whole town seemed to be watching the commotion.

Ever since they got to Creede, things had been going so well. Banjo worried that beating the New Orleans Kid in public would spoil everyone's goodwill. People might go elsewhere to gamble, like down to Bat's place. There might even be a public outcry. If the mood turned against him, Soapy could get run right out of town again, like Denver.

After all, Soapy had caned John Arkins, editor of the *Rocky Mountain News*, in the middle of a crowded street, just like this. And there was the editor of the *Creede Candle*, a pudgy man named Lute Johnson, standing near a snow bank. The last thing they needed was bad press.

Deciding against the cane, Banjo went over and whispered in Soapy's ear.

"Let's go easy this time. Too many eyes."

Instead, Soapy flipped over the New Orleans Kid's table and scattered his nutshells.

Grabbing a fistful of blonde hair, Soapy yanked the boy off the boardwalk and dragged him into the cold wet mud.

"What does that say?" Soapy said, pointing at the Orleans Club sign.

"The Orleans Club," the Kid replied, gritting his teeth. "And I'm the New Orleans Kid."

"Well, this is my club and my town."

He tightened his grip on the Kid's scalp, causing him to yelp.

Joe Palmer appeared from the alley, suspenders dangling. He was still holding his newspaper but dropped it when he saw the blond boy pinned on the ground, Soapy Smith twisting his hair, and all the people watching it happen.

Joe raced over.

"Easy, Soapy."

He gently pried Soapy's hand out of the Kid's hair.

"Don't you worry. We'll get him out of your sight."

Quickly, Joe grabbed one of the Kid's arms, and Banjo got the other, and together they yanked him to his feet.

"Let me go!" the Kid protested, and turned to glare at Soapy. "You pulled my hair, you scoundrel."

Seething, Soapy remained where he was, standing in the center of the avenue. He looked at his fist, and then wiggled his fingers. Several long blond hairs glided gently into the mud.

The Kid was enraged. "How dare you. I will gun you down for this."

"Shut up," Joe whispered tersely.

Though his eyes were watery from having his hair yanked out by the roots, the Kid recognized Joe Palmer from before.

"Hey, I know you."

Banjo gave him a jerk.

"Shut your damn mouth. You just called out Soapy Smith. Be glad you ain't dead."

The Kid writhed in their grips.

"You got no right to lay hands on me. What about my gear?"

"You ain't getting it back."

They dragged him all the way down to the train depot. Patting him down, Joe extracted a handful of silver dollars.

"Hey, those are mine."

But Joe took the coins and went into the ticket office.

"When's the next train?"

The station agent, seated behind the counter in his usual place, pointed at the chalk board with the schedule written on it.

"Noon, it says."

Joe looked up at the wall clock.

"It's quarter after. Did we miss it?"

"No, it's late. And close the door, you're letting all the heat out."

Sighing, Joe placed all the silver dollars on the counter.

"See that kid? Make sure he's on that train."

"Why would I do that? Is he incapable, or a nitwit?"

"He's a bother. Just make sure he leaves or Soapy will have something to say."

Joe slammed the door.

Held tight by Banjo's firm grip, the New Orleans Kid gave up the struggle. Instead, he began studying them both closely.

"Gonna remember your faces."

Joe sighed.

"Just don't come back."

CHAPTER 55

Davis held the boards while LG knocked in the nails. So far, they had completed a holding pen for their stock and framed in four walls for the meat market. A light flurry had started, and snowflakes were beginning to whirl in the air.

While they were working, Joe and Banjo walked up.

"I hope you can get this roof done before the weather turns ugly," Joe mentioned.

Davis looked up through the ceiling beams and eyed the clouds. "Hope so, too."

Then, without asking, Joe stepped through the door frame and whistled at all the lumber.

"What is this going to be, anyhow?"

Banjo came in, too, but stopped in the doorway. He was so tall, the top of his hat scraped the crossbeam. But there was something different in the air. When they had rode out to the cow camp to contract beef for the Orleans Club, they had been friendly. Now, they both had a queer look on their faces.

LG quit pounding but held onto his hammer.

"This is a meat market. We are going to sell beef right here."

"Well, that's good news," Joe replied with a satisfied nod. "That sure makes procuring beef for the Orleans Club easy. You two sure have gone the extra mile to keep us supplied. I bet poor Bat wishes he had a beef supplier as faithful as you two."

"You'll be happy to know he does," LG told him.

Joe grinned, but it was a hard grin.

"Don't tell me you're selling beef to Bat. Soapy wouldn't like that very much."

"Well, pard, we sell beef. That's what we do."

Pursing his lips, Joe appeared to wrestle with his thoughts for a moment.

"What's wrong with that?" Davis asked.

Joe scooped up a handful of nails from a pail, and let them trickle through his fingers.

"It's just that Soapy don't want you selling to anyone else."

LG kept an eye on Banjo, who still loomed in the doorway.

Snowflakes continued to flutter out of the sky, settling on the pine boards, their hat brims and dusting the floor.

"You see, if you sell meat to everyone, that will cut into Soapy's restaurant sales," Joe explained. "People might stop dropping in for a meal. And that ain't good for business."

LG shrugged.

"But it's good for our business."

Joe itched his chin.

"The only way to resolve this, as far as I can see, is you're gonna have to pay Soapy. We can call it rent, if you'd like."

Getting irritated, LG gripped the hammer a little tighter.

"I already paid the full purchase price for this lot. Why would I pay rent to anybody, let alone Soapy Smith?"

Joe looked around again, and nodded thoughtfully.

"This is a smart location you got. All kinds of folk pass right by here, in and out of the canyon. All them miners coming into town for a bite. They'll be stopping here long before they get down to Soapy's place. Buy their own cuts, cook it themselves. Hell, they might even eat at Bat's if they know he's serving fresh steak."

"I ain't gonna pay rent to nobody," LG informed him. "Go tell Soapy Smith to look to his own properties for rent money."

Joe shook his head sadly.

"Alright then, I'll tell him."

He turned and stepped between the studs and out into the fresh white powder. He left a line of muddy footprints as he walked off. Without a word, Banjo backed out of the doorway and followed along.

Halfway down the road, Joe paused and looked back.

"Do you got fire insurance?"

Then he laughed—but it was an ugly laugh.

CHAPTER 56

RICO

The sun had just dipped behind Expectation Mountain when the train chugged through Rico depot. There was a small knot of people milling around on the platform. One kid was scraping off the fresh snowfall with a big tin shovel.

A gray-bearded prospector with a sweat-stained hat struck up a conversation with a young, cleanly dressed fellow who was sitting on a valise in his socks, busy rubbing grease on a pair of rubber boots.

"Two o'clock. Right on time," the old prospector said. "Where you headed anyway?"

"Telluride."

The old man looked both amused and annoyed.

"What in the heck are you doing?"

The young fellow sitting on the valise looked confused.

"Why, I am making these boots waterproof," he answered, and then hesitated. "Isn't that what you're supposed to do?"

The prospector guffawed and pointed at a horse.

"Ask him. He knows more about gold panning than you do."

Riding in the cab of the engine, Kahopi and Bear Claw Lip stood at the controls—even though they did not know how to operate them. But that did not matter. Controlling the train was of no interest to them.

As the train rolled past the platform, Bear Claw Lip ran out on top of the coal car and let out as bloodcurdling a war cry as he could muster. Then he hurled the flagman's body onto the platform.

"Whoa, now! Did you slip, partner?" the prospector asked the flagman.

But the flagman was dead.

Bear Claw Lip continued his war cry and danced back and forth on the coal. His voice rose above the steam engine's hissing and carried loudly in the brisk winter air. Then he produced both the engineer and the coal shoveler, both dead, and hurled them off the train as well.

At that, everyone standing around on the platform of Rico station, waiting for the two o'clock train, realized what was happening.

"Injuns!" the old prospector cried. "Injun attack!"

Then he ran for it, and the young man who was waterproofing
his waterproof boots, skipped after him in his socks.

The train continued to move down the tracks. It passed slowly
through Rico without stopping. White Owl hung off the caboose,
shaking his fist in the air. Greasewood could be seen, seated inside,
peering through the window, sipping coffee. While some people
ducked down behind the platform, and others slipped inside the
nearby saloon, many townsfolk simply paused to watch it roll past
like some kind of macabre street theatre.

From the safety of the saloon, the prospector shook his head in
disbelief.

"Why, there hasn't been an injun attack for a decade."

— PART 8 —

CHAPTER 57

WINTER 1860
DENVER

Augusta pulled the covers up to her chin.

"Gussie!" Horace pleaded. "You've been in bed for more than a week."

"It's called influenza and some folks find it quite fatal."

"You seem sprightly enough to me."

"There's the door," she replied. "Look yourself out."

He went for the door but had to step around Maxcy, who was sword-fighting himself with a stick in each hand.

"I'm going to get the wagon hitched."

"You're wasting your time."

Stepping out into the hotel hall, Horace rapped on Nathaniel's door.

"Did Augusta throw you out again?"

Pushing past him, Horace went over to a table and spread out the napkin map.

"Look at this!" he said, excited. "There is gold right here, on a big river. Mr. Kelley is walking straight in—but if we cut up from the south, we can get a wagon in there. We'll need to fill half the wagons with feed for our stock, take a shovel for the snow and a saw to cut a road through the trees, but we can do it."

Nathaniel looked unconvinced.

"Why don't we just wait for the snow to melt?"

But Horace was too worked up.

"No, sir. We wait, and there won't be nothing left to find. That weasel George Stevens is getting a party together, right this very moment. The race is on."

Nathaniel looked at the napkin map again.

"I don't see how we can beat them."

But Horace waved his arms around.

"We'll have a head start. He won't expect us to leave in a snow-storm. It'll be days before he realizes we're gone. Besides, come springtime, this whole *town* will be heading up there. All I know is we just can't wait."

CHAPTER 58

SPRING 1892
LEADVILLE

It was when the tea was served that Maxcy realized Wheezy Jones was not going to appear this time. With a growing sense of apprehension, he realized he would be the only male at the tea party. Maxcy silently reproved himself for coming at all. The only reason he went was that it was hosted by the Knights of Labor president's wife. But Sylvander Sawney, like Wheezy Jones and all the other husbands, was absent.

Selma Sawney's sitting room was awash in white. The decorations and ribbon, the cookies and cucumber sandwiches, the doilies and draperies, and scads of flower pots, were all white. To his shock, Baby Doe, Maggie Brown, Janey Campion, and Selma herself were all wearing their *wedding* dresses. To make matters worse, no one had informed him of the color, and he had arrived in a black dinner jacket.

"That is such a lovely dress," Maggie said, gripping Janey's arm. "Isn't this lovely?"

Janey nodded enthusiastically.

"What a wonderful excuse to wear our wedding dresses again—a White Tea! I can't imagine any other occasion, can you? Mine has been locked in a trunk in my boudoir for two decades. It smelled like cedar and it took me all week to air it out."

"Well, it just looks lovely," Maggie assured her, though its seams were clearly under duress.

Handing Maxcy a cup of tea, Selma Sawney looked over his attire with obvious disapproval. Embarrassed, Maxcy said nothing. He started to take a sip, but noticed the hot tea was saturated with cream. He guessed it was meant to make the tea look white, like everything else. Maxcy normally took his tea with sugar, but cream made his throat feel gummy.

"Thank you, ma'am."

He took the smallest of sips.

"Poor Maxcy, all alone," Janey said. "I don't know what happened to my brother; he should have been here already. Perhaps he'll still come, but I doubt it. You must feel so singular."

Baby Doe nibbled on a cucumber sandwich.

"Practicing his juggle, I do hope," she muttered.

Janey looked at her, askance.

"My brother is an *expert*. He's been juggling since he was twelve."

"Perhaps he should have stopped when he *grew up*. That was the most ridiculous thing I've ever seen."

Selma glared at Baby Doe.

"Where's your ninety-thousand-dollar necklace?" she asked bitterly. "You prance around in that gaudy thing every chance you get."

Baby Doe touched her bare neck and glared back.

"Jealous!"

As softly as he could, Maxcy cleared his throat. He wondered how he could sneak into the kitchen for a glass of water. His throat was, indeed, feeling gummy. He looked around the sitting room. Four ladies in their wedding dresses, and here he was, dressed like a groom!

"I feel like Joseph Smith at his nuptials," he joked.

The room got very silent.

"I'm sure you could run off with Selma," Baby Doe said in an icy tone. "Sylvander won't complain. He might even pay you to do it."

Face tightening, Selma took a delicate sip of milky tea.

"Remind me, which wedding dress is this?" she asked, looking Baby Doe up and down. "How many do you own again?"

"More tea?" questioned Maggie Brown to no one in particular.

Feeling horribly out of place, Maxcy eased forward to get up.

"I apologize. Perhaps I should go."

Springing to action, Maggie circled the room with the cookie platter.

"Try one of these," she offered. "They're absolutely delectable. I got them from the bakery on Harrison Street first thing this morning. You know the one, Janey. They make those spectacular croissants. All the pastries they make are spectacular. Wouldn't you say?"

Janey smiled, but her heart was clearly not in it.

"They're lovely, dear."

Stopping in front of Maxcy, Maggie held the tray out with a hopeful expression. He shifted in his seat, hesitating to take one.

He also eyed the door.

"I do apologize, I know this tea has been on the calendar, and I do thank you for the invitation, but I should see if my father needs me."

"But you must try a cookie before you go. They are spectacular."

Then, she took one and pressed it into his palm.

"Tell us about your..." she began, but was too flustered to come up with anything.

Feeling bad for her, and for everything in general, Maxcy tasted the frosting.

"Look! Poor Maggie is ashen," Baby Doe announced, then glared at her nemesis, Selma. "Bravo, dear. You Sawneys really know how to spoil a party."

She extended her leg and kicked Selma, causing her to spill her tea.

Scrambling to her feet, Selma checked for stains.

"You're lucky that didn't get on my dress!"

"If it had, I'm sure the first thing you would do is call for a tea strike. That seems to be the Sawney way."

Baby Doe stood up and smirked in triumph.

But Selma was not quashed.

"The price of silver is dropping like a stone—lower and lower. Much like Horace's standards when he first met you."

Baby Doe slapped her and yelled, "Trollop!"

Selma's eyelids narrowed into seething slits.

"When silver bottoms out and the world goes to heck, the Silver King's mines will be worthless . . . and I can't wait to see you begging in the street for something to eat."

With that, she flung her cucumber sandwich at Baby Doe.

Enraged, Baby Doe launched herself at Selma, but Selma was limber and raced for the kitchen.

CHAPTER 59

"Let's take this conversation to my hotel," Horace suggested. "We can continue over glasses of Old Nectar."

He was standing in John Campion's tiny office on Harrison Street, which was right next door to the bakery that both their wives frequented. The room was cluttered with boxes and paperwork. Mine diagrams were pasted all over the walls.

Campion was seated behind a big oak desk, which took up most of the room. When he heard the comment, he grimaced.

"We ain't doing this at *your* place."

Horace looked offended.

"What's wrong with my parlor? Full service food and drinks."

Campion opened a drawer and took out a pipe and began tamping in tobacco.

"I'm not going to arbitrate a miners' strike sitting in a puddle of leak."

Once his pipe was lit, he glanced at a clock.

"We got time for snacks. You want some knockwurst? I got some in the icebox."

Irritated, Horace sat down. He looked around at all the disarray. It reminded him how disarrayed the silver club party had been. He still could barely believe that Campion had brought in his own brother-in-law to juggle oranges for entertainment.

"You should have paid the bill for some fireworks, and there wouldn't be a strike in the first place. Why in the world would you hire Wheezy Jones? And you let that fellow manage your biggest mine?"

Campion looked sheepish.

"He is my wife's kid brother. I had no choice."

They both sat in silence while the minutes ticked by.

Finally, Sylvander Sawney, president of the Knights of Labor miners' union, appeared in the doorway.

Campion waved him in.

"Syl, come on in here. How's your poor feet? You want some knockwurst?"

But Sylvander was in no mood for small talk.

"What the hell are you two up to? All them workers are about to go on strike, so don't drag this out with tall tales."

Campion puffed on his pipe and nodded agreeably.

"None of us wants to be in here for a month of Sundays, so let's get right to it. Horace, tell the man we meant no harm."

Horace spread his hands in apology.

"I'm not quite sure what happened. We were trying to do a good thing."

"There's a hundred different mines out that door, with a hundred different owners," Sylvander explained. "You can't just decree a wage increase like that. Certainly not without speaking to me first."

"And that's why we're here now. So we can straighten this out."

"I heard rumors of a wage slash. Very persuasive rumors."

Campion slapped the desk with his fist.

"From who?"

But Sylvander simply folded his arms, looking unflappable.

Getting up with a friendly shrug, Horace offered Sylvander his chair.

"We could be eating steak and potatoes at my hotel, but John wanted to meet in this cramped little pigpen."

Campion slapped his desk again.

"I'd fire that bartender if I were you. I knew he was spying on us."

But Sylvander shook his head.

"It wasn't the bartender . . . it was his carriage driver."

Shocked, Horace sat back down.

"What? That's impossible."

"Either way, it was still an ugly lie," Campion stated.

"Back to the point," Horace said. "What about offering everyone a pay raise? We need this silver club to work."

Sylvander's eyes narrowed.

"Why?"

"Politics," Horace said. "The price of silver is a battleground in Washington. They want to shut us all down. You, me, and everybody here. We just want to guide the votes a little bit. Senator Teller himself asked us to get a silver club started."

Campion puffed on his pipe.

"This is bigger than all of us," he added.

Sylvander thought it over, and his face softened.

"I do wish we could offer all the men a raise. Given the hazards and rigors of the job."

"So we are in agreement," Campion said and opened up the icebox. "Let's celebrate."

"But where's that four bucks a day coming from?" Sylvander asked and looked between them. "Your pocket, or his?"

CHAPTER 60

CREEDE

Caked in wet snow, LG and Davis shook out their coats and hats in the foyer of the Denver Exchange.

"At least we got the meat market roofed," LG remarked. "At this rate, we can open up for business in a day or two."

But Davis was already distracted. All the game tables in the Denver Exchange were pushed back against the walls. It was Saturday night, and every Saturday night Bat refereed a boxing match between Billy Woods and a challenger. A snowstorm had moved in, but that hadn't affected the attendance.

"Look at this crowd. Who's Billy Woods gonna pummel tonight?"

Before LG could answer, Bob Ford turned around and scowled.

"Billy's gonna be the one who gets pummeled."

"You're flat wrong. He's the heavyweight champion of Colorado," Davis told him. "I haven't seen him lose once since I been here."

Davis suddenly recognized he was speaking to Bob Ford. With his black eyes and scuffed up skin, he was almost unrecognizable.

"Looks like *you* got pummeled."

Giving them a sneer, Bob looked around the room until he spotted the other fighter.

"There's the pugilist you should put your money on. I certainly am."

They looked across the room and saw who Bob was talking about.

"What's so special about him?" LG asked. "He looks kind of wispy to me."

Bob snickered.

"It's your dumb luck."

Just then, Joe Palmer appeared with two mugs of beer and handed one to Bob.

"Two thousand bucks—I bet it all on Killer Jake Kilrain," he said and slurped the foam. "All these stupid sons of bitches are betting on Billy Woods. We're gonna be rich!"

Bob looked around to see who was listening, but no one was.

"Billy's got the sniffles," he confided to LG and Davis. "Kilrain is gonna whup him senseless."

Joe pinched Bob's elbow, and Bob recoiled, spilling some beer suds down his sleeve.

"You pinched me!"

"Don't blab," Joe muttered and wagged his finger at LG and Davis. "And don't you two go blabbing, neither."

Heading towards the betting table, Davis glanced back darkly.

"I don't trust those two at all."

"I'm placing my money on Billy Woods," LG said.

"Me too."

Calling for quiet, Bat Masterson held up a stopwatch and a revolver.

"Gentlemen," he shouted. "It is time."

Billy Woods stood up and began dancing around, his hands wrapped in leather gloves, pumping the air viciously. His opponent did the same.

"Tonight, it's Billy Woods, heavyweight champ, versus Killer Jake Kilrain."

Everyone in the Denver Exchange cheered.

Bat aimed the gun at the rafters and pulled the trigger.

The two fighters rushed in and began throwing jabs. Each time Billy punched his opponent, the crowd applauded. But Kilrain never went down.

"He can take any punishment Billy can throw at him," Bob Ford said, sidling up next to Davis again.

Joe Palmer came over, too. He was grinning, even though he kept spilling his beer.

Kilrain charged Billy and hit him in the face, causing his nose to spurt blood.

"Did you see that?" Joe said. "A blow on the smeller!"

Bat called the round and the two men retreated to their corners for a quick rest.

"Who did you bet on?" Bob asked Davis.

"Billy."

Cracking up, Bob put his arm around Davis's shoulder.

"You better start drinking. You'll want to be full blown drunk before this is over. It'll be easier to part with your money that way."

Joe burst out laughing.

It was clear they had both taken their own advice and were already quite drunk.

Bat pointed the gun at the roof again and pulled the trigger.

Getting his nose walloped had enraged Billy Woods. He wiped the blood off his face with his glove, and then rushed Kilrain. He began pounding away, and before Bat could call the round, Kilrain fell to the floor.

Billy jumped on him, but Kilrain threw him off and got back up again.

Bat called the round again.

After ten rounds, Killer Jake Kilrain's eyes were so puffed over, he could barely see. Billy Woods, sniffles or not, was aggressive and confident. More than once, Kilrain fell to the floor, but each time managed to rise up before Bat could count him out. Every time he went down, the crowd cheered—except for Bob Ford and Joe Palmer.

"Get up, you fool!" Bob shouted.

Joe stood by, silent now. His smile was gone, and so was his beer.

It was in the eleventh round that Killer Jake Kilrain became careless. Billy dodged every punch he threw, and started hitting the man's kidneys until his gloves sagged. As soon as he dropped his guard, Billy Woods caught him square on the chin. Kilrain collapsed.

It was over.

"Get up!" Bob cried, stunned, and stepped into the ring to yell at him.

But Bat had already called the fight.

Elbowing his way over to the bar, Joe ordered another mug of beer and drank it straight down.

"What was that?" Bob screamed at Kilrain, but the man was unconscious. "Billy was sick as a dog this morning. There's no way he could have won in a square fight."

He glared at Bat Masterson.

"This whole fight was rigged!"

CHAPTER 61

Bursting out of the Denver Exchange, Bob and Joe were too drunk to notice how deep the fresh snow was, or how cold it had become. They were fuming mad. Rushing around in the light of the streetlamps, Bob squinted at shadowy figures roaming the street.

"That damn fight was rigged," he shouted. "But you knew that, didn't you?"

The shadowy figures sensed trouble and steered around them.

"Yeah, you better watch out."

Joe bent over and almost vomited, but somehow held it in.

"We paid good money for that booze," Bob warned him. "Don't you spew it out. Not one drop."

Breathing the cool air deep in his lungs, Joe straightened up. The sky overhead was black, and snowflakes were still falling. He stuck out his tongue to catch some.

"Two thousand bucks, gone up the flume," he lamented, staring up into the night. Not one snowflake landed in his mouth, but instead, they got in his eyes and made him blink.

"He threw that fight," Bob repeated. "That was shady."

Joe was miserable.

"I'm broke. I ain't got enough to buy breakfast."

Whipping around, Bob noticed another dark figure looming nearby.

"That's him . . . Kilrain!" he exclaimed, and yanked out his pistol. "I ought to kill you, you cheat."

He fired at the dark figure—but it turned out to be a wood post.

Joe Palmer thought it was hilarious, and shook his head in disbelief.

"You can't shoot worth a dern. How'd you ever kill Jesse James?"

Clenching his jaw, Bob Ford shook the gun in Joe's face.

"Are you blind? I hit that damn post like a bull's eye."

But Joe just laughed at him, which made Bob even more angry than he already was. With his fingertips, Bob probed his forehead. He suspected the purple vein was sticking up.

Then he pointed his pistol at the nearest street lamp and pulled the trigger.

The glass globe shattered and the flame went out. In the silence of the snowfall, the gunshot seemed extra loud. It rang up and down the street. Some of the shadowy figures turned out to be actual people, who ran away and hid.

Feeling a little better now, Joe drew his own handgun and aimed at a street lamp. He pulled the trigger, but missed. He must have hit a window, because they heard glass tinkle somewhere in the darkness.

"I killed Jesse James!" Bob shouted at the world. "And I'll kill Jake Kilrain, and even Bat Masterson if I need to!"

Strutting through the snow, Bob shot out the lamp that Joe missed. It popped and went out. He cocked the trigger and fired again, destroying a third one, and then a fourth.

The gunshots echoed off the buildings and canyon cliffs.

Chasing after him, Joe pointed his gun at the street lamps, too, and fired until his gun clicked. He fumbled in his pocket for extra bullets.

"I lost two thousand on that fight. I'll shoot them both dead before you do."

Bob turned and spat at him.

"I lost *three* thousand, you fool."

Watching from the safety of Zang's Hotel, Parson Tom Uzzell breathed in relief. In the warm but dimly lit lobby, the preacher took off his old derby hat and used his finger to scoop the snow out of the narrow brim.

Rising up slowly from behind the counter, Zang looked nervous. "They gone?"

Parson Tom smiled gently.

"You are safe, as am I, by the good grace and almighty hand of Providence."

There was a hole in the plate-glass window from one of Joe Palmer's wild shots.

"Lady Luck," Zang said, relieved. "Tent out back is one dollar, one night."

The parson smiled at him again.

He had spent the last two days riding in the back of a hay wagon, covered by a tarp and sneezing regularly. Between the snowstorm and the darkness, and the loneliness of the pine, Parson Tom felt like death was a grand possibility. But the Lord Himself guided the wagon driver directly to the silver camp of Creede, without error or setback. And from what he just witnessed, in terms of debauchery, curses, and violence, the good parson was reminded that Providence had predetermined his safe arrival with a purpose in mind.

"Run ye to and fro through the streets of Jerusalem," he said, quoting Jeremiah. "And see if ye can find a man, if there be any, that seeketh the truth . . . and I will pardon it."

Reaching into his frock, Parson Tom removed three dollar bills.

"I shall stay tonight and the morrow, and depart on the third day."

The Chinaman took the money.

"Tent out back."

"Of course."

Putting his derby back on his head, Parson Tom headed back outside to find the tent. The bark of gunfire continued to pop from somewhere up the dark street. The steep rocky canyon walls flashed momentarily with each gunshot.

"Either it is a well-arranged universe or a chaos huddled together," he said to himself, this time quoting Aurelius. "But still a universe."

CHAPTER 62

Kneeling on his bedding in front of the cast-iron stove, Walker fed more sticks into the fire before settling in for the night.

The snow was coming down hard now.

LG and Davis had been in town for days on end. They were busy constructing the meat market. Walker had never been alone this long in his life. It took some determination not to succumb to fear, but he was determined to prove he was a reliable cowhand. But every night when the shadows fell, the forest became a spooky place.

"I wonder if they're coming back tonight?" he said aloud. "Probably not. Only a fool would be caught out in this storm."

It was something his father, Til, always said. Every time a blizzard rolled through. *Only a fool would be caught out in this storm.*

Their family home in Garo was situated in a wide, gentle valley. Without any trees to break the wind, it could get a little nerve-racking when the weather turned ugly. In high winds, the whole house creaked like it was going to crumble. But it never did. In a blizzard, Walker liked to stare out the kitchen window and watch the bunkhouse and corral vanish in the white haze like a lost city.

He peeked outside again but couldn't see much in the darkness.

A snowdrift had collected against the tent, and it was still coming down.

"This must be what it's like to live in a lost city," he mumbled. "When it gets lost."

Pulling the blanket up to his chin, Walker stared at the canvas ceiling. Orange shadows flickered. Without LG and Davis bickering about something, it was so quiet. He listened hard, but the only thing to hear was the fire crackling. Walker knew the shaggy cattle were happy, but he did worry about the horses—with one exception.

"If the Salty Jackass gets froze to death, I won't shed a tear."

Earlier in the day, before the storm came in, Walker had taken one last ride around the pasture. He noticed the wheel team horses huddled under a big spruce. Then, without warning, the mule pitched and took off. She must have bloated when he saddled her, because the whole rig slid sideways. Walker fell off and tumbled in the soft snow. By the time he got to his feet, the mule was already back at the tent. Walker had to walk all the way across the pasture, and he groused the whole time.

"I hate that dern mule," he said and must have repeated it a hundred times.

To top it off, when he got back to camp, the Salty Jackass took a bite out of his sleeve. It was his nice Sunrise orange shirt. First, she bloated and spun the saddle, and then, after walking all the way across the pasture in the deep snow, she tore up his good shirt.

Everyone he knew talked up mules—how sure-footed they were, how friendly they were.

"Not the Salty Jackass," Walker said and fed some more sticks into the old cast-iron stove. "She's out to bleed me."

Getting up on his elbows, he twisted around so he could reach an old tin candle box. He used it to store important things, like his earnings. He took it out and counted the cash. LG was giving him a dollar a day. So far, he had earned eleven dollars. A new horse would cost him thirty or more. He did the arithmetic in his head and sighed.

"I'm gonna have to put up with that dang mule for a while longer."

He stacked the bills inside the candle box and put it back.

Even though he had eaten supper already, he wished he had something tasty to eat. This was mainly because he messed up the recipe when he tried to make sourdough biscuits. He had never made them before, but the way LG talked, it sounded easy.

"Use the old pickle keg to mix the dough," LG had explained before he left. "Fill it with some water, cut up a potato, and add in a yeast cake with a handful of sugar. Then the flour. Mix it up good and there you go."

Walker did everything just like he was told. But, when he went to check on it, the dough was flat. That was the first clue something was wrong. It was supposed to rise. Undaunted, he went ahead and cooked it in the Dutch oven anyway. But at the first bite, he knew he had fouled up the recipe. Somehow, he must have mistaken a soap cake for a yeast cake. It took a lot of butter and syrup to make those biscuits go down.

It was still silent outside.

There was no wind, just falling snow.

Walker wondered how long Davis and LG would be gone. He wasn't sure how long it took to construct a meat market. As each day went by, he got a little more lonesome.

He also wished he had some candy. The last sweet he'd had was the peppermint stick from the Arbuckles package. It had tasted good, but because it was packaged inside the coffee beans, it tasted like peppermint coffee. While Walker did drink coffee, he always preferred lemonade if he could get it. His mother made the best lemonade in the world. She used sugar, too, and it was always sweet as candy.

The only saving grace was the maple syrup, which was sweet. He put it on everything. Eggs, potatoes, canned corn, canned peaches—and, of course, the soapy biscuits.

His mind often wandered back to Chubb's store in Garo. There was a whole row of jars with nothing but candy. There were peppermint sticks, like the one in the coffee beans, but other flavors, too— blueberry, strawberry, orange, and more. Cherry was his favorite. His least favorite was anise. But if he happened to find some in his present predicament, he would certainly eat it without hesitation.

But there were no sweets hidden in the tent. Walker had already rooted around, just in case there might be. He checked everywhere—in the horse grain, the corn meal sack, and he even double checked the Arbuckles bag, just in case.

To be thorough, he even re-stacked the wood pile, and sifted his fingers through the ash pail. Who knows, maybe LG or Davis had hidden their treats so the other couldn't find them easily. Of course, Walker was partly glad there was nothing to find. What if he did find a secret hiding place full of candy? Would it be considered stealing to eat some without permission? Or would it be considered fair game? Finders keepers?

CHAPTER 63

ROCKY MOUNTAINS

The sky was black and the moon was rising in the east when the train crested the high windswept pass. It was in the new moonlight that Kahopi suddenly spotted the tall rocky pillar to the west, standing out among the most jagged peaks he had ever seen. The pillar rose from among them like a lone sentinel, stretching high into the starry expanse. And in that moment, he felt a deep shudder in his body.

He could not take his eyes from the pillar.

"What is that?" Kahopi asked Greasewood.

"Ah, that is the Lizard Head."

The sense of shock that washed over Kahopi was so strong, he felt he might faint. He swooned and pressed his forehead against the window glass. It was very cool to the touch and the chill made him feel better.

"Are you not well?" Greasewood asked.

It was their turn to sit in the caboose. Earlier, they both climbed into the cupola, for there were two seats. From the cupola windows, they had a clear view of all the train cars and the steam engine. It was like a watchtower. Both Kahopi and Greasewood were mesmerized by the wilderness views, and were nearly lulled to sleep by the rhythmic rocking of the train and the falling darkness.

During the course of the evening, as the train chugged along and slowly gained elevation and took them higher into the backcountry, the four men took turns. Two would remain in the engine cab shoveling coal to keep the train moving, while two would rest in the caboose. For now, White Owl and Bear Claw Lip were up front. From the cupola windows, Kahopi and Greasewood could easily see them. The boiler fire glowed brightly whenever they shoveled in coal.

"I am a member of the Lizard Clan," Kahopi whispered.

Greasewood became solemn.

Taking a pinch of cornmeal from his waist belt pouch, Kahopi held it in his right hand and breathed a silent prayer to the Star-and-Moon Deity for good luck and prosperity.

When he was done, Kahopi glanced over at the Ute, who was also staring at the Lizard Head. Greasewood had a soft smile on his face.

"The Lizard Head means we are almost there," Greasewood said with quiet satisfaction. "The Valley of the Hanging Waterfalls."

Kahopi knew the Utes were seeking their old hunting grounds and had mentioned the Lizard Head was a landmark. But Kahopi had no idea what the Lizard Head was until he saw it. He was certainly not expecting this majestic, soaring rock pillar glowing in the moonlight. Kahopi was stunned. What else could this be, other than a sign that he was in the right place? Most likely, somewhere very close by, Kahopi would find the Whites digging like ants—as the Spider Woman had said, in her cryptic fashion.

The moonlight gave the large rock formation a ghostly appearance. The snow made the terrain seem ghostly, too. Kahopi wondered if this was a vision or a trance. It certainly felt like a dream world. There was a power in the air. He could feel it, quite intensely, and from the way Greasewood reacted to seeing the Lizard Head, it was clear he felt the power, too. Even if they both had different reasons and different paths.

The train slowed as it crested the high windswept pass.

At this elevation, there was only gnarled brush and plenty of snowpack. Bits of ice whirled in the air and shimmered.

Kahopi wondered if this was where the Cloud-People lived. Indeed, he saw some lurking among the peaks, watching the train pass.

Greasewood pointed straight ahead.

"Down there is the river valley. My people's traditional hunting grounds. We have nearly arrived."

This was auspicious. Kahopi was glad that he had not struck out on his own. He was glad he had stayed with these three Utes. He had been worried at first that they were witches, or Two-Hearts. A Two-Heart would have led him *away* from his destination. But their destination was in the same direction as Kahopi's. Their journey was a shared path.

Tawa had led him faithfully.

This realization made Kahopi feel warm inside. If only his brother and uncles and grandfather and aunts, and everyone else back in the village, could be made to understand this one simple truth. For it was they who first nicknamed him Kahopi. *Kahopi* meant *not peaceable*. It was a disgrace to be called such a thing. Even though it was his father who had first done a disgraceful thing—dumping in the *sipapu*. They should have called *him* kahopi.

It was unfair.

The day his father disappeared, Kahopi was still a child, and it was a confusing thing to understand. When he first heard what his father had done, Kahopi thought it was immensely funny. His aunt explained how his father had gotten very drunk during the Soyal ceremony and left a turd in the *sipapu*. Kahopi laughed out loud. His aunt became very stern, but he continued to laugh about it. Then she went and told his uncles, who in turn told his grandfather, and his brother, and his sister's husband—and soon everyone in the village knew. Before he knew it, Kahopi had a reputation as being one of the naughtiest boys.

His relatives began to abuse him, pinching him on the buttocks to remind him not to dump in the sacred places. After meals they would pinch him. When they were out hunting rabbits, they would pinch him. Kahopi soon regretted ever joking about the matter. But they would not let him forget. It got so bad that he took to sleeping alone on the mesa at night.

As the years passed, nothing changed. But Kahopi wanted everything to change.

So when the Spider Woman told him where his father was buried, he knew he had to find him and give him a proper burial. He could guess the Spider Woman, in her anger, did not put a burial ladder in his grave. Perhaps she even locked his coffin or did not put any food inside. If Kahopi could find him and bury him properly, his father could then find his way to the Skeleton House, join his ancestors, and be happy.

If he could accomplish such a great deed, Kahopi knew he would receive a special blessing and his own luck would change. The village would celebrate his return. He would be welcome once again. And he would no longer be called Kahopi.

— PART 9 —

CHAPTER 64

WINTER 1860
COLORADO CITY

The only sound was the wagon wheels crunching through the frosty sage and yucca.

It was after midnight and the stars were brilliant.

Horace was wearing two coats to keep warm. He wished he wasn't sitting alone on the driving bench on such a chilly night. Augusta, though she had a willowy frame, was warm to sit next to—bodily, if not conversationally. But ever since they left Denver, she had remained curled up in the back, buried under a pile of quilts.

Since she was so sick, Maxcy rode with Nathaniel in the little buckboard. Every time Horace glanced back and saw the little boy, he chuckled. Not only was Maxcy bundled up in several coats, but he was also wearing every other spare piece of clothing they owned. Maxcy wore Horace's extra shirts, three scarves, two pairs of mittens, and even one of Augusta's skirts. He looked like a pile of laundry.

They were heading south. In the starlight, the mountains seemed like an immense, forbidding wall on his right.

They saw Colorado Springs, but Horace didn't want to stop until they got to Colorado City. It was a small town, just a handful of structures, but it was closer to where they wanted to be—near a cleft in the foothills. Mr. Kelley's map was crude but clear. Head straight up that pass until they struck a big river, then follow it upstream.

The wagon crested a final hilltop and below, in the starlight, were the rooftops of Colorado City.

Just then, a big white streak zipped across the sky.

"A shooting star," Horace whispered, feeling lucky.

Nathaniel's white pony also saw the shooting star and spooked, taking off at a gallop. As the buckboard shot past, Horace watched it career and bump and jostle down the slope. Finally, it tipped over and shattered into pieces. Nathaniel went sailing, Maxcy rolled like a tumbleweed, and the white pony raced off into the darkness.

The oxen, ever reliable, didn't care. They plodded along like nothing happened.

As quick as he could, Horace parked the wagon and ran down the hill. He spotted Nathaniel panting and bleeding from the nose.

"Where's Maxcy?" Horace asked.

Then he spotted the little boy, wedged up against a cactus. Checking him over, Horace was relieved to find him uninjured. In fact, Maxcy smiled.

"Fun, Poppa!"

The buckboard was in splinters. Angry, Nathaniel grabbed one of the big spoked wheels and spun it.

"If that was a casino wheel, you might have won something," Horace joked.

He looked back up at his own wagon, a silhouette on the hilltop.

"I don't even think she woke up," Horace mentioned, but Nathaniel wasn't feeling chatty.

Horace clapped him on the shoulder.

"Just walk on into town and meet me at the hotel."

Once they all got there, Nathaniel and Horace carried Augusta inside on a litter of blankets. The hotel clerk smiled when he saw them, even though Nathaniel's face was caked with blood and Augusta looked like a perspiring corpse.

"Ah! Here for the soda spring, I see."

"The what?" Horace asked.

"The soda spring," he answered, and then realized Horace did not know what he was talking about. "Why, it's a magical healing spring—just up the road. Folks come with all sorts of ailments. Meningitis, tuberculosis, the heaves, the squirts."

"What do we do there?" Horace asked.

"Soak in it. Drink it. Breathe in the vapors. It's magical."

CHAPTER 65

SPRING 1892
LEADVILLE

It was Sunday morning, and Horace made scrambled eggs to celebrate.

"What a close shave—the strike is off," Maxcy said, who was seated at the little table in the kitchen. "Three cheers for the Silver King."

He poured himself a third cup of coffee as Horace brought the eggs to the table, along with a loaf of bread, a knife, and a jar of pear jelly.

"You like that?" Horace asked. "It's French coffee. It's a little thin."

"Mother hates coffee. She thinks it makes me all jittery. So when I get actually get some, I drink it regardless."

Horace spooned some fresh eggs onto Maxcy's plate. He heard the sound of footsteps shuffling down the staircase and promptly got out two more dishes.

Staggering into the kitchen, Baby Doe looked rumpled and sleepy. She carried Silver Dollar, who looked well rested and spunky, and dropped her in the high chair.

"Necklace!" Silver Dollar shouted at Horace.

"It's gone. But I brought you something much better."

He dug in his pocket and pulled out a silver dollar.

"Necklace!" she shouted again, and hurled the coin into the bowl of yellow eggs.

Horace dug it out of the eggs and licked it off.

"Well, I guess it's mine, then."

Watching the whole conversation with dark, baggy eyes, Baby Doe aimed them at her daughter.

"Shush your little sauce-box. Momma has a headache, and unless *you* want one, you better shush it."

Silver Dollar glared back but did not try her luck.

Maxcy smiled at the little girl.

"Good morning."

Receiving no response from the child, he turned to Baby Doe.

"And good morning to you."

But Baby Doe yawned, folded her arms on the tabletop, and buried her face in her elbow. In a matter of seconds, she had nodded off.

Catching Maxcy's eye, Horace put a finger to his lips.

He spooned scrambled eggs onto a plate for his little daughter and placed it in front of her. The little girl grabbed a fistful and gnawed on it, smacking her lips.

Horace looked at Maxcy and winked.

"A rare moment. One sleeps, one eats, and neither speaks."

Meanwhile, Maxcy took another slow sip from his coffee cup, savoring it.

"You know, Mother only hates coffee because I happen to love it," Horace whispered.

"I thought she hated it because it's a stimulant."

Taking the knife, Horace cut two slices of wheat bread and spread pear jelly on them both. Silver Dollar ceased her egg chewing and her studious little eyes followed the sparkly jelly as he passed one to Maxcy.

"Why don't you stay up here? Forget about Denver. We'll drink stimulants every single day."

Maxcy smiled.

"That would be nice. But I don't know. Mother relies on me."

He started to take a bite of jellied bread, and seeing how intensely Silver Dollar's eyes were focused on it, Maxcy quickly handed it over.

Delighted, she slapped at the eggs until they were all on the floor. Then, with great care, she placed the jellied bread on the plate—and began mashing it into a gooey ball.

"I've built an empire up here," Horace said, still speaking softly. "If you stay, you could learn how to run things. Take over when I pony up at the Pearly Gates. Which could be any day now, considering the volatile nature of my housemates."

To make his argument more enticing, Horace pushed his plate across the table towards Maxcy, offering his own piece of jellied bread.

Maxcy smiled at his father, but then balked as he thought about telling Augusta he would not be returning to Denver.

"If I do, I'll have to let Mother know, of course. What a dreadful conversation."

Horace waved it off.

"Just send her a postal card."

CHAPTER 66

Gazing out the icy window of the Stray Horse Brewery, Big Ed rubbed his eyes with his knuckles. It was early, and Big Ed was not normally an early riser.

"You know what we're gonna do today? Go down the toboggan slide."

He was depressed. The strike had ended before it even began.

It had been a good plan, too. It was hard to imagine how Horace talked his way out of the predicament. Leadville was the mining capital of the West, but ironically, the pay was the worst. The mine managers, owners, and the investors had all gotten rich on the backs of the shaft workers, the trammers, and the pumpmen. Trying to scratch out a living on three bucks a day was basically impossible. Big Ed had been convinced that starting a miners' strike would be like tossing a match into a box of nitroglycerine. The whole town should have exploded.

When he heard the news, it was like someone punched him in the gut.

He was glad his brother wasn't around. He would be very disappointed.

"We can't," Dirty Johns mentioned. "They just shut it down."

"They did what!"

Big Ed felt sick. All he wanted to do was ride the toboggan and feel the wind in his face. He had never ridden it before, and now the one time he wanted to, it was closed.

"How can they shut it down?"

Even though the sun was barely up, Dirty Johns poured them each a tin mug full of beer.

"All the kids have done rode it a thousand times."

Feelings churned inside Big Ed. He felt like he might even cry, which was odd. He hadn't cried since he was a baby. Quickly, to combat the feeling, he drank the whole mug down. It made him feel woozy, but he didn't care.

Suddenly, Big Ed noticed that Dirty Johns was still wearing the expensive boots and trousers.

"Why are you still wearing all that stuff? You're going to get it filthy. Take those boots off! They cost me a hundred dollars."

But Dirty Johns held up his chin.

"It makes me look more respectable. People respect a man in fancy boots."

Big Ed looked him over again, scowling.

"Well, it don't look right."

Then, an idea struck him.

"Nitroglycerine . . . that's what I need."

Unsure what he was talking about, Dirty Johns said nothing.

Big Ed pushed his mug towards Dirty Johns.

"Fill it up."

"You don't want to handle no blasting powder when you're sauced, Ed."

"I said fill it up."

Even though Big Ed glared at Dirty Johns, he was feeling much better. Everyone knew how hazardous mines could be. Why not make things a little more hazardous?

"What would happen if there was a cave-in at the Lucy B.?"

"They'd shut it down, I suppose."

Big Ed chuckled.

"That was my first thought, as well."

Dirty Johns refilled the mug, and then leaned on the bar thoughtfully.

"You know what I think? We should install a Fairy Floss machine in here."

Choking on his beer, Big Ed shook his head in amazement.

"I should never have took you to Haw's party. Look at you! You get a fancy pair of boots and a clean pair of trousers, and now you want a Fairy Floss machine. We'll have to change your name, next. How about Sweet Tooth? We can't be calling you Dirty Johns if you don't wear no dirty johns."

"I thought it was tasty, that's all."

Big Ed reached over the bar and mussed up his hair.

"You're a dope fiend for that Fairy Floss."

"Don't do that!"

Furious, Dirty Johns went over to the water barrel. He dipped his hands in the water, and patted his stringy hair back into place.

"Maybe I'll go work for Horace Tabor," he threatened. "I bet he won't muss my hair or criticize my dress."

Finishing his beer, Big Ed headed over to the coat pegs. The second beer made him feel even more woozy, but that was okay.

"All this fancy talk is going to your head, Sweet Tooth."

"Don't call me names."

As Big Ed put on his coat and gloves, his face got ugly.

"If it's beneath your dignity to work for me, go work for Haw. Drive that fancy carriage around. Iron the wrinkles out of his shirt cuffs. Taste the champagne, make sure it's bubbly enough. But Horace Tabor would never hire someone like you. He knows, like everybody else under the sun, that a hog in a silk waistcoat is still just a hog. This is the best fixed job you'll ever get, so quit whining about that stupid candy machine."

— CHAPTER 67 —

CREEDE

Whenever a blizzard passed through town, Bat knew the Denver Exchange would fill up like a bunkhouse. It didn't help that Joe Palmer and Bob Ford spent half the night shooting up the town. Between the snowfall and wild gunshots, everyone who bet on the fight never went home. They simply bedded down on the floor to wait it out. Bat didn't even bother trying to put the tables back into place.

Billy Woods stretched out behind the bar. Killer Jake Kilrain slept in the storeroom. Bat wanted the two of them as far apart as possible in case they decided to trade boxing gloves for six-guns.

At first, Bat intended to smuggle Kilrain out the back as soon as the fight was over, but by then the snow was too deep. Now, seeing it in the morning light, Bat wondered if he should go ahead and try to get a wagon through. The man was smashed up pretty bad and needed proper doctoring, but there was no physician in Creede.

Crossing carefully, so as not to step on the inert, Bat went into the kitchen to start brewing coffee. He filled up every water pot he could fit on the woodstove. While the water was heating, Bat went over to the big front windows. All the street lamps as far as he could see were shattered.

"Who won?" Bob Ford asked in a groggy voice.

Bat turned around, and spotted him propped up against a brass spittoon.

"You did."

Bob held his head in his hands but did not reply. Instead, he pressed his foot against Joe Palmer and shoved until Joe woke up.

Coming over, Bat knelt down.

"Is it all coming back yet?"

Sitting up and kneading his ear tenderly, Joe squinted in discomfort.

"I think someone slugged me."

Bat nodded.

"When you boys finally ran out of bullets, I went out and put a stop to it."

"Did you have to slug me?" Joe asked.

"I didn't have to," Bat replied. "But it felt right."

He smiled at them. It was a treat seeing Bob Ford so nauseous and immobile.

"Water's got to be boiling by now."

He disappeared into the kitchen again.

Getting up slowly, Joe put his hand against the wall for balance. He took a couple deep breaths to clear his head. Reaching down, he grabbed Bob by the arm and hauled him to his feet, and they both hobbled over to the nearest table.

LG snorted and his eyes flicked open. He sat up and looked around.

"Davey, wake up."

"I ain't asleep."

Bat came back out of the kitchen, bringing a coffee pot and several ceramic cups. LG and Davis crawled over to the table and watched as he poured.

"Careful, fellas, it's hot."

"I appreciate the warning," Joe said. "Though I don't recall a warning before you slugged me."

Other sprawled gamblers began to moan and roll around.

The scent of fresh coffee even roused Billy Woods, but just for a moment. He poked his bruised face up from behind the bar, long enough to see where he was, and sank back down.

Then the front door opened, and Parson Tom Uzzell came inside. He had to step over a snow drift in the doorway. It was a tall drift, but Parson Tom was tall. Seeing all the drunkards lying on the floor, except the Corner Pocket Drunk who had passed out on the pool table, he went straight to Bat Masterson—the only upright man among them.

Noticing the Bible in his hand, Bat looked him over in surprise.

"Are you in the right place?"

"The right place at the right time. My name is Parson Tom. This being Sunday, may I sermonize your patrons?"

"If you think it might help."

Bat grabbed an empty bourbon bottle. Using it like a gavel, he rapped loudly on the bar, eliciting a chorus of doleful groans.

"Gentlemen, this kind man is going to preach the gospel. Hats off!"

Then, he looked at Parson Tom apologetically.

"The closest thing to a pulpit we got is the pool table."

But the Corner Pocket Drunk was still on the table, and so was a smear of urine on its velvety surface.

"This will do fine," he said, remaining where he was.

Bat nodded, took off his bowler hat, and took a seat against the wall.

Parson Tom cleared his throat and held up his Bible.

"Examine yourselves, whether ye be in the faith, or whether ye be reprobates."

Thumbing open the Scriptures, he peeled back the thin pages, searching for a particular passage. As he did, Bob buried his face in his hands.

"Lord have mercy," he said. "Preaching gives me a headache."

The parson cleared his throat again.

"What man of you, having a hundred sheep, if he loses one of them, doth not leave the ninety and nine in the wilderness, and go after that which is lost, until he finds it?"

LG raised his hand like a schoolboy.

"I know a man who lost all one hundred. Due to hailstones the size of a cue ball."

CHAPTER 68

Parson Tom gazed around the room. Mostly everyone had fallen back asleep. He decided to try a second parable.

"Perhaps you've heard that a certain man had two sons."

Bob Ford groaned and slapped the tabletop.

But Parson Tom was not deterred.

"The younger son took his inheritance and squandered it on strong drink and riotous living. But then, there arose a mighty famine in the land. He found labor in the fields feeding swine, and he yearned to fill his belly with the husks the swine consumed."

When he heard that, Joe Palmer perked up.

"Me too. I lost all my money on booze and a bad wager. I ain't got enough left to buy breakfast."

He peered under the table, looking for husks or anything else edible.

"Finally, he came to himself," the parson continued. "'How many of my father's hired servants have bread to spare?' he said. 'I will go to my father, and say unto him, I have sinned against heaven and before thee.' So he arose, and went home, but when he was yet a great way off, his father saw him and had compassion. He ran to him and kissed his cheek. 'Bring forth the best robe, and put a ring on his hand, and shoes on his feet. And bring hither the fatted calf, and kill it. Let us eat and be merry, for this son of mine was dead, and is alive again. He was lost, and is found.'"

Having heard enough, Bob stood up and hurled his coffee cup at the parson, but missed.

"This is the most interminable lecture I've ever been subjected to."

Deciding to wind it down, Parson Tom spread his hands to give a benediction.

"According to the Proverbs, 'Good understanding giveth favor, but the way of the transgressor is hard.' Let us now sing that great hymn, Rock of Ages."

Joe turned to Bob.

"Did you hear that? I think I am a transgressor. That may be why I feel so bleak."

Sinking back into his chair, Bob wagged his finger in Joe's face.

"You feel bleak 'cause you lost all your money and you're dead broke."

The parson began singing the first stanza. Feeling embarrassed, Joe wished he knew the words. He tried to guess what they were and sang along.

But Bob was appalled.

"You sound like a cow giving birth."

When the hymn was finished, Bat stepped forward and stood next to Parson Tom.

"That was a fine sermon, wasn't it, boys? And to show our gratitude, we're going to pass the hat."

He went around the room, holding his bowler upside down. Those who were awake rummaged through their pockets, dropping in crumpled bills and sticky coins. Bat came over and gave it to Parson Tom, who accepted it gratefully.

"This is a wonderful offering, sir. It will be used to build a church. God bless you all."

Crossing the room, he stepped over the drunkards of the Denver Exchange, opened the door, and vanished in the bright morning light.

After he was gone, Bob Ford guffawed.

"The fatted calf sure got the rotten end of that deal."

Joe was feeling guilty. The parson's story might as well have been about him. He had bet all his money on Killer Jake Kilrain and lost it all. And now, here he was, penniless. Unable to even buy a strip of bacon. The mere mention of swine made Joe yearn for bacon.

"How much was in that hat?" he called to Bat.

Walking over, Bat shrugged.

"I can't say for sure."

"Well, whatever it was, it wasn't enough."

Seeing that Joe was feeling bad about the money, Bat sat down at the table.

Bob gave him a dirty look.

"That fight was rigged," he muttered.

He got up and went to the bar.

Ignoring the comment, Bat smiled at Joe in a fatherly way.

"What do you want to do about it?"

"He deserves double what he got," Joe replied, massaging his tender ear. "Let's double it."

After giving it some thought, Bat shrugged.

"We can't double it if we don't know how much it was to start with."

Feeling even more guilty, Joe laid his head on the table.

"We just shortchanged a preacher," he moaned. "That has got to be a sin for sure."

Bat put a hand on his shoulder.

"Why don't you just go ask him how much, so we can double it."

Sitting up straight, Joe looked mortified at the suggestion.

"I can't do that! Besides, he's probably halfway to Telluride by now."

Still lying in a puddle of his own urine, the Corner Pocket Drunk suddenly woke up.

"That preacher is staying at Zang's Hotel—in the tent out back," he said in a surprisingly lucid voice, then passed out again.

"Here's what you do," Bat told Joe. "Wait until it gets dark. After the parson says his prayers, sneak in there and count the money. Once we know how much it is, we'll pass the hat again."

CHAPTER 69

Someone must have told Zang that his tent was poorly staked, because when Joe tried to crawl underneath the sidewall, the canvas was tight as a drum.

"Of *course*," he muttered. "Now that I don't live here, Zang fixes the dern tent."

Joe was alone in the darkness, lying flat in the snow. He tried to wiggle his way underneath the tent wall but couldn't do it.

Getting to his feet, Joe jammed his hands in his coat. He had lost his gloves. They were probably underneath one of the game tables in the Denver Exchange. Or maybe Bob had played a trick on him while he was passed out and dropped them into the spittoon. That sounded like something Bob would do.

As expected, the wind was screaming down the snowy slope behind the hotel, peppering him with ice crystals. His face and hands were red as tomatoes.

"I've had all of that wind I can take."

In his boot was a gutting knife. He always kept it hidden there, in case he got into a fight and dropped his gun. He took it out and cut a big slice in the canvas.

Crawling inside, Joe was relieved to get out of the wind.

It was very dark, and it was nearly impossible to see.

Joe held his breath and remained motionless.

As his eyes adjusted to the dim light, he saw Parson Tom sound asleep on a cot. The man's breathing was slow and deep. Joe waited patiently to make sure. It also gave him more time for his eyes to work better. He spotted the parson's frock hanging on a peg, along with his round derby hat. Sneaking over, he reached in the coat pocket, but it was empty!

Joe felt sick.

There was now no question—only a true transgressor would cut his way into a preacher's tent.

If the parson woke up, Joe could say he had simply snuck in to count the money. After all, it was the truth. But, more likely, the parson would think Joe was robbing him. A genuine hellfire curse would be his reward.

There was a crate next to the cot.

Joe spotted the parson's pants, and underneath the pants, Joe saw the Bible. What better place to conceal church money?

So he tiptoed over and, with great care, lifted the pants so he could get at the Bible. As he did, he heard a jingle in the pocket.

It was the money!

The parson heard the jingle, too, and his breathing stopped.

Joe held his own breath, and felt a chill run down his spine.

He had to get out of there! There was no time to count the money. Dashing through the slit in the tent wall, Joe ran as fast as he could. It was only when he got to the Denver Exchange, that he realized he was carrying the parson's pants.

"Oh, Lord!" Joe exclaimed.

He stopped and looked down the street at Zang's Hotel. Should he go back?

The wind picked up, and his face and hands began to sting again. There was no time to think anymore. He had to get inside where it was warm. Feeling terrible, Joe flung open the door and went inside.

"What do you got there?" Billy Woods shouted from the bar. His eyes were a little swollen, and everything looked blurry.

Bat, who was sponging soapy water all over the pool table, looked up and saw who it was.

"Did you count it?"

"No," Joe replied, and held up the pants. "But the money is in here."

Bat dropped the sponge in shock.

"You stole the man's pants?"

Billy Woods started laughing, but then pressed his hand on his ribcage and gasped in pain.

Walking over to the bar, Joe started to scoop the bills and coins from the pockets, but his fingers were too cold to work properly. So he left the parson's pants on the bar top, and went over to the woodstove.

Drying his hands on a towel, Bat and Billy sorted the money and added it up.

"Seventy-five even," Bat announced.

Jeff Argyle, manning his station at the faro table, looked shocked.

"You better take those pants back."

"I can't go back there," Joe stated. "He'll think I was a robber and curse me for sure."

Joe didn't know what to do. It seemed like everything he did went wrong.

Meanwhile, Bat climbed up on the bar to get everyone's attention.

"Get out your money. We're taking up a collection for Parson Tom and I expect everyone here to pitch in."

But Jeff Argyle was skeptical.

"It don't matter how much money you raise now," he said, staring at Joe. "You're going to burn in hell."

CHAPTER 70

ROCKY MOUNTAINS

No one seemed to be inside. There was no smoke coming from the chimney. The pole corral had no stock in it and though there were many tracks to be seen, none were fresh. Several hours had passed as they watched the log cabin and no one had come or gone or made any noise.

Even so, Kahopi wanted to wait to see for sure.

"I'm going in," Bear Claw Lip grumbled. "It's too cold to be sitting out here for no reason."

Rushing the front door, the Ute rammed it with full force. However, the door was very stout.

Kahopi, Greasewood and White Owl remained huddled behind a line of frozen willow bushes. They watched, peering through the network of thin reddish branches.

Rubbing his shoulder, Bear Claw Lip stalked back and forth in clear frustration. Then he went around the cabin to see what he could see. Snow had sloughed off the roof and formed big crusty snowdrifts, and there were many icicles on the eaves. There was a window, but it was very tiny.

Going back to the door, he beat on it several times with his fist. Finally, Bear Claw Lip glared at the willows.

"You three look like a bunch of little bunnies," he shouted.

Greasewood rose up.

"I guess that racket you made would have stirred up anyone sleeping inside."

Boldly, he approached the cabin and rattled the door latch.

"If we can get in there, we can light a fire in that fireplace and get warm."

Kahopi shivered. He was very cold. It never got so chilly down on the mesa. A warm night in this cabin sounded very nice. The train caboose had been plenty warm. He was sad they had to abandon it, but when the boiler ran out of water the train was no good anymore.

Running to the nearest tree, Bear Claw Lip grabbed onto a long limb and bent and heaved at it. It bowed and snapped with a loud *crack*, as loud as a gun.

The cabin was a small structure. It was made of thick pine logs that were chinked together with a hard white substance. Bear Claw Lip ran over to the window and, using the thick branch like a spear, launched it straight through the glass. The window shattered.

"None too soon," he said, triumphant. "Look, here comes the storm."

The sky had been dark and threatening all day. They never saw the sun once.

This fact made Kahopi very nervous. Not seeing the sun was bad luck. All day, he felt uneasy, as if something was not right. Now, quite suddenly, thick snowflakes dropped from the sky and fluttered all around them and the wind picked up and the snow stuck in his hair and caught on his eyelashes and he had to squint.

Bear Claw Lip examined the broken window. The frame itself was not very large. Also, the glass had shattered into plates with sharp edges.

"You are small," he said to White Owl. "Crawl in there and un-latch the door. And hurry up!"

With great care, the boy began worming through the window frame.

"What is taking so long?"

Impatient, Bear Claw Lip grabbed the boy's ankles and shoved him inside. White Owl disappeared, and they heard him land on the floor. They also heard him yelp in pain.

Greasewood was quite concerned.

"What happened? Are you hurt?"

But there was no response.

Meanwhile, Bear Claw Lip ran around and banged on the oak door.

"Hurry up!" he shouted.

But there was no response.

The snow fell harder and harder, and Kahopi became very ner-vous. It was hard to remain calm with the Cloud-People so angry. But he was also wary about the strange little cabin.

"It is very dark inside," he whispered. "Perhaps an evil spirit was hiding in there and attacked him."

They all grew quiet and listened.

The snowflakes continued to swirl.

"Look!"

Greasewood pointed at the bottom of the window frame. One shard of glass was red with fresh blood. He turned and frowned at Bear Claw Lip.

"You shoved him, and now he is cut."

Unconcerned, Bear Claw Lip merely shrugged.

"It's just a little slice," he said, then hollered in the dark window, "Open that door!"

"How do you know it's just a little slice? It could be a big slice."

They heard White Owl moan and knock something over. When he got the front door open, they all rushed inside to get out of the snow and wind. Kahopi came last, still cautious about evil spirits that might be lurking in the dark.

"Are you alright?" Greasewood asked, and studied the boy in the dim light.

"I think so."

There was blood dripping from his forearm and legs.

"That bed is mine," Bear Claw Lip called out.

There was a lantern on the table as well as a box of matches. Fumbling with a match, he got the lantern lit while Greasewood helped the boy staunch the bleeding.

At last, Kahopi relaxed. They were inside, and he did not see any evil spirits. The lantern light was bright, and made him feel safe.

"Let's get a fire going," Greasewood said, having finished with the boy's bandages.

There was a fireplace in the back wall. As Greasewood began picking through a dry woodpile in the corner, Bear Claw Lip rooted around the cabin.

"Look what I found," he said, examining jars on the kitchen dresser. "Peanuts and coffee."

Then he spotted something else, on the top shelf. There was a glass bottle hidden among the crockery. He reached up and grabbed it.

"What does this say?"

Kahopi came over and examined the label.

"*For headache, foul breath, no energy, constipation. Prickly Ash Bitters.*"

"Must be a decrepit old woman who lives here," Bear Claw Lip said. Then he pointed at Greasewood. "You better drink some of this—quick."

Ignoring him, Greasewood knelt and blew softly on the flames until a good fire flared up.

Hobbling over to the dresser, White Owl grabbed the peanut jar. He took it over to a chair by the fireplace and ate quietly, staring into the yellow flames.

Kahopi was still very chilled. There was a sheepskin blanket folded up on a bench, so he picked it up. Beneath it was a new coat!

The coat was warmer than his thin old jacket, so he put it on. Feeling weary, he curled up on a rug near the fire, pulled the blanket over his shoulders, and fell into a deep sleep.

Immediately, Kahopi began to dream.

The cabin went pitch black. Kahopi sensed a presence standing over him. He quivered, nervous it was an evil spirit. In the hearth, a new fire suddenly roared to life with strange green-and-blue flames that illuminated the entire room. Careful not to move, Kahopi rolled his eyes the best he could and saw Bear Claw Lip sound asleep on the bed, and White Owl and Greasewood curled up in sheepskin blankets on the floor nearby.

There was someone standing right over him!

Kahopi saw it was a tall man wearing a large ceremonial mask and costume. He had long black hair that flowed down past his shoulders. A prayer feather was tied in his hair, and the man wore a dancing costume and a sash wrapped around his waist. He also had bracelets and necklaces—all decorated with beautiful turquoise beads.

"Sit up and come with me," the man said. "We must travel now, before the sun rises, so I can show you something. I am your Guardian Spirit and I have been protecting you from evil all your life. I will guard you on this journey as well."

Getting to his feet, Kahopi followed the man outside. The moon was high and bright and the sky was clear of any clouds and the stars were brighter than he had ever seen. They began walking west and suddenly Kahopi no longer felt the ground because he was floating.

Swooping above the treetops, they flew over the shadowy forest and over the river and railroad tracks towards the tall, jagged peaks, which shined in the silver light. They picked up speed and shot across the sky like an arrow.

Kahopi suddenly spotted the tall rocky pillar that he had first seen from a distance the other day—the Lizard Head. That was where they were headed. Kahopi was pushed up through the air all the way to the top of the pillar. It was exhilarating to watch the rock pass by silently as he was carried straight up its steep sides. Together, they alighted on the top, which was clear of snow and flat like a table. A large circle of corn-meal was sprinkled around the outer edge.

His Guardian Spirit took out a bone whistle and blew it. The sound was loud and shrill.

The stars twinkled and blazed, and Kahopi heard a great clap like thunder in the sky and suddenly a man appeared on the Lizard Head with them. He was small but serene and strong to behold.

"This is the Star-and-Moon Deity," his Guardian Spirit told him.

A second time, he blew the bone whistle, and another man with wings flew up and stood by them. Kahopi knew it was the Hawk Deity and needed no introduction.

"We have been expecting you," the Star-and-Moon Deity said. "There is much to see and we must hurry."

Feeling something he couldn't see lift him up and carry him, Kahopi followed the others as they stepped off the Lizard Head and traveled through the air. His stomach fluttered the moment they left the pillar, for the ground was far, far below, and if he were to fall it would surely mean death.

The Star-and-Moon Deity led the way and together they floated over the rolling hills and forests, swept along in the wind. There were tall mountains everywhere and looking back, Kahopi tried to spot where the cabin might be. But all he saw in that direction were dark trees stretching away.

The Lizard Head was soon behind them, now just a silhouette against the starry sky.

"Look down there. What do you see?"

Kahopi looked. There was a long narrow valley running east and west, and at its eastern end it ended in a bowl surrounded by tall mountain ridges and cliffs. An icy river stretched along the valley bottom, glittering in the bright starlight.

"I see a large village in the bowl beneath the cliffs. I see a big waterfall pouring off the cliff right above the village. And all along the river, men move about in droves."

"This is the Valley of the Hanging Waterfalls," his Guardian Spirit explained. "All of these people are Two-Hearts—witches and sorcerers who steal the lives of their relatives and neighbors so that they may live longer and postpone their own death."

"What are they doing here?" Kahopi asked.

"They are holding an underworld convention," the Star-and-Moon Deity revealed.

Kahopi spotted a black crow. It circled the village in silence, watching the Two-Hearts go about their business.

Then Kahopi noticed some of the Two-Hearts were scratching around at the base of the cliff near the waterfall.

"This is a terrible lot—mean and dangerous," the Star-and-Moon Deity observed. "But from way up here in the sky, don't they look like harmless little ants?"

Then Kahopi awoke with bells ringing in his ears.

— PART 10 —

— CHAPTER 71 —

SPRING 1860
THE SODA SPRING

"I wonder if Gussie feels good enough to bake some bread tonight?"

The wagon creaked along.

Horace lay sprawled in the wagon bed, nursing his sore hands. It had been a long day of tree cutting, and they were almost done chopping a road up the mountain pass. His palms were raw, and he poked at a blister flap.

"If she does, I hope she makes cinnamon bread—like she did back in Kansas," Nathaniel said from the driving bench. "I've had dreams about how tasty it is. And then I wake up, and all we got is jerky."

The clear sky was changing colors from blue to orange. At dusk, the forest became dim and shadowy, but peaceful. Horace loved to watch the sun go down in the mountains. It was different than sundown on the plains.

Nathaniel twisted around and looked back up their new road.

"How much further till we reach Kelley's Diggings?"

Horace thought about it.

"I'd say another day or two and we'll be over the pass. But on the other side is the Bayou Salado, whatever that is. Kelley said all the old trappers used to go up there in the old days."

"What were they trapping? Alligators?"

Horace shrugged.

"I don't know."

"I grew up in Tallahassee, and I know what a bayou is. It's a swamp full of alligators."

Sitting up straight, Horace grabbed the shotgun. Peering into the shadows, he looked at the dark forest with new eyes.

"Well, I hope you are wrong about that."

By the time the wagon rolled into their camp at the soda spring, the first stars were twinkling. Augusta was hunched over the fire with a stick, pushing around the embers. As soon as she saw them, she crossed her arms and scowled.

"You fools took the shotgun."

Horace slid out of the wagon, and began taking off his boots and socks to check for more blisters.

"You sound like your old self again," he told her. "That magic water sure did its work."

She pointed a finger at the soda spring.

"There were some dirty Utes here this afternoon."

"Lots of folks come for a bath, Gussie—injuns too," Horace assured her.

He looked over at the spring gurgling in the gloom, but no one was there.

Sliding slowly down off the bench, Nathaniel yawned and stretched.

"Remember what that fellow at the hotel said?" he mentioned. "They think the bubbles are their Great Spirit. They come to hear what he has to say."

Augusta trained her steely-eyed glare on him.

"Is that right? Well, their Great Spirit must be as generous as he is conversational. He gave them a fine looking white pony. It looked a lot like yours."

Nathaniel, in mid-yawn, froze.

"They got my horse?"

Whipping around, Augusta jabbed her finger into Horace's chest.

"And they snuck off with my cinnamon bread."

Nathaniel could not believe all the bad news he was hearing at once.

Alarmed at the situation, Horace grabbed the shotgun again, but Augusta merely rolled her eyes.

"Oh, Horace, it's over. They're gone. All day long, they lazed about the soda spring and ogled me. Now I know why. What a bunch of sneaks."

"Well, it ain't my fault."

She jabbed him again.

"If I had that shotgun, they would have minded their manners."

Propping the weapon against the wheel, Horace took off his hat and blotted his sweaty forehead with a handkerchief. He suddenly felt irritated. After spending days on end sawing down trees to make a road to make traveling safe for her, here she was complaining about a missing loaf of bread.

"Well, without it, all we'd have for defense was the whipsaw. What if a bear tried to eat us? Or an alligator?"

She gave him her most corrosive frown.

"What if them injuns had murdered me? And what about Maxcy? What if they murdered Maxcy?"

His eyes went to her handbag.

"But you got those two fancy pistols—two secret pistols I never knew about."

Shocked, Augusta took a step back.

"Don't bring my father into this! You have always despised him, Horace. And you always look for reasons to speak lowly of him. What an ugly thing to say."

CHAPTER 72

SPRING 1892
LEADVILLE

At 11:30 p.m. the night shift came up for dinner. When no one was around, Big Ed slipped inside the shaft house at the Lucy B. Mine.

"Don't you ring that bucket bell," he hissed at Dirty Johns.

"I ain't gonna ring no bell."

As carefully as he could, Big Ed set a box of Giant Powder in the bucket and crawled in with it. He held his breath, waiting to see if it was going to explode or not. When it didn't, he nodded silently at Dirty Johns, who pulled the machine lever, activating the cable spool.

With a jarring clunk, the bucket began to lower, and Big Ed gaped in terror.

"*Easy!*" he whispered at Dirty Johns before he lost sight of him.

He wore a candle affixed to his hat. In the yellow pall of the flame, he could see the timbers that lined the shaft. As the bucket descended, Big Ed tried counting the tiers as a distraction, but he couldn't stop thinking about the nitroglycerin between his ankles.

The ride down seemed to take an eternity.

Big Ed held his breath until he got dizzy, and tried to hold as still as possible. He knew all the stories. Blasting powder was not very stable. Even the dynamite factory, which made the powder, had blown itself up on several occasions. He was no chemist, but Big Ed knew a soft touch was absolutely vital.

With another jarring clunk, the bucket came to rest at the bottom of the shaft.

Looking around, Big Ed saw no one. He was relieved. The whole night crew was up on the surface taking a meal, and he wasn't sure how much time he had.

Carefully, he lifted the box of Giant Powder.

Snow was falling in big white flakes up on the surface. But below ground, in the tunnel, it was surprisingly warm.

There were several drift tunnels leading in different directions, and they were all pitch black. Each one had a set of tram rails extending off into the darkness. There were ore carts, too, obviously abandoned at the dinner bell.

"This must be the path down to Hades itself," he muttered, feeling the hair on his neck rise.

Not sure which passage to take, Big Ed chose the one in the middle.

The candle on his hat lit up the darkness and made the rock walls glitter. With every step, shadows jumped and dodged around him.

He heard water dripping and trickling, echoing, and his footsteps seemed very loud in the stillness.

Going deeper into the drift shaft, Big Ed noticed the ceiling getting lower. He passed several side tunnels, which had been filled in with rubble. Going farther, he passed another one, barely big enough for a man to squat in. The entrance was framed in with timber, and there was a mechanical water pump on the ground, humming.

He could hear water gurgling through a series of iron pipes that ran out of the hole and then alongside the rails to a sump pit. Just a stone's throw past this small side tunnel, the main tunnel came to an end. Several pickaxes were lying on the ground, as well as a sledgehammer and a spike.

"Good a place as any," he whispered, and set the box of Giant Powder on the ground among the tools.

Feeling his neck hairs tingle again, Big Ed took a deep breath to calm his fears. He had a long fuse coiled around his shoulder, and when he tried to set it up, he noticed his hands were trembling.

The hum and trickle of the water pump was noisy, but it also made him feel less alone.

"Better you than me," he told the pump.

Uncoiling the fuse, Big Ed stretched it out as far as it would go. Then he pressed one end, with a deft touch, into the nitroglycerin. As he was kneeling, hot wax leaked off his hat and burnt the back of his hand. He gasped, but kept his hands steady.

Backing up, slowly, he sighed in relief and wiped the sweat off his forehead.

"I'm going to get dead drunk blue after this."

He pulled out a box of matches, swallowed, and then carefully struck a match. He watched it flare for a couple quick seconds, then it evened out into a nice simple yellow flame.

"Here we go."

He knelt down and did it.

The fuse caught, like a sparkler, and Big Ed knew the clock was ticking.

"Fire in the hole," he mumbled, then turned around and ran for it.

He dodged ore carts, and leapt over tools and pieces of lumber and rock.

Wavy, flickering shadows were everywhere, making him feel a little wobbly and he kept bumping into the walls. But he kept moving and leapt into the bucket.

"Now, Dirty Johns!" he half-shouted, half-hissed. *"Go, go, go!"*

Instantly, the thick steel cable vibrated and the bucket glided upwards.

CHAPTER 73

The alarm bell at the Lucy B. Mine rang and rang, waking up half of Leadville. Horace's house was close by, and he sprung out of bed when he heard it.

"What's happened?" Baby Doe called out, startled from her sleep.

"Nothing good, I can tell you that."

Pulling on his trousers and boots, Horace raced down the staircase and grabbed his coat. As he threaded his arms through the sleeves, he glanced out the windows to see what he could see.

"All the lights are on at the Lucy B.," he shouted up the stairs. "I'm heading over—you stay here!"

He heard Silver Dollar wake up and start to cry.

Clutching his coat, Horace didn't waste time with the buttons. The Lucy B. was right up the street and it only took him a few moments to get there. Men were racing around, shouting and hollering, and the bell continued to clang.

Rushing into the shaft house, Horace spotted Wheezy Jones, who looked like a treed cat.

"There was an explosion," Jones explained. "The whole thing is flooding."

Horace surveyed the room while Jones babbled about the dinner fare.

"We were all eating dinner. It was sourdough bread, bologna, and cheese. And my sister had sent over a bunch of vanilla cookies with frosting."

The bucket was down, and men were gathered around the shaft, peering nervously into the dark void.

"Where's John?" Horace asked.

"Mr. Campion? I ain't seen him."

Horace went over and elbowed his way in so he could look down the shaft.

"Turn on the lights so they can see down there!"

"There ain't none. All we got is candles."

"You mean to say Campion is too cheap to install electrical lights down in the tunnels?"

But Wheezy Jones's eyes seemed to glaze over.

The cable reeled in and brought the bucket back to the surface. A man leapt out, looking grim.

"Boss!" he said, urgently pulling at Jones's jacket. "Boss! The center line caved in, and the water's rushing in fast! Ore carts are flipped over and bobbing around like corks. The tram rails are all twisted. And the pumpmen are too scared to even go down there."

"*Tommyknockers,*" Wheezy Jones whispered to Horace.

Horace tore off his hat and swatted the wall.

"This ain't ghosts, I can promise you that. And it ain't just bad luck, either."

But Wheezy Jones still had that glazed look.

"It ain't ghosts!" Horace repeated.

At that moment, Maxcy appeared in the doorway. Horace spotted him and waved.

"We have a saboteur," Horace informed him.

"What can I do?"

Horace put his arm around his shoulder and pivoted to face Wheezy Jones.

"Did you hear what my son just said?" he asked the befuddled mine manager. "*What can I do,* he says. That is a pragmatic attitude. One which you seem to lack."

"The frosting was vanilla," Wheezy Jones said again.

"Maxcy, run over to John Campion's home and see if you can rouse him from his precious dreams. This is his mine, his problem."

Spinning on his heel, Maxcy trotted through the door and into the night.

"What is your name?" Horace asked the miner who had come up from the shaft.

"I'm only a trammer, Mr. Tabor. Isn't this awful, sir?"

"Yes it is. Now, where is the telephone?"

The trammer led him into Wheezy Jones's office. The telephone was sitting on the desk with a piece of wool in the mouthpiece to keep the diaphragm from freezing up. Horace picked up the earpiece, rang the bell button to wake the switchboard operator, and leaned close to talk.

"Hello? It's me, Horace Tabor. Would you ring the Matchless Mine? I need to speak to the Major immediately."

He nodded to dismiss the trammer, who ran off.

"Major!" he shouted, through the wool. "I need you to bring all the reliable pumpmen you can find over to the Lucy B., right away. It's flooding, and it may be too late already."

Horace hung up the earpiece and went over to the doorway to watch the ruckus. The miners were arguing about who should go down—if anyone. Wheezy Jones stood off to one side, looking limp.

Horace thought about it. Who *was* the enemy? Someone was desperate to derail the silver club meeting. And when that failed, they outright sabotaged the Lucy B. Horace needed the entire city functioning like a well-oiled machine when it came time to vote in a new president of the United States. The miners huddled around the bucket, arguing about tommyknockers and bad luck—but Horace knew it was neither.

Just then, Maxcy appeared with John Campion.

"Well done, my boy," Horace said. "Even under pressure, a Tabor gets results."

Campion looked around in confusion, clearly frustrated at being awoken after bedtime. His normally pointy goat-beard was smooshed flat.

"What is going on here?"

"Your mine has been blown to hell," Horace told him. "And you slept right through it."

Unamused, Campion pointed at Wheezy Jones.

"Get over here!"

But Horace yelled, too.

"Do not come over here!"

Then he spoke in a rational and calm voice.

"The cavalry is on its way. The Major is bringing over my best engineers and pumpmen. We'll see if this thing can be saved."

Finding his biggest producing mine flooded, John Campion's first impulse was to fire Wheezy Jones. But Janey would not like that.

CHAPTER 74

CREEDE

While LG shoveled snow off the meat market roof in the morning sun, Davis walked to the train depot to check the mail.

"What a weekend," he said when he saw the station agent. "How about you? Any excitement?"

"The missus baked an angel food cake. And then a bobcat killed our chickens."

Davis went over to the blazing potbelly stove to warm up.

"Now we don't got no eggs," the station agent complained. "Which is bad when it comes to baking cake."

"That is unfortunate."

"Yes, it is. She bakes an excellent angel food."

The station agent, like usual, was sitting behind his desk. He held up the latest edition of the *Creede Candle*.

"It says here some nitwit stole Parson Tom's pants last night. There was seventy-five dollars in the pockets."

Davis's back was sore from sleeping on the meat market floor all night. He backed up to the stove to see if heat would help his soreness.

"Oh, that's too bad," he commented. "The parson gave a fine sermon; I heard it myself. Did the mail arrive on the early train? Or was there a caterpillar on the tracks, or a mighty zephyr, what might slow it down?"

Folding the newspaper, the station agent rifled through a canvas postal sack. He pulled out a letter and handed it to him.

"You are in luck. It arrived on time."

Davis's face lit up when he examined the letter.

"This is from the XIT, in Texas. I bet it's my old pard Lee."

Once he got it open, he shook his head in complete surprise.

"Well, land's sakes! This is from Colonel Boyce. He is the ranch boss. They got three million acres down there. Can you believe that?"

With one hand, he massaged his lower back, while he read the letter's contents.

Suddenly, Davis got pale.

"What does it say?" the station agent asked.

"Lee got killed."

"Was it a bobcat?"

Davis stuck the letter inside the crown of his hat, and put it on his head.

"I have to go," he said, and went out the door.

Jogging up the street, Davis hurried back to the meat market. When he got there, he found LG up on the awning hammering cedar shingles into place. Davis went over to the ladder and looked up.

"I got poor news," he called.

Seeing how sad he looked, LG climbed right down.

"What's the poor news?"

"I got a letter from Colonel Boyce at the XIT. Lee's cutting horse stuck both front feet in a hole, running across the Yellow Houses Pasture. Lee got throwed and broke his neck. He's dead."

Feeling weak, Davis sat down.

LG sat down next to him.

"I am sorry to hear that," he said. "Lee was a top beef hand. One of the few who knew how to twist the Blocker loop. That is some bad luck."

Davis stared into his hat.

"The best man to ever jingle an XIT spur. Or a B-Cross spur, for that matter. We were best of friends. This is sorrowful information."

LG held out the hammer.

"We can get that awning finished up today," he said. "Between the two of us."

But, instead of taking the hammer, Davis got up and went to the stock pen behind the building, where his horse Big Sunday was napping.

Taking the reins, he climbed into the saddle and began heading down the street.

"It'll take me two days, then, all by myself," LG called. "Long as it don't hail."

Davis glanced back.

"That poor sheepherder never got a funeral. Still froze in a snow-drift till spring arrives," he said. "I am going down to the panhandle. I'll see to it Lee gets properly eulogized in a timely fashion."

CHAPTER 75

The front door to the Denver Exchange burst open, and Parson Tom marched inside—and he was livid. The only thing he had on between his frock coat and riding boots was his apple-red long underwear.

"You, sir, are a black character!" he announced, singling out Joe Palmer.

Instantly, all the gambling and drinking and chatter stopped.

"You are but a little soul bearing up a corpse," he shouted, reciting the Stoics. "Childish! Bestial! Fraudulent! Tyrannical!"

Terrified, Joe scurried around the bar and ducked behind Billy Woods.

"An abscess on the universe!"

"Help me, Bat!"

But Bat, standing by the casino wheel, had a big smile on his face.

"Babylon is fallen—it has become the habitation of devils, the hold of every foul spirit, and a cage of every unclean and hateful bird."

Parson Tom waved his elbows like wings, pursed his lips like a beak, and stomped around the room.

"Cuckaw! Cuckaw!"

Joe felt sick about the whole thing. The parson was storming about, in a theological rage, all because he accidentally stole the man's pants.

"Help me, Bat!" he cried out again. "Tell him it was all a mistake!"

To Jeff Argyle's shock, the parson suddenly overturned the faro table.

"Money changers! Den of iniquity! The zeal of thine house hath eaten me up!"

He kicked at the playing cards and scattered the chips.

"Why, Reverend. What transpired that's got you all riled up?" Bat asked, acting coy.

Parson Tom pointed an accusing finger at Joe again.

"That vile goat hath purloined the church money—while I slept."

Then, he ran across the room and circled behind the bar. Like a rabbit, Billy Woods hopped over to escape, and Joe Palmer, eyes wide, scrambled right after him.

Darting back around, Parson Tom proceeded to chase his prey around the pool table.

"Oh, me!" Joe cried.

They raced around the table one way, and then raced around the other way. Finally, Bat Masterson intervened and got in between them. The angry parson stopped and glared, breathing heavily.

In the lull, everyone in the Denver Exchange erupted into laughter, clapping and hooting.

Parson Tom looked around, confused.

"What is happening here?"

Bat looked slightly embarrassed.

"Sorry, preacher. This is all just a bunch of mischief."

He waved at Billy.

"Give the man his pants back."

Opening the safe behind the bar, Billy Woods held up the missing trousers.

When he got his pants back, Parson Tom checked the pockets. They were stuffed full of cash. Confused, he looked at Bat for an explanation.

"We sent poor Joe over to count your money so we could double it."

"This is more than double."

Parson Tom tried counting it, but his mind was too scattered to keep track.

"There's got to be at least seven hundred dollars here."

He pulled on his trousers and looked around, amazed.

"Well, I am grateful. A little perturbed, but grateful."

Stepping towards Joe, he extended his hand in peace.

"I mistook you for a villain."

Joe shook it but still felt sick about the whole thing.

CHAPTER 76

"I still feel like a transgressor," Joe said.

Jeff Argyle and Billy Woods picked up the faro table and set it upright. Argyle was still nervous about the parson and avoided looking at him directly.

"Well, you look like one, if that helps," Bat joked.

Billy put his arm around Joe, and pointed at the front door.

"You just need some fresh air."

Parson Tom was overwhelmed by the money. He kept patting his overstuffed pockets in disbelief, as if it all might vanish in a puff of smoke.

Kneeling down, Argyle began to pick up the scattered play chips and cards, and copper pennies. At least the abacus wasn't damaged. He hoped Joe would indeed go outside—and take the evangelist with him. The man's presence was too unnerving.

"Fresh air will do you good," Argyle called. "Both of you."

The parson gazed from Jeff Argyle to Joe Palmer to the front door. Looking more like himself again, he marched over and gripped the door latch.

"Behold, I stand at the door and knock," he said, quoting John the Revelator. "If any man hear my voice, open the door."

Then he opened the door. Instantly, sunlight streamed into the dim room and lit up the haze of cigar smoke, like a scene from the *Apocalypse* itself.

Joe blinked.

Maybe the cold fresh air would do him some good after all.

It had been a long, long night.

Passing through the doorway, Joe took a few hesitant steps in the crunchy snow. He held his hand up against the sun. It was so bright he had to close his eyes for a moment. That was the moment the New Orleans Kid had been waiting for. He stood up from his hiding place across the street in a stack of cut lumber and pointed a pistol at Joe Palmer.

"Direct from the muggy climes of Louisiana!" he shouted, and fired.

Joe's hand shook with the impact, and his thumb exploded.

Dropping flat, Joe rolled through the snow to find cover and dodge any more gunfire.

Stepping out of the Denver Exchange, Parson Tom watched him roll away—and then looked up to see the New Orleans Kid, with his scraggly blonde hair, cocking his pistol again.

Bat appeared in the doorway, grabbed the parson, and yanked him back inside the building.

The Kid fired again, kicking up a blast of snow near Joe, who ended his roll behind the nearest lamppost. The street lamp, of course, had been shot out during Joe and Bob's shooting spree. The glass globe on top was gone. Every single one along the street had been shot out, and now Joe himself had been shot, too.

"Told you I'd kill you dead!" the Kid called and took a third shot.

The bullet hit the wall behind Joe, leaving a white pockmark in the wood.

Luckily, Joe was wearing his gun belt and went to draw his Colt 45. Strangely, when he palmed the grip, his hand slid right off. He fumbled a second time to pull out his revolver, and then noticed his thumb was gone. The skin was torn and he saw a bone nub in the middle with red blood leaking out. Big gooey drops fell in the white snow.

The Kid decided the stack of lumber was no longer useful and climbed out. Hunching over, he jogged a few steps and ducked behind a barrel of salt. Popping up, he rested his shooting arm on top so he could aim better. His arm was quivering with excitement, and he wanted to ensure his shots were straight.

"You're a dead man," he yelled at Joe.

He closed one eye and took a breath before pulling the trigger.

Joe heard a pop right next to his head and jerked away. It felt like a bee sting. Touching his ear, he noticed his ear lobe was missing.

Reaching over with his good hand, Joe drew the Colt successfully and, with his remaining thumb, rocked back the hammer. He rolled through the snow a little further, and then hopped up to a crouch. He was not as good at shooting with his off hand, but at least he was confident he could hold the ivory grips properly. He fired at the New Orleans Kid, but the shot went wide.

The Kid didn't know Joe was shooting with his off-hand, however, and ducked behind the barrel of salt again.

Getting up, Joe hustled down the boardwalk and dropped behind a buckboard. He glanced at the wheel team. The two horses were nervous, he could tell. Joe pressed his bloody hand against his chest, to keep it from leaking as bad. The horses nickered uncomfortably, their eyes wide.

Joe spotted the Kid peeking out from his hiding place.

Resting the gun barrel on the wheel spokes, and angling the gun sights, Joe squeezed the trigger.

The gun barked, the horses spooked, the wagon lurched, and the wheel spun—knocking Joe's gun out of his hand.

Howling, the New Orleans Kid stood straight up and arched his back in pain.

Joe's gun hadn't fallen far. He dove and grabbed it, but by then the Kid had recovered from the hit and ducked back down.

"You made a big fat mistake!" Joe shouted.

"You did!" the Kid replied from behind the barrel of salt.

The door opened behind the New Orleans Kid, and the lone prospector of great fortune, JJ Dore, who had attempted to sell Joe Palmer a fake mine claim for a hundred bucks at the pool table in the Orleans Club, appeared and slapped the door jamb in anger. It was his buckboard, with a spade and pick in the back—his tools of deception—and now it was rattling up the street.

"Hey!" he barked at Joe. "You spooked my horses."

But when JJ Dore saw Joe's gun pointed in his direction, he looked horrified.

"Don't shoot me," he yelled, and jumped back inside the building. "I'll give you your hundred bucks back!"

"It's not you I'm aiming at," Joe replied. "And I never gave you a dime."

But JJ Dore slammed the door and was gone.

In fact, looking around, everyone was gone.

The street had cleared at the sound of all the gunshots.

Up and down the white, icy road, Joe noticed faces in every window, and people peering around corners, everywhere he looked.

This was the second time in as many days that he had cleared Main Street Creede with his Colt 45.

Suddenly, the New Orleans Kid dashed down the boardwalk, his blond hair flopping, and took another shot.

Joe felt his sleeve pop and leapt to the side, but it was too late.

"Quit shootin' at me, dammit!" he said, and fired back.

He caught the Kid in the ankle, and the boy tripped and sprawled.

Joe fired again, but missed, and the snow erupted by his face.

The New Orleans Kid, using his elbows, crawled like a crab behind a frozen water trough. He poked up and pulled the trigger, but it just clicked. He pulled it a second time, the cylinder rotated, but it clicked again. All the bullets were spent.

Joe squinted in the bright light, and tried to see what kind of pistol the Kid had.

The Kid opened up his gun and shook out all the old casings. Joe frowned. It was a newer revolver—one of those where the cylinder swung out to the side. That made reloading a quick process, at least compared to Joe's. He had an old side-loader, and it took longer.

Joe checked his arm. His sleeve was torn and he had been nicked. Blood trickled down inside, and his skin felt hot. But it didn't seem to be too bad of a wound.

So, he got to his feet and headed straight towards the water trough.

But the Kid heard his boots crunching in the snow. He only managed to thumb in a couple bullets, but he pushed the cylinder back into place and jumped into the open.

"Gotcha, you skunk!" Joe shouted and aimed.

The Kid pulled his trigger faster, but his shot went low and caught Joe in the shin.

Collapsing hard on the icy road, Joe almost lost his gun. Blinking in pain, he wrestled to get his bearings. He spotted the trough again, and shot at it, splintering the wood.

But the Kid was already halfway down the street. Though his ankle was ruined, he hobbled quickly along the boardwalk, grabbing the broken street lamps for balance.

Joe Palmer blinked again. His vision was blurry. He had hit his head on the ice.

He only had one shot left.

Getting up, Joe chased after the New Orleans Kid, hobbling like a cripple, too.

The Kid was just up ahead.

He had made it all the way down to the Hardware & Stoves and was clinging to the clock post out front like a drunk. His face was contorted, and blond hair dangled in his eyes.

Even though his vision was still blurry, the clock face was big enough Joe could read it from a distance. It was only nine o'clock in the morning.

Just beyond the hardware store were all the tent saloons of Tent Town. In Joe's foggy head, they looked like a sea of ice cream cones, all propped upside-down.

The Kid saw him coming and his mouth moved, but Joe didn't hear any sound come out.

When Joe was a kid, his favorite thing in the whole wide world was ice cream. His mother made it from the cow's milk which Joe collected. It would occur every summer on his little sister Henrietta's birthday.

It made Joe bitter about his own birth date, being in the dead of winter.

"How come she gets ice cream on her birthday?" Joe asked one time. "Why, she doesn't she even milk them cows. But I do."

"She's too little," Mother replied. "And I don't want her little white dress to get dirty."

"Then why can't we have ice cream on *my* birthday?" Joe demanded. "I do all the work. I deserve the ice cream, not her."

"It's too cold for ice cream on your birthday."

In a huff, Joe left the kitchen and went outside. He spotted his little sister under the clothesline, which was strung between the water well and the outhouse. She was standing in the tall green grass, pulling the petals off a yellow daisy.

He went up and slapped her.

She screamed and ran, and Joe chased after her. However, Henrietta was short and lithe, and darted between the wet dungarees and linens like a hummingbird. Joe was big and clunky, and got tangled in the wet things. When he got loose, Joe saw her disappear inside the house. He sprinted after her, getting more and more angry when he considered all the privileges she got to enjoy.

Racing into the kitchen, Joe found Henrietta, in her little white dress, clinging to her mother's leg like a drunk. Her face was contorted and blonde hair dangled in her eyes.

Mother reached up on the cabinet for the switch she used whenever Joe talked sass or got into trouble. She took it down and dragged him outside.

From the corner of his eye, he saw Henrietta saying something. Her mouth moved, but Joe didn't hear any sound come out.

A shadow fell over him. It was Mother, raising the switch high above her head.

Joe cowered and squinted.

"No!" he pleaded. "Don't!"

He felt the switch hit his shoulder, and it stung really bad, and his ears rang.

Falling down, Joe lay in the soft green grass, staring up at the clouds, and tears began rolling down his cheeks.

CHAPTER 77

Joe clenched his fist, trying to grab a handful of grass. But there was no grass. It was only plush green velvet.

His eyes came into focus.

Then Joe realized he was lying on the pool table in the Orleans Club. His right hand was wrapped in a blood-soaked cloth. His shirt was gone—he was bare chested, and white linen strips had been wrapped clear around his shoulder and chest, and he saw more rolled tight around his arm and shin.

"Don't try to sit up."

Joe turned his head.

Soapy Smith was sitting nearby, looking tired. The whole place was empty. Joe had never seen it empty since they opened for business. Day and night, no matter the time, it was full of folks gambling their earnings away.

"Soapy?" Joe called out, afraid that his shoulder had suddenly caught fire. It felt like it was burning, and he pressed his hand on it to put out the flames. But there were no flames.

Getting up, Soapy came over and put his hand on Joe's forehead.

"You're pale as a ghost," Soapy commented. "But you ain't a ghost. You're lucky."

He picked up a clean cloth and wiped Joe's eyes and cheeks.

"Mollie is in the kitchen warming up some soup. Don't let her see you bawling like this."

Joe sniffed a couple times, and with his good hand took the cloth.

Sitting back down in his chair, Soapy sighed.

"You had me worried."

Wiping his eyes, Joe tried to remember everything. His head was hazy and he looked around the room for Mother or Henrietta. His heart was racing, and he felt confused.

"He got away, Joe," Soapy said. "Stole a horse and ran off down the tracks. He was pretty banged up, so I expect he'll be dead before the sun rises. Where's he gonna go, anyhow? Stupid kid."

Joe remembered. He was talking about the New Orleans Kid.

"He won't be running no shell games," Soapy added. "That's for damn sure."

At that, Joe began to cry again. He pressed the cloth to his eyes. Soapy leaned forward, concerned.

"What's wrong? Where does it hurt?"

But Joe shook his head sadly.

"I'm sorry, Soapy," he whispered. "I truly am. I should have warned you about that Kid. Back when he first came to town."

Soapy smiled.

"How could you know he was out there running a shell game? You were in the crapper when he showed up, remember?"

Joe hid his eyes in the cloth.

"It was Bob," he said in a low voice. "He sent that Kid over on purpose."

Soapy stood up slowly, his face getting ugly.

"Bob Ford sent that Kid over on purpose?"

"The New Orleans Kid was running his shell game outside Bob's hotel. It was the day after you caned him, and he was pretty hot about it. So, he tricked that Kid into setting up in front of your club."

Holding his breath, Joe peeked out of the cloth.

"I'm so sorry, Soapy. It's my fault. I should have warned you, but it slipped my mind."

Walking around the pool table, Soapy balled his hands into fists.

"I'm sorry, Soapy," Joe repeated, almost inaudibly.

Soapy punched the wall, causing it to rattle, and a lantern almost fell down.

"I am gonna beat his brains out."

Then he tore the big brown bearskin off the wall and flung it, and ripped down a rack of antlers and smashed them on the floorboards.

Hearing the racket, Mollie ran out of the kitchen.

"Is Joe dead?" she asked, worried. "Did he die?"

Joe sat straight up, and she squeaked in fear.

"I ain't dead, Mollie. It's okay."

She sighed in relief, and then turned to Soapy. But when Mollie saw the look on his face, she spun on her heel and went right back in the kitchen without another word.

Grabbing the edge of the pool table, Soapy squeezed it until his knuckles turned white.

Joe pressed his thumb stump against his chest. He looked remorseful.

"If I could do it all over again, I would."

Soapy looked up but didn't reply.

"Can we just let this go? Please?"

"Let it go?" Soapy growled. "Don't you see? Bob Ford did this to you! He sent that Kid over to my club. He knew what I'd do. And now that Kid went after you . . . and nearly killed you dead! This is Bob's fault. All of it. Don't defend him anymore. I don't wanna hear it."

Joe hung his head.

"The way of the transgressor is hard."

Breathing heavy, Soapy glared at him.

"What?"

"That's in the Good Book. We're transgressors, Soapy, you and I. We only make things worse and harder on ourselves. Don't you see that? Let's just let Bob be. Can we?"

Sinking into his chair, Soapy's face softened.

"You are an enigma, Joe. An enigma."

Joe looked confused.

"Is that good?"

Studying Joe's watery eyes and bloody bandages and his missing thumb, Soapy nodded.

"I like enigmas."

Then he rubbed his forehead like he had a headache and sighed.

"I want you to stay away from him," he said, gently. "You hear me?"

Then he twisted around and tried to see in the kitchen.

"Is that soup done?"

They heard a clatter and then Mollie reappeared. Nervous, she looked at them—first at Soapy, and then at Joe.

"You still want it?" she asked.

"Of course we do," Soapy told her. "Bring three, and sit here with us. Besides, Joe needs a pretty girl to help him hold his spoon. God knows I ain't gonna do it."

He gave her a charming smile, and she smiled back.

"Okay then!"

CHAPTER 78

TELLURIDE

"You were just a little spud back then," Greasewood told White Owl.

They took slow steps through the deep snow. It was too soft in the afternoon sun to support their weight. Each step took immense effort, since in some places the snow was waist deep. The air was thin, too, and they gasped to get enough of it.

"But *I* was old enough. I remember everything," Bear Claw Lip muttered. "*You want our land. You want our country. You tried to take it in pieces and now you want it all.* That is what the chief told the general."

Greasewood was surprised.

"For someone with a mangled lip, you sure have a good memory."

At the top of a slope, they paused to catch their breath.

Ever since they left the cabin, they decided to play it safe. They stayed within sight of the train tracks but kept to the forest. After seeing the Lizard Head, they knew the traditional hunting grounds were very close. Great stealth was required now.

As they were resting, a passenger train came up the rails. Through the windows, they could plainly see there were many White people inside. It eased past and descended into the valley, and they soon lost sight of it among the trees.

Somewhere up ahead it blew its haunting, airy whistle. The hairs on Kahopi's neck stood up. He felt his ears begin to ring and a strange feeling came over him. He knew something important was about to happen.

"We must be very close," Greasewood whispered.

Indeed, at the crest of the next ridge, they found themselves looking down at the ancient river valley.

Greasewood's face fell.

"It is completely overrun."

Even Bear Claw Lip seemed dismayed.

Everywhere in the snowy valley, up and down the river, even speckled among the trees, were cabins and shacks and tents and people coming and going, and riders riding, and smokestacks spraying sooty smoke into the sky.

"Listen to all that noise," Greasewood lamented.

He felt like it was all hopeless, and shrugged.

"What can we do here? This was a mistake."

Had it not been for his Guardian Spirit showing him in a dream that the valley was overrun with Two-Hearts, Kahopi would have also felt shock and dismay. His ears continued to ring as he observed all the activity. He, at least, had been warned.

However, his dream was meant for him alone, so of course he couldn't share it with the Utes. Perhaps they would understand, and perhaps not. They had their own reasons for reaching this place. Kahopi was there for one special reason—to find his father. He knew that if he could finally find him and bury him properly, not only could his father go in peace to the Skeleton House, but the disgrace Kahopi felt would finally be resolved. He wanted so badly to get back on the Sun Trail again.

They saw the same passenger train in the distance. It emerged from the forest and made a wide turn along the riverbank. It chugged towards the end of the valley, towards a heap of buildings and poles and cables clustered beneath the tall cliffs, and a giant majestic waterfall. Long icicles dangled from the rocky ledges in many places.

Greasewood was despondent. He couldn't believe what he was witnessing.

"There must be thousands of them. They've built a damn city here."

Kahopi listened politely. He understood. He had experience with the Whites, too, back at the mesa. Traders, missionaries, nurses, government agents. It only took a short period of time, and they multiplied into a swarm.

Bear Claw Lip stood silent for a long time. His face was drawn as he studied the river valley and the state of things. Finally, he stirred.

"One, a dozen, or a thousand—the Ghost Dance will come true. But we must do our part."

He took out his knife and held it aloft.

Father, I come.
Brother, I come.
Mother, I come.

Climbing up on a granite block, White Owl stood tall and raised his arms in defiance.

"Give us back our arrows!" he cried. *"Give us back our arrows!"*
Casting aside his depression, Greasewood joined the dance.

Though they were within shouting distance of several Whites, no one noticed them dancing and no one heard their chants.

Kahopi looked to the sky. The sun was bright and the clouds were few. He knew Tawa had led him here.

Suddenly, Bear Claw Lip let out a war whoop and rushed down the steep hillside, among the aspen and pine. Like an antelope, he sped out into the open and headed straight for the nearest shack. It was made of logs and had been built right next to the cold river, which was half-frozen.

A Mexican man with a thick brown mustache was fishing. He stood on the icy embankment alone, and the running water must have been too loud, since he never realized Bear Claw Lip was approaching until it was too late.

The Ute grabbed the fisherman by the hair and plunged his knife into his back. The blade must have pierced the man's spirit and stolen his voice, because no sound came out of his mouth even though his lips moved.

Red blood squirted out each time Bear Claw Lip jabbed his knife. It wasn't long until the man ceased writhing and lay still.

Then Greasewood and White Owl ran over, too.

Kahopi took a last look at the branches overhead. He did not see the Hawk Deity as he hoped, but he was not too worried. He knew his Guardian Spirit was protecting him from evil. So, he stepped out into the cold sunlight and took a few brisk steps, then broke into a trot.

Together, they all dragged the body into the small shack.

"Look what I found. Four whole quarters!" Greasewood said, after searching the man's pockets.

"We don't need money," Bear Claw Lip said rudely. "We are not here to *buy* anything from these people. If you see something they own that you want, you don't need to worry about buying it."

He slapped Greasewood's hand and the quarters scattered on the floorboards.

"All you need is a knife or a gun now."

"I don't have either," Greasewood said. He looked upset and rubbed his hand.

White Owl frowned and glared, angry at Bear Claw Lip's bad behavior.

"You should honor your elders. Walk lightly."

"Only geese and old women walk lightly."

Bear Claw Lip let out another war cry and ran outside.

Kneeling, Kahopi quietly scooped up the coins and handed them back to the old Ute. With a kind smile, Greasewood gave two quarters to White Owl and two quarters to Kahopi.

"You keep these," Greasewood told them. "You have honored me. I will honor you."

Then, despite his rude behavior, the two Utes chased after Bear Claw Lip—leaving Kahopi alone in the fisherman's shack. Alone, except the fisherman's bloody body.

He sat down on a stool and pondered all he had seen.

The Utes were intent on purging the Valley of the Hanging Waterfalls and reclaiming it as their traditional hunting grounds. That was their reason for coming. But that was not why Kahopi was there. He had dreamed of this place, and the Star-and-Moon Deity himself had hinted at its significance.

Kahopi went outside again, then snuck over and hid in the willows.

There were White voices in the air. They seemed to come from all around him. Kahopi could also hear other sounds in the distance. Burros baying, metal clinking. The strangest sight was a long cable stretched up the cliffside, suspended in the air. Ore carts floated up and down—and Kahopi spotted White men way up there on the steep slope, digging!

In that moment, he decided to part company with the Utes. It was time to follow his own path.

— PART 11 —

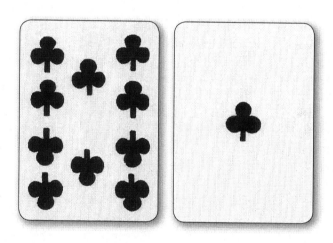

CHAPTER 79

SPRING 1860
THE BAYOU SALADO

It turned out the Bayou Salado was just a wide open, snow-swept meadow ringed in by mountain ranges. There was no swamp, and there were no alligators.

Horace parked the wagon next to a shallow frozen pond.

It was a warm afternoon, and there was a lot of slush. He tied flour sacks over his boots before he jumped down, to keep his feet dry. Looking back where they came, their wheel tracks were easy to see. They were two dark lines in a vast white expanse.

"Such good boys," Horace said, petting the oxen.

He scooped out a handful of oats and fed it to them.

When she saw what he was doing, Augusta frowned.

"Don't waste all the feed."

"Oh, Gussie. They deserve a treat."

She walked over and watched as they ate. Their big noses snuffled Horace's palm, searching for more.

"Now look. Your hand is slimy. Go wash up."

Ignoring her, Horace walked over to the water's edge and broke the ice with his boot. Then he brought the oxen over for a drink, but they only sniffed at it.

"Can you believe Mr. Kelley and his crew came in on foot?" Horace asked. "Guns, shovels, gold pans, food, tent. They carried everything on their backs."

The sun was starting to arc down directly in front of them. Augusta shaded her eyes and examined their surroundings. She saw no footprints, only coyote tracks.

"Well, they didn't come through here."

"Keep looking. I bet we can spot their campfire smoke from here."

Seeing no smoke, Augusta walked over and gave him her trademark steely glare.

"I thought you said we were close."

"Look . . . my hand is all slimy," Horace joked and pinched her sleeve.

Pulling away, Augusta shrieked. But reluctantly a smile spread across her face.

"You know I hate ox slobber."

Letting her go, Horace knelt down at the water's edge and washed his hands.

"Drink this up, boys," he said to the oxen.

He leaned down and took a sip himself, but then spit it right back out.

"This is salt water! No wonder they don't want it."

Augusta walked around the wagon and checked the water barrel.

"This thing is solid ice," she noted. "We'll have to melt snow in the frying pan."

Suddenly, she held her finger to her lips and frantically waved Horace over.

"Come look at this."

Inside the wagon bed, underneath the hooped canvas canopy, Nathaniel was snoring. Little Maxcy was there, too, snuggled up and snoring along with him.

"A couple of bedbugs," she whispered.

He peered in over her shoulder.

"A couple of lazybones, you mean. Who is going to help me with the tent?"

"Leave them alone," she said softly, and threaded her arm through her husband's. "I will help. Let them sleep."

He shrugged.

"We need to shovel this slush back so we ain't walking in it."

The shovel, along with all their tools and cooking pans, was strapped onto the side of the wagon. Everything was held in place by a web of knots.

As Horace freed the shovel, Augusta crossed her arms.

"All I ever hear is that constant clanging and it is driving me mad. Find a better place for all these things."

"What's Maxcy going to think?" Horace replied. "I told him we borrowed Santa's sleigh. He thinks we're going to the North Pole."

"I'm sick of listening to all this clanging around."

"Maxcy likes it."

He dug the slushy snow away from the wagon and made a nice flat spot. Meanwhile, careful not to wake the two sleeping inside, she pulled out the food box.

"Can you find the matches?" Horace asked. "I'm going to get us some wood."

There was a clump of brittle, gnarled pine trees nearby—barely taller than the wagon. Horace went over and began snapping off branches, but instead of looking for the matches, Augusta followed him.

"We're lost, aren't we?" she asked.

He reached out and grabbed her forearm.

"Ox slobber," he joked.

"Tell me you have a new plan, Horace. That little napkin map is useless. I say we turn back right now."

"No, Gussie. I do have a plan. Here, I'll prove it."

He sorted through the branches and picked out the straightest one he could find. Planting one tip on the snowy ground, Horace pointed the other end straight up at the sky.

"Genghis Khan did this to cross the Alps," he told her. "And Alexander the Great found the Rubicon this way, too."

Augusta put her hands on her hips.

"Hannibal crossed the Alps, and Julius Caesar crossed the Rubicon. You better not be doing what I think you're doing."

"Lady Fortune, show us the way!" Horace called and dropped the stick.

It fell on its side, pointing toward the setting sun.

CHAPTER 80

SPRING 1892
LEADVILLE

"Maxcy, you displayed grit and aptitude," Horace told his son. "The way you handled yourself at the Lucy B. was admirable. Not like that pouf, Wheezy Jones."

They were sitting in the Tabor Grand Hotel parlor, sipping Old Nectar.

Maxcy twitched his mustache and glanced around awkwardly.

"I may need to take my boots off."

"Why do you say that?"

Maxcy leaned over and checked his soles.

"I must have stepped in horse pee. I apologize for the malodor."

Sinking back into his big leather chair, Horace gave him a dismissive wave.

"It's okay, son. You are of Tabor blood. That means royalty. And royalty don't need to take off their boots, no matter what they stepped in."

He caught the attention of the new waitress.

"My dear, what is your name?"

"Jenny."

"Well, Jenny, can you bring us a couple cigars? The Cubans, please."

"Yes, Mr. Tabor."

She darted off.

"Don't think I didn't notice how quick you were to help, Maxcy. You got there quick and did what needed to be done. Campion himself was still in his bedclothes. And here we were, two Tabors side by side, taking care of business. That's how it should be."

Maxcy smiled softly.

"I was glad to help."

Jenny returned with two big cigars and handed them to Horace.

"Lovely, dear," he said, and gave her a silver dollar.

"Why, thank you, Mr. Tabor."

"Off you go, now."

After she left, Horace leaned forward and cupped his hand around his mouth so he could whisper at Maxcy.

"There are spies in my employ."

Maxcy leaned in, too, listening.

Horace's eyes followed the waitress across the room. She went over to a serving cart, and took out a platter of caviar and oysters.

Relaxing in his chair, Maxcy struck a match and got his cigar going. Then he grinned sheepishly.

"Do you think Mother has realized by now that I'm not in Colorado Springs on a business trip?"

"I am surprised she hasn't let loose the hounds yet," Horace said. "Don't go back down there, Maxcy. Not yet. How would you like a job instead? Working here for me."

They heard a tinkle of laughter.

Horace cringed and looked around, realizing he'd lost sight of the waitress. Then he spotted her laughing it up with the bartender and sighed in relief.

"It's someone in here, I'm sure of it."

"The spy?"

"That girl is new, but that don't mean nothing. The bartender has worked here for a couple years, but for all I know it's him."

He struck a match and got his own cigar going. He blew the rich smoke straight up at the ceiling.

"What do you know about mixed drinks?"

"Not much," Maxcy replied. "Given Mother's stance on alcohol."

Horace snorted.

"It doesn't matter. You can be the new hotel parlor manager."

From where they sat, through the plate glass, the Lucy B. Mine was in plain sight. It was closing in on five o'clock, but there would be no shift-change bell ring. Despite all of Horace's best engineers and pumpmen working around the clock, they could not stop the water from filling the tunnels and shafts. The mine was flooded.

"Campion thinks they'll have that thing pumped out in a month," Horace said, staring outside. "He's wrong. It'll take a year, maybe longer."

Maxcy followed his father's gaze. The tall, ornate lampposts at the Lucy B. stuck up as high as the headframe. It was an odd mixture of the rustic and the decorative. Normally crawling with workers, the mine was as empty as a cemetery.

"It's sad," he replied. "And all those miners out of work, too."

Horace cupped his hand over his mouth again.

"Parlor manager is just a front," he whispered. "Find out who the spy is."

He winked and sat up straight.

"Jenny!" Horace called. "More Old Nectar, please."

She smiled and waved and brought over the decanter.

CHAPTER 81

"Hey Ed," a miner said. "You signing on?"

"To what?" Big Ed asked.

"The silver club, of course."

"Get out of here!"

But the man, confused at the hostile response, simply turned back to his beer bottle. The Stray Horse Brewery was full of miners, celebrating their wage increase and good fortune. Half of them were from the Matchless, which made Big Ed mad. It was like a slap in the face, having Haw's boys here in his own brewery, celebrating the success of the Leadville Silver Club.

He took a napkin and rooted around for a pencil.

"Take this down to the Western Union," he muttered, writing out a short message.

Dirty Johns frowned.

"Why me?"

Big Ed handed him the napkin.

"Cuz you look more respectable than me," he said sarcastically. "Now get on down there and wait for a reply. But don't loiter out front. The laundry ladies are not friendly at all."

"Haw head in clouds; stars ain't lining up; seeking advice," Dirty Johns read out loud. "Will he know what that means?"

"He'll know what it means."

The miner looked up from his bottle again.

"Join the silver club is *my* advice," he said. "All the boys did. We get four bucks a day now."

Big Ed strutted around the bar and took the man's beer bottle away.

"Get the hell out of here."

But the miner grabbed his beer bottle back and simply moved to another table.

Studying the napkin again, Dirty Johns looked confused.

"What *does* it mean?"

"It ain't something your booze-mangled mind can comprehend."

Then Ed flipped a quarter at him.

"Here's twenty-four cents for the wire and a penny for your trouble—now light out!"

Then, for no good reason, he gave Dirty Johns a hard shove into the wall.

When he regained his balance, Dirty Johns crumpled the napkin and threw it in Big Ed's face.

"Quit treating me poorly. Send that damn thing yourself."

He tore open the door and tried to dash outside. But Big Ed, giving chase, grabbed a handful of his expensive new suit coat before he could get through the doorway and whirled him into a table.

Sprawling on the floor, Dirty Johns rubbed his elbow—and was shocked to find his fancy sleeve had an ugly snag.

"You ruined my coat."

"I'll ruin more than that," Big Ed growled and straddled the man's knees. He yanked off his pricey new boots and hurled them over the bar.

"You don't deserve hundred-dollar boots."

"Those are mine!"

"Your stinky feet don't belong in them fancy boots."

Big Ed was a large man, and Dirty Johns was thoroughly pinned.

"Now take that napkin to the Western Union, or I swear to God, I will beat you senseless."

Getting up, Ed sniffed his fingers, gagged, and kicked him in the ribs.

"How is it that I give you hundred-dollar boots, and you don't put on fresh socks?"

Gasping for air, the unkempt man hugged the table leg and teared up.

The miners in the room had stopped celebrating and were watching in silence. Ignoring them all, Big Ed grabbed his coat and went outside. The cold temperature was refreshing—although somehow the scent of Dirty John's filthy socks seemed to follow him like a cloud.

Big Ed was tired of things stinking. The miners' strike had been a failure. Even the Lucy B. cave-in didn't seem to make much of a difference. The Leadville Silver Club was a success. And now, he could barely get Dirty Johns to take a simple message down to the telegraph office.

"This whole town stinks," Big Ed mumbled to himself. "I hate it here."

It was true. He used to love Leadville, back when he had a gang and influence. He used to have a grip on the city. Now his grip was gone, and even the weak-willed Dirty Johns was sassing him.

He hoped Soapy Smith would have some good advice.

— CHAPTER 82 —

CREEDE

When Walker saw LG ride into the glen, he whistled and danced around the cook fire.

"A whole week," he said while LG unsaddled. "I ran them cows for a whole week, all by myself. I was so lonesome I named 'em all, every single one. Watch out for that one over there, with the evil eye. His name is Evil Eye. I know what to expect of him at all times and all places. He may be no good, but that dang mule is still worse."

After he cut his horse loose in the pasture, LG went straight for the coffee pot.

"A week? Shoot, that's a vacation."

He filled a tin cup and took a sip.

"Back in '84, I once spent a whole winter all alone in a line shack up in Wyoming."

He took out a package of cigarettes.

"All I had for company was a lanky little mouser. I cut a little hole in the wall, and that cat could come in or out whenever it suited him. At first, he was wild as a deer. But I trained him to come running when I rang the supper bell."

"Say, where is Davis?" Walker asked, cutting him off.

Striking a match, LG took a deep drag on the cigarette.

"Texas."

He peered closely at Walker's face.

"That penciling on your lip makes you look like a pretty tough character. I might mistake you for a rustler."

Walker cautiously rubbed his peachy whiskers.

"Does it look bad?"

"From now on, when you ride up on me, be sure to call out, 'It's me.'"

"Okay, I will."

LG took another sip of hot black coffee.

"That's tasty."

"I parched the beans beforehand, like you told me."

"Good man."

"Why's he in Texas?"

"His old pard crossed the Great Divide. In the permanent sense. Davey's gone down there to say a prayer over the man's grave."

He stood over the cook fire and pointed at the Dutch oven, nestled in the hot coals.

"What's for breakfast?"

Walker ran over and lifted the lid.

"I made up some potatoes and eggs," he said, proud that something he cooked turned out right. He picked up a spoon and a tin plate. "I'll dip it out for you."

"Go get the butter and syrup."

Walker stopped in mid-spoon.

"I ran out."

"Of butter or syrup?" LG asked, mortified.

Walker got quiet for a moment.

"Should I still dip some out?"

LG flicked his cigarette into the snow.

"I suppose."

Filling a plate with food, Walker handed it to him, then grabbed the coffee pot and topped off LG's cup.

"How long will he be gone?"

LG shrugged and chewed in silence.

"I've never known anyone who died before," Walker said. "That makes me feel a little lightheaded, just thinking about it."

He looked up at the branches overhead. Several magpies were watching, as they always did whenever he had food cooking.

"That dern mule bit a hole in my sleeve."

Walker was wearing his coat, and he slid his arm out long enough to reveal the damage.

LG examined the torn fabric.

"That is the rankest mule I ever met. Billy overcharged me for that thing."

He finished up his eggs and potatoes and set the plate on a rock. One of the magpies swooped down and landed near them.

"With Davey gone, it's up to us to run this outfit. The construction is all done in town, and all I need to do now is drive some of these beeves up there and skin them suckers. Once I get enough cuts of beef hung, I'll open the store and drum up some business."

The magpie hopped closer and cawed.

"That means you're ranch boss again," LG added.

Walker's face fell.

"All by myself?"

"Yep."

Turning pale, the boy stared into the flames.

"How long will that be? A day or two?"

"Tell you what," LG said, patting him on the shoulder. "I'll go stock up on syrup and butter tomorrow."

He reached into his pocket and pulled out the Pinheads again.

"You need a smoke?"

Taking one, Walker put it in his mouth.

"Now you really look like a hard case," LG said and squinted at him as if he couldn't see very well. "Is that you?"

Walker smiled and almost dropped the cigarette from his mouth.

"Yeah, it's me."

CHAPTER 83

The Denver Exchange had a peculiar odor. It was a mix of tobacco smoke, kitchen fume, pepper fart, and body onion. Whenever LG stepped inside, it was always an adjustment from the pine and fresh mountain air.

Like usual, Billy Woods was working the bar, Jeff Argyle was dealing faro, and Bat Masterson was roaming the game floor making sure there was no trouble.

Then, near the poker table, Frank Oliver began pulling at Ella Diamond's dress like he planned to remove it. Seeing the scuffle, Billy Woods rushed over and punched Frank Oliver in the nose.

While that was happening, the Corner Pocket Drunk successfully executed an intricate ricochet shot and Bat Masterson couldn't believe his eyes.

"Billy, did you see that!" he shouted. "He made that shot but can't even enunciate his own name."

But Billy was too busy dealing with Frank Oliver.

"No, I did not. Because I am involved in fisticuffs with this lecherous gambler."

Frank Oliver, whose lip was split wide open, crawled around the poker table, out of Billy's sight.

"Get back out here," Billy said, shaking his fists.

Then Frank Oliver rose up again, pointing a pistol.

"You're dead, Billy Woods!"

However, before he could pull the trigger, Bat sprung on him from behind and wrestled the gun from his hand.

"Settle down," Bat said and thunked him on the head with the barrel of his own gun.

Frank Oliver collapsed on the floor.

Immediately, Billy checked on Ella Diamond.

"I apologize for that fool's behavior," he told her. "He had no business hassling you like that."

With a coquettish smile, Ella Diamond pinched Billy's cheek.

"Franky is just drunk."

"Drunk ain't no excuse for handling you improper."

"I'll let you boys hash things out. I gotta get back to Soapy's place before it gets dark. I'm singing a special song tonight."

She pinched him again and walked past LG, disappearing with a wave. The door closed with a bang.

LG whistled and clapped, like the curtain had just fallen at an opera house.

"Every time I come in this place," he said. "It's always something."

Grabbing the unconscious gambler by the boots, Bat and Billy dragged him towards the kitchen.

"Why, that fellow's half your size, Billy," LG pointed out.

Billy grinned.

"He may be small, but he's a live one."

"Looked like it."

"Well, he can sleep it off in the slop heap out back."

Bat and Billy dragged him all the way through the kitchen to the back entrance, and LG helped with the door. In addition to several outhouses, the alleyway was filled with muddy piles of trash, deer legs, fish heads, cow guts, cabbage and banks of crusty, yellow snow.

"Who eats all this cabbage?" LG asked, poking some with his boot.

Bat shrugged.

"Nobody, that's why it's all back here."

"Then why do you serve it?"

Bat shrugged again.

"I have no earthly idea."

They dumped Frank Oliver in the sludge.

"You here to gamble or drink?" Bat asked LG.

"Neither," he answered. "I just opened my meat market for business. Let me know when you need a cut of meat. All you gotta do is send someone down the street instead of all the way out to our cow camp."

Bat pointed at the cow guts.

"That will make the cook happy. He don't got to butcher cattle back here no more."

CHAPTER 84

There were easily two thousand people living in Creede, but only three hundred turned out to vote for a mayor. But in Soapy's mind, it didn't matter how many showed up and cast a ballot. It was all rigged anyhow.

It didn't matter what names people wrote down. Once all the votes were inside the ballot box, the little pieces of paper were secretly swapped out. The ballot box had a special hinged bottom, and Joe Simmons was hidden beneath the platform. After the last vote was cast, Soapy rapped on the podium three times. It only took a moment for Simmons to replace all the vote papers.

"Let's see what the tally is," Soapy announced, and began counting.

Old Man Tripp stood on the platform next to two other candidates. There was the boss of the Amethyst Mine, who wanted to be mayor so he could enforce a lower price on woodstoves. And there was the owner of the Hardware & Stoves store, who wanted to be mayor, too, just to keep the Amethyst boss from winning.

Soapy pretended to count, and recount the total. Finally, he quieted the crowd and pointed at Tripp.

"Mr. Osgood Tripp wins mayor!" Soapy announced. "You all know him. He is a fine, upstanding citizen. Come on over here."

Old Man Tripp, with a neatly trimmed beard, Mason's pin, and new suspenders, paraded across the small platform and waved. Soapy made a big show of shaking his hand and smiling.

"As the first mayor of Creede, what do you want to do?" he asked.

"I should think the first order of business is to elect a street commissioner," Tripp told the crowd. "Every time a horse dies, folks just leave it to rot."

Soapy applauded.

"What else does a street commissioner do?" he asked.

Trying to remember his lines, Old Man Tripp suddenly snapped his fingers.

"He shall license all saloons, theatrical shows, and street games," he said, winking at Soapy. "For instance, no one can operate a shell game without a proper license."

"That sounds like a fine idea," Soapy agreed.

He turned to address the crowd.

"Now, just for doing your civic duty, everyone here is invited to my place for one free shot of rye whiskey. And be sure to sign up for the Creede Silver Club. You get a second free shot if you do."

The boss of the Amethyst Mine turned to the Hardware & Stoves owner and punched him in the gut.

While the people dispersed, Simmons crawled out from beneath the small platform, and wiped the mud off his knees.

"That could not have gone better," he said, holding up a canvas sack. "And now we got plenty of therapeutic papers for the privy."

Banjo stared at Soapy with a fresh look of admiration.

"Just a short time ago, you were being run out of Denver," he noted in amazement. "And now here you are, running the show. I am amazed at what you can accomplish when you set your mind to it."

Soapy put his hand on Banjo's shoulder.

"I do run the show. And I want every Jack and Jill working these streets to pay their dues," he said. "That includes Bat Masterson."

"I'll take care of it," Banjo said proudly.

"And you," Soapy said, turning to Joe Palmer. "Get that meat market in line."

Joe nodded but said nothing.

Soapy noticed his sullen demeanor, a hangover from the gunfight with the New Orleans Kid, but Joe's mood did not dampen Soapy's. He was pleased as he could be with how well things were going.

At that moment, the telegrapher ran up and handed Soapy a message.

"*Haw head in clouds; stars ain't lining up; seeking advice.* Who is this from?"

"Big Ed Burns. Over in Leadville," answered the telegrapher. "What should I tell him?"

Soapy folded the paper and dropped it in the ballot box.

"Tell him, 'Shoot for the stars.' That's what I do."

CHAPTER 85

TELLURIDE

Slipping quietly through the front door of Adams' Grocery, Kahopi spotted an unusual sight. Here in this remote high country town, deep in the cold snowy winter, in this random little room, were mounds of oranges, lemons, apples, cranberries and cherries! It was so shocking to see all the fresh fruit he forgot why he came in.

A man in an apron stood behind a counter.

"You're lucky you dropped in," he said and held up a glass jar. "Look what came in, just today. Chow-Chow."

Brushing the snowflakes from his coat and face, Kahopi looked around in wonder.

Oranges were a rare treat on the mesa where he grew up. He was lucky to eat one on a special occasion, or when the missionaries came and spoke. He never ate an orange quickly but always savored every bite, for he never knew when he would get a chance to eat another.

"I know folks love it," the Aproned Man said. "Simply mouthwatering. A tasty blend of select, pickled vegetables in a spicy mustard dressing. Goes well with just about anything."

Kahopi glanced back outside nervously.

Heavy gray clouds were rolling up the valley, and snow was falling heavily. The Cloud-People were angry with him for coming here. The Valley of the Hanging Waterfalls was clearly a sacred and strange place.

Then, a White woman in a thick skirt and wide brimmed hat came inside.

"Pardon me, did my order arrive?"

"Yes, ma'am. It's in the store room. And you may be tantalized to learn I just got in a limited supply of Chow-Chow—just today."

Just today. He kept saying that peculiar phrase. Kahopi wondered what it meant.

Then the Aproned Man guided the woman through an archway and Kahopi was left alone.

Kahopi did not trust Whites. He was raised to distrust them. And in his dream, he was reminded that many of them are Two-Hearts, wicked and full of deceit.

However, the Aproned Man was truthful in saying that he was lucky to have dropped in. The snowflakes were falling so thick that Kahopi was terrified he would get buried alive and suffocated by an evil spirit. The sight of the fresh fruit caused him to forget, for a brief spell, that he had narrowly avoided death.

Pressing his hand on the glass, Kahopi looked outside again. It was like someone hung a white sheet over the window. He could see nothing. The Cloud-People were not playing games today.

He left the window and walked around the tables, mesmerized. There was so much here!

Fruits, green vegetables—and even sweet potatoes. In such an inhospitable place. None of these things could possibly grow in a place like this. Not naturally. Only witches could make that happen, and with such abundance. The Aproned Man must certainly be a witch. This was a dangerous place to be.

Just then, the two Whites returned from the store room.

"I'll have my boy load your wagon if you will pull around to the side of the building."

"But you have no eggs?" the woman asked.

The Aproned Man looked sheepish.

"I'm afraid I've sold out."

"I have no choice. I'll have to go to the Vienna Bakery and see if they have any. And in this weather!"

To Kahopi's shock, the woman in the wide hat and thick skirt simply opened the door and strolled into the blizzard. Instantly, she vanished.

"Now, sir. What can I assist you with?"

Kahopi could hardly stop from staring at everything. Then something among the vegetables caught his eye.

"You have the red bitter stalks," he said, trembling.

The man seemed confused. Then, he saw what Kahopi was looking at.

"You mean rhubarb. Yes, I do. How much would you like?"

How much would he like? Such abundance! And of course a witch who had a magic room full of fresh foods running contrary to the season would certainly have an unending supply of the red bitter stalks.

The Aproned Man picked up the rhubarb crate and set it on the table.

"It is a little expensive. Twenty-five cents for a pound. But you can't get this anywhere else."

This was the blackest of magic.

The red bitter stalks seemed to hum. Kahopi could hear it. He could feel the vibrations in the air. The large green leaves, which had not been removed, brought death to those who consumed them. Did this Two-Heart offer poison to all who crossed his threshold? Were all his customers killers?

"They make a wonderful pie."

The witch spoke in riddles.

Struggling to understand, Kahopi weighed his options. He could try to escape. He could run out the door to seek safety. But with such heavy snowfall, in the very depths of the Two-Hearts hive, there was no true safety. Only deadly traps at every turn.

The other option was to pretend to be a Two-Heart and purchase the red bitter stalks. Then the Aproned Man might let him leave without killing him.

"We've also got celery relish."

"I will take the red bitter stalks," he said with gravity. "And an orange."

"I'll throw the orange in for free, since it's storming so bad. That comes to twenty-five cents."

Taking out one of the quarters that Greasewood had given him, Kahopi set it on the counter and took his purchases over to the window. He sat on the floor and examined what he had bought.

But, then he noticed the witch was watching his every move. The Aproned Man suddenly smiled at him. It was peculiar, and made Kahopi's heart race. It seemed he was looking directly into his heart. Kahopi felt a chill until finally the Aproned Man averted his powerful gaze.

"No rush. You can wait here until it stops storming."

As soon as he turned away, Kahopi felt great relief.

With his heart still pounding, Kahopi carefully tore off a fistful of rhubarb leaves and put them in his coat pocket. He may need the powerful magic of the red bitter stalks to escape this terrifying place.

When his breathing returned to normal, he began to peel the orange.

However, before he could even remove the rind, the door burst open and several White men rushed inside, looking wild as cougars. Their eyes immediately settled on Kahopi, who sat on the floor unwrapping his orange.

"Another one. Grab him!"

The men surrounded Kahopi, yanked him to his feet and tussled him around violently.

What an awful fix he was in!

Kahopi began to wiggle and cry out, but they dragged him through the doorway, into the white swirling blizzard. He realized this was the end. It was so obvious, now. The Cloud-People had sent the blizzard to trap him until he could be caught—and it had worked.

— PART 12 —

CHAPTER 86

SPRING 1860
THE BAYOU SALADO

When morning arrived, there was a strange burro standing in the ashes.

"Horace," Augusta whispered, tugging at his shirt to wake him. "Horace!"

"What is it?"

"I think the Utes are back."

He scrambled into his boots, grabbed the shotgun, and leapt outside the tent.

"There ain't no one out here," he called. "Just this burro."

Taking a handful of oats, Horace examined the animal while it ate.

"Poor fellow. His leg hair is all scorched. He must have saw the fire in the darkness and wandered in to get warm."

The scraggly animal had a saddle strapped on, but no one was in it.

When it had eaten all the oats out of Horace's hand, it *hee-hawed*.

Nathaniel, who was camping inside the covered wagon, poked his head outside to see what was going on.

"That's what we all need," he said, irritated. "A honking donkey before I even get my first cup of coffee."

Horace got a second handful of oats.

"If you like it so much, you can ride it from here on in."

"I will ride that beast," Nathaniel said. "This wagon is pretty cramped."

But Augusta burst from the tent and ran straight to the burro and climbed into the saddle.

"That rickety wagon is shaking my teeth loose. And I am sick of those pots and pans clanging constantly."

Nathaniel squirmed out of his quilts and began to climb out of the wagon.

"Make any coffee yet?"

But Augusta shook her head.

"No, and there won't be. We're leaving right now. The Utes stole my cinnamon bread, so I'm stealing their burro. And as soon as we find water that ain't salty, we'll make coffee."

Looking around, Nathaniel did not see any Utes—or anyone else.

"They stole my white pony."

Meanwhile, Horace was rooting through the food box. He found the coffee pot and went to stoke up the fire in the fire pit.

"I'm going to melt some snow and get some coffee before we go anywhere," he told them.

Ignoring him, Augusta *hi-yawed* at the burro and took off at a rough trot.

Watching her go, Horace called after her, "Some poor prospector lost that thing."

Giving up, he dropped the pot back into the food box.

"Help me get this tent down."

As the scraggly burro with the burnt legs ran off with Augusta, the two of them broke down the camp and got the oxen back in the traces. Maxcy was hungry, so Horace gave him some antelope jerky to gnaw on.

It wasn't long before the burro slowed to a crawl. The oxen, as slow as they were, caught up easily. The sun was hanging low in the clear blue sky when they reached the far side of the Bayou Salado. Horace spotted a cleft in a low ridge, and they passed through wooded hillsides until the slope gently angled down into a big river valley.

"This is it—the river we've been looking for. All we got to do is head upstream."

Looking to the north, Horace spotted a black trickle of smoke in the distance.

"Look, Gussie!"

Seeing the smoke in the sky, Augusta became suspicious.

"I hope they ain't being burnt out."

For the first time in a long time, Horace felt proud. *What a journey,* he thought. It all started in a filthy little sod house on the Kansas prairie. And now, here they were, deep in the Rocky Mountains, at the headwaters of what was being called the Arkansas River—and everything was about to change.

"I can't wait to be rich," Nathaniel mentioned.

As the wagon got closer and closer, the more excited they became.

Finally, the Tabor party arrived at Kelley's Diggings.

But there were no heaps of gold.

Only piles and piles of black mud—and a half dozen weeping, wild-eyed men.

"You survived!" Kelley shouted, rushing up to Horace. "For the love of God, do you have anything to eat?"

Horace was shocked.

Kelley's camp was small and grimy. There were two windblown, saggy tents. Bonfires were crackling along the frozen riverbank, next to a long series of sluice boxes. But it was the black mud that caught Horace's eye. It was heaped up everywhere there wasn't snow. But he saw nothing that glittered gold.

Sliding off the burro, Augusta began passing out jerky, dried fruit, and cans of vegetables.

"If you men will be patient, I'll bake up a loaf of cinnamon bread, too."

Nathaniel nudged Kelley with his elbow.

"You're in for a real treat. She makes a tasty cinnamon bread."

But Kelley had a mouthful of dried prunes and did not reply.

CHAPTER 87

SPRING 1892
LEADVILLE

"Well, there's Indian Oil, Pulmonary Syrup, and Oriental Invigorator," said the druggist. He placed a row of medicine bottles on the counter, and then plucked another one off a high shelf.

"Then we've got Swift's Specific. The label itself reads, 'It's not one of the old worn-out, potash, mercury, sarsaparilla, thousand doses-for-a-shilling medicine.' No, sir, I can vouch for that. And it says right here, it cured a woman and her child. That's quite a testimonial."

Wheezy Jones dabbed his nose.

"Just the Bronchial Pellets. I'll see if they help."

"If it doesn't have some kind of positive effect on your nasal leakage, come back and try one of these."

"I will, thank you."

Stepping outside into the fresh air, Wheezy Jones blinked in the sunshine. The druggist's shop was on the second floor of the Midland Depot, and the morning sun, just starting to peek above Mosquito Pass, lit up the landing in its bright beam.

The bright beam not only blinded Wheezy Jones from the danger he was in, but it also illuminated his frame so distinctly, Big Ed had no trouble drawing a bead on him with his Sharps Big Fifty buffalo rifle.

When he squeezed the trigger, Wheezy Jones's entire head vaporized in a crimson spray, and the vial of Bronchial Pellets fell from his grip and rolled down the wooden stairs, clunking like a metronome the whole way down.

"Shoot for the stars," Big Ed mumbled, who was crouching on top of the train caboose a short distance away.

The caboose of the Colorado Midland train was the perfect blind for an early morning ambush. The train had sat all night, and the first departure wasn't scheduled to leave until after breakfast. The train crew was still off eating in the Tabor Hotel, and the depot was more or less empty. Plus, the caboose viewport stuck up high enough from the rooftop that Big Ed could hide behind it comfortably, as well as prop his rifle on the roof for a sure shot.

There was also a convenient series of ladder rungs leading straight to the ground, and Big Ed got down quickly. Once his feet hit the gravel, he was off like a jackrabbit.

Alarmed at the loud gunshot, the druggist hustled to the entryway and opened the door. There, he saw Wheezy Jones' headless body lying on the landing, motionless in the morning sun.

"Oh, dear Lord!"

Going back inside, he immediately gathered every vial of Bronchial Pellets he could find and dumped them in the dustbin.

CHAPTER 88

Dabbing her nose with a handkerchief, Janey Campion was inconsolable.

"He was just a dumb, drippy kid," she howled. "He ought never have been put in charge of nothing."

John Campion didn't like being around weeping women, especially his own wife, so he snuck out the front door. When she heard the door latch click, Selma Sawney glared over her shoulder.

"Just like a man."

They were in Janey's sitting room, among a pile of pillows on the sofa. All around them, scattered on the floor, were damp, wadded handkerchiefs.

"He couldn't even run that mine, why would they make him run that silver club?" Janey asked, tears pouring down her cheeks. "Now he's . . . he's . . ."

But she couldn't say it out loud and began gasping hysterically.

"Hush, hush," Selma said softly, pressing a cool rag to her forehead. "If you work yourself up anymore, you might faint."

Without bothering to knock, Baby Doe burst through the front door and rushed over to the sofa. Her face was creased with concern, and she carried a wicker basket full of pastries.

"Oh, poor Janey! I brought blueberry muffins."

She set them on the table.

But Selma gave her a withering frown.

"You think muffins will help?"

"They're from the bakery on Harrison."

Selma could not believe what she was hearing. She stood up and put her hands on her hips.

"Her brother was shot in the skull. Now he doesn't even have a skull. You are the most insensitive person I have ever met."

Fearing a slap, as Selma was a known slapper, Baby Doe took the initiative and slapped her first.

Stunned, for a moment, Selma touched her tingling cheek. Then, she rushed over to the table and grabbed the basket of blueberry muffins. Baby Doe watched her warily.

"Don't you touch those."

"Oh, Wheezy . . ." Janey wheezed, scratching at her corset.

Rushing to intercept Selma, Baby Doe's feet got tangled in a pile of moist handkerchiefs, and she tripped onto the floor. Selma, seeing her enemy go down, raised the basket above her head and heaved it towards the ceiling. Blueberry muffins from the bakery on Harrison cascaded through the air and burst into crumbles on the Persian rug.

Since she was already down there, Baby Doe grabbed Selma's ankles and yanked.

Landing hard among the bready bits, Selma cried out in rage.

Jumping up from the sofa, Janey hurled her hanky furiously at the women.

"Stop it! My brother is *dead.* He's dead and I'll never see him again!"

Selma sat up, rubbing her ankles.

"And we all know why," Selma muttered, in a vile way. "Don't we, Mrs. *Tabor*?"

Baby Doe sat up, too.

"What does that mean?"

Still breathing heavily, but much more calm, Janey looked down on her with disgust.

"Blueberry muffins don't make up for what your husband did."

"What did my husband do?"

Janey and Selma looked at each other, sharing the moment.

Getting to her feet, Baby Doe brushed the crumbs off her skirt and smoothed her rumpled sleeves.

"What a thing to say," she muttered darkly. "And to think, I went all the way down to the Harrison Street bakery. The line was quite long this morning, let me tell you what."

Brooding, she kicked at the mess of handkerchiefs on the floor.

Selma got to her feet, gingerly. She examined Janey, who looked hollow and frail, and hugged her. The grieving woman buried her face in Selma's shoulder.

"Despite all the signs, Horace set up that silver club no matter what, didn't he?" Selma said. "Don't forget—Sylvander tells me everything."

"And now poor Wheezy is . . . is . . ."

Janey trailed off again.

The color drained from Baby Doe's cheeks.

"I can't believe you think Horace had anything to do with this," she said.

Selma sneered.

"He doesn't care that John's mine got blasted or Janey's brother got plugged. None of that slows Horace Tabor down one bit. And you'd defend him no matter what he gets away with. All because he owns half this town and you get to be rich."

"You Sawneys are jealous of his success," Baby Doe said, but without much force.

Seeing Janey so completely shattered by sorrow, and the pile of handkerchiefs—the same kind Wheezy Jones always carried—made her feel terrible.

Undeterred, Selma wagged her finger in Baby Doe's face.

"If silver crashes, Horace will be broke and Janey's brother will have died for nothing."

Picking up her wicket basket, Baby Doe marched for the door.

"And if Horace goes broke, there won't be no more fancy pastries from the Harrison Street bakery, or ninety-thousand-dollar Isabella Necklaces. Baby Doe will be off like a little bird, fluttering about, looking for a new branch to light upon."

CHAPTER 89

CREEDE

Since it was early on a Monday morning, Banjo suspected the Denver Exchange would be a little slow. He wanted to get in and out of there with as few problems as he could. His main problem was Billy Woods, since Billy was a prize fighter. So instead of going straight inside the saloon, Banjo went around back where he could observe the privy.

There were plenty of good hiding places in the alleyway, and he chose to lurk at the rear corner behind a big embankment of snow. It was almost as tall as Banjo, so he didn't even have to squat down.

The main difficulty with the snowbank was that it stank. The crust was riddled with yellow pee streaks. Beer bottles and cigar stubs made it look like a porcupine. While the whole alley reeked of rotting food and decomposing cow guts, the snowbank generated its own special perfume. So Banjo found a cigar stub that was still decent and lit it.

After he had waited for the better part of an hour, Banjo noticed a hat sticking out of the snowbank. Since he was bored, he grabbed it and broke it free from the ice. He regretted it as soon as he did, however, because there was a face underneath. It was the Swedish sheepherder. He looked pretty tattered. His face was a mess of scrapes and bruises and covered in a spider web of frozen blood.

It was unsightly, so Banjo tried to hang the hat back over his face. Unfortunately, it kept sliding off and he couldn't get it to stick in place. He tried several times.

Looking around, Banjo considered his other options. There was the privy itself, but he didn't want to hide behind that. Other than that, there were only rubbish heaps of various sorts, and he would have to crouch, or lie down flat, to hide successfully.

So, Banjo gave up and stayed where he was.

It was spooky, though, staring at the sheepherder's face in the snowbank. The longer he stood there, the more jittery Banjo became. His decided he hated the alleyway behind the Denver Exchange and promised himself he would never go back there again—just as soon as he was done.

The back door opened, and Billy Woods walked out and marched straight into the privy. As soon as he went inside, Banjo hustled back around the building. This was his moment, and he had to move quickly. He did not know how long Billy Woods took for his morning constitution.

Entering the Denver Exchange, Banjo looked around. The game room was quiet, as he had hoped. There were a few sleepy all-night gamblers huddled over coffee cups. The Corner Pocket Drunk was propped up in a chair near the pool table. Bat Masterson was right beside him, gripping the young man's hair as he retched, guiding the upchuck into a cast iron spittoon.

"There you are, amigo," Bat soothed. "Maybe you will be able to tell me your name, once you get it all out."

As luck would have it, Bat had his back to the door. Moving as stealthily as he could, Banjo slid up behind him, seized the man's throat, and began to squeeze.

Writhing, Bat furiously elbowed and twisted and Banjo nearly lost his grip. They banged into the faro table, knocking it over. Playing cards flew everywhere.

Banjo was taller than Bat and had a sinewy strength that surprised most people. It certainly surprised Bat, who, try as he may, could not break free.

Leaning hard, Banjo pressed him to his knees.

"Soapy wants his weekly cut," Banjo whispered in his ear. "You hear me?"

Though his face was turning purple, Bat was still conscious and thrashed. But Banjo's grip was firm.

"This is the only warning you get," Banjo said, and gave his neck an extra squeeze.

Someone punched Banjo in the kidney. The pain was explosive. He let go immediately and spun around to see who hit him. It was Billy Woods.

"Say your prayers, string bean."

But instead of praying, Banjo sprang for Billy's neck—hoping to choke him, too. But the bartender batted his arms away and began pummeling his face.

Billy's fist felt like it was made of stone. Banjo felt his nose snap, his lips split, and then his eyesight exploded into a flash of starbursts as if a dozen photographers had just caught the moment.

And that was all he remembered.

When he finally came to, Banjo's vision was blurry and his head ached terribly.

He moaned.

Gently, he touched his eyes, but they were too tender to rub. He tried to sit up. Even though he knew his nose was broken, he could still detect scents because the smell of the alleyway was keen. He was lying in muck, and his pillow was a pile of cabbage.

"Dern it all."

With a great deal of effort, Banjo got to his knees.

His eyes were so watery it was hard to see. Even so, he felt a desperate desire to get out of the alley as fast as possible. But when Banjo stood up straight, he swooned. Leaning against the privy, he waited for his head to clear.

Blood leaked off his face, leaving a trail of red sprinkles in the filthy snow.

He didn't know how long he had been lying there, but Banjo began to shiver. When his teeth chattered, fresh pain shot through his jaw like electricity. He gasped.

Stumbling, he made it over to the big snowbank.

He grabbed onto it for balance and found himself face-to-face with the Swedish sheepherder.

"I bet I look like you do."

"You don't," said a voice, causing Banjo's heart to skip.

He whirled around and squinted.

"Who said that?"

A blurry figure was standing nearby, whizzing on a pile of mule deer legs.

"You look worse than he does."

Tucking everything back into place, the man came over.

His footsteps seemed loud to Banjo, squishing in the cabbage.

"Shush, please," Banjo whispered, his head throbbing.

"It's me—JJ Dore. And who is this frozen fellow?"

Banjo grimaced.

"I said *shush*," he pleaded. "That's just the sheepherder. The one that got hailed to death. They buried him here, till spring."

With his head swimming, Banjo needed help. He reached out and gripped JJ Dore by the arm. Banjo suddenly recalled who the man was. He was the one who tried to sell Joe Palmer a false gold claim for a hundred bucks at the Orleans Club on its opening night.

"Walk me back to Soapy's, would you?"

JJ kept staring at the dead man's face, poking out of the snowbank.

"Boy, if you didn't know better, you might think this was a Neanderthal froze in the ice."

"Come on, would you?"

"Okay," JJ replied. "Hang on to my arm."

They headed down the alley, slowly, since Banjo's eyesight was unclear and there were many hazards to negotiate. He also found it hard to breathe without sharp pains radiating throughout his abdomen. Banjo just wanted a quiet place to rest. A place that was dark, with a bed. A place that didn't reek of waste and rubbish.

"If I found a Neanderthal, would you pay a whole quarter to see it? Or just a dime? Which do you think is more reasonable?"

"I'll pay you a hundred dollars to shut the hell up."

CHAPTER 90

With the sun down, the meat market had closed for the day. Joe Palmer was not surprised, but he had wanted to wait for dark to make his move. He checked the front door. It was locked, so he peered through the windows to see if anyone was inside. There were no lamps or candles burning inside. Not even the orange glow of a cigarette. He went around to the stock pen out back, but it was empty, too.

That meant LG would be back at his cow camp in the forest. But that was okay with Joe. It would be a better place to say what he had to say, anyhow. In case things got violent.

Joe limped over to the town livery and got his horse out of the corral. His shin was still mending, ever since the New Orleans Kid shot him up. The leg wound was more of a graze than anything, but it still made walking a chore. So Joe was glad for a chance to ride horseback.

Tacking up, he rode the horse down the street—past the telegraph office, the Cliff Hotel, the Denver Exchange, the Orleans Club, Zang's Hotel, past the Hardware & Stoves store, and on into Tent Town.

He stopped by the Mexican Lady's tent, just in case LG was there. But he wasn't, so Joe bought some fresh tortillas. Then he stepped in the Bonanza, which sold beer bottles, but LG was not there, either. So Joe bought a bottle of beer.

"What happened to your ear?" the Bonanza man asked.

"Same thing that happened to my thumb," Joe replied, holding up his hand.

The Bonanza man looked him over.

Joe knew he looked pretty rough.

He climbed back in the saddle and let the horse pick its way down the road while he ate tortillas and sipped beer.

It was a pleasant feeling, he thought, riding along past all the campfires and lanterns and coal oil lamps. The fiery glow made everything look mysterious. In the day, Tent Town looked much less mysterious. In fact, lately, every time he passed through during the day, the lack of mystery made Joe sad. In the stark light of the sun, it was just a bunch of gritty, saggy hovels and passed-out drunks.

"The way of the transgressor," Joe mumbled to himself.

He hadn't been on a bender, with Bob Ford or anyone else, ever since the preacher's sermon. The thought of hard whiskey after hard whiskey made him feel hollow inside for some reason.

Even the beer tasted sour.

He tossed the bottle onto the train tracks.

Grabbing the reins with his good hand, Joe pointed his horse across the rails. Away from Creede, the night closed in quickly. The moon was only a sliver, but the sky was clear and constellations filled the expanse overhead.

In the starlight, the cattle trail was easy to follow. It was a black muddy line in the soft white snow.

The trail soon left the river valley and cut up into the forest. Joe clucked his tongue to keep his horse moving, since it was pitch black in the trees. It wasn't too much farther.

Joe had wisely bundled up. He pulled his scarf tight around his throat, and his hat low. He had purchased a pair of winter chaps made of shaggy lamb's wool soon after the demise of the Swedish sheepherder. They kept his legs warm on nights like this.

"There it is," he whispered.

In the dark, a short distance ahead, he spotted a yellow flicker.

"Got to be his cook fire."

Suddenly, Joe's horse stopped and wouldn't go further.

Getting down, he felt around in the darkness. There was a strand of wire running across the trail entrance. He felt along, trying to figure out how to get through.

"How do you get in here?"

Fumbling with the wire, he sighed and gave up.

"I can't see a dern thing."

Hunching over, Joe crawled through and snuck forward on foot. It was hard to be too stealthy with a limp, but somehow he managed it. Halfway across the snowy cattle pasture, he pulled out his revolver. It was better to cock the hammer before he ever got close, in case LG heard the click.

Slinking up on the fire, Joe paused, listening.

Then someone came out of the tent, holding a small pickle barrel, and sat down on a stump.

"Why, it's Garo," Joe mumbled.

Pinching up wads of dough from the pickle barrel, Walker dropped them into the Dutch oven.

"I used a yeast cake this time," Walker said.

Joe squinted and looked at the tent. But there was no movement. Then he pointed the gun at the trees, but nothing moved there either.

"He will be glad to know that," Walker added.

Who is he talking to? Joe wondered, straining to make out any movement in the darkness. But no one spoke, and no one appeared.

Joe was confused.

"Soapy biscuits," Walker said and clucked his tongue wryly. "What a greenhorn."

Then Joe realized that Walker was only talking to himself. LG was not there. Nobody was. *It's just the kid.*

Slowly, Joe uncocked the hammer and somehow lowered it without making any noise. He suppressed a chuckle as he watched Walker chat with himself. The boy listed off the proper ingredients for sourdough biscuits from memory, and when he got to the yeast cakes, he stopped and dwelt on it.

"Not soap cakes, stupid. Yeast cakes."

Joe hoped his horse was still standing where he left it. He realized he forgot to hobble it, and that particular horse had a reputation for wandering off. As quietly as he could, Joe Palmer turned around and retraced his steps.

CHAPTER 91

When Big Ed stepped off the early train in Creede, the first question he asked the station agent was "Where's the biggest saloon in town?"

"That would be the Denver Exchange," the station agent said, peering over his newspaper. "We only got one street. Just walk up towards the big cliff and you'll see it."

"He just exchanged Denver for Creede," Big Ed grinned. "That's funny he calls it that."

But the station agent wasn't listening.

Big Ed headed up the avenue until he found the Denver Exchange. But when he looked around the game room, to his surprise, he did not see Soapy Smith—or any of the Smith Gang at all.

"You here to eat or gamble?" Bat Masterson asked.

Big Ed looked around again.

"Is Soapy here?"

As soon as he said that, Bat's face turned ugly.

"Why in the hell are you looking *here* for that SOB?"

Confused, Big Ed scratched his chin.

"I guess I was expecting this to be Soapy's saloon. But it ain't, I guess."

"No, it sure as hell ain't," Bat replied.

At the poker table, LG turned around and laughed.

"You're in the wrong establishment, friend. And if I was you, I wouldn't mention that ol' boy's name again. Not to Bat, anyhow."

All the gamblers in the room stopped what they were doing and watched to see what Bat Masterson would do. Jeff Argyle leapt up from the faro table and ran over to escort Big Ed back outside.

"You want the Orleans Club. Go up the street a little farther."

Looking like he might burst, Bat flexed his fingers and cracked his knuckles. Then he pointed at his neck, which was purple.

"You see this? Tell Smith I'll wring *his* neck if I ever see him again."

Ushering Big Ed out the door, Jeff Argyle was nervous. He didn't want his faro table to get flipped over again. It seemed like every time he turned around, his table got tossed.

He patted Big Ed on the shoulder.

"Now, don't come back."

Without arguing, Big Ed left the Denver Exchange and walked up the road. Sure enough, the Orleans Club was just a few doors down, and he had no trouble finding it. He peeked through the big plate glass window first and spotted Soapy Smith chatting with Mollie at the piano.

Knowing that he was in the right place this time, Big Ed strolled confidently through the front door.

"Soapy Smith!" he shouted with a wide grin.

Joe Simmons, standing behind the bar, immediately cocked a pistol and pointed it at his head.

"Don't shoot," Big Ed cried, and held up his hands.

Coming closer, Simmons pressed the gun barrel against Big Ed's ear.

"Walk," he said.

They crossed the room over to the dance floor, where Soapy and Mollie were standing.

"Well, if it isn't Big Ed Burns in the flesh," Soapy said, but looked him over with contempt. "The fat, droopy flesh. I figured you'd be the new king of Leadville by now. Don't tell me you hung up your fiddle?"

Feeling awkward at the greeting, Big Ed gulped.

"I find it hard to play fiddle with a gun in my ear."

Soapy nodded, and Simmons removed the barrel from his ear canal. But he stayed close.

"Hey, dummy!" Mollie said with a giggle.

Staring at her for a moment, Big Ed remembered.

"You're the girl from Haw's hotel."

She smiled and gave him a flirty wave.

"Yep."

Soapy turned and headed for the backroom.

"In the back."

Simmons poked Ed with the gun barrel, and they followed.

Banjo, who was lying on a cot, sat up as soon as they came inside. His face was lumpy and bruised, and he could barely get one puffy eye open wide enough to see.

"Didn't mean to interrupt your nap," Soapy said, sarcastically.

Banjo quietly got up and stood against the wall.

"I took your advice," Big Ed told Soapy.

"What advice?"

"*Shoot for the stars,*" Big Ed replied, with a sly grin. "And I shot the star straight to hell!"

Soapy looked around.

"What the hell is he talkin' about?"

"That's what you told the telegrapher," Simmons recalled. "After we elected Old Man Tripp mayor. That's what you told him."

Big Ed's smile faltered a little.

"Who did you shoot to hell?" Soapy asked.

There was a tap on the door.

Soapy looked even more irritated.

"Now, who the hell is *that?*"

Simmons checked, and let Joe Palmer in.

Joe averted his eyes and quietly took his place next to Banjo.

"And where have you been?" Soapy asked him. "You were supposed to report in last night about that meat market."

But Joe looked down at the floor.

"I shot Wheezy Jones," Big Ed explained. "Blasted his damn head clean off."

Walking up to Joe, Soapy looked him in the eye.

"Tell me you did what I told you."

Joe looked bleak.

"He wasn't there last night and didn't show up for work this morning, neither. I waited for him to come unlock the door, but he never showed. I don't know where he is."

Soapy stepped over to study Big Ed.

"Who is Wheezy Jones and why did you blast his head off?"

Sensing he wasn't communicating correctly, Big Ed took a deep breath to clear his mind.

"Wheezy Jones was the president of the Leadville Silver Club. I knew we had to shut it down, so I did what you said. I shot the star."

Soapy's face scrunched up.

"You did what?" he said, shocked. "I thought you were having a tiff with Horace Tabor!"

Big Ed frowned.

"Well, I was. He was trying to be the boss. Why, he even tried to talk tough with me. Called me names! You remember what a soft underbelly he had. Well, Haw tried to get tough so I put him in his place. And did us all a favor, too."

"How did you do us all a favor?"

Forcing a creasy-eyed smile, Big Ed put his hand on Soapy's shoulder.

"Politics. Haw thought he was pulling the strings. But it was me who pulled that string. His little silver club just went belly up. This gold camp you got going . . . it is the right place at the right time."

Knocking his arm away, Soapy couldn't believe what he was hearing.

"Are you a complete dunce?"

He slapped Big Ed in the face.

"We need a silver club in Leadville. We need silver to get the votes. And this ain't a gold camp—*it's a damn silver camp.*"

Big Ed looked astonished.

"What? I thought you told me to do that."

"I didn't tell you to do anything," Soapy shouted, and slapped him again. "Do you know what you've done? Leadville is the biggest city in the west. If Horace Tabor's silver club fails to get the votes, this whole damn country falls apart like a house of cards. All these silver towns and camps and mines will be broke. This one, too!"

Using his gun, Simmons thunked Big Ed on the back of the head. Collapsing, he rolled onto the floor, and Soapy kicked him in the ribs.

"You are dumber than a post. My God!"

CHAPTER 92

TELLURIDE

When Kahopi was dragged through the door, he was met with a roar of angry shouts.

The lobby of the Sheridan Hotel in Telluride was packed with people. The three Utes—Bear Claw Lip, Greasewood, and White Owl—were sitting on the floor, handcuffed.

The Aproned Man from the grocery followed along and came inside.

There was a long mahogany bar along one wall. Standing there, an older, refined-looking gentleman with thin hair and piercing eyes held his hand up, and the room quieted down.

"Now, who is this?" he demanded.

The men holding Kahopi shook him a couple times, but he remained silent.

"Found this one hiding out in Adams' store."

Striding over, the gentleman looked Kahopi up and down severely.

"You realize who this is?" Kahopi's captor said. "This is Mr. Otto Mears and he owns the whole Rio Grande Southern Railroad."

They pushed Kahopi to his knees.

"Which you hijacked. You stole a whole train and kilt a whole crew."

At that, the crowd roared.

"Hang them dusky devils!"

Bottles were thrown, and people spat at the Utes.

Mr. Mears studied the three captives lying on the floor, and then looked at Kahopi again. A quizzical look crossed his face.

"The boys in Rico say it was a bunch of Utes who stole the Number Nine," he said.

"That's right."

"Kill 'em!"

Someone rushed forward and pressed a hot cigar into Greasewood's chest.

Mears pointed at Kahopi.

"Where did you find that one?"

The Aproned Man answered.

"He was in my store. He bought an orange and some rhubarb. He was polite and paid for everything."

"We saw him through the plate glass," the captor said. "Hiding like a skunk."

"He didn't seem like he was hiding to me," the Aproned Man said. "He was a paying customer. By the way, I received a bulk order of Chow-Chow for anyone interested. It came in, just today."

Otto Mears thought it over.

"Sheriff Beattie," he called to a man with a badge. "This one is not a Ute. He is a Hopi—just look at him. Plus, those other three got blood all over them."

The sheriff examined Kahopi closely.

"You are right, no blood," he confirmed. "Was he armed?"

The man who held Kahopi blinked.

"Well . . . no."

"And he was a polite customer, Mr. Adams?" asked Mr. Mears.

"Yes sir," the Aproned Man replied. "He gave me twenty-five cents."

Otto Mears turned to the sheriff.

"Last month, those damn cowboys at the Pittsburg Cattle Company hoaxed me. Told me there was a gold strike just across the border—right where the government put the Ute tribe. Long story short, the cowboys concocted the whole thing so they could get them injuns off the land. They want it for grazing."

The sheriff scratched his head.

"I don't follow."

"They tried to trick the government and get them Utes moved— by tricking everyone into thinking there was a new gold rush out there. I even sent in surveyors to scout out a rail line. No wonder these men jumped my train."

Then he pointed at Greasewood, Bear Claw Lip, and White Owl.

"This is some kind of land-grab protest."

The sheriff nodded.

"What do you want me to do?"

"Arrest these three and I will press charges," he said. Then he pointed at Kahopi. "Cut that one loose."

The crowd erupted again. There were oaths and spitting.

"If anyone wants Chow-Chow come by my store," mentioned the Aproned Man.

Sheriff Beattie waved over his deputies.

"Lock them up before they get killed foully. And clear all these scamps out of here before some fool knocks over a lantern and burns this place to the ground."

Then he grabbed Kahopi by the arm and pushed him through the door.

Kahopi braced himself for the suffocating snows and the fury of the Cloud-People.

But nothing happened.

In fact, when he opened his eyes and looked he realized the sky was clear and blue. The dark clouds were racing each other to see which could climb over the tall mountains first. They flew right over the big waterfall and vanished. The Cloud-People, in their cotton masks and white robes, had relented.

"Let's go," the sheriff said and marched him briskly down the street. "You ain't safe here. Even if you did nothing, it won't matter to them railroad men or half this town. You are an injun—and injuns just killed some folks."

Even though he felt great relief, Kahopi was confused why the Star-and-Moon Deity had led him to this town. The very bowels of the Two-Hearts' underworld convention was a very evil place, and he could guess the Spider Woman was laughing at his folly.

Then he spotted the black crow.

It was standing in the frozen street picking at a bread rind. It must have been invisible to the Whites, because the miners kept walking right past without taking notice. The crow was certainly the Evil Power. It was watching everything, and must have led the witches right to him in the grocery. But Kahopi knew his Guardian Spirit was watching, too, and got him out of that fix.

Kahopi felt bad for the three Utes. Their prospects did not look good. The mob in the hotel was very angry and wanted to abuse them. If it weren't for Kahopi's good luck, he too would be getting abused at that very moment. Back home, in his village beneath the mesa, when a horse was found in the wrong cornfield, grazing at the fresh sprouts, sometimes the animal would have its ear cut off. It was punishment for trespassing, and the animal would learn its lesson good that way. It was only right to expect something similar was in store for the Utes.

"What are you doing here anyway?" the sheriff asked.

"Looking for my father."

Giving him a side glance, the sheriff kept up his brisk pace.

Their footsteps crunched and squeaked on the cold packed snow.

Kahopi breathed deeply. The fresh air in his lungs quickened his spirit again. He felt very relieved to be out in the open again. The hotel lobby had been very crowded. Open spaces were far more preferable than crowded hotel lobbies.

"The people here dig like ants," Kahopi said, feeling confused.

"Ain't the only place."

Sheriff Beattie led him further down the street.

They passed a miner who had a half dozen burros in tow. In addition to full panniers, each burro had a long plank of lumber tied to its back. Kahopi looked at them sadly as he passed. Most of them ignored Kahopi and flicked their long ears. But the last one in line looked up at him, square in the eye. Kahopi winked at the beast. They understood each other. They were both carrying burdens tied on by others. They were both being led somewhere they did not want to go.

"Inside," the sheriff said.

It was the train depot.

The terminus. The mountains rose high and the trains could go no further. Kahopi had reached his own terminus. His long journey ended here and he, too, could go no further. He had come all this way, endured much hardship and adventure, and now he was unsure what would become of him. It was true White people were deceitful. Also, it was well known that the Two-Heart society was very powerful and caused much evil in the world. Perhaps this was a dirty trick, and he would be led outside of town and murdered.

The station house was warm. There was a bench against the wall, and the sheriff made Kahopi sit down.

"Put this injun on the first train you can. Mr. Mears will comp his ticket."

The station agent peered over the desk at Kahopi, then up at a wall clock.

"Pulls out in twenty minutes."

"Which direction? Ridgway or Durango?" Sheriff Beattie asked.

"Ridgway."

The sheriff sat down next to Kahopi and sighed.

"Where you go from there is up to you. Just don't come back to Telluride."

Leaning over his desk, the station agent looked suspicious.

"Is he dangerous?"

The sheriff thought about it and shrugged.

"Not quite sure."

"Then you better ride with him. Mr. Mears doesn't want any more violence on his trains."

The outbound train was parked at the platform. There were four passenger cars total, all of which were empty. Many people came to Telluride looking for fortune, but not many left. A small twist of smoke rose from the stack and the engine creaked and hissed.

Kahopi stared out the window hopefully, trying to get a look at the tree branches. He took out a pinch of cornmeal and held it in his hand, silently praying that the Hawk Deity might swoop in and carry him to safety.

PART 13

CHAPTER 93

SPRING 1860
KELLEY'S DIGGINGS

It was late, and Horace fought to keep his eyes open.

"You did a good thing, Gussie, giving that cinnamon bread away free of charge," Horace said and gave her hand a squeeze.

They were in their tent, buried beneath quilts, staring at the ceiling.

"It was the right thing to do," she replied. "These men are on the verge of starvation."

"How much should we charge per loaf, do you think, from now on?"

But Augusta didn't like that.

"It's too soon to charge. These men are skinny as ghosts."

"Don't let Maxcy hear you say that," he said softly. "He's fearful of ghosts."

"He didn't hear me. He's in dream land."

Horace sat up.

"I need to check on the fire."

He had staked a claim on a side stream near the Arkansas River that they called Cache Creek. Kelley's group had made such a mess along the main river. Horace decided to try his luck at a different location. Nathaniel, too, had staked his own claim a little farther upstream. Just like in Kansas, they were neighbors once again. But instead of homesteaders, they were gold miners.

It was their first night, and Horace didn't want to waste it sleeping. Since Cache Creek was frozen solid, he had built a bonfire on the bank. That way, once the ice melted back, he could start panning for gold.

Leaning into the lamplight, Horace checked his pocket watch. It was a quarter past midnight.

"Don't make any noise," Augusta told him. "You'll wake Maxcy."

Sliding carefully out of the quilts, Horace pulled on his cold boots.

The stream's bank was still solid ice, and the gravel was as hard as a brick. He threw a log on the fire and stoked the coals.

Disappointed in the slow progress, Horace went back inside and pulled his boots off again.

Just as he crawled into bed, they heard Kelley's voice at the door.

"Hello, the Tabor residence!"

Horace put his boots on again, and let the man into the tent.

"Shush when you talk, because I don't want Maxcy to wake up," Augusta warned them.

Taking off his hat, Kelley knelt down by the quilts with pleading eyes.

"I do hate to be a bother, on your first night and whatnot."

He paused, trying to find the right words.

"Spit it out," Augusta hissed from the blankets. "And then get out."

"Yes, you are right. I apologize beforehand, and I shall be brief," he said. "Sadly, we killed off all the mule deer. The rabbits are all ate up, too. The boys have been eating bark off the aspens and boot leather for dessert."

Horace, seeing where this was going, nodded, and considered how much extra food they had. Mistaking his reflection for hesitation, Kelley got down on both knees, and laced his fingers together like a penitent sinner.

"There's another party just up the river, on the next side creek. They're all out of food, as well," he said, frowning. "It's that damn George Stevens, and I fear they are eyeing us for meat."

Horace was confused.

"But you don't have any meat. Surely you told them that."

"No, I mean, they're eyeing *us* for meat," he clarified, and hiked up his pants leg. "Here's a drumstick, for instance."

Augusta put on her eyeglasses to see what he was talking about.

"We're all too weak to hike out for supplies. Not to mention, there has been one snowstorm after the other. Plus, if I'm honest, no one wants to abandon their claim rashly."

Augusta was irked at the logic.

"Rashly? They're facing emaciation, starvation, and cannibalization. What a bunch of fools."

Kelley shrugged his shoulders.

"That is true. But it is, unfortunately, the actual state of affairs."

Looking uneasy, Horace wondered how they could truly help. He wanted to. But, he also knew they had already used up quite a bit of their own supplies. They didn't have enough food to make it until the spring thaw, and had planned on shooting deer to get by. Now, after learning all the deer in the area had been hunted out, Horace felt his gut knot up.

"This is quite a conundrum."

He turned to face Augusta.

"How long can we survive on bread?"

"I only have so much flour, Horace. I can't bake enough for everybody."

Kelley wrung his hat into a twist.

"I hate to be a bother," he said, again. "Yet, I do see a solution—readily at hand."

He swallowed, and itched his forehead.

"Spit it out," Augusta hissed again.

"There are two big bags of meat right outside, on the sharp end of your wagon."

Horace sat up, stunned at the suggestion.

"The oxen? The *boys?*"

Kelley pulled up his pants leg, displaying his drumstick again.

"It's them or us, really. I hate to say it, but that sure would provide a lot of feed for a lot of mouths. We'd make it for sure, every last one of us."

"Not the boys," Horace mumbled, sickened at the thought of eating the faithful oxen.

But Augusta, ever the practical one, nodded in sympathy.

"That may be our only option, Horace. And if survival is the issue . . ."

She rolled over and uncovered her son's face. Despite the conversation, the boy had remained sound asleep beneath the quilts. She petted his hair.

"What about *Maxcy?*" she whispered. "Do you want to see him go hungry? Or eat shoe leather?"

Getting out of bed, Horace began pacing around the tent in his socks.

"We'll pay you in gold," Kelley added, still crouched on his knees. "Name your price. Although I must confess, none of us have struck it rich yet. The creek bed is nothing but thick black sand. It gums up the sluice boxes and it is a damn chore to work with."

CHAPTER 94

SPRING 1892
LEADVILLE

"You look blue," Horace told Maxcy.

It was lunchtime, and Horace had come home to eat, only to find Maxcy sitting at the kitchen table staring at an envelope.

Baby Doe was fixing lunch, and when Horace came in she shook a butter knife at him.

"Don't bother him, Horace. I'm making us sandwiches, so go away. You'll irritate our digestion. Unless you brought the Isabella Necklace back. Or is it still locked in the hotel safe where your two-year-old daughter can't find it?"

Horace walked over to the hutch to see what she was making.

Picking up a small circular tin can, Horace was horrified to see the label.

"This is ox tongue!"

Maxcy perked up.

"We used to have oxen when I was a kid. Remember that, Pop?"

"You cannot serve ox meat," Horace informed Baby Doe.

But she snatched it back and slammed it so hard on the countertop that pickle juice sloshed out.

Horace went to the table and sat down heavily—but then deflated.

"I remember the boys," he said and moaned.

Reaching across the table, Maxcy squeezed his hand.

"It's from Mother," he said, indicating the letter.

Horace moaned again.

"This is for you, Maxcy," Baby Doe said, and set a plate down. She smiled, though her eyes were still hard. "It's got mustard."

"I like mustard."

"I could never eat the boys," Horace mentioned.

He held his hand up to block the sight of the sandwich. It had been thirty years, but the memories were still quite fresh.

Unfazed, Maxcy took a bite of the sandwich.

"Mother is mad. She wants me to come home."

"Why, you *are* home," Horace assured him.

Baby Doe began spreading mustard on another slice of bread.

"Horace never eats ox sandwiches. He likes boiled beef with mushrooms and cheese."

"Mother likes the Denver Sandwich," Maxcy told her. "You know, when they put an omelet in it."

Hearing that, Baby Doe turned on him.

"Don't mention that old crow. You two are spoiling lunch."

Maxcy gave her a sincere but apologetic smile.

"I have to talk to my father about this, though," he said. "It demands attention."

"You don't have to discuss her meal preferences."

She speared another piece of ox from the tin can and finished making another sandwich.

"What is Mother threatening to do?" Horace asked.

"Nothing. She's taking the opposite approach. She will *promote* me—to manager of the whole boarding house—on the condition that I leave Leadville immediately."

Horace frowned.

"Well, what were you doing there before?"

"Operating the telephones, mainly."

Leaning back in his chair, Horace folded his arms.

"I'll make you manager of the entire Tabor Grand Hotel."

"That's too much, Pop," Maxcy replied sheepishly. "You've already made me the parlor manager."

"That's nothing. You deserve to run the whole place. And what would you rather run . . . a first-class luxury hotel, or a ratty old boarding house in Denver?"

Baby Doe pointed the mustard knife at the walls.

"It's worth forty thousand dollars. Unlike this dump."

"Where is Silver Dollar?" Horace snapped, pointing at the high chair. "Did you forget about her?"

But Baby Doe ignored the question and ate her sandwich.

"Mother is pretty mad," Maxcy went on.

Horace leaned across the table with an imploring look.

"I need you here with me. We need to find out who is sabotaging the silver club. Who caved in the Lucy B.? Who shot Wheezy Jones? I need you, Maxcy. You are the only one I can trust."

Maxcy took another bite of his sandwich and chewed slowly, reflecting on the situation.

Horace sighed and collapsed in his chair.

"Do you want to go back to Denver?"

Maxcy gave his father a half-smile.

"No. But don't tell Mother I said that."

"Baby Doe!" Horace said and slapped the tabletop in victory. "Meet the new manager of the Tabor Grand Hotel!"

But she had already left the room.

Getting up from his seat, Horace rooted through the pantry.

"Where does she keep the mushrooms and cheese?"

CHAPTER 95

They heard a knock at the front door. Horace went into the foyer and peeked through the curtains. It was Dirty Johns.

"What are you doing here?" Horace asked, cracking the door open.

Taking off his nice stovepipe hat, Dirty Johns looked remorseful. "I know who's been doing all these terrible deeds."

Opening the door all the way, Horace waved him inside.

"Hurry up," he whispered, glancing up the staircase. "Before the woman sees you."

He hustled Dirty Johns around the corner and into the kitchen. As soon as he saw Maxcy, who looked very much like a young Horace, Dirty Johns looked startled.

"I forgot there was two of you."

"Just tell us what you know," Horace said.

Sinking into the chair next to Maxcy, Dirty Johns placed his hat on the tabletop and stared at it sorrowfully.

"It's Big Ed."

Horace's eyebrows shot up.

"What!" he exclaimed. "Why, that little pecker milk. Where is he right now? The brewery?"

But Dirty Johns shook his head.

"No, he's long gone."

Horace paced the kitchen, furious.

"I should have run him out of Leadville years ago," he muttered. "But why? Why would he bet against the silver club? That don't make sense."

Maxcy gave Dirty Johns a reassuring pat on the forearm.

"You did right, coming to us and telling the truth."

Horace punched the air several times, frustrated at the revelation.

"I'm not sure why, but I know he did it," Dirty Johns continued. "He started the bad rumors and caused the strike. He planted blasting powder in the Lucy B., and he shot your man in the head."

Pushing his plate aside, Maxcy studied him carefully.

"That man he shot was not only the mine manager at the Lucy B., but he was also the silver club president. The reason why is politics."

Dirty Johns looked even more mournful.

"Ed sure is a bad man," he said.

"We have to find him," Horace said, feeling flustered. "We'll need a posse. I never raised a posse before. We need to think about how to do that. And hire a tracker. Who knows where he went!"

Dirty Johns glanced up.

"Ed went to Creede."

Relieved, Horace clapped him on the back.

"Thank you, sir. That is valuable information."

Brightening at his last comment, Dirty Johns looked at Horace hopefully.

"How valuable?"

Hearing that, Horace slid into the seat across from him and grew somber.

"What would you like?"

Dirty Johns grinned and revealed a row of rotten teeth nubs.

"A Fairy Floss machine. For inside the Stray Horse. I could put it next to the bar."

CHAPTER 96

CREEDE

Though it was a chore to butcher all by himself, LG decided it couldn't wait. The cooks at the Denver Exchange, Orleans Club, Cliff Hotel, and Zang's Hotel had all stopped by to place orders.

"How long does it take to spade dirt onto a dead man?" he wondered, up to his arms in blood.

He looked around the room at his handiwork. He had skinned several steers and hung the biggest cuts from the rafters. The meat market, at long last, looked like a meat market. Including the awning with its cedar shingles.

"I deserve a day off," he said, talking to a steer head. "Maybe play some poker."

He was starting to lose track of the days. How long had Walker been by himself at the cow camp? LG couldn't quite recall, but he wasn't concerned. It was good for the boy. It would toughen him up. He'd learn to run things on his own. That was the cowboy's life anyhow—there was a lot of alone time running cattle. It was good for him to learn that now, because it would serve him well later at other ranches. The boy could wind up in a line shack, or tooling on a windmill all by himself, or repairing water tanks, or stuck on night guard a hundred nights in a row. Plus, the more time Walker spent working the cow camp, the less time LG had to. He liked being in town. He liked people, chatting, and evening poker games. And he liked being close to the Mexican Lady—which meant frijoles for lunch and flautas for supper, every day of the week if he wanted it.

Dragging a wet haunch into the smoke room, LG knew his back was going to be sore.

Suddenly he heard someone knocking on the store window. Stoking up the fire pit, he went out to see who it was.

It was Bob Ford.

"Hey!" Bob shouted and rapped on the glass again.

LG grabbed a rag and wiped his hands off the best he could, and then let him in.

"I need to buy some meat."

"You bet," LG said.

Walking around the room, Bob examined all the cuts dangling from the rafters.

"You all by yourself tonight?"

"Yep. My pard will be back soon. He's off burying the dead."

Bob walked around until he found the biggest haunch.

"This one looks good. I'll take it."

He saw another one that caught his eye and poked it with his finger.

"This one, too."

He grinned, like he had a secret.

"Just put 'em somewhere, and I'll bring a wagon over in the morning."

"You must be hungry," LG quipped.

"You won't blab, will you?" Bob asked.

LG shrugged.

"Who would I tell?"

"Not that fool Soapy Smith, or any of his stinkin' crew."

LG shrugged again.

"Want to know something?" Bob asked. "I'm gonna open my own saloon."

"Let's celebrate."

Pulling out his package of Pinheads, LG offered Bob a cigarette.

"You hear about Soapy Smith, fixing that election?" Bob said as he lit up his cigarette. "I am sick of that sort o' shit."

"The vote for mayor?" LG asked. "I suppose."

"He thinks he runs this town and can do whatever he wants."

He took a deep, nervous puff.

Bob's eyes kept shooting to the door, as if he expected Soapy to barge in at any moment.

"If you're opening a saloon, you'll need more than just a couple slabs," LG told him. "I can provide a steady supply of beef."

"I'll need it. My saloon will be the biggest and busiest in this whole canyon."

Bob went over to the window and pointed across the street. The gas street lamps were still broken, but in the starlight they could make out the silhouette of a new frame building, going up nearby.

"That yours?" LG asked.

"I brought my own construction crew up from Walsenburg. Boys I can trust. Boys who won't blab."

Suddenly, Bob's face turned to stone. "Are you in his pocket, too?"

LG finished his cigarette and flicked the stub into the street. "He sent his boys over to lean on me. They threatened to burn me out if I didn't pay."

"That son of a bitch," Bob muttered.

He relaxed a little, but kept his eyes on the door. He finished his own cigarette and flicked it.

"I'll bring the wagon by tomorrow night, after it gets dark. Don't you blab!"

CHAPTER 97

Draining his shot glass in one gulp, the lone prospector of great fortune, JJ Dore, waved at Simmons—who promptly brought over the bottle for a refill. But strangely, JJ Dore put his palm over the shot glass.

"You don't want more?" Simmons asked, confused.

"Yes, I do—but first I got to tell you something that will boggle your mind."

He sniffed and glanced around to see who was listening.

Simmons found his guile ridiculous.

"There ain't no one around, JJ. Just move your dang hand."

But JJ did not move his hand.

"This will be music to your ears, I assure you."

"Let me guess. You got a bridge in China you wanna sell me."

"Now, I am just a lone prospector, but a man of great fortune . . ."

Taking a fresh shot glass off the shelf, Simmons poured himself a drink.

Unperturbed at his obvious disinterest, JJ continued.

"I was out prospecting this weekend, up a little draw off the Rio Grande, and I struck a find more valuable than half the mines in Creede."

"Is that so?" said Simmons. "Now let me guess . . . all I have to do is pay you a modest fee and you'll sell it to me?"

Still untroubled by his skepticism, JJ carried on.

"I happened to notice something sticking out of the dirt and mud, which caught my attention. There had been a recent rock slide, which unmasked this object from its earthy tomb. And when I got close, I saw a piece of stone in the shape of a man's bare foot—toes and all. Spellbound, I took my spade and gently dug out the soil . . . and do you know what I found?"

"Jack and the beanstalk?"

"*A petrified, prehistoric human being!*"

Simmons poured himself a second shot and gulped it down.

"A Neanderthal," JJ said. "In perfect condition, turned to stone by the passage of time. Can you believe that?"

"If you had gone with Jack and the beanstalk, I would've said yes."

Chuckling, JJ shook his head.

"You're funny, Simmons. But I'll be the last one laughing. Because I'm gonna set up a tent and charge everyone a quarter for a quick peek at this archaeological find of the century."

Tiring of the man's penchant for fables, Simmons began to walk away.

"A quarter sounds like an awful lot for a quick peek at a stone hoax."

But seeing Soapy emerge from the backroom, Simmons lit up. He waved him over to the bar, urgently.

"Tell Soapy everything you just told me," he said to JJ. "He needs a good laugh."

CHAPTER 98

"Where did JJ find this thing?" Simmons wondered, in amazement.

"A junkyard in Denver," Soapy said.

Lying flat on its back, on a bed of burlap sacks filled with straw, was JJ Dore's petrified Neanderthal. Soapy, Simmons, Joe and Banjo all stared at it, as if it might move at any moment.

"Gives me the willies," Simmons said.

They had converted the backroom of the Orleans Club into a shadowy, somber exhibit. To help create the right atmosphere, and obscure the obvious, the windows were papered over—and the only light came from two flickering kerosene lamps. Soapy even used soot to blacken the glass flues.

"Did JJ sell it for a hundred bucks?" Joe asked. "He's always trying to get a hundred bucks."

Soapy shrugged.

"I gave him enough to shut him up and get out of town."

"I could have shut him up," Banjo said weakly.

Soapy looked him over.

"We ought to lay you out, and charge people a quarter to see that mashed up face. But this ain't no freak show."

Joe snickered.

"Why don't you two go outside? And pass out those handbills," Soapy told them. "The first showing starts in an hour, and I want to see a line all the way down the street."

They quietly slipped out the door, leaving Simmons and Soapy alone with it.

"The Petrified Man," Soapy said eerily.

Simmons shuddered.

"This whole setup makes the hair on my neck stand up straight."

"You always were scared of your own shadow."

"Only when it moves."

Simmons opened the door and went back to man the bar.

The Petrified Man was a tall creature, with long arms and splayed feet, and a mummified expression. It could certainly pass as an archaeological wonder, in the right conditions, even though it was made of concrete.

The common miner was gullible. Whether it was mesmerists or witchcraft, poltergeists or prehistoric ape-men, there was always some superstition Soapy could use to turn a profit. Maybe, when this con ran its course, he might create a haunted mine. That would be easy enough. With Joe's missing thumb and ear and Banjo's busted face, they could pass as spooks in a dark tunnel.

Soapy needed to figure out what he was going to do with Big Ed Burns. At the moment, the fool was tied up in the cellar. Perhaps, people would pay even more money to walk through a *legitimate* haunted mine—Soapy could turn Big Ed into a real ghost with a quick gunshot or a twist of the knife. Or drop him down a deep, dark shaft.

"Wouldn't be the first time," he mumbled.

Soapy could only hope Big Ed's mistakes in Leadville hadn't been too serious. Soapy knew Horace Tabor. Their paths had crossed in the past. Back then, the man had no intestinal fortitude. But from the sound of things, the Silver King had toughened up a bit. So, maybe all was not lost. Perhaps Horace could fix whatever Ed had broken. November was still far enough away they could still get ahead of the vote.

The cellar was right below the backroom. Big Ed was gagged, but every now and then he would kick or moan. Kneeling, Soapy knocked on the floorboards and listened. Immediately, he heard Big Ed flop around.

"Shut up down there!"

If it got too distracting, Soapy could always chloroform him. Or, given the spooky nature of the Petrified Man exhibit, the sounds of muffled fear emanating from the floorboards might just add a certain *je ne sais quoi* to the whole experience. He might even get away with charging thirty cents.

CHAPTER 99

TELLURIDE

Lulled by the train's swaying motion, Kahopi fought to keep his eyes open. It was not safe to nap, even though he desperately wanted to. He tried counting the number of seats to keep awake. He knew there was a good chance he was being taken to the Underworld Kiva and it was best to be alert.

"It's gonna be awhile," Sheriff Beattie told him. "Might as well relax."

It was just the two of them in the entire passenger car. A ticket agent passed after the train left Telluride but didn't say anything to them and never came back through.

The train moved slowly, following the icy river right through the Utes' traditional hunting grounds. Kahopi was sitting by a window. He looked out across the snow-covered slopes. High above, among the big snowy peaks, he caught one last glimpse of the Lizard Head. It was high and far away, and when the train entered a canyon, the giant stone pillar vanished from view.

Kahopi knew what to expect. The Two-Hearts would try and initiate him into their society. They would try and persuade him and tell him how happy he would be if he joined them. But Kahopi knew better. He struggled to remember what his father told him long ago, should just such a situation arise. Despite his jokes and foolish behavior, his father had given him valuable advice when he was a child. There would be ceremonial questions with secret answers, and Kahopi needed to answer precisely to preserve his life and stay on the Sun Trail. He hoped he could remember the right answers when the time came.

"I could eat," the sheriff muttered.

He got up and walked to the back of the car, opened the door, and went into the next car. After a minute or so, he returned and sat down again. The sheriff looked at Kahopi and gave him a soft look.

"He's gonna bring us some grub."

It struck Kahopi that he never got to eat his orange. The Whites captured him while he was still peeling it.

The sheriff stretched and crossed his legs.

"They only got one damn dining car on the whole line."

He scratched his chin.

"They only hook that up when the rich folk ride."

Sitting in silence, Kahopi began counting seats again but gave up after a while. He turned his attention back out the window. The river was much closer now. The banks were frozen. In many places, the ice stretched across to the other side, as if trying to smother the water. In fact, there were places where the ice succeeded. One part of the river was completely covered with snow and ice—except for holes, in which Kahopi could see the water sputtering. That was how he felt. Like the ice had been struggling to cover him over, to smother him, and it almost succeeded. The window in the train was like a hole in the ice. He could see out, but he was trapped and could only sputter.

The ticket agent returned. He carried a plate, three mugs and a kettle. He walked with care, since his hands were quite full.

"Johnny cake, onions, and beef. And apples for dessert," he told them. "Railroad don't provide passenger meals on this stretch. Never on the outbound at this time of day, not when it's dead like this. At least they keep the caboose stocked with some basics. And of course, we got the stove back there to keep the coffee going. This beef here, I brung from home. You're welcome to it."

The sheriff took the plate.

Taking one of the small yellow cakes, he held it out to Kahopi.

"Better take on a good bite. We won't make Ridgway for a couple more hours."

Kahopi had no intention of eating anything these men gave him. It was sure to be poisoned. But when he caught a whiff of the yellow cake, he realized it was made of corn. Corn was one of the true Hopi foods. Like beans and spinach and squash, the old Hopi foods were preferable. They were satisfying in ways the White people's fancy foods could never be. So Kahopi took the yellow cake and tasted it. He was not worried now. The Corn Mother would protect him from any witch's poison.

The ticket agent sat across the aisle and started filling the mugs with steaming hot coffee, then passed them around.

"What's going to happen to them Utes?" he wondered.

The sheriff took a cautious taste.

"Ooo—that's good."

"Just like Jesse James," the agent went on. "I can't believe they robbed one of our trains. And I knew them boys. I used to run the broom on Emmit's crew last summer. He would holler like a grizzly if I didn't sweep up that soot, and sweep it up quick. But I learned to sweep up real good, let me tell you."

The coffee did smell tasty and Kahopi decided to risk it, since the sheriff and ticket agent were both drinking from the same kettle. It warmed his insides. Also, the corn cake was dry and the coffee helped wash it down.

"We were the very first crew to ride over the Ophir Loop trestle last summer," the agent continued. "I about shat myself. That big ol' bridge! You could drop a penny and count to ten and if it hit the ground you'd never know. And boy was it long. Four hundred and seventy-six feet of ass-puckering terror—every inch felt like a mile. Emmit didn't have to holler that day. I just kept my head down and swept like a madman till we made it to the other side. He had to holler to get me to *quit.*"

The ticket agent chuckled.

"That's real good beef, by the way," he noted, pointing at it. "My wife boiled it up just last night. She likes to add chili peppers. That's her secret. Most ladies just use salt to season it up. But she likes to add the peppers. And I do like it that way."

Using his fingers, the sheriff tore off a big piece. He tasted the cold meat.

"Yep," he said.

Turning to Kahopi, the ticket agent whistled in disbelief.

"Wrong place at the wrong time. Count yourself lucky you ain't invited to the necktie party. Them injuns got to be swingin' by now."

Kahopi ignored him and continued staring out the window. The tracks crossed the river on a small, stout timber bridge. The train slowed as it crossed and then made a narrow turn. It creaked and rocked and all three of them held their cups aloft.

"Whoa! You almost spilled on your coat!" the agent said to Kahopi. "You know, I just bought a new coat at the OK shop, just like yours, and I would hate to get it spilled on. My wife makes all my clothes herself, so when I showed up with a store-bought coat, she was mad as a bull seeing red. I told her they sell pre-stitched jackets at the OK shop and a lot of folks buy 'em. But she still didn't care for it. All the fellows who work the creeks and freeze all day seem to own one. Although I can't say I ever seen an injun work a sluice. You got a claim on the river?"

Sheriff Beattie scowled.

"You don't ask a man his business."

"No, no, you're right, Sheriff. Never ask a man his business. Not polite. I apologize. Probably works up at the Smuggler-Union. Most everybody winds up there sooner or later."

The sheriff scowled.

"If he did, he don't no more."

"I hear you, I hear you. Stay away from Telluride," the ticket agent chuckled. *To-Hell-You-Ride!*"

He took the kettle and offered them more coffee.

"Well, it ain't the end of the world. Plenty of other places to go. They're pulling silver ore out of the ground just about everywhere. Leadville's big. Cripple Creek. Silverton, of course. Big new strike at a camp they call Creede."

He snapped his fingers.

"Sheriff, you hear what they found up in Creede? Some ol' boy dug up a petrified corpse and they got it on display. Parade folks through there at twenty-five cents a head. I wish I could see it with my own eyes. They find dinosaur bones and seashells and all kinds of crazy things up in these mountains. Now they found a damn Java Man."

This news was so shocking that Kahopi sat straight up and splashed coffee all over his coat.

"There it is!" the station agent said with a good-natured smile. "Sooner or later, everyone spills on the train."

— PART 14 —

CHAPTER 100

SPRING 1860
KELLEY'S DIGGINGS

"Black magic, black death, black widow spiders . . . Black*beard.*"
As soon as Horace said that, Maxcy flicked his fingers.

"Pirates!" he yelled. "Doubloons!"

They were sitting on a heap of black muddy sand, and Maxcy started raking his fingers through it, searching for buried treasure.

"Nothing good comes in black, Maxcy," Horace continued. "You see a black cat, you turn the other way. Black clouds, black bears—it's all the same."

The dense black sand of Cache Creek was causing him nothing but headaches. The entire creek bed was filled with it. Every spadeful came up with the same heavy, pitch-black silt. When he dumped it in the sluice box, instead of rinsing gently over the riffles, it clogged the whole thing up. It could only have been worse if he dumped in molasses.

Seeing his boy digging for pirate gold made Horace feel less miserable.

Reaching into his vest pocket, Horace palmed a copper penny and when Maxcy turned his back, he buried it in the mud.

"Maxcy—check over here."

Horace stood up, and brushed off his trousers. The seat of his pants were damp, and so were his knees and pant legs. Placer mining was cold, wet work. He picked up a stone and hurled it over the frozen creek. It punched a hole in a crusty snowbank and vanished.

The bonfire, at least, had worked. The ice around the fire had melted, exposing the stream water. Horace was able to pan for gold, and also drink from it. It was nice to have a source of fresh water and not have to melt snow in the frying pan.

It was also nice to have fresh meat.

"Sorry, boys," Horace mumbled.

The oxen had been butchered, and the meat was drying. It was an enormous amount of food, plenty for the whole camp. There was so much, Horace even invited George Stevens and his party to come down to the Kelley Diggings and share a meal. He even gave them a whole side of ox to take back. It helped smooth over the claim-jump tension, as well as quench any thoughts of meat raiding or murder.

George Stevens had been so grateful, he brought a bottle of absinthe to share. Horace had never tasted the potent liquor before, and it was very strong. It was also very green. Stevens offered a short, strange, but unique toast as they drank: "Smother the parrot!"

Just as Maxcy discovered the copper penny in the black sand, George Stevens himself hiked up Cache Creek.

"Look, pirate gold," Maxcy said, showing him the coin.

"That's quite a find," Stevens replied. "The propensity for good luck must run in the Tabor family. If it weren't for you all, we'd be skeletons by now. Rich skeletons, I might add."

Maxcy's eyes grew big, at the mention of skeletons.

"Are you a ghost?"

Horace put his arm around the young boy.

"It's okay, son. There's no such thing as ghosts."

Stevens smiled.

"Horace, I want you to know how much me and the fellas appreciate the ox meat. That was a very generous gesture."

"All my friends call me Haw," Horace said, and they shook hands.

"Well, Haw, I ain't lying when I say we were pretty desperate."

Horace shook his head in disbelief.

"They said you were eating aspen bark and boot leather. I wish we had more to offer."

Stevens looked around, to make sure no one was eavesdropping. Augusta was in the tent and Nathaniel was upstream working his own claim.

"I hear your bride bakes bread."

"That is true," Horace admitted. "It's quite popular down here. Especially her cinnamon bread."

"I wanted to show my gratitude for the help and friendship you've shown. Don't tell Kelley, but we have found high grade colors at our camp. And not just a twinkle of dust, like down here. We find *nuggets!* We're rich already. It's the California gold rush, all over again, but no one knows it yet. You are welcome to come on up and join us. Remember—just don't tell Kelley, because I hate his guts."

Horace looked doubtful.

"All this black sand is wearing me down. Do you have the same problem up there?"

Peering into the sluice box, George Stevens grinned.

"Not at all. Why don't you come on up? It is only a day's travel upriver. When you see a bald mountain, turn up the next gulch. You'll see the smoke from our fires when you get close. Just come on in. We'd love to have your company—and share in the wealth."

He dipped his hand into the black mud, and squeezed it through his fingers.

Maxcy watched, fascinated. He picked up a handful of mud, too, and squeezed it through his own fingers.

"Or you can stay here, I suppose."

CHAPTER 101

SPRING 1892
LEADVILLE

"What happened?" Maxcy asked, sinking down into a zebra-striped chair.

Seated behind the large mahogany desk in his hotel office, Horace looked absolutely crestfallen. There were dark bags under his eyes, and his thin hair looked wispier than usual.

"She's threatening divorce."

Maxcy scratched his head, trying to think of something compassionate to say.

"That's awful."

Horace nodded, barely.

"She wants half of everything, right now, in cash," he said. "She don't want shares or promissory notes, or anything on paper. Either cash—or *gold*, if you can believe she said that!"

The safe behind the desk was open, and Horace was holding the Isabella Necklace.

Maxcy was not sure what was going on, exactly, or what to say, or how to say it. He had never seen his father looking so morose before, and it made him uncomfortable. When Maxcy was a kid, he remembered his father and his mother, Augusta, fought a lot. They argued over everything—and then one day, they got a divorce. Ever since Maxcy had come to Leadville, he had seen Horace and Baby Doe argue over everything, too.

"I'm sure whatever spooked her, it's only a misunderstanding," Maxcy said, trying to say something optimistic. "It will be alright."

Horace, looking pained, held up the necklace.

"Do you think she married me for my money?"

"No, of course not."

Horace cringed.

"She's gone, Maxcy. She packed up and left the house, right after the ox tongue sandwich fiasco. She took Silver Dollar and checked into a hotel room."

Maxcy looked around.

"Here?"

Horace cringed again.

"At the Delaware."

John Campion owned the Delaware Hotel and had built it directly across the street from the Tabor Grand Hotel. They could see it through the windows.

"I'm sure once she cools off, everything will be fine," Maxcy said.

Cradling the necklace like a cat, Horace began to pet it, softly.

There was a knock, and the telegrapher from the Western Union stuck his head through the doorway.

"You wanted to send a message, sir?"

Horace nodded, miserably.

"Face-to-face is better," Maxcy said. "Maybe you should just go over there in person."

Putting the Isabella Necklace back in the safe, Horace went around the big mahogany desk and handed the telegrapher a silver dollar.

"Wire Bat Masterson in Creede. Ask him if he's seen Big Ed Burns."

"Certainly," the man replied and tipped his hat.

"And let me know the minute you get a reply!" Horace added.

Pausing at the window, Horace stared forlornly at the Delaware Hotel.

"Which room do you think she's in?"

Maxcy got up and stood beside him.

Horace's office was situated on the third floor of the Tabor Grand. If someone were to look up from the street, there would be no mystery where it was located. The entire building was made of red brick, except the corner room where the office was. It rose up above the rooftop like a white shining tower, with a big American flag flapping on top to mark the spot.

Nothing else in Leadville reached such glorious heights.

Until John Campion built the Delaware.

"That stupid Campion, putting his hotel right there," Horace grumbled. "Not only is it an eyesore, but it blocks my view of half the Mosquito Range. And now my wife is holed up inside that thing. I am going to buy it, tear it down, and rip out the foundations."

Then he began to weep.

"What did I do wrong?"

Maxcy put his arm around him.

"Oh, Pop."

"It was that damn sandwich," Horace said. "I didn't want to eat the boys."

"Of course not. No one can blame you for that."

Clearing his throat, Horace began pacing around the room.

"Big Ed shot Wheezy Jones, and I want him arrested and tried for murder. I know Bat Masterson will be glad to help. He was a lawman once."

Maxcy sank into the zebra chair again. His father's office was fancy. It had everything—a telephone, gas lighting, a colorful hand-woven rug from Kathmandu, an ivory elephant tusk from Zimbabwe, and a French mantle clock with a silver rooster on top.

"What do we do about the silver club?" Maxcy asked. "This whole city is on pins and needles. Maybe we should give up on it until things settle down."

"Campion don't want nothing to do with it, that's for certain," Horace grumbled.

Digging a handkerchief out of a drawer, he wiped his watery eyes—and then held it up.

"Poor fellow. But that's what a buffalo gun will do to a man's head. Now, he's dabbing his nose at the Lord's Supper."

CHAPTER 102

CREEDE

When the stock car door opened, a flood of burros came rushing down the ramp—and one horse. It was Davis's horse, Big Sunday.

"Look at 'em run!" LG said.

Davis was perched on the fence, and after they all ran by he jumped down and shook out his rope. He walked around the stock-yard until he cornered the sorrel.

"Spill your loop on him, so we can eat supper," LG called.

"All you ever talk about is food," Davis yelled back.

A group of three muleskinners came over and stood next to LG, with arms crossed. They were all dressed the same—canvas pants, rumpled hats, buckskin gloves, and matching mustaches. None of them looked happy.

"When are you gonna fix these stockyards?" one of them asked. LG shrugged.

"It still holds 'em in, don't it?"

The man spat tobacco juice on the ground.

"The yard is too big without them cross-fences. Dern burros are hard to catch. They run circles around us."

"Get a pail of grain and shake it," LG told him. "They'll follow you like the pied piper."

"Why don't you just fix the dern yard and I won't have to."

Once Davis roped Big Sunday, he led him out and saddled him. As he tugged on the cinch strap, the muleskinners climbed over the fence rails and began chasing the burros.

LG led Specter over to the depot stairs so he could get his foot in the stirrup a little easier.

"I heard the Mexican Lady made up a batch of chorizo."

"Lee got buried fine, beneath a yellow sunset. Thanks for asking."

"Forgot how sensitive you were. What else did you learn down there?"

Davis put on the headstall and worked the bit into Big Sunday's mouth.

"They told me the XIT is gonna trail cattle up to Montana again this summer. Five herds, two thousand head each."

LG looked surprised.

"They're still trailing herds north? How do they get past all the settlements on the plains? Can't be much open range left."

"Colonel Boyce says it ain't all barbed wire yet. Once they get up in Wyoming, it's still open prairie as far as the eye can see," Davis said, and then looked around curiously. "Where's Walker?"

"Where do you think? He's been ranch boss ever since you left. And, you'll be glad to hear, I got the meat market open all by myself, and business is booming."

"You left the kid all alone at our cow camp this whole time?"

"More or less."

Davis got up on Big Sunday, and they walked their horses into Tent Town.

"That poor kid must be going loco, all by himself."

"He's an expert biscuit shooter now. Not only can you eat them, but you can wash with them."

Not caring to pursue the matter further, Davis didn't ask what he meant.

"I got a wire this morning from the Houston stockyards," LG told him. "We got a herd of she-stock coming up the rails. It'll arrive in a week or so. And just in time, 'cause we're selling beef quicker than I can skin it."

Davis looked back at the Creede stockyards. The cross-fences were still lying flat, and the muleskinners were running around trying to flush the burros into one corner. But the burros refused to be caught.

"Maybe we should fix those cross-fences after all."

CHAPTER 103

As soon as Davis told him he could take the day off, Walker wasted no time and threw a saddle on the Salty Jackass. Almost forgetting his money, he ran inside the tent and retrieved his earnings from the tin candle box.

"You heading into town?" Davis asked.

Walker, grinning from ear to ear, packed his cash in his saddlebag, and then jumped on the mule's back.

"I sure am!" he exclaimed.

"Alright, then. Have fun."

"I sure will!"

Then he lambed his bootheels into the mule's sides and crossed the pasture at a dead run. The mule seemed just as excited as he was and didn't even try to pitch him off. They only slowed down long enough to get through the wire gate, and once they were through, picked up speed again and shot down the forest trail.

By the time they made it to the train depot, the Salty Jackass was walking slow and breathing heavy. Which was okay with Walker. A spent mule was far less dangerous than a fresh mule. And he was sick of being thrown.

Pointing his reins up the street, Walker looked around in wonder. The last time he came through was the supply run in the buckboard. Coming in alone, with a whole day to himself and his own money to spend, was a completely different feeling. He noticed things that he hadn't noticed before. There was a boot shop, for instance. Walker's boots were tolerable. But a new pair of boots sure would be nice.

"I wonder how much a new pair costs?" he thought out loud. "I better not go in there—it'll be a temptation."

He had been saving for a new horse. He wanted a friendly, reliable saddle mount that didn't pitch, and had finally saved enough to buy one—but not much else.

Then, a set of spurs in the window caught his eye. They were made of silver and brass, and twinkled in the light.

"I need a closer look at those."

He didn't have any spurs of his own, and without spurs the Salty Jackass could give him all the trouble in the world and there was nothing he could do about it. With a pair of new, twinkly, silver-and-brass spurs, Walker could break him of that nonsense for good. Better late than never.

Leaving the mule to take a nap at the hitching post, Walker went inside.

"It smells like bananas in here," he said in surprise.

"Your nose ain't lying," replied the boot maker. He pointed at a wooden barrel. "I soak the leather in banana oil. Makes it easier to tool."

"Have you ever tried banana taffy?" Walker asked. "You should try it sometime. It's very chewy. I haven't had taffy for a long ol' time. Boy, that sure sounds good."

He went over to the shelves and looked around, especially at a pair of tall riding boots with bright green shafts, arched scallops, and pull-straps.

"Try those on," the boot maker said. "See what you think."

Walker tried the boots on, as well as the silver spurs.

"How much you asking?"

"Twenty for the boots. Ten for the spurs."

Without hesitating, Walker counted out thirty dollars in cash, and strode out the door wearing his new get-up.

Walker felt like a real cowboy. He also felt like getting some banana taffy. The livery stable was right across the street, so he led the sleepy mule over and left him in the yard. It cost a whole dollar to leave him there, but it was worth it.

Excited to see the town, Walker headed up the boardwalk, pausing to look in every window he passed. His new boots made a nice firm clopping sound, and his new shiny spurs jingled.

Going inside the General Merchandise, Walker came back out with a paper sack full of banana taffy, candy corn, peppermint puffs, and lemon drops. He also had a separate sack filled with cherry hard candies, his all-time favorite.

Hearing piano music, Walker went inside the Orleans Club.

He gawked. The place was alive with laughter, chatter—and a pretty lady sitting right on top of the piano, singing a song! Walker had never been in a saloon before, but the smell of sizzling steak erased any doubts he had.

Simmons saw the boy come in the door.

"You look like a card sharp to me," he told Walker, smiling at his new green boots. "You gotta be here for some poker."

"No, I'm a cowboy."

Walker had his pant legs tucked in his boots, so everyone would know he was a cowpuncher. He was surprised the man had misjudged his vocation so drastically.

"Can I buy a meal?" Walker asked.

"Come with me, cowboy."

Simmons led him over to a small square table near the piano.

"Who is that?" Walker asked.

"That's Ella Diamond. She can carry a tune, can't she?"

"I would say so."

"Steak and a beer sound about right?" Simmons asked, still grinning.

Walker, trying to act casual, simply nodded.

Setting his candy sacks on the table, he took a look around. The game tables were crowded, and so was the bar. Then he suddenly caught sight of Mollie on the dance floor. A short, skinny miner was dancing with her, but was clearly too drunk to do more than sway.

Mollie saw him watching, and she waved.

"A dollar a dance!" she hollered.

He waved back.

"Look, it's Garo," Joe Palmer said, limping by with a handful of dried-out jerky strips.

Walker was pleased to see a familiar face.

"Is that the deer you shot on the train?"

"Hell, no! And I ain't never gonna shoot another deer again, as long as I live."

He wove past Mollie on the dance floor and took the jerky into the backroom. A moment later, Simmons came out of the kitchen with a plate of steak and bread, and a bottle of beer.

"Five bucks."

"Why is everything so costly in this town?" Walker asked, but gave him the five dollars.

Simmons laughed.

"It's a boomtown, kid."

There was a loud yell from the backroom, and the sounds of scuffling. Mollie heard it, too, and let go of the skinny drunk, who, with no one to support him, collapsed on the dance floor.

Suddenly, the backroom door burst open and Big Ed Burns, looking as wild-eyed as a feral cat, came rushing out. He raced straight across the dance floor, leapt over the fallen miner, and rammed his full weight into Simmons—who went flying as if he had been hit by an elephant.

As he tumbled to the floor, Simmons's forehead struck the edge of Walker's table.

The boy managed to grab his plate and jump out of the way at the last second. Unfortunately, his beer bottle hit the floor and his candy scattered like marbles.

"Holy Moses!" Walker cried, his new silver spurs jingling.

Big Ed kept right on moving, knocking everyone out of his way with hard, vicious shoves. He disappeared out the front door. Then, Joe emerged from the backroom, looking dazed.

"Where did he go?"

"Help!" Simmons cried. "I can't see a thing!"

He had a jagged gash right across his forehead. Red blood poured down his face and covered his eyes.

"Dammit," Joe shouted and pulled his Colt 45. "Where's Banjo?"

Simmons, rolling around on the floor, was in too much pain to care.

"Hell if I know!"

Despite his bad shin, Joe Palmer hopped the drunk miner, flew across the game room, and ran out into the street.

Shaking his head in disbelief, Walker sat back down and cut into his five-dollar steak.

"This is one wild outfit!" he marveled. "The smoke, hair, and fire flies—and don't you forget it!"

CHAPTER 104

Panting, Joe leaned against one of the street lamps to give his bad shin a rest.

"When is somebody gonna fix these things?" he muttered.

He glanced around, trying to spot Big Ed Burns. The three muleskinners were leading their string of burros up the street. The one in front had a pail of grain and shook it like a maraca.

"Where did he go?" Joe shouted, waving his pistol. "Did you see him?"

Giving Joe a hard glare, the muleskinners kept on going.

"Don't point that in my direction!" said the leader, spitting tobacco juice.

"Don't you spook this string," another added. "I ain't chasing no more dern burros today."

Lowering his gun, Joe blinked a few times to clear his vision. Big Ed had a strong punch, and his skull throbbed terribly. To make matters worse, Big Ed had socked him in his bad ear.

Joe realized that the muleskinners were coming from the direction of the depot but acted unruffled. If Big Ed had run past them, he probably would have scared their jack train, and there would have been some *hee-hawing*. All the burros seemed calm, so Joe deduced that Big Ed had gone in the other direction, deeper into the canyon. The road led to Jim Town and the mines tucked up on the slopes, but it didn't go much farther than that.

"There ain't nowhere for him to go," Joe said and chuckled. "Like a fat, cornered rat."

He limped up the street.

Though his head pulsed in pain, Joe tried to stay alert. Perhaps Ed was hiding in a doorway, or an alley, or in the back of a wagon. There were a hundred places to hide. Poking his head in the Cliff Hotel lobby, Joe waved at the clerk.

"Did you see him?"

"Who?"

"Big guy, running scared?"

The clerk looked confused.

"Never mind," Joe said, and hustled back outside.

He crossed the street and burst into the Western Union, flashing his Colt 45 around. The telegrapher dove behind the counter, but no one else was in the tiny office.

"Sorry," Joe yelled and left.

He looked through the window at the meat market, but it was closed up tight. Turning around, Joe noticed a brand new building across the street. The wallboards were made of bright, raw lumber, and he could smell the pine sap from across the way.

Crossing the road, Joe barged inside.

There were a couple carpenters, busy fashioning a long countertop out of blue spruce.

And Bob Ford was seated at a table playing solitaire.

"Anyone break in here?" Joe asked, glancing around the room.

Bob got up, a grin spreading across his face.

"If they did, I'd whomp the hell out of 'em. Now, who you looking for?"

Joe took a second look around.

"Are you building a bar? Is this a saloon?"

Bob lifted up a bottle.

"You look all played out. Why don't you sit down and rest. You want a whiskey?"

Joe frowned. He hobbled over to watch the carpenters, examining everything.

"Please don't tell me you're building a saloon, Bob. Soapy will bury you alive—after he skins you alive!"

Bob just smiled, but it was a tense smile.

"That con man. Thinks he is the king of Creede or something."

"But he is," Joe insisted. "He got Old Man Tripp elected mayor. All these places on Main Street pay him a weekly cut. Even Tent Town. Even the Mexican Lady! What do you think is gonna happen when he finds out about this?"

"Let's see what the cards have to say."

Bob sauntered back over to the table and picked up a card.

"The king of clubs," he said, showing it to Joe. "Why, hell, that's me."

Staring at him in shock, Joe could only shake his head in amazement.

"You don't give up easy, do you."

Bob uncorked the whiskey bottle and took a swig.

"Sure you don't want any? You look like you could use a slug."

Joe turned and started to leave. His shin hurt, along with his ear, but he had no intention of letting Big Ed get away.

He paused in the doorway and held up his Colt 45.

"Make sure you got one of these behind the bar at all times. And post a lookout. Soapy will be coming for you."

Walking over to the bar, Bob pointed at a big mirror hanging on the wall.

"That big glass on the wall is my lookout."

Then his face turned stony.

"He won't get a chance to kill me, not if I see him first."

He took another swig.

"What did I ever do to that prick, anyhow? Out there, on the plains, out East, and everywhere else, I was famous for killing Jesse James. Famous! But then folks got to hating me. Jealous of my success. Twisted it all up, like I'm the one to blame. But I wasn't looking for trouble. I done my best to avoid trouble. I come up here to this quiet little silver camp in the middle of nowhere. Try to live my life. But I was hardly here a week before the word spread . . . *Bob Ford's in town!* And the hatin' began all over again."

Joe's skull was still pounding, and it was hard to listen to one of Bob's speeches when he wasn't drunk.

"Then this fool Soapy Smith gallops in, making trouble for me. Tell me, Joe. What did I ever do to deserve such meanness?"

Joe Palmer sighed and shrugged his shoulders wearily.

"All I know is I got to hunt down Big Ed."

CHAPTER 105

It was very late in the night.

Kicking steps in the snow so he wouldn't slip, Kahopi snuck down the slope beside Zang's Hotel. It was steep and slick, but he made it down without trouble.

Creeping around the big canvas tent behind the hotel, Kahopi paused and listened.

The kitchen door in the rear of the building creaked open. A beam of yellow light shined out, illuminating the trash heap. Kahopi froze in the shadows, watching. An Oriental girl came out and dumped a pail of steaming cow guts upside down. Failing to notice him, she went back inside and closed the door.

Without making a sound, Kahopi darted to the corner of the building and peeked into the street.

Dark figures roamed about.

Voices carried.

Noises floated in the crisp night air, like in a dream.

The moon, just a sliver, crept higher and higher. Like a squinting eye, it, too, peeked into the street.

Kneeling in the darkness, Kahopi fastened a prayer feather to his hair. Then, he laid a second prayer feather on the ground. He prayed to the Star-and-Moon Deity to watch over him and to give him success. He took a pinch of muddy snow and rubbed a little on his chest, face and limbs.

Somewhere, in this small canyon town, he hoped to find his father—whom the Spider Woman had turned into clay. What a harsh punishment for such a minor misdeed!

In what little light the moon offered, Kahopi studied the town.

He immediately noticed something peculiar.

Even though many windows shined in the darkness like floating sun-yellow squares, the street itself was very dark. There was a long line of street lamps running right up the road—but, strangely, every single one was broken. It was as if someone did not want Kahopi to see the street. As if someone did not want him to walk up this road at all.

Suddenly, he felt absolutely certain that this was his true path.

The Spider Woman had tried many, many things to discourage him from completing his journey. But he was wise to her tricks now! If she did not want him to walk up this road, then he most certainly would.

Glancing up at the squinting moon for strength, Kahopi stepped out boldly.

He was on an important journey.

He could not be scared off so easily now.

Kahopi began walking up the dangerous shadow path. Mysterious voices punctuated the air all around him. Dark figures marched alongside him, like souls marching to the Skeleton House. He began to wonder if he was in a dream after all. Perhaps he had fallen asleep. He was very tired, after all.

Once Kahopi had been cast out of Telluride by the sheriff, he traveled east towards the rising sun. When all else seemed confusing, Kahopi always looked to Tawa, his faithful guide. Why stop trusting him? After three days and three nights of frozen wilderness, icy alpine lakes, and snow-swept mountain passes, Kahopi spotted the big cliff. When he saw it, his ears started ringing loudly—and he knew he had arrived. But he was exhausted. Maybe he had fallen asleep! This did feel like a dream. Or perhaps he had gone down into the underworld without knowing it, and was marching to the Skeleton House along with these departed souls.

Suddenly, Kahopi saw another dark figure up ahead, holding a flaming torch.

It was Masau'u, the bloody-headed Fire Spirit.

The god of death himself.

"Come see the wonder—the Petrified Man!" beckoned Masau'u.

Kahopi's ears began to ring again, as they always did when something important was about to happen. The hair on his arms stood up and cold shivers ran through him. His family back at the mesa warned him that meeting the Fiery Spirit up close meant death. Simply seeing his firebrand from a distance was dangerous. And here he was, face-to-face! Even if he tried, Kahopi knew he could not turn away. Masau'u's power was too strong.

A small crowd gathered around the god of death and his flaming torch. They stared at him as if in a trance and, like Kahopi, were powerless to escape.

"For a mere twenty-five cents, come inside and gaze upon the terrifying lineaments of the forerunner of the Java Man, from whom we are descended," said Masau'u in a commanding voice. "Who here has the nerve it takes? Who here has the guts?"

He was standing in front of a dark doorway—the entrance to his shrine.

Lofting the torch high, Masau'u held out his hand expectantly.

A boy in his teens, about the same age as White Owl, stepped forward.

"This is my very last quarter," the boy said, sadly. "I guess I am stuck with the Salty Jackass forever."

Masau'u accepted his offering.

"Money well spent. Who is next?"

Kahopi remembered he still had one quarter left—*the exact amount required!* Bear Claw Lip had sneered at the money, claimed money was unnecessary. That was certainly true for Bear Claw Lip, who was probably dead. The dead did not need money. But Kahopi had found the money useful. And now, he needed exactly twenty-five cents to gain entry to Masau'u's dark shrine.

Trembling, Kahopi placed the coin in the Fiery Spirit's palm.

"That'll do. You may enter."

Crossing the threshold, Kahopi went inside. As he moved through the darkness, he quietly sprinkled a trail of cornmeal on the floor. Behind him, others followed him into the shrine. All of them lined up next to a row of candles, which stretched across the dark floor.

"You scared?" the boy asked.

Kahopi shifted nervously but did not respond.

The boy rubbed his hands on his pants.

"The Petrified Man! I've been looking forward to this all day. My palms are sweaty. Do you want a piece of banana taffy?"

He held out a small item wrapped in white waxy paper.

Kahopi took it but placed it in his pocket—in case the boy was a witch, trying to poison him.

Behind them, Kahopi could hear Masau'u collecting quarters. Finally, he came in. Floating past his victims, Masau'u waved his flaming torch, revealing a second door, hidden in the shadows!

"I am about to unlock the mystery of the ages. Gird your loins . . . cuz there ain't no turning back."

He stuck the key in the lock, making a loud *click.*

Slowly, Masau'u, the Fiery Spirit, the god of death, pushed it open, and led the way into the secret chamber.

The boy followed without hesitation. On his heels, Kahopi stepped carefully over the threshold and looked around, amazed.

Two kerosene lamps cast orange flickers about the room. Shadows rushed among them, dodging and twisting. But Kahopi's eyes were fixed on the body of his father, stretched out on a mattress of straw. Though sinister and vindictive, the Spider Woman had not lied! She had indeed turned him back into clay, and hidden him here in this small mountain town, where the Whites dug like ants.

Masau'u began speaking, his voice deep and thick, but Kahopi was not listening. Taking a prayer feather, he slid it into his father's hand, which was as hard as rock.

"Alright everyone, that's it!" Masau'u announced. "Let's head back out to the bar. Whiskey is half price, and the first one's free."

He led the way out of the secret chamber, and once they were all out, he locked the door.

Kahopi felt panicked. He had only gotten a short glimpse of his father! It was so dark, he could barely even see his face! He hesitated, looking back at the secret chamber, yearning to go back in. But Masau'u had sealed it shut.

The group gathered at a wooden counter, like cattle at a trough.

Masau'u went around, and began pouring amber liquid into small glass cups. Watching the others gulp down the "whiskey," Kahopi knew they were fools. They would be dead by morning. The bloody-headed god of death even poured a glass for Kahopi, but Kahopi did not touch it.

"You gonna drink that?" Masau'u asked, trying to frighten him. "If you don't, I will."

Kahopi placed an old corncob on the bar and a pinch of meal.

"Great Masau'u, accept my gifts. It has been a long and dangerous trip. At last I have come. Please, allow me to bury my father."

Chuckling, the Fiery Spirit turned away and began pouring more poison for the others.

"Come back tomorrow night, if you dare."

Kahopi knew he was in great danger. He had to fight for his life, or he would certainly lose it. Thinking quickly, he reached into his pocket and tore off a leaf from the red bitter stalks. When Masau'u wasn't looking, he shredded it and mashed it in the bottom of his whiskey, with his finger. Then, staring hard at Masau'u, Kahopi secretly projected snake venom into the Fiery Spirit's heart.

"I warned you!" Coming back over, he grabbed Kahopi's glass and drank it down. Then he realized he had swallowed something besides whiskey and coughed.

"What was in here?" Masau'u asked, licking his lips.

Leaping away, Kahopi dashed to the front entrance and rammed the door with his shoulder. It flew open, and he disappeared into the night.

PART 15

CHAPTER 106

SPRING 1860
CALIFORNIA GULCH

When the Tabor party arrived in California Gulch, George Stevens could barely contain himself. As soon as he spotted their covered wagon, being pulled by an unfortunate burro with scorched fetlocks, George Stevens pointed a revolver to the sky and fired.

"Hot damn, boys!" he shouted, hollering up the gulch. "You fellas get down there and help push that wagon. The bread lady is here!"

Several men came running. They were all dressed in filthy brown dungarees with droopy hats and suspenders. Without even shaking hands or doffing hats, they started pushing the wagon right up the gulch.

"Look how nice this road is," Horace commented, marveling at the craftsmanship.

"A road this nice must have taken some serious effort," Nathaniel said. "Look, they even blasted out the stumps. It's smooth as glass."

Clearly, the Stevens party had been busy. The wagon road stretched all the way up the gulch from the river valley, making for easy access—as if it had been made just for them.

"You are welcome to stake a claim anywhere there ain't one already," George Stevens told Horace. "But, in hopes you might join us, me and the fellas already built your wife a cabin right here in camp. We even built a chimney out of river stones."

Flattered, Augusta went inside and looked around.

"Why, it appears they've built me a bakery, Horace."

The men lined up, with their hats in hand.

"The boys even hung a stained-glass window in the front wall," Stevens pointed out.

Sure enough, there was a stained-glass window. It had the image of a red tulip in the middle.

Augusta gave them a warm smile.

"Why, that's lovely."

The three men, standing in a line, beamed in her praise.

"Can we help you unload your baking supplies, ma'am?" one man offered.

"Will you be baking a bread today, ma'am?" another asked.

"I chopped you a cord o' wood, ma'am," a third added. "For baking."

George Stevens clapped his hands and hollered again.

"Tonight, we'll open up the absinthe, boys. This calls for a celebration."

While the men helped Augusta get her baking items transferred into the cabin, George Stevens invited Horace for a walk along the creek. Maxcy followed along, flinging stones in the water.

"We call this California Gulch. Like the gold rush."

"Yes, that's what you told me," Horace said. "That was the sales pitch. Nuggets and such."

The Stevens party, like the Kelley diggings, had bonfires burning to keep the water flowing. And like the Kelley site, it was a mess. Tents, crates, tin cans, liquor bottles, frying pans, tools, and gear were all over the place. The ox meat, at least, was hung up in tidy strips, drying on a clothesline.

"This part of the stream is mine," Stevens said. "And up there is where one of the boys washed up the first nugget. You should have been there! He looked at me and said, 'We've got California in this dern pan.' That's how we come up with the name."

Horace tried to imagine it. A smile slowly spread across his face.

"What a find."

But then his heart stopped—all along the gravel bank, near the sluices and rocker boxes, were mounds and mounds of black, silty sand.

"Blackbeard!" Maxcy shouted. He rushed over and grabbed a handful, and it oozed through his fingers. "Doubloons!"

A cold shiver ran through Horace's gut.

As Maxcy dug around for buried treasure, Horace ran over to the nearest sluice box. It was thoroughly gummed up with the evil, black mud.

"I thought you said there wasn't sand any up here," he said, looking around hopelessly.

George Stevens gave him a blank look.

"That sand? Oh, it's everywhere."

Looking aghast, Horace stared at him in disbelief.

"Tell me you got a special way of separating it out? Surely, you do. There must be a trick?"

"Oh, no. It's just miserable, slow work."

Horace sat on the icy embankment and looked up at the sky. It was pale and blue, with scattered wispy clouds. That was how he felt. Pale, blue, scattered and wispy. All at the same time.

"Did you really find a gold nugget?"

"Oh, yes, Abe found one . . . last year."

Burying his face in his hands, Horace felt woozy.

It was like the Universe did not want him to find gold.

When he first read the article in the *Kansas Tribune*, describing gold in the mountains, the paper made it sound like it was easy to find. As if all you had to do was sled down a slope with outstretched arms, and you would gather enough to buy a castle and live like a king.

Horace wished he could live in a castle like a king.

He had lived in a shoddy sod house with the hot Kansas wind, but that was not a castle. Neither was the hotel room in Denver, which smelled of sickly cheese soup. The soda spring was no castle, and neither was the covered wagon, which they had lived out of for weeks on end.

A king would not be foiled by a crafty cuss called the Old-timer. A king would not lose a pony and a loaf of cinnamon bread to a bunch of sneaky Utes. A king would not be duped by hungry, desperate, competitive, and very nearly cannibalistic, prospectors.

A king would have gold, and loads of it.

Now here he was, in the very heart of Rocky Mountain gold country, one of the very first to arrive, in the dead of winter with three feet of snow on the ground—and there was no gold.

Only black sludge.

Perhaps he could build a castle out of black sludge.

Horace sighed, feeling like his soul had wilted and fluttered away like a crumpled piece of paper in the wind. He watched Maxcy digging in futility, searching for pirate doubloons that didn't exist. Horace could relate. That was exactly what he was doing. Digging and digging, but there was nothing to find.

"Does your wife know how to make banana bread?" Stevens asked. "I have had a craving for banana bread so bad I can taste it. And we heard talk of cinnamon bread."

It had not been that long ago when Horace, after being duped by the Old-timer, walked into a dim tavern in Denver with its fiery red lantern light, and been given the old horse laugh. That weasel, George Stevens himself, had led the taunts.

"I am a fool," Horace mumbled. "The greatest of fools."

CHAPTER 107

SPRING 1892
LEADVILLE

John Campion was shocked to find Horace curled up on the colorful hand-woven rug from Kathmandu, blubbering.

"She's leaving me, John. And I can't talk no sense into her."

Tears leaked from his eyes. Then he reached out and gripped Campion's ankle.

"Just tell me which room she's staying in?"

Maxcy, who was standing by the coat rack, came close and whispered in Campion's ear.

"It's really not a good time."

"Yes, I can see that with my own two eyes," he replied, disgusted.

Campion knelt down, and dangled a sheaf of papers in front of the Silver King.

"You want the Lucy B.?"

Opening his eyes, Horace blinked and sniffled.

"I want my Baby Doe."

Frowning, Campion wiggled the paperwork like he was wiggling a carrot in front of a stubborn donkey.

"Name your price, sign the papers, and it's yours. That damn thing is stopped up like a whore's bathtub. The boys say it will take a year or more just to pump it out. And none of them want to run it, or the silver club, neither . . . and I can't blame 'em."

He looked up at Maxcy.

"Talk some sense into him."

Maxcy knelt down next to his father, and put his hand on Horace's shoulder.

"Pop, should we buy it or not? What do you think?"

Squeezing his eyes shut tight, Horace rolled up in a ball and pulled his coat over his head.

"I *can't* think, Maxcy. I'm in too much pain."

Taking the paperwork, Maxcy went over to the big mahogany desk to look for a fountain pen. Circling around the blubbering Silver King, Campion followed Maxcy around the desk and peered over his shoulder while he signed.

"Good luck finding someone to run your little club, Horace," Campion grouched. "Find someone with thick skin. Especially around the head region."

The telegrapher peered through the doorway.

"Mr. Tabor?"

Horace groaned, Campion marched out, and Maxcy sighed.

Handing the telegrapher a silver dollar, the younger Mr. Tabor unfurled the message.

"Good news at least," he said, relieved, and knelt on the rug by his father. "Bat Masterson says he saw Big Ed. He says he showed up in Creede a few days ago, and no one's seen him leave."

But Horace was still distraught, with his head still buried in his coat.

"Now, Bat also says there is no sheriff in Creede, so we're on our own."

But realizing that everything he said was falling on deaf ears, Maxcy gave up trying. It was clear that his father was in bad shape. It was the worst possible time for an emotional collapse, but nonetheless, it had occurred.

Maxcy squeezed his father's shoulder in a loving manner.

"Don't worry, Pop. I'll take care of this. It isn't over yet—and neither is your marriage."

CHAPTER 108

CREEDE

"It's just pneumonia," Soapy said cheerfully. "Couple more days, you'll be up again."

But Joe Simmons did not look like he would be getting up anytime soon. His skin was colorless, speckled with beads of perspiration, and he cradled a tin pail. The black crusty scab that ran across his forehead did not help, either. He looked downright miserable.

As soon as Simmons began blasting puke, Soapy excused himself. He hurried down the dim stairwell and stepped into the lobby. As soon as he saw Soapy, Zang brought over a steaming cup of coffee.

"Very good, Zang. Now, take another cup of coffee upstairs," Soapy said. "Coffee—you understand? Just coffee. No food. No eggs. You got it?"

Smiling, Zang nodded and bowed.

"No coffee," he said and dashed into the kitchen.

Just as Soapy took a big sip, Zang came back out and raced past him, carrying a plate of vinegar pie and calf's head jelly. Soapy saw what he had, but Zang zipped up the stairs before he could swallow and speak.

"Damnit, Zang!" Soapy said, almost choking . . . but it was too late.

He heard Simmons's door open and slam shut.

"Poor sucker is gonna need a bigger pail."

Taking his cup with him, Soapy went outside into the fresh, brisk air. At some point, it had snowed a little. It was only six in the morning, and he had been awake all night playing faro at the Orleans Club.

Playing faro at his own club was a dreary affair. It was a lot more fun to gamble at Bat's place because Bat didn't rig the game tables. At Soapy's place, everything was rigged. But ever since Banjo tried squeezing Bat for a weekly cut, and failed, things had been a little tense between the two of them.

Soapy was mad at Banjo, and Joe Palmer, too. The meat market still wasn't paying its dues any more than Bat was. Plus, Big Ed had slipped right through Joe Palmer's fingers. Of course, Joe was missing a finger, but that was no excuse. Now Simmons was down, too. All his men were either sick, maimed, or battered to bruises. Old Man Tripp was the only one who was whole and healthy, but he was busy being the fake mayor. Soapy felt like he had to do everything himself—tend bar, run the game tables, and give the Petrified Man spiel—until Simmons got better.

The hotel door squeaked, and Zang came outside—with a worried look on his face.

"What happened? Did he throw up on your shoes?"

The Chinaman lowered his eyes.

"No coffee."

Soapy was confused. But he was always confused when he tried to have a conversation with the man.

"*No coffee,*" Zang repeated, more firmly.

"Did you run out? What are you saying, Zang? Just walk your yellow ass down the street and buy some more beans."

But Zang pointed up at the second floor windows. He was pointing at Simmons's window.

Dropping his cup in the snow, Soapy charged up the stairwell as fast as he could. But as soon as he went into Joe Simmons's room, he knew the man was dead. The vomit pail was full of blood, and there was bloody foam oozing out of his mouth.

"Oh, my God! Joe!" Soapy shouted. "Wake up!"

But he did not wake up, nor would he ever again.

CHAPTER 109

"That is *fantastic* news," Bob Ford said and clapped his hands.

But Joe Palmer laid his head on the new spruce bar in Bob's saloon.

"No . . . it's terrible news."

The two carpenters were sitting in a pile of sawdust eating bologna and crackers. Bob danced an awkward, impromptu jig. Then, he ran over and snatched a piece of bologna from their lunch box and waved it in the air.

"That old boy is dead meat!"

Joe was in no mood for Bob's poor humor.

"That ain't nice. Simmons was Soapy's best friend since childhood. He's sick to death about it, and you ought to show some respect."

But Bob Ford ate the bologna instead.

"I ain't ever seen him so blue before," Joe went on. "He closed the Orleans Club. No gambling, no dancing, no drinking. He even shut down the Petrified Man. I'm worried about him."

But Bob flung open the front door and ran out into the street, shooting his revolver in the air.

"He ate my bologna," one of the carpenters muttered.

The other one scooted the lunch box behind him, protectively.

"Don't let him see the gingerbread."

A moment later, Bob came back inside with Lute Johnson, editor of the *Creede Candle*.

"Look who I found."

"Don't you dare!" Joe warned him.

But Bob pulled out a chair, wiped the sawdust off, and gave it to Lute.

"I've got a headline for you: *Bob Ford Takes Over Creede, And Soapy Smith Is A Petrified Man.*"

Seeing Joe's reaction, Bob burst out laughing.

"The look on your face! I wish I had a camera."

Taking out his pencil, Lute started jotting notes.

"Tell me more."

"Why, damn, Lute. Look around you," Bob told him. "This is the biggest saloon in Creede, and I aim to open these doors right away. Tomorrow, in fact."

He glared at the carpenters to convey the urgency.

As he spoke, Lute nodded and jotted.

"What are you calling it?"

"What else? *The Ford Exchange.* Tell people the games ain't rigged and the booze is free." Then he winked at Joe. "For anyone who says the password."

"And what is the password?" asked Lute.

"The King of Clubs."

"That's four words."

Bob waved irritably.

"Just write it down, Lute."

Getting up, Joe stalked out the door.

"You are mean spirited, Bob," he said over his shoulder. "I don't know why I spend any time with you."

CHAPTER 110

Bat Masterson couldn't believe his eyes.

Looking haggard and lost, Soapy Smith himself eased into a seat at the faro table . . . in the Denver Exchange! Bat had his back to the door when it creaked open. But when he saw Billy Woods's jaw drop, and a hush swept the room, he swung around to see who it was.

There were still purple finger marks around Bat's neck—courtesy of Banjo Parker, and hence Soapy Smith by proxy. His first impulse was to throw him out, but the news about Joe Simmons's death was a major conversation topic. In fact, Bat first found out about it when he laid eyes on the newest edition of the *Creede Candle*. Lute Johnson ran an article about it, side by side with a story about Bob Ford's new saloon.

Soapy put a hundred-dollar stack of blue chips on the king card on the faro game layout. Jeff Argyle, realizing the gravity of the situation, said nothing. He just went to work, drawing cards. Every time Soapy lost, the despondent soap swindler didn't fuss or even react other than to put a fresh stack of chips on the king.

Seeing how miserable Soapy was, Bat brought over a whiskey sour and set it down.

"Sorry about your pard."

But Soapy's eyes were vacant.

"This drink is on me," Bat said, and slowly itched his throat. "How's that string bean healing up?"

Saying nothing, Soapy went ahead and took a small taste of the whiskey.

Feeling horribly uncomfortable, Jeff Argyle revealed the next two cards. The losing card was a king.

"House wins," he mumbled mechanically.

He reached out and swept Soapy's chips up, bracing the table with his other hand. *How many times,* he wondered, *is this table gonna get flipped?* Soapy seemed broken down, even wounded in the soul. But Jeff Argyle was still leery.

Immediately, Soapy bet another hundred dollars on the king.

"How much money do you plan on giving me tonight?" Bat asked him. He pointed at Jeff Argyle. "The bank is sitting at forty thousand tonight. If you got that much, put it down now. Get it over with. Then you can go home and leave us be."

But Soapy remained silent and merely stared at the cards.

"Alright, good luck," Bat said and headed to the bar.

When he got there, LG and Davis were both standing there, bottles in hand, mouths agape.

"You look like two birds on a wire," Bat told them.

LG whistled long and low.

"I thought for sure there was going to be fireworks. Rumor has it, you're a legend with the Colt 45."

Glancing back at the faro table, Bat shrugged off the comment.

"A man of my peculiar reputation can't go long without trouble," he said. "But, as you can plainly see . . . Soapy got the wind knocked out of his sails. No reason to worry."

He went behind the bar and chose a bottle for himself.

"Bottoms up."

However, the whole Denver Exchange did seem worried, despite Soapy's demeanor. It was as if every gambler and drinker in the room was holding their breath.

"It's quiet as a library in here," LG commented.

Davis raised his eyebrows.

"How would you know? Can you even read?"

LG swiped Davis's hat off his head and rooted around inside the crown.

"Give me one of your love letters and I'll prove it."

Then, noticing the pool table, Billy let out a dramatic sigh.

"Oh, no. There he goes again."

The Corner Pocket Drunk dropped his cue stick, crawled slowly onto the velvet, and collapsed.

"Let's get him off there before he fouls it up again."

Billy and Bat went over and laid him on the floor, but it was too late. Billy returned to the bar and got a rag and bucket.

"That kid wee'd on himself," he mentioned.

However, LG and Davis were still preoccupied with the faro table.

Soapy sat there for hours.

As the night wore on, no one even tried to unseat him. Several people walked over with a smile and a handful of play chips—until they saw who was sitting there. Including Frank Oliver, who was already "in his cups" before he ever came inside the building. He watched Soapy for a few minutes from a safe distance, and then wobbled over to the bar.

"All he does is stare at Jeff Argyle's hands," Frank noted and ordered a drink. "It's like his neck is broke and all he came move is his eyeballs. Except when he drops another heap of chips on that dang king card. I guarantee you, that man knows full well how the cards run. Boy, he must have got hit on the head or something."

Leaning close, Davis whispered in his ear.

"His best friend just keeled over dead. It's in the paper and everything."

Frank Oliver frowned and looked around drunkenly.

"Really? You're pulling my leg."

Billy Woods pulled out a newspaper from behind the bar. He tapped the front page.

"It's right there."

Frank Oliver glared at Billy Woods, since they hated each other. But, he took the paper and wobbled back to his table.

"I hear you got another shipment of beeves coming in," Bat mentioned to LG.

"I promised you a steady supply of steak, and I aim to please."

"I guess I'm surprised you succeeded in running cattle up here in the middle of winter. I had my doubts."

Suddenly, they heard Soapy Smith yell at Jeff Argyle.

"You *pull* that card . . . or you'll be pulling cards in hell!"

Bat ran over and found Soapy Smith on his feet, face blister-red, with a revolver jammed against the dealer's cheek.

"Hold on!" Bat shouted. "What happened?"

"If Bat Masterson tells me to pull it, then I'll pull it," Jeff Argyle said, sweating. "He's counting cards, Bat."

Examining the table, Bat saw forty thousand dollars' worth of chips on the "High Card" placard.

"He's been watching me deal this whole time. We're down to the last card and he switched his bet at the last minute. If I turn it over, he wins the whole bank!"

Everyone was watching.

Soapy's eyes were locked on Jeff Argyle, and he grinded the barrel harder into his cheek.

But Bat backed off with an easy laugh.

"Just pull the card, Argyle. If he wins, he wins. The man could use a little good luck today."

Moving extremely slow, Jeff Argyle pulled out the last card and turned it over.

"High card wins," he said.

Soapy put the pistol back in his coat and relaxed.

He rubbed his eyes.

It was obvious he was exhausted and consumed with grief. Bat angled back to the bar as casually as possible, but kept checking over his shoulder as he walked. When he passed by Frank Oliver's table, Frank reached out and pinched his coat tail.

"If that was me, you would have chunked me out the back door."

Bat shook him off and kept going. But Frank Oliver was mad. He jumped up, knocking his chair over.

"Hey Soapy! Why don't you go down to the Ford Exchange and scam Bob Ford next."

Soapy was in the middle of scraping all the blue chips into a big pile.

He froze.

"Shut up, Frank!" Billy hollered.

But Frank Oliver, instead, wobbled over to the faro table and dropped the newspaper in front of Soapy. Then he leaned close and squinted.

"Bob's right. He *does* look kind of petrified."

Soapy eyes went dark, and he slid his hand back into his coat pocket.

"What did you say?"

Too drunk to realize he was going for his gun, Frank kept talking.

"You mean you didn't see this yet?"

He pointed at the headlines. Soapy grabbed the paper. As soon as he saw the article on Bob Ford's new saloon, his eyes grew even darker.

"Let's cash you out," Bat suggested.

Frank Oliver turned around and wobbled back to his seat, unaware of how close to death he had come.

Opening the safe behind the bar, Bat counted out eighty thousand dollars. He put it in a cotton sack, and gave it to Soapy Smith. The Denver Exchange was silent. Everyone was waiting to see what would happen.

But Soapy simply took the money sack and left.

Bat took off his hat and wiped his forehead with a handkerchief.

"Things are about to go lickety-bang."

CHAPTER 111

"Heave!" Joe shouted.

Together, he and Banjo swung the Petrified Man and let go. The heavy concrete figure rolled downhill, through the snow and gravel, and slid to a stop at the bottom of a pit. Breathing hard, they both leaned over, hands on knees, until they caught their breath.

"That thing weighs a ton."

They were out in the forest at a played-out, abandoned mine. Banjo rubbed his neck and groaned. Joe glanced at him sideways.

"Sorry to say it, but I would have put my money on Billy Woods."

Banjo shrugged.

"I can barely breathe. My nose is crooked and full of scabs. He smashed my eyes so bad, they're all swoll up. Hurts like the dickens."

Joe agreed.

"It's like I'm staring into a couple walnuts."

Self-conscious, Banjo pulled his hat down low.

Then, looking back into the pit, Joe pointed at the Petrified Man.

"Look at that, his hand broke off."

Then he frowned, remembering his own ruined hand. It was hard to hold onto things without a thumb.

"I suppose we ought to cover him up."

They had both brought shovels, but suddenly Joe flung his in the pit. The more he thought about it, the madder he got. He could barely hold onto a fork now, let alone use a shovel.

"Forget it. I want to eat lunch."

He turned around and started heading back down the trail.

Banjo took his own shovel and tossed it in the pit, too. He trotted after Joe into the pines.

The sound of their bootsteps dwindled and faded away.

A hawk glided down from the cold blue sky and softly settled on a tree branch near the mine. Taking this as a sign that the danger had passed, Kahopi emerged from his hiding place.

Except for the clink of picks carrying from across the canyon, the forest was silent.

Shaking with fear, Kahopi crept over to the edge and peered into the pit. There, staring up at the cloudless expanse and the blazing sun directly overhead, was his father. Kahopi felt a strange sense overwhelm him. A mixture of joy, sadness, guilt, and relief.

Tears welled up and fell to the ground like raindrops.

The path had been long and dangerous. But even in his most confusing and hopeless moments, Tawa had come through. The Hawk Deity had come through. His Guardian Spirit had come through. Despite everything, he had persevered and, at long last, arrived at his destination. Nothing could stop him. Not the Spider Woman's cunning riddles, or the Six-Point-Cloud-People's storms. Not the Evil Power's influence, Masau'u's schemes, or the treachery of the Two-Hearts he encountered along the way.

Kahopi had succeeded.

He sat for a while, marveling, as many thoughts passed through his mind.

Finally, after a while, Kahopi got up and collected long straight branches to fashion into a grave ladder. He used twine that he found among the mine timbers to bind it together. Sliding into the pit, Kahopi propped it against the slope so his father's spirit could climb out and travel to the Skeleton House.

He found an old flour sack in a trash heap and crawled down into the pit. Kahopi placed it over his father's face, as a mask, to represent a cloud. Then he caught a bunny, prepared it, and left it by his father's body for a meal. Finally, he placed a pinch of sacred cornmeal in his father's good hand, along with a prayer feather and a necklace of white beads around his neck.

"Go now to the House of the Dead, greet our loved ones, and feel no more shame," Kahopi told him. "Return often with the clouds and drop some rain on the mesa. And when I reach the helpless stage and get too old to plant corn, I will join you."

After he climbed out of the pit, Kahopi walked around the rim four times and sprinkled cornmeal eastward.

The Hawk Deity was still on the branch, overseeing the burial. He nodded in approval, spread his majestic wings, and took flight.

— PART 16 —

CHAPTER 112

SUMMER 1860
CALIFORNIA GULCH

"Haw, you're lucky you braved the elements and staked an early claim," said George Stevens. "If you had waited till now to leave Denver, you'd be the last to arrive."

They were sitting in a saloon made entirely of pine boughs. Stevens was watching Horace learn how to play three-card Monte. So far, he had lost fifty bucks.

"Plus, we would have had to eat the Kelley party."

Hoping it was a joke, Horace forced a polite chuckle.

The dealer laid out three new cards.

"It's no different than a shell game," Horace said. "This should be easy . . . so why haven't I won a dime?"

"In a span of one month's time, this little gold camp exploded from you, me, and a handful of men, into a thousand and counting!" George Stevens said, eyes shining. Then he whispered in Horace's ear. "I already got so much gold, I could pack up tomorrow and never work another day in my life."

Giving up on the Monte game, Horace went over to the bar to buy a drink. Stevens followed him right over.

"How does it feel to be rich, Haw?"

Horace looked pained.

"I don't know how it feels, 'cause I ain't rich. It's that black sand! My sluice box is gummed up so bad I don't know what to do. Gives me a headache just talking about it."

He paid for a whiskey and took a tiny sip. These days, Horace always sipped it as slow as he possibly could. The drink lasted longer, and he wasted less money as the evening wore on.

"I just lost fifty dollars on a card game no more complicated than a slap in the face."

George Stevens ordered a shot, too, but drank it all at once.

"How do you deal with that black sticky sludge, George?"

"Maybe my claim is just a bigger producer, Haw. Tell you what. You sell me yours, and I'll pay you a steady wage to work it."

"I ain't falling for that."

Stevens gave his arm a pinch.

"Well, I suppose you got a steady wage coming in from your wife's bakery. What's that like? When your woman brings in more money than you do. I imagine it's pretty humiliating."

Abandoning his slow-sip policy, Horace gulped it down. Then, while he was counting out coins for a second drink, he heard a distinct silky voice.

"Hello, hello."

Turning around, he saw it was Miss Red Stockings, the only other woman in camp.

Whereas Augusta ran a profitable bakery, Red Stockings ran a profitable boudoir.

When he saw her, Horace turned as red as her stockings.

"Don't let Augusta see you two talking," Stevens said, wagging his finger. "She has a temper, from what I've seen."

Red Stockings smiled at Horace and tugged on the end of his mustache.

"I don't mean no harm."

George Stevens tugged on the other end of Horace's mustache.

"Which do you like better, Haw . . . Augusta's bread or Red's stockings?"

"I bet he likes my stockings," said Red.

Wiggling free, Horace darted over to the Monte table. But it was too late. At the worst possible moment, Augusta had walked through the door.

"Horace!"

Scratching at the air like a cat, she turned around and stormed off down the muddy road.

George Stevens, who had ducked behind the bar, popped back up again and laughed like it was the funniest thing he had ever seen.

"Even Shakespeare couldn't have thought that up."

Running to the pine bough wall, Horace tried to pry the branches apart to see where his wife was headed.

"Let me buy you an absinthe, Haw."

Was it worth it? When he wasn't fighting the black sands in his sluice box, Horace was fighting with Augusta. How much of life, Horace wondered, when stripped of its existential veneer, could be distilled down to the simple concept of a battle? Was there anything that came easy? Or did every single decision he make take him further and further away from his true destiny?

George Stevens held up a glass full of the green absinthe.

"Smother the parrot!"

CHAPTER 113

SPRING 1892
LEADVILLE

As soon as Major Bohn stepped into the Tabor Grand Hotel office, he realized that the Silver King had lost his mind. He was on his hands and knees, crawling around on the colorful carpet from Kathmandu.

"Is he nibbling at the rug?"

Maxcy had the telephone receiver pressed against his ear. He looked up from the big mahogany desk and shrugged helplessly.

"Baby Doe wants a divorce," he explained, covering the mouthpiece with his fingers. "I'm ringing the stables."

Gently, the Major nudged Horace with the toe of his boot. But instead of making a coherent reply, Horace, choking on his own tears, bellowed like a cow.

"King Nebuchadnezzar ate grass for seven years," the Major commented. "How long will the Silver King be like this?"

Suddenly, Maxcy got through.

"Can you get Horace's carriage ready?" he asked. "We'll be going to the train depot."

Hanging up, Maxcy gave the Major a baleful smile.

"I apologize for the hastiness. But given the circumstances, and speaking on behalf of my father—we need you to take over the silver club. And the Lucy B. Mine."

Maxcy held his breath, hoping the Major would agree.

Everything seemed off the rails. His father was emotionally hamstrung, his step-mother was mad, his real mother was mad, the silver club was flailing, the Lucy B. was flooded, and somehow it had all landed squarely on his shoulders to resolve. But at the same time, it was all infinitely more gratifying, and thrilling, than spending his days running the phones at Augusta's boarding house.

In that moment, Maxcy knew he would never return to Denver.

He also knew the Major already had his plate full. But he decided to rope him in anyhow.

"I know that managing the Matchless Mine, my father's shining star, is a big job all by itself. But the Lucy B. can be saved, and so can the silver club. And you, Major, are the only man who can make it happen. My father respects and trusts you—and so do I."

Maxcy stepped around Horace, and extended his hand to the Major.

"Plus, you'll get a big raise."

The Major brightened and they shook hands.

"I won't let you down, Mr. Tabor."

Then Maxcy ran down the hall, shot down the staircase, and went straight to the hotel stables. The driver was waiting for him. Maxcy leapt inside and slammed the door.

"Midland Depot!" the driver shouted, and popped the reins.

As the carriage bumped along, racing down Harrison Street, Maxcy leaned back and sighed. He had no idea how he was going to fix all these problems—but he wanted to. In one quick conversation, he had solved the crisis at both the Lucy B. and the silver club. Perhaps one quick conversation was all it would take to resolve his father's marital fiasco, too, but that would have to wait until he got back.

The next thing on Maxcy's list of resolutions was to arrest Big Ed Burns.

CHAPTER 114

CREEDE

Seeing Soapy pat his coat pocket, the one where he kept his revolver, Joe Palmer became alarmed.

Lute Johnson, editor of the *Creede Candle*, had just stepped inside the Orleans Club. He had his notepad and pencil and was innocently looking around. Concerned the man was about to get shot in the gut, Joe raced across the game room to intercept him.

"Hey, Lute, I think you're in the wrong place," he said, blocking his path. "Why don't you head back outside?"

Lute looked confused.

"I am in the right place. Is Soapy Smith here?"

But Joe shook his head firmly.

"Nope."

Then Lute spotted him at the bar, pouring himself a shot of rye.

"Joe, you may need some spectacles. He's standing right there."

Walking over, Lute wiggled his pencil.

"Can I get a quote, Mr. Smith?" he asked. "Bob Ford just opened his own saloon—the Ford Exchange. That is now the third such business in Creede, not to mention all the little one-jug saloons all over Tent Town. How do you feel about the growing competition?"

Soapy turned and looked at him with concern in his eyes.

"Why, didn't you hear the news about poor Bob?"

"What news?"

Soapy gripped Lute's shoulder.

"Why, Bob's dead."

Looking shocked, Lute started nodding and jotting.

"I just spoke with him this morning! Oh dear. Can you provide any details?"

Soapy made a big sad frown.

"Poor fellow. I'm not sure how it happened, but he is deader than a post. They found his body swinging from the rafters in his brand new place just this very morning. If you skitter on over there, you can see it for yourself. His face is all blotchy and his tongue is black. Of course, that is how he regularly appeared prior to death, so that may or may not be relevant to the article."

Writing everything down word for word, Lute sprinted for the door.

Lute was pudgy, and running was an activity he preferred to avoid. But, it seemed like every day now, there was something vital happening in Creede. This week's edition was going to be particularly juicy with Bob Ford's swinging body. It would be better than when Joe Simmons died, or when the Petrified Man was discovered, or when the Parson's pants had been stolen.

When he got to the Ford Exchange, Lute burst through the door and looked up at the ceiling.

"Don't barge in like that!" Bob shouted. "Unless you wanna die!"

He was peeping up from behind the bar, pointing a pistol.

Lute dropped his pencil and notepad and held his hands straight up in the air.

"Please don't kill me."

Slowly, Bob stood up. His big eyes looked sunken and wild. When he realized it was only Lute, he laid his gun on the lacquered spruce surface and waved him over.

"Get over here and spend some money."

The saloon was almost empty, except the Corner Pocket Drunk. He had come to break in Bob's new pool table. Oblivious to what was going on, he mumbled something unintelligible and for some reason tapped the cue stick against the eight ball.

Sitting down on a stool, Lute stared at Bob with a confused expression on his face.

"What are you gawking at?" Bob demanded.

"Well, I heard you were dead and came to check on you."

Choosing his favorite brand from among the liquor bottles, Bob popped the cork and took a quick swig.

"Hell no, I ain't dead. That's a load of manure. What stupid son told you that?"

"I just heard it from Soapy Smith not five minutes ago. He told me you were swinging from the rafters."

Bob's wild eyes rolled between Lute and the front door. He let out a giddy, shrill laugh.

"You are pretty gullible for a newspaperman."

Lute looked offended.

"I was just checking my facts by coming over here."

"Well, you got the facts wrong."

Bob took another swig and licked his lips.

Feeling like something was off, Lute turned around and looked at the front door himself.

"I wonder why Soapy Smith told me that?"

CHAPTER 115

The Ford Exchange, being made of nothing but pine and spruce, burned to the ground within a few minutes. Orange flames flickered and roared and lit up the night. The fire cast such a bright glow that, had they been repaired, the gas street lamps would have been completely unnecessary.

Hearing shouts, Bob Ford woke up and gazed out his hotel window. Seeing that his brand new saloon was roaring, Bob pulled on his boots, grabbed his gun, and rushed down the stairs as fast as he could.

The Cliff Hotel clerk was standing in the doorway watching the excitement. When he saw Bob coming down the stairs, wearing his bed clothes and boots, he jumped out of the way.

"Move!" Bob howled, although the clerk was already out of his way.

He raced down the street, but it was too late.

The water wagon was already there, and the firemen were throwing buckets. But the building was lost. It seemed like the whole town had turned out for the event. People poured out of the Orleans Club and the Denver Exchange to see what was happening.

"Oh, how sad," commented Ella Diamond.

Hearing what she said, Billy Woods immediately put his arm around her.

"Don't feel blue, honey."

Frank Oliver tried to put his arm around her, too, but bumped arms with Billy Woods.

"Get off her, you damn fool!" Frank shouted.

He was drunk, as usual, and glared at Billy with red, watery eyes. But Billy kept his arm where it was.

"Go to hell," he told Frank.

Hopping up and down, Bob Ford pointed at the flames.

"My saloon!"

Seeing the look on his face, Ella gave Bob a sad but kind smile.

"Didn't you just build that a couple days ago?"

Bob could not stand still.

"Six whole days."

"Why don't *you* go to hell?" Frank Oliver said to Billy Woods.

Then he pulled out a pistol and shot Billy in the head.

At the gunshot, Ella jerked, startled, and then clasped onto Billy's arm. But Billy went weak, and he was too heavy for her, and he slowly sank to the ground.

Ella Diamond, horrified, began to scream.

Frank Oliver tried to put his arm around her once again, but found that her piercing shriek was too loud. Dropping the gun, he put his fingers in his ears and took a wobbly step back.

Bob Ford was too preoccupied watching his saloon burn to care about Billy Woods. He went over to the water wagon. The inferno raged and crackled, and everyone with a free hand was either filling buckets, passing buckets, or dumping buckets. A few people were even shoveling snow into the flames. Bat Masterson and Jeff Argyle were there, as were LG and Davis.

"Grab a bucket, Bob!" Bat shouted. "If we don't stop it here, the whole town will go up in flames."

But Bob was as distraught about his saloon as Ella Diamond was about Billy Woods.

"It smells like an ocean of kerosene," Bat added, trying to get Bob's attention again. "It's a good thing you weren't in there. You'd be dead."

Blinking in the smoke, Bob sniffed the air a little closer. There was indeed a distinct scent of kerosene in the air. Then he remembered what Soapy Smith had told Lute Johnson.

"Soapy's trying to kill me! I know it was him, beyond a shadow of a doubt."

Turning around, Bob started searching for Soapy Smith. But he didn't see him, or any of his gang. Drawing his pistol, Bob ran straight down to the Orleans Club and peeked through the windows. But the place was empty.

CHAPTER 116

White ash fluttered down like impure snowflakes.

The smell of smoke was everywhere.

Joe Palmer's shin had never really healed after being shot by the New Orleans Kid. Some days were better than others, but he had been limping ever since. He often found himself moving at a gentle mosey, but at the moment, he was hustling to keep up with Soapy Smith.

"Slow down!" Joe begged, wincing with each step. "Haven't we done enough damage for one night? We should hole up somewhere and lay low."

"Here!" Soapy muttered and handed him his cane. "Use this and shut your mouth."

Moving quickly through the smoke and haze, Soapy didn't slow down until they reached the train depot. He climbed the stairs and looked back at the town.

Flames rose up high.

The entire downtown area was engulfed in the fire, and the glow lit up the entire canyon. The big cliff, rising above the buildings, was clearly visible even though it was well after dark.

"Do you see Banjo?" Joe asked from the ground. His shin felt like it was on fire, too. "I can't climb those steps."

Soapy's eyes were hard.

"You better be able to climb up in a saddle by the time he brings those damn horses."

Joe looked stung.

"Of course I can ride, Soapy. It's just that my leg is acting up from all this rushing around."

"As long as you can point a gun and pull the trigger, that's all I care about."

Taking a seat on the bottom step, Joe massaged his tender leg. He looked up at his boss with sad eyes.

"We sure done plenty enough already, don't you think?" Joe said. "Let's leave them cowboys alone."

"If you had done what I said in the first place, I wouldn't have to do nothing," Soapy groused. "And since Banjo botched it, I need to beat some sense into Bat Masterson next. I swear! I can't rely on you two no more."

In the distance, he spotted Banjo lead three horses out of the livery.

"Took him long enough."

With a painful groan, Joe got back up and leaned heavily on Soapy's cane.

Behind them, the midnight train came chugging across the bridge above the Rio Grande. Its headlight shined in the blackness, like a bright white star. The train rolled towards the depot, hissing and squealing, and then braked to a stop.

"Why don't we get on that train right now," Joe suggested. "We can go to Cripple Creek and start all over. How about a fresh start, Soapy? No one knows us there. We could even use fake names."

But Soapy couldn't believe what he was hearing.

"Why in the hell would I wanna do that?"

Joe motioned at the massive inferno.

"Just a matter of time till they figure out it was us. I don't want to wind up in jail, do you? And why make things worse?"

After studying him for a moment, Soapy burst out laughing.

"Ever since that preacher came through, you been going knock-kneed on me."

Joe shrugged.

"Ain't you sick and tired of all this?"

Men and women poured out of the passenger car but stopped on the platform to gawk at the flames. Everywhere in Creede, people ran around in alarm. Miners, gamblers, and drunks coughed in the smoke and cried out. Even among the tents, there was chaos. The Mexican Lady was trying to tie a basket of green chilies onto a skittish burro. The Bonanza saloon keeper, carrying a box of beer bottles, climbed into a waiting wagon. The corral fence at the livery suddenly went down. Mules nickered, burros brayed, and the entire herd charged off into the night.

Soapy grinned, but it had no mirth in it.

"Tired of what?"

Joe turned away.

"You look like a gargoyle up there with that wicked smile."

Then, the station agent tapped Soapy on the shoulder.

"This gentleman is looking for Bat Masterson," he said. "You know everybody in this town, so I figured you might have seen him."

"Hello, my name is Maxcy Tabor," said Maxcy.

Soapy examined his face closely—the walrus mustache and receding hair.

"Do I know you?"

"No, I don't think so. I've never been to Creede before," he replied. "I live up in Leadville."

Then it dawned on Soapy.

"Tabor from Leadville. You related to Horace?"

"Yes, sir. He's my father and I work for him. I am the manager of the Tabor Grand Hotel."

Soapy reached out and shook his hand.

"Well how do you do?" he said, and gave Joe a subtle wink. "So Horace Tabor sent his son on the midnight train to find Bat Masterson. Did you hear that Joe? Horace Tabor and Bat Masterson are thick as thieves. Hand me my cane."

Joe paled.

"But I need it to lean on."

Turning to face him, Soapy held out his hand and snapped his fingers.

"You know, when I was a kid I could never snap my fingers like that," Maxcy said, thinking back. "All I could do was flick them."

Feeling weary of it all, Joe sighed and handed Soapy the cane.

"You won't be meeting Bat Masterson tonight," Soapy told Maxcy, and then whacked him in the forehead. "You came a long way for nothing."

Looking stunned, Maxcy's eyes went out of focus.

Soapy whacked him again, and Maxcy fell to the platform.

The station agent, shocked, took a few steps back and waved his arms.

"What are you doing?" he shouted. "Stop this right now."

But Soapy did not stop whacking Maxcy. He continued to beat him, and beat him some more, and the blood flowed. The crowd of train passengers were torn, not sure which spectacle to watch—the conflagration or the caning? One young man, eyes wide, dragged his terrified wife and luggage right back aboard the train.

The white ash kept falling from the night sky.

When Soapy finished the beating, he glared at the station agent and the crowd on the platform.

"I will not stand for underhanded collusions to unseat me," he announced.

Grabbing Maxcy by the heels, he dragged him across the platform. Leaving a streak of smudgy blood, he pulled Maxcy into the passenger car and propped him up in a seat by the window.

"Tell Horace I said hello."

CHAPTER 117

"Use the nippers," Soapy said.

Fishing out a pair of blacksmith nippers from his saddle bags, Banjo slid off his palomino. Stepping through the cold snow, he reached out in the darkness and snipped the barbed wire.

"I'm snagged, Soap," Banjo said, his sleeve caught.

"Get down there and help, Joe."

Without complaining, Joe got down and went over. After he freed Banjo's sleeve, he glanced up at Soapy—just a dark silhouette, towering on his horse against the starlit sky.

Joe peeled back the wire so they could pass through.

The pasture was pitch black, but the smell of cattle was strong. He tugged his neck scarf up over his nose and crawled back up in the saddle. He would always hate the smell of cattle. Even more after all this was through.

Soapy's voice floated in the dark.

"Lead the way."

Even though his stomach was in knots, Joe had no choice. He didn't want to be there at all. He wished he could leave. He wished he could say it all out loud but knew it was too late.

"Look up ahead. That's their camp."

On the far side of the pasture, they could see a soft reddish glimmer. It was the cook fire, but it had burned down to just a bed of hot coals.

Soapy paused, listening. There was a soft breeze rattling the treetops, and he heard an owl hoot.

"Let your horse have its head," Joe recommended in a whisper. "Dang cows are everywhere."

They walked their horses slowly. The surface of the snow was frozen and it made a crusty crunch with each step. Just as Joe said, there were cows bedded down everywhere.

Taking out his revolver, Soapy cocked the hammer. The metallic *click* was loud. Hearing it, Banjo drew his weapon, too.

"Get your gun out, Joe," Soapy said.

They rode up on the fire ring. Up close, they could just barely make out the tent. The canvas looked red in the glow of the coals.

All three of them eased off their horses, and Soapy leaned close to whisper. Joe could feel his hot breath.

"When they come runnin' out, you pull that damn trigger—understand?"

"Okay."

"And hold onto your reins," Soapy added. "If you lose your horse, you're walking back."

The owl hooted again.

Soapy aimed his gun at the tent, and so did Banjo.

Reluctantly, Joe did the same.

Without another word, Soapy fired his pistol once.

A hole appeared in the canvas wall, and the tent wall fluttered with the impact.

Behind them, several startled Highlanders rose up and dashed across the pasture, snorting in fear.

They waited, but no one emerged from the tent.

"I bet they're in town fighting the flames," Joe whispered, gesturing at the horizon.

Above the tree line, they could easily see the orange light from town. Creede was on fire.

Soapy knelt down by the fire ring and warmed his hands.

"Banjo, take those nippers and cut every strand of wire you can find. And I want those cattle spooked and scattered, and nothing left for them cowboys to come back to."

He stood up and aimed his gun at the tent again.

"And I mean nothing."

Firing his gun over and over, Soapy shot up the tent until he ran out of bullets. The canvas popped and danced and swayed. Inside, a bullet dinged off the stove and they heard an anguished cry.

"What was that?" Joe said.

They paused, listening.

Slowly, the door flap opened and Walker stumbled out.

Blood was leaking down his hip, and he pressed his hands over the wound.

"Oh, please, no!" Joe shouted, his face white. "You shot Garo!"

Soapy ignored him and began reloading. But Joe ran and grabbed the boy, supporting him so he wouldn't collapse.

"What do we do?" Joe yelled.

Soapy finished thumbing in new bullets and looked up.

"Burn that tent down and scatter them cows."

Then he yelled at Banjo, who hadn't moved.

"I said cut those wires!"

Charging out into the pasture, Soapy fired his gun in the air. In the muzzle flashes, they could see sleepy cows leap up and bolt away in fright. The gunshots barked and echoed, and soon the whole herd was milling around the pasture in chaos. The deep pounding of heavy hooves made the ground tremble like an earthquake.

Soapy kept firing. The wheel team ran by, among the cattle, and Soapy shot the horses dead.

In the yellow sparks, his face was lit, and once again Joe glimpsed that empty gargoyle smile.

CHAPTER 118

To purify himself, Kahopi took off all his clothes and rubbed snow all over his body. He hung his clothes in the smoke of juniper and piñon sap, and let it waft over him, too.

After a while, he got dressed and checked his snares. He found a squirrel and cooked it.

Traveling alone through such rough country, one great challenge was catching enough birds or small animals to keep from starving. Kahopi's thoughts often turned to the secret meeting place of the Two-Hearts, and the witch who governed the room of fruits and vegetables, which were out of season and out of place.

Kahopi shuddered when he considered such powerful magic. Yet his mouth watered as he thought about it, too. He wished he had a couple oranges. Even one orange would make him happy. It was wise to not be too greedy. Being greedy brought bad luck.

Once the sun set, his eyes grew heavy and Kahopi began to dream.

He was in his field, near the mesa, tending his lambs, when he saw a man dressed in white. As he got closer, he realized it was his Guardian Spirit. He carried a square shield with him. It had a round patch of buckskin sewn in the middle.

"I must show you something important," the Spirit said, and he laid the shield flat on the ground. "Step onto the Sun Shield with me."

Together, they stepped onto the Sun Shield.

They spiraled aloft, floating in the air on the shield. Up over the mesa they went, and across the ruddy landscape, with its draws and sandstone formations and clusters of rocks. Mile after mile they traveled, and in the blink of an eye, they arrived at the Grand Canyon.

They hovered over the confluence of two rivers, and as he studied the waters, Kahopi gasped. The waters parted and he could see down into the underworld! His father was walking around, alive and happy, eating an ear of fresh corn.

"In four days, he will come up and become one of the Six-Point-Cloud-People."

Kahopi turned to the Spirit and thanked him for his protection.

"You have watched over me, even in my time of loneliness, when no one else cared one whit whether I lived or died."

The Sun Shield turned around in the sky and carried them back toward the mesa. When they flew over it, his Guardian Spirit pointed down—and there was Masau'u, the bloody-headed god of death, sitting on a ledge.

"When you return to the village, you may have to sleep on the mesa again if the people don't accept you. But always sleep on the sun side . . . or else Masau'u will catch you and make you a prisoner in the House of the Dead."

"He almost did once," Kahopi said, remembering his close call with the Fiery Spirit. "But I was lucky and escaped."

When he woke up, the smell of smoke was strong. His body was cold. Kahopi pulled the blanket around his shoulders as tight as he could. In the silence, he watched as the dark sky turned red in the east.

— PART 17 —

CHAPTER 119

AUTUMN 1860
CALIFORNIA GULCH

It took a lot of convincing to get Augusta to attend Red Stockings' farewell party. It was late in the season. The winter snows were coming, and everyone knew it. A farewell party was just the thing, now that it was time to bid California Gulch a very temporary goodbye.

"Is she watching?" Horace whispered to George Stevens.

Stevens had a bottle of absinthe and kept glugging it down.

But even squinting through the liquor haze, he could not tell if Horace's distempered wife was watching or not. He spotted her, standing over in the dim corner, straight as a poker rod—or at least George Stevens thought so. He was almost certain it was Augusta Tabor. Or perhaps a coat rack.

"Nope, you're fine, Haw."

Horace released the air in his lungs, and blotted his forehead with a hanky. Red Stockings was about three feet away, flirting with all the miners.

"Augusta told me not to even look at Red, or she'll divorce me."

"That girl is the jammiest bit of jam I have ever seen." George Stevens commented.

Nathaniel came over and shook hands with both of them.

"I am heading out with the sunrise. What about you, George?"

"Guess how much gold I have accumulated this summer?" Stevens said, ignoring the question.

Without waiting for a reply, he leaned in and jabbed Nathaniel with an elbow.

"Two hundred and thirty-nine pounds of gold—*pounds!*"

Horace gaped.

"How? What I found will barely fill up a tobacco pouch. I hate those black sands."

Stevens poured more absinthe into his mouth.

As it went down, Horace peered into his mouth.

"Your teeth are as green as grass."

But George Stevens was on cloud nine.

"And just now, some dumb puke paid me five hundred dollars for my claim."

He drew out a wad of cash from his pocket and waved it in the air. Then his eyelids fluttered, as he tried in vain to see clearly.

"Haw, point me at the Monte table and give me a shove."

Seeing the money in his hand, Horace felt even more depressed.

"I suppose I could sell you my claim," he said, eyeing the cash.

"Ha!" laughed George Stevens.

And with that, he jiggled off towards what he thought looked an awful lot like the Monte table.

Horace was in shock. His own claim was a sad, sad joke. Lady Luck had not done him any favors.

"You don't got no more absinthe?" George Stevens shouted, having somehow arrived at the bar. "Good thing I'm leaving, cuz this place has run out of every dern commodity known to man."

Suddenly, Horace had an epiphany.

He looked around feverishly for Augusta. She was not standing in the corner after all, but was seated on a sawn tree stump, sipping hot tea.

"Gussie, Gussie!" he called and raced towards her. "We need to open a supply store. With axes, picks, shovels and lanterns, ponchos and rubber boots . . ."

He gasped for breath as he listed off everything he could think of.

"We can sell coffee pots, frying pans, tin plates, blankets, blasting powder and fuses!"

Augusta's face softened as she listened. Sometimes, Horace seemed like a little boy. Especially when he got excited. In fact, he had the same look on his face that Maxcy did when he dug for pirate doubloons or picked the legs off a spider. The two of them were like peas in a pod.

It was becoming clear that most people in California Gulch were coming up dead broke. Only a few people, like George Stevens, seemed to strike it rich. All summer long, with the talk of a gold rush, a steady stream of new miners appeared every day. Most of them had no clue what they were doing. They all seemed to show up without much equipment, or any good sense for that matter. Which was why she did so well with the bakery. Perhaps Horace was onto something.

"But everyone is packing up and heading to the plains," Augusta pointed out gently. "We should go, too. The first snow will fall in a matter of days."

Horace paced around, unable to stand still.

"But if we hole up here all winter, we'll be waiting for them when they come back in the spring. With a store full of supplies."

He knelt by the stump she was sitting on, and gripped her hands in his.

"Don't you remember when we first got here? They needed food. Their clothes were rags. Their boots had holes. They were in such a rush to strike it rich, they left too early and didn't bring the right gear. We should be right here waiting, because the same thing will happen all over again."

Augusta looked skeptical.

"I won't lie to you, it's a good idea," she said and meant it. "But we have to stay alive in the process. We'll be snowed in if we stay— this might as well be the North Pole."

"Maxcy will like that. He'll think it's Christmas every day."

Giving her hand a final squeeze, Horace sprung to his feet.

"I have to race to Denver and buy all the supplies I can and race back before the heavy snows fall. I have to leave right now!"

But she grabbed his arm and stopped him.

"Just in case you get slowed down, you better patch up our cabin before you go. The chinks in the logs are big enough to crawl through. I don't want Maxcy to catch a chill."

Dashing out of the building made of pine boughs, Horace sprinted up the gulch.

The day was late, but there was still plenty of light in the crisp autumn sky.

The aspen trees still had their leaves, but they had turned yellow. He had no time to waste. But Horace knew he had found his destiny. The Universe was a cruel teacher, but at long last he had figured it out.

Jabbing a shovel into a mucky pile of black sand, Horace filled a hand cart to the brim. Wheeling it over to the cabin, he scooped it up with his bare hands and patted it in between the logs.

"At least this is good for something," he muttered.

CHAPTER 120

SPRING 1892
LEADVILLE

When Maxcy was brought into the foyer, unconscious on a stretcher, Horace's heart froze in his chest.

"Take him upstairs to the bedroom."

His mind wheeling, Horace was so shocked that he forgot to close the front door. He couldn't believe it. Maxcy's face was bruised and bloody—his eyes were closed and he made no sound or movement.

Horace's eyes lingered on the handrail leading up the staircase. It was made of expensive cherrywood, heavily varnished, and glistened in the afternoon sunbeams. Every single day, the maid polished it with a soft cotton rag and linseed oil. It took a solid hour to do it right, including the spindles. She never complained, but that was because Horace gave her an extra silver dollar each time. Waiting patiently for her to finish, Horace would faithfully produce the coin out of his vest pocket and hand it to her. But, for some reason, he couldn't picture her face in his mind at the moment. It was blurry. Or recall her name. What was her name?

Taking slow steps, Horace walked over to the staircase and ran his hand over the shiny smooth wood.

There were no sunbeams today.

"Horace?" Baby Doe asked, gently.

She seemed to appear from nowhere and touched his shoulder.

"It's me, Baby Doe."

Turning slowly, Horace looked at her for a moment, blinking, and then took a silver dollar out of his vest pocket and handed it to her.

With a forgiving smile, Baby Doe took the silver coin from his fingers.

"It's okay, Horace. He'll be alright."

But for some reason, Baby Doe's face was blurry, too, just like the maid's face in his memory. He felt lightheaded.

A soft fabric touched his face—she was blotting his tears.

"Maxcy is hurt, bad," he said and began to tremble.

She led him into the kitchen and helped him into a chair. It was quieter in the kitchen. They could still hear the doctor's voice, but it was muffled. Footsteps raced up and down the staircase, and there were urgent shouts and whispers.

Horace began to hyperventilate. He clawed at his chest and looked terrified.

"It's okay, Horace. I'm right here."

Baby Doe undid his necktie, removed his emerald stick pin, and loosened his collar. Then she went and dipped out a cup of water and held it to his lips. He drank, but choked and sputtered, and then started to get up.

"I have to go to the hotel. The Isabella Necklace is in my office, in the safe," he said. "I want you to have it forever."

She shushed him gently and put her arms around him.

CHAPTER 121

When Augusta arrived in Leadville, she brought along her own physician and an entourage of assistants.

"I'm taking him to Denver," she told Horace matter-of-factly. "He will be treated at the hospital with the best care possible. Don't argue with me, Horace."

But Horace did not argue. And neither did Baby Doe, although she eyed Augusta with suspicion the moment she appeared at the door.

"He's up the stairs," Horace told her. "In the bedroom."

Augusta marched right up the staircase without another word. Her assistants and physician went with her. Within a few short minutes, they brought Maxcy back down to the foyer on a white cotton stretcher and paused to allow for goodbyes.

Avoiding his bludgeoned face, Horace's eyes drifted down to his son's hand.

"Why, his knuckles are swollen up like grapes."

The doctor looked grim.

"He must have held his hand up to protect himself."

Going quietly to the door, Augusta turned the handle and pulled it open.

Cool air drifted in. But it was spring air, fresh air, and a there was even a bluejay singing a song on the porch.

Horace looked past her, through the doorway, at the shining white mountains. They dominated the view from the porch. Such majestic beauty. Every morning on his way to work, Horace paused and soaked it all in. The grandeur inspired him, and every day he was thankful just to see it. It inspired him, it thrilled and strengthened him, and made him want to strive for the best in life. Whether it was gold or silver or hotels or politics—or his family.

He turned his gaze from the mountains, to Augusta's steely blue eyes, to Maxcy's swollen hand.

"Remember when we first came here?" he said. "Those big peaks. The snow was so deep we had to shovel our way across South Park, and all the way up the Arkansas River. Remember, Gussie? It was all so vast and wild and unknown. And what did find? All that terrible black sand."

Augusta sighed softly and blotted her eyes with a kerchief.

The physician looked stern and impatient but said nothing.

"I used to bury copper pennies. Maxcy would use his fingers and dig around looking for pirate gold. He was so happy when he found it."

Augusta gave him a genuine, loving smile.

"I recall, Horace."

He softly touched Maxcy's damaged hand, and then smoothed the hair on his head. It was thin and receding, just like his was.

Bending down, Horace kissed his son's forehead.

CHAPTER 122

DENVER

Now that Maxcy was in capable hands, Augusta felt absolutely drained. Stepping outside of his hospital room into the hallway, she spotted a bench and collapsed.

The train ride from Leadville had seemed interminable. Every bump and jostle made Maxcy moan. And every time he moaned, she felt a stabbing pain in her chest. Her throat was sore, too, from whispering and crying and asking the physician if there was anything else that could be done.

"May I sit here?"

Augusta looked up to see a blonde woman she had never met before.

Nodding, Augusta scooted over to make room.

"You look as unhappy as I do," the woman said. Her voice was also raw.

Smiling mechanically, Augusta took out a silk handkerchief and started to wipe her eyes, but they were dry.

"I guess I've cried so much I don't have any more tears left to shed."

She offered the hanky, but the blonde woman stared at it bleakly.

"I'm afraid I ran out of tears, myself."

Augusta tucked it back in her belt.

"I guess neither of us need that, then."

"My name is Laura."

Augusta nodded politely.

"Augusta," she said, and then decided against it. "Please call me Gussie."

They sat in silence for a moment.

"Who are you here for?" Laura asked.

"My son. He's been beaten rather badly, I'm afraid."

Laura frowned.

"My son is in the next room. He's been shot in the waist. He's only fifteen."

Augusta grabbed her hand and squeezed.

"Who would do such a thing?"

But Laura shook her head, sadly.

"My throat is too sore to talk about it."

"I understand."

They held hands and stared at the wall. There was an oil paint-ing hanging in between the two rooms. It was the Battle of the Little Bighorn. General George Custer was right in the middle of the swirling chaos, dressed in blue, with his long golden locks and two big pistols, coughing up puffs of white smoke.

"He just wanted to be a cowboy," Laura said finally. "To ride a horse and rope cattle, just like his father. The day he left, Til took him down to Chubb Newitt's general store to buy him a brand new shirt and some candy for the train ride. Now he's lying in a hospital bed."

Listening, Augusta could only shake her head.

"Gussie, why is there so much evil in the world?" Laura asked.

But Augusta could not say.

CHAPTER 123

LEADVILLE

Rage replaced Horace's sorrow.

A telegraph message from Bat Masterson revealed who Maxcy's assailant was—Soapy Smith. At first, Horace was shocked. His gut reaction was to blame Big Ed Burns. After all, Maxcy had gone to Creede to arrest Big Ed. But Bat was adamant that no one in Creede had even seen Big Ed for quite some time. Regardless, Maxcy never even got the chance to hunt him down.

The station agent was right there when it happened, along with a dozen other witnesses. There was no doubt. It was Soapy Smith.

Horace had spent enough time with the man, in the past, to know what he was capable of.

But Horace was also capable.

In the old days, he used to quake when Soapy came to see him in Leadville. The man had a fearful way about him. Whatever Soapy wanted, Soapy got. But after what he did to Maxcy, everything changed.

"Everyone got a carbine?" Horace called out.

He had called for a posse. A group of men from the Matchless Mine had gathered at the Midland Depot with Winchesters and Remingtons. Major Bohn was there, too, waving his steel sword.

"If you don't got a gun, bring a blade," he said.

One of the pumpmen presented a little pocket pistol.

"My wife gave me this Deringer."

"This is a Vigilance Committee," Horace scolded him. "We're going after Soapy Smith. Someone get this fellow a gun powerful enough to blow a man's head off."

For a fleeting moment, Horace felt guilty about his choice of words.

He turned and glanced up at the landing where the drug store was—the very place where Wheezy Jones had his own head blown off.

CHAPTER 124

CREEDE

When Horace stepped off the train in Creede, he paused and examined the platform. He saw dark streaks across the pine boards and instantly knew it was Maxcy's blood. As he knelt down, a man in a lavender corduroy suit came up and knelt beside him.

"Horace Tabor? My name is Bat Masterson."

"I don't understand all this," Horace said. "Why would Soapy Smith hurt my son?"

Bat took off his bowler hat and held it over his chest.

"I can't say. He burned down half the town, as well."

Horace, the Major, and the pumpmen from the Matchless Mine followed Bat as he guided them from the depot, through Tent Town, into Creede. The smell of burnt wood was strong.

The sun was out and powerful. The snow on the slopes had begun to melt and soften. The road itself was almost too soft to walk on. The mud sucked at their heels with every step.

"Soapy's been hiding out in his club," Bat mentioned. "My boys have the building surrounded, so he ain't going nowhere. But I'm sure he knows you're here, so we ought to go in expecting a war."

True enough, most the wood-framed buildings in Creede had burnt down. Half the Denver Exchange, too, was charred and blistered. Blackened boards and beams twisted up in the sky. Even the big cliff was gray with soot. A row of unhappy shopkeepers sat on the boardwalk, sipping from flasks and smoking cigarettes.

The Ford Exchange, the Cliff Hotel, the livery stable, the boot-maker, horseshoe shop, and the Hardware & Stoves—it was all gone.

The front of the Orleans Club was singed, but otherwise unaffected.

Bat pulled Horace aside.

"The problem is, we ain't got no legal proof he did any of this. The only thing we got him, dead to rights, is accosting your son on the train platform. So the best we can do is make a citizen's arrest and ship him down to Denver for trial."

Horace looked implacable.

"I hope he comes out shooting."

Bat nodded.

"I expect he will."

They crossed the street and filed into an alley, where they could safely observe the Orleans Club. There, they met a group of men, the citizens of Creede, waiting and watching.

"I don't know how many men he's got in there," Bat said and peered out of the alleyway.

Raising his voice, he called across the street.

"Come on out of there, Soapy. It's over!"

CHAPTER 125

DURANGO

The smell of cooking bacon smelled good. Kahopi was hungry and decided to ask if he could have some. Two Mexicans were sitting on crates near the railroad tracks, eating breakfast.

"What is this town?" Kahopi asked.

"Durango," one said and handed him a tin plate heaped with bacon and scrambled eggs.

Kahopi sat down on a canvas tarp, crossed his legs, and ate. Even though it was White food, and not the good old Hopi foods he was raised on, like corn and beans and squash, it still tasted good. He had been living for many days on pine nuts, rabbit, and ptarmigan, which were easy to catch. But even though they were easy to catch, they were hard to spot. So the bacon and eggs tasted especially good.

The Mexican man who gave him the food looked him over closely.

"Do you know those injuns?"

Kahopi bit into a piece of bacon.

"Which ones?"

"Those three in jail."

Kahopi shrugged.

"I did not hear about that."

Setting his plate down, the man wiped his fingers on his trousers and handed Kahopi a newspaper.

"What does it say?" he asked, since he was busy eating.

"Dismissed for lack of evidence. The judge set 'em free last night."

"What did they do?"

"Stole a train and murdered the engineers."

Kahopi finished off the bacon. It was crispy and very savory. Then he scooped up the eggs in his hands and ate them, too.

"You gobbled that right up. You want more?"

Picking up the frying pan, the Mexican man scraped the last of the scrambled eggs onto Kahopi's plate.

"The judge ordered the sheriff to put them injuns on a wagon and get them out of town. The whole town was mad about it."

"I imagine so."

Kahopi ate every bite and licked the plate.

"They were going to put them on the train, since it's quicker, but Mr. Mears refused to allow it. He owns the train. Do you want a cigarette?"

He offered Kahopi a cigarette. They sat around the fire and smoked. The second Mexican never said a word. Kahopi wondered if his tongue had been cut out or something. Or perhaps he was born mute.

"Where are you headed?"

"Back to the mesa," Kahopi replied.

"I don't know where that is, but you may want to skirt around Durango. The people may mistake you for one of them injuns, and hang you from a tree."

PART 18

CHAPTER 126

SUMMER 1876
CALIFORNIA GULCH

"The best thing about an afternoon drizzle is that it cuts down on the dust," Alvinus said. "Plus everything smells so damn fresh."

"You buy out anybody else today?" Horace asked.

Alvinus was a miner, and a strange one at that. He had been buying up defunct gold mines all over California Gulch.

It was still a busy place. Cabins and tents were everywhere. Summer after summer, the camp grew so big, they gave it a new name—Oro City. "Oro" was Spanish for gold, but the gold seemed to be playing out. Which was what made Alvinus strange.

"Some fellas up in Stray Horse Gulch sold out just this morning," the man said, looking pleased.

Horace shook his head.

"You are an odd duck, my friend."

They were standing in the muddy road, just outside of Horace's supply store.

Alvinus climbed down from his wagon—which was filled with the hateful black sands of California Gulch.

"Have my shovels come in?"

"Tomorrow, I expect," Horace said.

Alvinus cast a glance at Augusta's bakery, which was nearby.

"I wonder if my bread is ready? I've got a long day ahead of me, and these oxen are slow as sin."

Every day or so, Alvinus drove by with a big load of black sand and ordered a basket of bread. It was another strange thing.

"Where are you dumping all this wretched mud anyhow?" Horace asked, dumbfounded. "I don't know why you go to all the trouble of hauling this junk so far away."

Alvinus leaned against the wagon and smiled a curious smile.

But Horace wasn't done complaining.

"I hate this dang mud. It's why I gave up gold mining to begin with! I don't know why anyone would want to ruin their sluices, or clog up their rocker boxes. What a nightmare. I'm so glad I quit."

He pointed at the store.

"This is my gold mine. We're doing so well, we're gonna open up a second store at the other end of the gulch. Maxcy will run that one. Between the two stores and Gussie's bakery, things are looking good."

Alvinus reached into the wagon and dug his fingers in the thick black silt.

"I haul this all the way to Colorado Springs—down your old wagon road, in fact. From there, I put it on a train for Saint Louis."

Scratching his wispy hair, Horace was flabbergasted.

"Why in the world would you do that?"

"I guess I can let the cat out of the bag," Alvinus said, eyes twinkling. "All this black sand? It is lead carbonate—and it's *chock full of silver.*"

Horace turned pale.

"The closest silver smelter is way out in Saint Louis," Alvinus explained. "But I don't mind."

He spread his arms and embraced the world.

"This whole place is one big silver lode."

The bakery door banged open, and Augusta came out with a basket of cinnamon bread.

"This is still hot, Alvinus," she said and brought him the basket. "It just came out of the oven."

Then she noticed her husband.

Horace's mouth was moving, but no sounds were coming out.

"What's wrong with you?" she asked. "Did you swallow a bug?"

CHAPTER 127

SPRING 1892
DENVER

Parson Tom tapped on the hospital door.

Til and Laura Blancett, who were sitting in chairs next to Walker's bed, stood up and waved him in.

"I understand this lad was shot in Creede," the parson said. "I spent some time up there this winter, and I know it is full of villains. I trust he is recovering well?"

But Laura looked down at the floor.

Til went over and spoke softly in the parson's ear.

"He hasn't said one word since he got shot."

Walker, lying in bed, was staring out the window. It was propped open to let in the fresh warm air. He had an open view across the rooftops of Denver. The sun was shining, and some kids were shouting and playing down in the street.

"Perhaps I might speak with him."

Til took Laura by the arm and led her into the hallway. Once they were in the hallway, Parson Tom went over and sat down. He sighed and patted the boy's hand. But Walker continued to stare outside.

"A cucumber is bitter? Throw it away. There are briars in the road? Then turn aside. But do not ask, why were such things made in the world. It is our duty to leave another man's wrongful act where it is."

He smiled serenely.

"A Roman emperor wrote that—though the knowledge does not make it less painful to experience."

Leaning back in the chair, Parson Tom noticed there was a new crisp white shirt hanging on a coat hook. Beside it was Walker's old orange shirt—with a torn sleeve and dried bloodstains.

"I can't believe they stole my trousers."

With that, Parson Tom got up and left the room.

After he was gone, Til poked his head through the doorway.

"I brought you a bottle of root beer."

Walker slowly sat up, wincing at the pain, but held out his hand.

"And you have visitors," Til added as his son took a sip of the root beer.

It was LG and Davis. They were dressed like they always did, in riding boots with jingle-bobs, canvas trousers, and wide brimmed hats. They smelled of horses. They seemed out of place in the hospital, with its doctors and sick people all dressed in white.

"Look what we got here," LG said. "A real old-fashioned, first-class cowpuncher. He handled some hard-looking rustlers, all by himself."

Davis whistled, impressed. "He wasn't even armed."

Right behind them, Laura Blancett brought in a chocolate cake. She smiled and set it carefully on the night table. She had a basket hooked over her arm and handed everyone a small plate and a fork.

"I was waiting for the right moment," she explained and began slicing it up. "Emmanuel baked this cake as soon as he heard you were in the hospital."

Til nudged his son.

"Emmanuel says chocolate cake always makes him feel better whenever he gets shot by rustlers."

Laura clenched her jaw.

"Til, that is not funny."

But Walker thought it was funny and laughed.

CHAPTER 128

CREEDE

Through the plate glass windows, Soapy could see them all.

It was a motley bunch.

Of course, a posse wouldn't be a posse without Bat Masterson, lurking in the alleyway in his purple suit. But where was the ever faithful Billy Woods?

Horace Tabor was very recognizable, too, with that big walrus mustache. Soapy wasn't surprised to see him in Creede—given he just beat the hell out of his only son.

Soapy was surprised to see the Corner Pocket Drunk positioned on the blackened rooftop directly across the street. His aim, predictably, appeared to bobble and drift. Lute Johnson, looking ridiculous with his notepad and pencil, was up there, too.

When he spotted Zang brandishing an old muzzleloader, Soapy felt a little betrayed.

"Probably thinks he's on a duck hunt."

The Orleans Club was empty and silent. Soapy walked over to the bar and poured a shot of rye.

"No more lollygagging!" Bat called. "You don't get another warning."

Horace led his men out of the alley and they lined up in the street, leveling their rifles at the club.

Soapy held the little glass up, starting to toast his own good luck.

But no words came out.

He was alone. Mollie and Ella Diamond had left town after the fire, and so had the entire gang. Joe, Banjo, and Old Man Tripp— they were all worried about getting hung, after the fire and the cow camp. Joe had been particularly dismayed after the kid got shot.

"That was an accident," Soapy said out loud, though no one was there to hear it.

They had all abandoned him.

Even his best friend had left him for good.

"I wouldn't be here all by myself if you hadn't coughed yourself dead."

"I see you in there!" Horace shouted. "Come on out."

Soapy hurled his glass of rye against the wall. It erupted, and broken glass tinkled onto the floorboards.

"Let's shove the booze across the boards!"

Marching across the game room, he unlocked the door and stepped out into the sunshine.

Horace worked the lever action on his rifle, chambering a live round, and gripped the stock tight.

"You're under arrest."

Soapy casually produced a cigar and lit it.

"Why? I didn't do nothing wrong."

Emerging from the alley, Bat stepped into the sunshine.

"That suit sure does shine," Soapy told him. "Always a snappy dresser."

"Where's your boys?" Bat replied, eyeing the Orleans Club. "Where's that string bean? And your fake mayor?"

Soapy waved him off.

"Nobody's here but me."

Bob Ford jumped out from behind a barrel of salt and applauded.

"The show is over! Gonna miss you like a hole in the head."

At that, Soapy smiled.

"I'll keep that in mind, Bob."

He started strolling down the street, smoking his cigar.

Shocked at his brazen behavior, Horace poked the barrel of his Winchester in Soapy's back.

"Stop right there or I'll shoot you dead."

But Soapy kept walking, and even waved at the gunmen on the rooftops.

"All I'm guilty of is being affable," he said. "You ain't got proof of nothing."

Like a parade, Horace Tabor and Bat Masterson, Bob Ford and Major Bohn, and the rest of the posse trailed behind Soapy Smith. He led them right down Main Street Creede, all the way to the train depot.

Horace grit his teeth when Soapy crossed the platform and stepped on the streaks of dried blood—Maxcy's blood.

"You beat my son right here in front of a dozen folks."

"It was pretty dark that night, Haw," Soapy retorted. "Too damn smoky for folks to see anything clear."

The station agent peered out of his office. But when he saw Soapy Smith, Horace and Bat, and all the gunmen, he darted back inside and shut the door.

"That station agent saw what you did," Horace said. "He'll testify in court."

But Soapy laughed.

"That fellow is scared of his own shadow. What are the odds he'll be too scared to testify?"

The train was sitting on the tracks. Steam hissed from the engine.

Soapy walked over to the passenger car and went inside.

They saw him take a seat by the window and wave goodbye.

Horace was in disbelief. He looked at Bat for help.

"Are we just going to let him walk away like this?"

"Ain't much we can do, besides hanging him without a trial."

Then Bob Ford went over to the train car, and pressed a playing card flat against the glass. It was the king of clubs.

"I guess I'm the king of Creede after all. Go to hell!"

The train eased out of the station and crossed the Rio Grande. It didn't take long before it disappeared in the forest. Horace, Bat, and the others watched the plume of smoke twist up, drift, and vanish in the clear blue sky.

— PART 19 —

CHAPTER 129

SUMMER 1892
DENVER

It was three a.m. and the Tivoli Club was empty.

Joe Palmer looked around. The police were gone, and so were the customers. They had raided the place and charged Soapy with a "wine room crime." They had to make something up, because there were no real crimes they could prove. But it did not matter, because Soapy knew the judge and got the charge dropped. Yet it had been enough to scare off the gamblers and boozers—at least for a while.

Soapy was seated at a round wood table, playing solitaire by lamp light and smoking a cigar. His brother Bascomb was slumped on a sofa. Soapy gave up on the game and began flicking cards at his brother, but he was dead drunk and could not be roused.

"Nothing changes, does it?" Soapy asked.

But Joe felt different about that.

He was on the sofa next to Bascomb. He had not slept all night, waiting to see if the police might reappear. He felt strange from pure exhaustion—from everything that had happened. His body felt like it was filled with lead. Soapy looked tired, too. Joe wondered if he should say anything, but decided against it.

The front door opened and Banjo walked in with a stranger.

"Who's there?" Joe asked warily, trying to see if it was a policeman.

But it wasn't.

When Soapy saw who it was, he smiled.

"That is Edward O'Kelley," he said.

Soapy waved the man over to his table.

"Banjo, get us some coffee."

O'Kelley, eyes dark, took a seat across from Soapy.

"Where is he?" he growled.

"The man you're looking for has a saloon in Creede," Soapy told him. "Well, he *had* a saloon. It just burned to the ground. Yet I imagine he's still dawdling around up there. He's known for his dawdling."

Banjo brought coffee and a plate of hot doughnuts from the kitchen.

Soapy snapped his fingers, as if he had a fresh idea.

"Get this man a shotgun and a box of shells."

Reaching behind the bar, Banjo brought out the gun and ammunition.

"I'm gonna get that coward," said Edward O'Kelley. He filled his pocket with the shells, hid the gun in his long coat, and left without touching his coffee.

Bascomb was still slumped on the sofa, covered in playing cards and dead to the world.

The smell of hot pastries and coffee got to Joe. He joined Soapy at the table, and ate a doughnut.

"Who was that?"

"Did you know Jesse James had a cousin?"

Joe shrugged. "No."

"He is going to be famous for killing Bob Ford."

When he said that, Joe felt sick to his stomach.

"What! I thought we were done with all that."

He slammed his fist on the table.

"What are you mad about?" Soapy wondered.

"I thought you had woke up—woke up to all this violence. Nothing good ever comes from it. Look what happened! After all we done and been through. I can't believe you want to make things worse."

Soapy took a sip of coffee.

"Jesse James married Edward O'Kelley's cousin. Bob Ford killed Jesse James and left her a widow. That's a family matter and an old score to settle."

"You could have left it all alone."

Joe held up his bad hand—the one missing a thumb.

"See this? And now I got a limp when I walk. All for what?"

"One hell of a good time, I'd say."

Frustrated, Joe sighed and rubbed his eyes.

"The way of the transgressor is hard."

"What does that mean?"

Joe stood up and headed for the door.

"Where are you going?" Soapy asked.

The anger in Joe's eyes faded.

"You just burnt down a whole town, beat a poor man senseless just for saying hello, and gutshot that kid in the woods. And now you want Bob Ford dead, too? The way of the transgressor is hard. Those words come from the Good Lord himself."

Soapy took off his hat and held it over his heart.

"You are absolutely right, Joe. A divine truth has been revealed from on high. The way of the transgressor *is* hard . . . hard to quit."

Going outside, Joe Palmer went straight to the train station, but he realized he still had no money. He slapped the brick wall in frustration.

— CHAPTER 130 —

CREEDE

Bob's new tent saloon was in business for a mere three days prior to catastrophe.

"Hello, Bob."

Hearing his name, Bob Ford turned around and saw Edward O'Kelley pointing a double-barreled shotgun at his throat.

Ever since Soapy Smith left Creede, Bob realized he had no real competition. Not only did the Ford Exchange burn to the ground, but Bat Masterson's club, the Denver Exchange, had also burnt pretty good. Bat even left town, and of course Billy Woods was dead.

The quickest way to get back in the game was to build a new saloon. But Bob didn't want to waste time building an entire wood-frame building. It had taken weeks to build the original Ford Exchange, but it had only been open six days before it went up in smoke.

It all left him pretty short on funds, too.

This left him little choice but to head on down to Tent Town and set up a canvas saloon.

However, Bob wanted his saloon to be the biggest and best of all. So, he bought some lumber and a hammer, and constructed a simple square skeleton frame himself. Then he took three old tents, from the Amethyst Mine, and stitched the canvas over the frame to make one large tent saloon. None of the other one-jug saloons in Tent Town could compare. Certainly not the Bonanza, which only served bottled beer in an area the size of a wagon wheel.

Unfortunately, Bob did not have enough money to buy a new mirror to hang above the bar. Which is why he didn't see Edward O'Kelley step through the front door, walk up behind him, and train the shotgun on his throat. He did see Edward O'Kelley pull both triggers, but that was the last thing he saw.

The buckshot blast nearly severed his head from his body.

It was the middle of the day, around noon, when it happened. The drinkers in the room, enjoying a lazy afternoon, produced knives and frantically cut through the walls in order to flee. But Edward O'Kelley only had one victim in mind that day, and he immediately took off running, too.

CHAPTER 131

TERRITORY OF ARIZONA

One day, not long after he had returned to the mesa, Kahopi dropped by his sister's house to see if she had any oranges. When Kahopi arrived, he found her near the fireplace baking yellow piki bread.

She was wearing a striped shawl and had a squash blossom in her hair.

"Why are you dressed up?"

"There will be a Katcina dance in the kiva tonight. We are celebrating your return home."

"Do you have any oranges?"

"There are melons and peaches. However, do not eat more than one. I am bringing it all to the dance and we will need lots of food."

She indicated a basket filled with squash, melons, and peaches.

Kahopi examined the peaches and chose the largest one. As he was eating it, his sister's husband came through the doorway. When he saw Kahopi, he snuck up behind him and slapped his anus.

"Are you going to leave a loaf in the kiva tonight?" he asked and chortled.

"Shut up," Kahopi said, frowning deeply. "I'm getting tired of your mischief."

He took the fruit and went up on the rooftop to finish it. As he went, he heard his sister shout for him to come back.

"He's just teasing you."

But Kahopi was frustrated. He yearned for a good name again. What would it take? He wanted to stay on the Sun Trail by being good and wise and not react to taunts. But he was tired of the jokes. Ever since he returned to the mesa, his friends and family began picking on him, all over again—as if he hadn't even been gone for a single minute.

But Kahopi had gone. He had taken a brave journey, well beyond the village and the mesa. He traveled through strange lands with strange powers. Very few of the People ever left the area, except for occasional trips to collect salt, or water during a drought.

It seemed unfair, after all that had happened, to have to endure the same old ridicule.

There was plenty of evil in the world, as it was. Most of it was caused by Two-Hearts, of course. Sickness, strife, misfortune. Two-Hearts were everywhere, even in the village. Kahopi secretly suspected that some of his neighbors were Two-Hearts. Maybe even some of his relatives.

But Kahopi knew nothing good could come from worry.

It only brought bad luck.

He stood up and hurled the peach pit as far as he could.

— EPILOGUE —

CHAPTER 132

AUTUMN 1893
LEADVILLE

"What's this?" Horace asked, but he already knew the answer.

"It's corned beef," Baby Doe said. "It's all we can afford."

Sitting in her high chair, Silver Dollar grabbed a fistful of corned beef and threw it at her father's face.

"No, Silver," Horace said, wiping the mash off his cheek. "Very bad manners."

But Silver Dollar was unhappy.

"Necklace!" she yelled and flung another handful.

"I sold it to pay for this corned beef!"

Getting up from the table, Horace wanted to pace. Unfortunately, their new housing was not spacious enough to allow for pacing. It was a tiny one-room shack at the Matchless Mine.

Baby Doe pointed at the door.

"Go outside and cool off."

So Horace went for a walk around the property—but instantly got depressed. The Matchless Mine was silent. The ore cars were empty. The bucket was rusting on the headframe. Instead of burros and miners and pick axes and dynamite, there was only the sound of cawing crows and the wind in the branches.

The aspens were bare.

The leaves had seemed to simply fall off overnight. The trees changed from green and healthy one day to empty and barren the next—it had been the same story with Horace's bank account following the presidential election.

Heading back to the cabin, Horace saw Baby Doe waiting for him in the doorway. She had a kitchen knife and was notching the wood.

"What are you doing?"

She smiled, trying to be optimistic.

"Every Sunday, I cut a notch in the door jamb. When we strike it rich again, we'll buy a forty-thousand-dollar mansion and look back and see how long we lived like poor people."

Horace itched his mustache.

"You need a haircut and a proper shave," she added. "You're turning into one of these scraggly trammers, Horace."

He sat down on an old, dented, five-gallon can.

"I'm sixty-five years old," he lamented. "I work for two dollars and fifty cents a day. I push ore carts up and down the rails."

Baby Doe rubbed his shoulders.

Then she leaned down and whispered in his ear, "Go get me a newspaper."

Horace frowned.

"I don't want to read anymore headlines. Those damn Democrats."

The election hadn't gone his way. The silver club had failed. The wrong man became president, and the price of silver crashed. Everyone called it the Silver Panic, and half the country plunged into financial ruin—including the Silver King himself, Horace "Haw" Tabor.

Every bank in Leadville folded. People withdrew every penny they could get. All but a handful of the mines closed down. The ones that stayed open were the gold mines, of course.

Horace had to sell everything—the Tabor Opera House, the Tabor Grand Hotel, the Tabor Hose Company, the Tabor Amalgamation Mill, and his shares in the Telephone Company and the Gas Illumination Company. And their house, too.

But Horace kept the Matchless Mine.

He hoped, against all odds, that one day the Democrats might see the light and recognize all the damage they caused. But that was about as likely as the moon falling from the sky.

So, Horace hoped to get rich again by mining. But so far, things were looking bleak.

"I am going to take Silver Dollar for a walk along the railroad tracks and look for coal," Baby Doe said. "When you get back with the newspaper, you can help me paste it on the walls, for wallpaper. I want to spruce this place up before winter sets in."

"Maybe we should move to Denver," he suggested. "I could spend more time with Maxcy."

"Where would we live—Augusta's boarding house? Maxcy can come up *here* if he wants to visit."

Then she gave her husband a peck on the cheek.

"Why don't you try panning for gold?"

But that caused Horace to leap off the five-gallon can.

"These streambeds are nothing but black sand! You don't know. You don't understand."

Baby Doe started to go back inside but paused in the doorway. She looked back at him and shrugged.

"Then go get me a newspaper."

He began marching down the gravel road. On foot, it took a good hour to get to town from the Matchless Mine. But the quiet walk was peaceful and helped him clear his head. The autumn air had a crisp refreshing feel, like it always did in the high country. The surrounding peaks were already capped in snow, and the creeks were starting to ice up.

Back in the old days, when he had a little extra money, Horace used to "grubstake" miners. He would cover their startup costs, like a mining pan and a shovel. If they found any silver or gold, Horace got to keep a percentage. That was how he got rich in the first place. But now, what kind of miner could he grubstake, even if he had the extra cash? It was a different era. Back then, there was so much to discover. Now, everything there was to find was found. And what was left, like silver, was worthless.

He bought the *Leadville Chronicle* and made it home before it got dark.

Baby Doe had found some coal on the railroad tracks and had a warm fire going in the cookstove.

— CHARACTER INDEX —

Greasewood	An old Ute who yearns for the good old days.
Dirty Johns	Big Ed's last remaining gang member. He is also the bartender at the Stray Horse Brewery in Leadville.
Wheezy Jones	He is Janey Campion's younger brother and the manager of the Lucy B. Mine in Leadville.
Kahopi	A Hopi who is on a quest to find his father.
Kelley	He has found gold deep in the Rocky Mountains but had to abandon the claim to avoid the winter snows. He is concerned that his rival, George Stevens, will steal his claim in the spring.
LG	Along with Davis, he runs the cow camp in Creede.
Bat Masterson	A former lawman, he now runs the Denver Exchange in Creede.
Otto Mears	Owner of the Rio Grande Southern Railroad. His trains run through the mountains of southwest Colorado—from Durango, through Rico and Telluride, up to Ridgway and back again.
Mollie	She works the silver camps as both a waitress and a dance hall girl.
Nathaniel	Horace's good friend and homestead neighbor. When Horace and Augusta leave Kansas to pan for gold in the Rockies, he goes along.
New Orleans Kid	He is a young shell game con artist who arrives in Creede.
Frank Oliver	A gambler, often inebriated, who likes to play in the Denver Exchange.
Joe Palmer	A longtime member of the Soapy Smith Gang.
Banjo Parker	One of Soapy Smith's gang members who often does the dirty work.
Selma Sawney	One of Leadville's high society ladies, and Baby Doe's arch rival. Her husband is the president of the miners' union in Leadville.
Sylvander Sawney	President of the Knights of Labor miners' union in Leadville.

Joe Simmons	An old childhood friend of Soapy's. They used to be cowboys in Texas when they were young—they even ran a saloon together, once upon a time.
Bascomb Smith	Soapy's younger brother. He runs the Tivoli Club in Denver in Soapy's absence.
Soapy Smith	Denver's most famous con man. He moves to Creede to set up a new operation, along with his gang.
George Stevens	A gold miner in early Denver who knows Kelley found gold along the Arkansas River—and wants to beat him to it.
Augusta Tabor	Horace's first wife. They have a son together named Maxcy.
Baby Doe Tabor	Horace's second wife. She is twenty years younger than he is. Together, they have a daughter named Silver Dollar.
Horace "Haw" Tabor	Also known as the Silver King of Leadville. Horace started out looking for gold in the Rocky Mountains but eventually became rich on silver.
Maxcy Tabor	Horace and Augusta's son who was born at their Kansas homestead and raised in early Leadville. After the divorce, he moved to Denver with his mother Augusta.
Silver Dollar Tabor	Horace and Baby Doe's young daughter. Even at a young age, she has developed a taste for the finer things in life.
Senator Henry M. Teller	The state senator of Colorado. He is concerned about the falling price of silver.
Old Man Tripp	The oldest member of the Soapy Smith gang.
Parson Tom Uzzell	A traveling evangelist who discovers that Creede is full of lost souls.
White Owl	A quiet, thoughtful teenage Ute. He has left the reservation with Greasewood and Bear Claw Lip.
Billy Woods	Bartender of the Denver Exchange in Creede. He is also a boxer, the heavyweight champion of Colorado.
Zang	A Chinaman who runs a hotel in Creede, in which the Smith Gang resides.

ABOUT THE AUTHOR

MARK MITTEN was born in Texas and raised in Colorado. He is a member of the Western Writers of America, and is known for his western novel *Sipping Whiskey in a Shallow Grave*. It was nominated for the 2013 Peacemaker Award. An experienced mountain climber, Mark has summited all 54 of Colorado's highest peaks. He and his wife Mary currently reside in Winsted, Minnesota.